the weather war

STORMS IN AMETHIR - BOOK 4

STEPHANIE A. CAIN

THE WEATHER WAR
Storms in Amethir: Book Four

This book is a work of fiction. Names, characters, and places are products of the author's imagination. Any resemblance to actual events or persons living or dead is purely coincidental.

ISBN: 978-1-944774-05-9
First Print Edition, September 2017
Published by Cathartes Press

BOOKS BY STEPHANIE A. CAIN

STORMS IN AMETHIR

Stormsinger
Stormshadow
Stormseer
The Weather War
Witchery's End (forthcoming)

FAITH AND FEALTY

Sow the Wind

CIRCLE CITY MAGIC

Shades of Circle City
Circle City Psychic (forthcoming)

FROM WORLD WEAVER PRESS

Equus: Rhonda Parrish's Magical Menageries #5

DEDICATION

For Jilly
—Eldry is entirely her fault

ACKNOWLEDGEMENTS

Thanks go first of all to Amanda McGuire, copy-editor beyond measure; and my father, who isn't afraid to tell me when the writing is sub-par.

Thanks also to Garrett Hutson, who offered important feedback on politics. (His mysteries are available in ebook and print format, and well worth the read!)

Thank you to Jillian Storm—discussion with her inspired the character of Eldry, and even if Eldry is a book late in showing up, I hope she's worth the wait!

Thank you to Nicole Cardiff, whose art amazes me with its detail and beauty. Thank you for envisioning my characters and bringing them to life!

Thank you to my tribe, both online and IRL: Twitter Monthly Writing Challenge folks, Midwest Writers Workshop folks, the IndyScribes, Jillian, Charity, Jared, Christopher, Patty Jansen, and Rachel Aaron.

Thank you to the Michigan Maritime Museum and the 2017 crew of *Friends Good Will*: Josh, John, Maggie, and Captain Zach, all of whom were generous with their time. Thank you particularly to the captain, who let me steer the ship and gave me a whole new understanding of tallships. #AllWoodAllGood

Thank you to the members of my small church: I know you all pray for my writing as well as other things, and I can't overestimate how grateful I am.

Thank you to my email subscribers, who are not only interested in the stories I make up, but also offer sore throat remedies when needed.

Thank you to Campaign Cartographer and ProFantasy, who provide the excellent software that enables me ~~to lose~~

~~countless hours mapmaking~~ create maps to share with my readers.

Thank you to Jenn and Trav, Lilliana, Dacia, the entire Daniel family, my co-workers, Tim Timmons, Ray Boomhower, Laura VanArendonk Baugh, and Kelly O'Dell Stanley.

Thank you most of all to my readers. You are the people who enable me to tell stories that matter to me, that I hope matter to you. You wait patiently for each book. And most of all—you make what I do mean something.

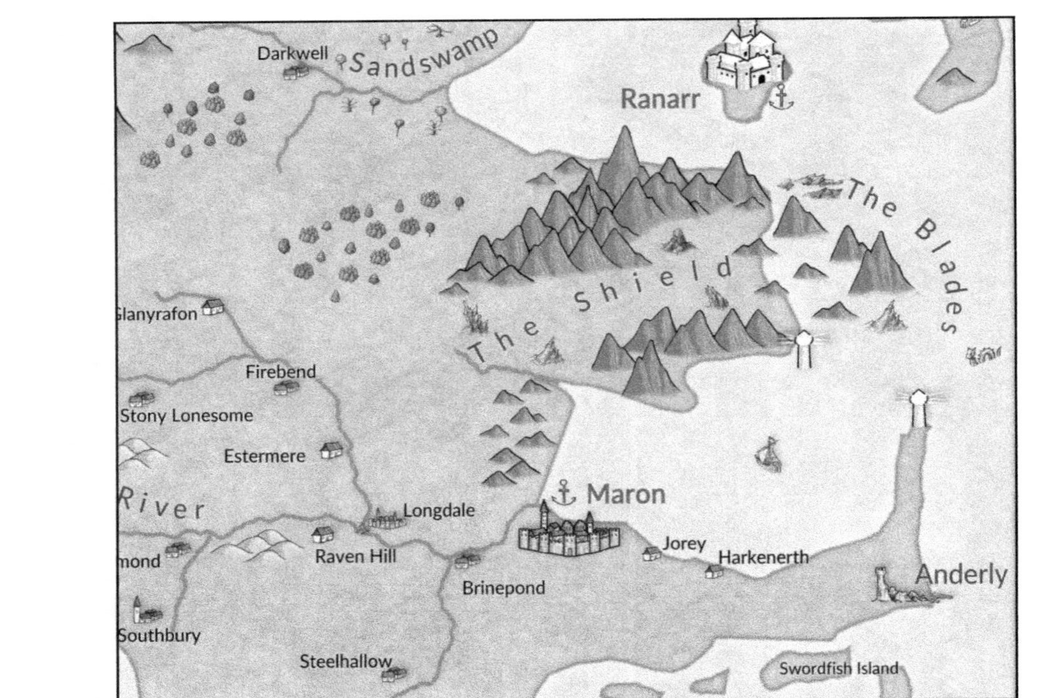

Darkwell
Sandswamp
Ranarr
The Shield
The Blades
Glanyrafon
Firebend
Stony Lonesome
Estermere
River
Longdale
mond
Raven Hill
Maron
Jorey
Harkenerth
Anderly
Brinepond
Southbury
Steelhallow
Swordfish Island

PROLOGUE

The driving rain slashed across Eldry's face. Her long hair was plastered to her cheeks, her dress clinging to her legs, tangling in them and making it hard to walk. She squinted up into the clouds, wincing as lightning tore a hole in the darkness.

The deck of the *Elana Bey* was pitching under her. Eldry lurched and staggered to catch her balance. The wind was howling through the bare rigging and reefed sails—the crew had chosen to heave to, though she thought they were regretting it now. She was certainly wishing they'd been able to outrun the storm. She'd deflected the worst of it, but the *Elana Bey*'s captain had told her there was no need to push it completely aside. She wished now that she had argued with him. But then, the storm was much more powerful than she had originally thought.

Eldry had only been sailing for a few months. She hadn't wanted this assignment, but her choices had been a ship or back to her home up the Gehb River into the mountains, and she never wanted to see Stony Lonesome ever again. That made the decision to sail to Tamnen an easy one.

The sailors were shouting at each other. Eldry couldn't hear what they were saying, but the urgency of their words had escalated into alarm. She turned just as something overhead *cracked* deafeningly.

Eldry staggered forward. The ship's mate had shoved her. Mouth open in a wordless cry of surprise, Eldry took several stumbling steps forward. A moment later a section of the mast crashed to the deck behind her. She spun to thank the ship's mate, but he was trapped under the mast. He'd saved her life—but he'd lost his own.

Eldry screamed in shock, staggering back against the railing. She gripped it as the deck lurched.

"Stormwitch!" The captain was next to her, fingers gripping her elbow so tightly they pinched. "Stormwitch! Turn the storm! Save us!"

Eldry stared at him with wide eyes. It took her a moment to comprehend that he'd changed his mind. She closed her gaping mouth and nodded.

It would be hard now. Harder than it would have been to turn it before it reached them. But she could do it. She might not be a stormcaller, but she was a powerful deflector. She clenched her fist around the large chunk of polished seaglass that hung from her neck. Trying to push away the distractions of the wind and pelting rain, she closed her eyes.

She could still see the flash of lightning through her eyelids, but a moment later she raised the mental walls that shut off the howling of the wind. She took deep breaths, trying to steady her racing heart. Fear would do her no good here. She needed control.

She extended her senses, finding the worst of the storm easily—it was right overhead. She could nudge the storm weatherward to get it past quickly, or she could nudge it to the side and carry the worst of it away from them.

"Eldry!" That was Rhys' voice. She tried to shrug him off, but strong hands shook her. "Eldry! We're going to die! You have to get belowdecks!"

Eldry's eyes popped open. "This is my job!" she snapped at him. She pushed him away. "Get below yourself."

"I'm not going without you."

She glared at her best friend. "Then stop distracting me and let me work."

She shouldn't have brought Rhys with her. He was no sailor, for all that he'd moved to the coast for her. He had supported her service at the stormwitch academy, but he didn't understand the work. He still didn't understand why she hated Stony Lonesome so much, why she'd sworn never to go back. But he was loyal, so she had invited him with her as a condition of her service.

It had been a mistake.

She closed her eyes again, stretching her senses out again. She would nudge the storm weatherward but she would also shift it a bit east. It couldn't hurt to do both, and it would probably make the *Elana Bey* safe sooner than doing just one shift. She stretched out her mental fingers, grasping the fringes of the storm and tugging gently.

The wind howled louder suddenly and Rhys screamed. She couldn't seem to seal off her attention well enough to block it. He was gripping her arm, pulling on her.

"Rhys, stop!" she shouted.

The world flashed into white.

Eldry reeled backwards, her hair whipping into her face. Her hands were tingling, crackling with pain so hot it seared them cold. The world crashed down on her, thunder so loud it was like an avalanche of boulders falling on her head.

As the crash faded away, she heard Rhys still screaming.

Eldry blinked her eyes frantically, willing herself to see anything but the white afterimages of that flash. When she did, she wished she couldn't.

Rhys was sprawled on the deck. His body spasmed, limbs flailing, his back arching away from the boards.

The voices of the crew merged together and swelled into a huge, monstrous thing. They were louder than the storm. Eldry's own scream was drowned out by Rhys'.

Rhys went still.

"*Rhys!*" she screamed, dropping to her knees beside him. Her fingers fumbled frantically at his throat. She held her breath until she found a pulse. It was thready and weak, but it was there. "Sea Lord Antos, preserve us," Eldry whispered, leaning down to put her arms around Rhys. She was the cause of his hurt. He would never have left Stony Lonesome if it weren't for her.

She buried her face against his chest, reaching out to gauge the storm's strength. The worst of it had passed east and weatherward of them. The ferocity of the wind lessened. She'd done it.

Which was why the wave caught her completely by surprise.

It washed over the deck, greedy water clutching at her. It tore Rhys from her grasp and she screamed. Then she realized it had swept her from the deck of the ship. She sucked in a deep breath. Then she was flying, flying, falling, and the sea was all.

1

Thunder rumbled low in the distance. Princess Azmei Corrone of Tamnen tucked her hair behind her ear and squinted. They'd been sailing for three weeks, and they probably another week to go. But they hadn't accounted for storms when they made their plans.

"Is that something we need to be worried about?" she asked, lifting her chin towards the thunder.

Beside her, Destar Thorne shrugged. "We're close to Amethirian waters, but not in them yet. Their storm season hasn't started. And the rest of us sailors just take the weather as it comes."

His tone didn't give away what he thought about that. Azmei looked at him curiously. "Have you ever sailed with a stormwitch?" she asked.

"Aye, twice now. Once after we thought you dead, when I conveyed the Amethirian ambassador from Ranarr to Tamnen City." His voice roughened. "He put the wind in our sails, right enough, but I didn't like it. Wasn't natural."

Azmei pressed her lips together, trying to shove down the guilt. She'd done the best she could. Not knowing where the threat against her family came from, she'd made what she thought to be the right decision. She'd known people would be hurt by it, but what else could she have done? If she hadn't gone into hiding, would her cousin Arisanat have succeeded in murdering her brother as well as her father? He might have destroyed the entire kingdom of Tamnen.

Destar cleared his throat. "The other time was longer ago, when I was ship's boy on my first mission. I was ten years old, and Prince Marsede and his father King Costa were trying to improve trade with Amethir. We sailed to Maron City with a trade proposal, and the king of Amethir wanted his message to get out of their waters before storm season. The stormwitch he sent with us was this tall old woman with fancy white braids, and she dressed and talked like a sailor."

Azmei smiled. "You liked her."

"She was impressive, no doubt about that. We knew less about the stormwitches back then. Thought they were half devil, with their magic abilities, and liable to send us all straight to the bottom if we defied them. She knew how to use our superstition against us, too." Destar chuckled. "But she was kind, for all that."

"I've only met a stormwitch a handful of times, and never seen one work," Azmei said. "I know they can create ice. Vistaren's stormwitch frosted a glass of wine for me once." She smiled softly, thinking about the circumstances. She had just learned that Vistaren loved men instead of women, dashing all her girlish notions of an epic love affair with her betrothed. The cold wine was a kindness he needn't have extended, considering how shocked she'd been at that revelation, and it had endeared him to her even more, though perhaps not in the way she had originally imagined.

"Do you know how things stand with Prince Vistaren?" Destar asked, his voice a low rumble.

Azmei glanced curiously at him. "In what way?"

Destar shrugged. "He wore the mourning black the full half a year for you. And he's not married in the three years since. But there are rumors that…" He trailed off and then coughed. "I know it's impertinent of me, princess. But did the two of you have an understanding?"

Azmei forced a smile. "He said he would honor our betrothal. I told him he shouldn't wait, that there were no certainties, but…" Her smile strengthened. "We don't love each other as a husband and wife might, but there is genuine affection there, Destar." Not to mention she was the only princess currently available.

"You have a unique gift of gathering allies to you, lass," Destar said. He rested a hand on her shoulder. "These two you've brought with you, they're not quite what I was expecting."

Azmei looked up at him, then followed his gaze to the railing, where a teenaged boy with dark hair stood staring out at the ocean. He stood an inch or two shy of six feet, with a nearly scrawny build, and his black hair flopped into his eyes. Azmei smiled.

"I imagine not," she said. "Nobody could expect Yar."

She took her leave of the captain and went to lean on the railing next to Yar. The boy was just as enamored of the ocean as he had been three weeks ago when he saw it for the first time. She supposed she couldn't blame him; Yar had grown up in a city of canals, but it was in the rugged western region of Tamnen, far from the ocean.

"It's so big," Yar said without looking at her.

"Bigger than all of Tamnen," she replied.

"And alive. So alive."

She just looked at him. He was the one who would know; Yar's life had been consumed by magic, perhaps since he was a baby, but definitely over the past half year. He'd been chosen as the Voice of Dragons, and it was partly because of Yar that they were making this journey halfway across the world.

"Does Xellax talk to you often?" she asked.

"All the time." He smiled, turning his silver eyes to hers. "She is treated well by your brother. She gets fat sheep to eat. She likes it."

Azmei laughed, pleased. "And that'll keep the people of Tamnen City under control, seeing a dragon lounging on the palace walls." Her cousin's rebellion had nearly succeeded. Razem said it would have succeeded if she and Yar hadn't arrived with the dragons when they did. Azmei thought her brother gave her too much credit, but she knew it had been a near thing. It wouldn't be bad for the citizens of Tamnen to have a living, fire-breathing reminder of the powerful allies her brother had.

Yar shrugged and looked back out to sea, which made Azmei smile again. In some ways he had changed so much from the boy troubled by Voices in his head, and in others, he was very much the same. He still had little interest in politics, and the smallest thing could fascinate him for hours.

Yar's shoulders moved as he heaved a sigh. "You wanted me to like you for who you are. When we met, I mean. Not your title." He glanced over at her, but Azmei just blinked at him, confused. "That's why you lied."

"Oh." Azmei felt a flush of embarrassment rush up her cheeks. "Yes." When they'd met, he'd been a teenage runaway who heard voices, and she'd been a gruff assassin who felt drawn to protect him despite the fact that she'd killed his grandfather and older brother. How far they'd come from where they started.

"But once I decided to like you," he continued, "you still didn't tell me." He cocked his head to one side. "To protect me. Since you knew my sister was dead. And you knew why she was dead."

Azmei was silent. He must have a reason for bringing this up, but she couldn't guess what it was, so she waited.

"Is that why you're avoiding Hawk now? To protect him?"

It was like a punch to the gut. Azmei stared at him, wondering how he'd noticed *that*, of all things, and why he thought he should bring it up. She knew he liked Hawk. Everyone liked Hawk. She certainly liked Hawk. But Yar didn't usually care about other people's relationships.

"I heard your brother ask you if you're still going to marry Vistaren," Yar elaborated, and Azmei's thoughts flashed back to the night, three weeks ago, when they'd all sat around the fire in the aftermath of Arisanat's failed rebellion.

"Then you also heard me say I plan to go back to Tamnen if I can," she said tartly.

Yar shrugged. "But I asked people. Well. I asked Ilzi.

She said you were betrothed, and maybe you still are. She said everyone knew it, so Hawk knew it. Knows it."

Azmei sighed and folded her arms across her chest, waiting.

"So you're not protecting him," Yar concluded. "You're being dumb."

Speechless, she glared at him. How dare he—

Yar shrugged. "You didn't want me to care about you being a princess. So I'll talk to you as Orya talked to me. And you're being dumb."

Azmei choked back a laugh. Of all the times for Yar to become observant. "Thank you," she said in a strangled tone. "I think."

Maybe she *was* being dumb. There was no knowing what would happen when they arrived in Amethir, but that was at least a week away. Practically speaking, it was difficult to avoid someone on a ship, even one as big as the *Victorious*, the flagship of her brother's navy.

And if she were honest with herself, she didn't like avoiding Hawk. She'd just been too cowardly to face the questions he would probably ask.

She found Hawk at the stern railing on the poop deck. He leaned on the railing, his right leg bent at the knee, which told her the old wound was bothering him. His hair, so dark a brown it was almost black, was scraped into a stubby tail at the base of his skull. His eyes squinted against the sunlight that still shone on them despite the dark clouds on the horizon.

She stopped a few steps away and cleared her throat, though he must have heard her coming. She had never met anyone as alert as Hawk, except her old training master Tanvel.

He didn't turn. For a moment she thought he was going to ignore her, which would be fair, considering the way she'd been acting. But finally he said, "Join me, princess."

"Don't," she said, leaning on the railing next to him, close enough that their shoulders touched.

He glanced sidelong at her. "Oh, are you being Azmei now?" There was no rancor in his voice, but Azmei felt a pang of shame anyway.

"I'm sorry," she said. She wanted to point out that she'd never had the luxury of a romantic relationship before. It wasn't like princesses were encouraged to fall in love with anyone before they were disposed of in a properly political marriage. And he ought to know—as everyone in the kingdom knew—that her properly political marriage hadn't exactly worked out the way she had expected.

Hawk sighed and slid his hand over to cover her fingers with his own. "So am I," he said, his voice soft. "I am having trouble finding my equilibrium."

Azmei sighed. "I know it must not seem like it, but I'm grateful you're here."

His smile was wry. "You have a funny way of showing it." But he lifted their joined hands so he could brush his lips against her fingers. She felt her stomach flutter.

"I don't know what I'm doing," she said. "This is all beyond me. Carrying a message for the dragons about the gods? Going to Amethir, where everyone except the prince thinks I'm dead?" She felt him go still and forced herself to continue. "Figuring out what's going to happen with my betrothal when we get there?"

Hawk's charcoal eyes were sad when he turned to look at her. "You know I wouldn't stand in your way," he murmured. "You signed a contract. You—you're the princess. I couldn't live with myself if I got between you and your duty."

Azmei frowned up at him. "To the hells with my duty. I died for my country three years ago. They ought to give me some leeway."

"I think they did. Three years' worth." Hawk sighed and looked back out at the water. "Life has never been easy, Az. Why would it start now?"

She squeezed her eyes shut, pretending they weren't stinging with tears. "Because I've never wanted anything as much as I want you," she whispered. "That ought to mean something."

She felt his arms go around her, pulling her against his chest. "It does," he said, his voice rough. "More than you can imagine. I'm just not sure if life really gives a damn."

Azmei gave a watery chuckle and slipped an arm around his waist. "He might not even want to go through with it. After all, he doesn't even love women. He might have found someone himself."

"And can he marry that hypothetical someone and produce heirs with him?" Hawk didn't sound convinced. "He'll go through with the treaty marriage, unless he's stupider than I think."

"Maybe the succession works differently in Amethir," Azmei said. "After all, in Tamnen, a prince who loved men wouldn't stay a prince very long."

"Unless he knew how to hide it very well," Hawk agreed. "But I have a feeling there are some things that are universal to politics." He leaned back, breaking the embrace. "What are those?"

It took Azmei a moment to realize he was changing the topic. Then she squinted out where he was pointing. In the distance, but rapidly approaching the *Victorious*, were massive black and white shapes, their sleek forms cutting through the water with astonishing speed.

From the crow's nest, a voice called, "Orca off the port stern!"

"Orca," Azmei said. "I've heard of them, but never seen them before."

Footsteps thudded across the deck, then Destar was at the railing with them, spyglass raised to his eye. "They've been more active lately," he said. "It's not their migration time yet. Must be the sirens are moving, but that's not normal, either. Especially in waters this deep." He glanced at Azmei. "Sirens are shallow-water beasties."

She shuddered. "Sirens—they eat people, don't they?"

"And whatever else they can catch," Destar agreed.

"S'why having orca around is a mixed blessing. They eat sirens, so you know if you go down, the orca'll probably keep you alive. But they usually mean there are sirens around too."

"If this is unusual," Azmei began, and Destar nodded.

"Been a lot of siren activity lately. I don't like it, what with your news about gods and conflict and the whole world about to shake."

Azmei exchanged a look with Hawk. "That's why we must reach Amethir as soon as possible," she said after a moment. Regardless of her doubts about seeing her betrothed again.

Azmei had thought finding justice for her family would mean she could relax. Instead, she had discovered that Tamnen no longer needed her to save it—but the whole world just might.

"Captain!" shouted the lookout from aloft. "Something's coming astern!"

Hawk's hand closed on Azmei's wrist a moment later. "That isn't an orca." His voice was tight.

Destar swore. "What in the seven hells—That doesn't look friendly."

Azmei leaned across the railing, shading her eyes. The orca had nearly reached them, and they weren't slowing. They parted to swim around the *Victorious* and one leapt into the air alongside them, blowing water in what Azmei thought must be an attempt at communication. Then the orca were past and she was staring at a long, sinuous shape speeding towards them.

"Is that—chasing the orca?" she asked. Teal scales flashed through the spray. She sucked in a breath. She didn't know what sirens looked like, but that was immense.

"It bloody well looks likes it." Destar grunted. "Gunners to stations!"

Azmei heard the order repeated by the gunners as they ran to man the guns. She had only sailed anywhere once before, and there had been no cannons involved that time.

She shifted her stance, wishing she were better skilled in a distance weapon.

"That looks suspiciously like it might be related to Yarrax," Hawk muttered next to her. Azmei cast a startled glance at him and then looked back at the monstrous beast bearing down on them.

It had scales of metallic teal and its body was serpentine, but the head that reared above the swells did have a remarkably draconian shape to it. The bone over the eye had the same flat shape and its jaw was filled with teeth that looked like they were at least as long as her arm. A fin-like crest began immediately behind its head and stretched along its neck to the point where it disappeared under the surface.

Azmei spun to look for her friend. "Yar!" she screamed. Her eyes found him a moment later and she saw it would do no good to talk to him; he had fallen back into a sitting position on the deck and his face had the vacant expression it took on when he was lost in one of his visions.

She turned to Destar. "Seadragons," she said. "What do they look—"

"Sleeping gods!" Destar interrupted. He was peering at the oncoming creature—which was much closer than it had been moments before. "You're right, lass. I've never seen one alive."

"I've never seen one at all, but that one doesn't look like it wants *us* to stay alive," Hawk put in.

"Take the princess amidships," Destar ordered. "Protect her with your life."

"The princess can protect herself," Azmei snapped, but she allowed Hawk to guide her away from the railing and towards the center of the ship. One hand fell to the dagger at her hip, but it was more for comfort than anything; it would be no use against a creature that immense.

"Don't argue in the middle of a battle, soldier," Hawk murmured. He loosened his sword in its sheath. "I should have taken Thorne up on his offer to learn to shoot."

"I still trust my steel over gunpowder." Azmei couldn't

tear her gaze away from the seadragon. Another minute and it would be on them. She registered that Destar was shouting orders to his crew, but she wasn't sure if they would get the cannon ready in time to make a difference.

She underestimated the crew of the *Victorious*. She could still taste her words on her lips when the first of the cannons roared. The deck shuddered underfoot as the acrid tang of gunpowder stung her nostrils. A plume of water rose several paces to the left of the seadragon. It bellowed but kept charging towards the ship.

Destar was shouting a correction. Azmei realized her fingers were tight on the hilt of her dagger. With an effort she loosened her grip. A second cannon fired and, this time, the aim was dead on.

Red fountained from a crease along the seadragon's neck. It bellowed again and dove under the surface. Azmei frowned. Surely it wasn't that easy to kill.

She could hear the gunners preparing for a second volley, cleaning the barrels and reloading. She exchanged a swift, anxious glance with Hawk and went back to scanning the surface of the ocean.

"Help Yar," Hawk snapped.

"What?" Azmei looked around. Yar had fallen prone on the deck, his heels drumming against the wood. She swore and dove for him. He could bite his tongue or even choke on it without intervention. Her heart was pounding as she worked her fingers between the back of his head and the planking. Where was the seadragon? Was it attacking him psychically somehow? The timing of his attack couldn't be a coincidence.

Steel rang over her head and she knew Hawk had drawn his sword. She took a deep breath, forcing away her fear. Hawk would guard her. Nothing would harm her if he could prevent it. And if he couldn't prevent it… Well, if he couldn't prevent it, she would die, and there was nothing to be done about it. She focused on cushioning Yar's head with one hand and trying to prise open his jaws with the other.

The ship rolled hard. Sailors to her right screamed and Azmei realized the starboard side of the ship was rising into the air. She couldn't look away from Yar's face, though. His eyes had rolled back into his head and his mouth was twisted into a silent scream. What was going on in his head?

Please, Silent God, whatever peace you may grant me, let me help him, she thought. It wasn't much of a prayer, but she wasn't much of a disciple, and the Silent God was surely used to her by now. She pulled her belt off with one hand and managed to force a length of leather between Yar's teeth. It was the most she could do.

She rocked back onto her heels and took a moment to look up at Hawk. His teeth were bared as he looked at something off the starboard side of the ship. His sword was raised, but he clearly knew as well as she did that it would do no good.

A cannon blast shook her and she swayed. She didn't have a free hand to catch herself, so she relied on her balance to keep from falling. Yar's face was strained and pale under his dark skin tone. Azmei wanted to swear. She hated feeling helpless.

"Yar," she called softly. "Yarrax." She licked her lips. "Please." She watched his face for a moment, then raised her voice. "Hawk, tell me what's happening."

"The dragon came up under the ship. Someone went over the rail. They've almost cut it in two with the cannons." He spit out the terse sentences like he was angry, but Azmei knew he was just being efficient. "Thorne has his pistol out."

Azmei bent over Yar, her head tilted so she could feel his breath puff against her cheek. She'd heard of people falling into fits and dying, though Yar had always come out of his all right. He'd been more coherent since joining with the dragons, though. She hadn't seen a fit this bad since they were in the desert still looking for whatever was causing the Voices in his head.

"Keep talking," she ordered.

Whatever Hawk said next was drowned out by a crack

of thunder splitting the sky. Half a beat later the cannons roared again. Azmei wondered if the seadragon was calling the storm somehow. She knew orca and their cousins were called stormsingers and had some sort of weather magic. Did seadragons have that magic too?

Yar suddenly tensed and went completely still under her touch. Azmei bent closer, watching his chest for several heartbeats until it lifted in a deep breath.

"Hold on!" Hawk shouted, and a hand gripped her shoulder so tightly it hurt.

The deck pitched under them. Azmei heard sailors screaming and someone's pistol barked nearby. She didn't think the tiny shot would make even a dent in the seadragon's thick hide. Destar's voice rose over the din, not shouting orders or even oaths, but just a wordless roar. The cannons belched again and again, and suddenly a bestial howl rose in the air.

The sound prickled her flesh and shook her bones. She felt hot spray against her cheek and lunged instinctively to shelter Yar from whatever was happening. Then someone hit the deck next to her, screaming in agony. Hawk's voice rose over her head, but she couldn't understand what he was saying. She squeezed her eyes shut in sudden fear. This was the end, wasn't it?

Fingers curled around hers. "Let me go, Az."

Her eyes flew open. Yar's swirly silver eyes were open and fixed on her face. He looked entirely coherent, and his jaw was set.

She shifted and sat back, releasing her grip on her belt. It dropped to the deck as Yar rolled to one side and from there to his feet in one fluid motion.

She glanced at the man on the deck next to her. His screams had dwindled to a low, sobbing moan. It was Destar, his cheek flayed open so deep she could see the bone. Her throat tightened.

"Avaunt!" Yar screamed. He was running at the railing, where the seadragon towered at least fifty feet above the deck. "I command! I, Voice of Dragons!"

Destar made a choked noise and Azmei looked down. She tore her jacket off and pressed it against his face, which made him scream again.

"I'm sorry," she gabbled. "I'm sorry, Destar, I'm sorry, I have to stop the blood!"

He didn't react, and after a few moments she felt him go limp under her hands. She checked to make sure she wasn't smothering him, then pressed the cloth hard against his cheek. She'd packed far more clothes than she actually needed, anyway. The jacket wouldn't be missed.

"The thing's actually listening," Hawk said, his voice resonant with wonder.

"What?" Azmei lifted her head and stared at Yar, whose slender form stood straight and strong against the towering silhouette of the seadragon.

"He told it to go away, and it—well, it hasn't gone away, but it's actually stopped attacking." Hawk rested a hand lightly on Azmei's shoulder. "I think it's listening to him."

Azmei looked back at Yar. When she'd met him, he'd been nothing more than a strange, skinny boy, taller than most, who lived half outside the world. Or perhaps it was half inside his head. Either way, he'd been out of sync with everyone else, and Azmei hadn't known quite what to think of him. All the same, she'd understood why Yar's sister had died—and attempted to kill—to protect him. There was something special about Yarrax Perslyn, and Azmei had not wanted to be the one to break it.

The seadragon apparently had that same desire. It arched its neck, peering down at the strange creature who dared challenge it. Yar's dark hair flew in the wind like a banner. He always had trouble meeting a person's gaze straight on, but he seemingly had no similar difficulty with the seadragon. His chin jutting out stubbornly, Yar had planted his feet wide, his hands on his hips, and appeared to be staring down the seadragon.

"Now!" cried the first mate's voice, and the starboard side cannons roared in unison. A cloud of smoke billowed from the cannons, obscuring Azmei's vision, but she heard the wild bellow of the seadragon. The ship pitched wildly and she was grateful for Hawk's fingers tightening on her shoulder. Beneath the other noises, she heard an agonized wail from Yarrax.

But it didn't matter. What mattered was Destar bleeding under her hand, the ship's deck slowly calming, the rumble of thunder suddenly retreating.

"They hurt it bad," Hawk said, his voice steady. "It's going. I'm going to leave you, Az. Yar needs help."

"Go," she said immediately. She trusted Hawk's instincts as much as she trusted her own. For that matter, Hawk had taken to Yar like an older brother to a younger. She knew he cared about the boy's well-being, and if he placed Yar's safety below Azmei's, it was only *just* below Azmei's.

Destar was disturbingly still under her hands. She leaned in, reassured herself he was still breathing, and sat up. "Healer!" she shouted.

Two sailors were with her at once, one of them already muttering under his breath. Azmei waited until he put his hand on the cloth over Destar's cheek, and then she sat back.

"We have him, princess," the other one said, and she nodded and stood.

She felt like she was waking from a nightmare as she focused on the action at the railing instead of right in front of her. Yar had fallen to his knees, clinging to the railing. On the deck near him, three soldiers were sprawled and writhing in various states of injury. Beyond the railing, the seadragon was flailing and thrashing in the ocean, which was now stained a dark purple-red.

Azmei gained her balance and staggered to Yar's side. "Yar—" she began, but he howled.

"Make them stop! Don't hurt it!" He turned his face

towards her, but his eyes were unfocused again.

"It was attacking us!" She looked at the seadragon again, though, and couldn't suppress the pang of pity that shook her. It had coiled in on itself like a dying serpent. Its throat was laid open, ragged edges of flesh gouting blood.

"Forced!" Yar howled. "Forced! Wrong!"

Azmei went to the rail and stared at the seadragon. Did Yar mean the seadragon had been forced to attack them? And if so, by what? Or whom? Were the gods already so awake they were trying to prevent the warning Yar carried? Or was some other power at work? Perhaps someone was trying to wake the gods faster? Or was it all a strange coincidence?

The seadragon gave a last, shrill shriek and slipped beneath the waves. Azmei couldn't see it, couldn't see if it kept sinking or if it was merely retreating. It left a purple-red blood slick on the surface of the sea.

"Princess?" The first mate's voice was tentative.

Azmei looked over her left shoulder at him. "What is it?"

"The captain, your highness. The healer isn't sure he'll live. Could you come?"

Azmei felt a horrible thrill along her limbs. She couldn't lose Destar! He'd been her teacher, her encourager, as well as her protector. Surely such a small injury wouldn't kill him.

"I'll come," she promised. She spared a final glance for Hawk, who was half supporting Yar, and then she followed the first mate belowdecks.

2

Eldry woke up on a barren stretch of sand, the sound of waves crashing in her ears. One side of her face was on fire. She couldn't see out of that eye. Her clothes were stuck to her, dried stiff with sea salt. What had happened?

She swept the gray landscape with the gaze from her good eye. She couldn't see anyone else. Not even animals, except a solitary gull winging overhead. The sky was gray too. A tumble of rocks in the distance was the only thing of interest on the whole beach.

Rhys, she thought suddenly. Had Rhys gone overboard too? Was he lying somewhere on the beach near her? Or had they saved him somehow? She thought of the way his heels had drummed against the deck, the high-pitched scream-ing…

Pain stabbed through her head, bringing her back from the too-vivid memories. She lifted her hand, muscles protest-ing, and touched her right cheek. Another throb of pain went through her and she flinched. Her tentative fingertips trailed up her cheekbone to her eye…and found a pulpy mess. The skin around her eye was swollen, and from the sticky feeling, there was blood. Something was definitely not right.

What had happened? Her breath came faster.

She gasped as the memory seized her. Rhys screaming. Rhys' body spasming, limbs flailing, his back arching away from the deck. The shouts of the crew. Her own cries, drowned out by Rhys'.

She curled up on the sand, burying her face in her arms and moaning. She'd done this to Rhys, dragging him away from Stony Lonesome, first to the capital and then to the sea. They'd grown up side by side, not blood siblings, but so close the villagers all called them the twins.

How could Rhys be gone?

Even worse was the knowledge, creeping and insidious, that it was her fault.

She shivered, sobbed, and then couldn't stop shivering.

"I couldn't save him," she whispered. Her fingers crept up to touch the bloody pulp of her eye again. "I didn't." She shook and dug one fingernail into her skin. It sent a spasm of pain through her head—a spasm like lightning. It felt horrible. It felt like she deserved it. "I couldn't save him."

She scraped at her face again. She craved the pain. The pain was her punishment for talking Rhys into leaving Amethir with her. She hadn't caused the storm, but he wouldn't have been on that ship if it weren't for her.

She'd just wanted to see something of the world. She hadn't expected anyone to get hurt.

She wasn't sure how long she'd been hearing the humming when she realized it was a real sound. Someone was on the beach with her. It couldn't be Rhys. Rhys couldn't be in any shape to hum. Eldry hunched further into herself. Maybe the person wouldn't see her. She didn't want anyone to see her.

But the humming was approaching her along a fairly direct path. It was a man's voice, she thought, though it wasn't deep. It was reedy.

"Oh, dear, dear, this won't do," said the person, and then she knew it was a man. "Just look at her. No wonder you said she needed to be fixed. Poor thing. She can't do anything like that."

Eldry squeezed her good eye shut. The fingers pressed into her bad eye felt the muscles twitch, but no eyelid moved to cover her eyeball. She wasn't certain her eyeball was there, actually.

"Yes, you did warn me. It was ugly, what happened. You're gracious to spare her. And striking at the ship that way—" The man broke off, chuckling gleefully. "What a fine joke! I'll have food for both of us to last months!"

Eldry knew he wasn't talking to her, but she didn't want to roll over and see who he was talking to.

"Here, lassie. Sit up. I know you're not sleeping." He snorted. "Well, she *isn't* sleeping. She's eavesdropping. Come, sit up."

At that last, a wizened old man stepped around in front of her. He propped his fists on bony hips and looked sternly down at her. "I know it hurts. We'll take a look at it. Tchk! That won't do. We can fix this. Better than new? Yes?" He looked away from her. "You'll do it, yes? I found her, after all. I have the glass. You'll fix her."

Eldry stared up at him, her breath coming faster. Who was he talking to? There was no one here but the two of them.

"Yes, yes," the man said, looking back at her. "It'll work beautifully. We'll need some wire. Oh, pretty wire." He started fishing around in a bag that hung at his side. "Let's see…"

He was mad. There was no other explanation for it. She shrank back. She could probably outrun him, if her legs weren't injured. But where would she go?

"You look thirsty. All that water and not any you can drink, eh?" The man cackled. "Here. Drink this. Drink up. You're probably dry as a bone, aren't you?" He pressed a flask into her hand. Eldry tried not to take it, but he curled her fingers around it.

When she turned her gaze to the flask, it looked ordinary. It didn't smell like anything other than being slightly musty. She *was* awfully thirsty. Maybe he was just a harmless beach comber, out looking for anything of value that washed up from the sea.

Too bad for him he found me instead, she thought ruefully. She lifted the flask and drank.

It tasted like musty water, too. Eldry started to relax. She'd been unfair to the poor man. He'd only wanted to help her. It must have been a shock for him to come across her like this.

Then she realized she was too relaxed. The flask seemed to weigh as much as a sword. She dropped it and stared at her enervated fingers.

"Wha d'you d…" she began, as the old man's face swung too close to hers. Then she felt herself being lowered to the ground.

"Don't worry," she heard. "I found you. Now I'll fix you."

***

When Eldry woke, she was surprised to find she actually hurt less than she had the last time. This time, she didn't have to work to remember what had happened. The old man was chattering on in his odd, one-sided conversation.

"She didn't want to let go, that's for certain. But you know best. You always do. It's a good thing you gave me plenty of healing herbs this time, though. If that ship hadn't happened along, there would have been danger of infection." He cackled then. "You aren't the healer, it isn't your strength! Trust me to know more about healing than you do."

Eldry inhaled. Her dry throat tickled and she began to cough.

"There, you woke her," the old man said. "She'll need a drink. Here, here you are. Drink now. This isn't sleepwater. It's wine. Nice strong wine. It'll warm you and keep you."

Eldry didn't want to drink, but he tipped the bottle to her lips and she didn't have much choice. She swallowed. To her relief, it really was just wine. It sent a flush of warmth through her. She glared up at the old man and then looked past him. For the first time she realized he had moved her. They were in a cave. The rough stone ceiling was uneven and low, and most of the light came from a steady lantern that burned on a niche near her feet.

"Who are you?" she rasped.

"Oh, no one important," he said, waving a hand. "The Scavenger, that's all. You washed up on my beach. Well, not my beach. Not exactly my beach. But close. Close enough. Yes!" He giggled. "Close enough that I could find you when he sent me. You're lucky, too! You were trying to take the rest of that eye out with your fingers! Better than if the gulls had found you, though."

That was when Eldry realized she could see him with both eyes. She tried to close her right eye and fresh pain tore through her head. She whimpered.

"Not that one, my dear," the man said. He patted her shoulder. "That one's a little different now. Better, though! Much better! And pretty, too. So pretty. I've always liked that piece, but I'd never found any project worthy of it. That's because he had you in mind for it from the beginning."

"Where's Rhys?"

"Rhys? I don't know. He didn't send me for Rhys. He sent me for you."

"Was there anyone else on the beach?"

The man shook his head. "I was just there to find you—and I did. I didn't notice anyone else."

"Why were you there to find me?" she whispered. "What did you do to me?"

"I fixed you!" He sounded impatient. "Well. You won't understand until I show you. Can you stand?"

She sat up slowly, discovered that she *could*, and nodded. Once she was on her feet, the man hopped down the cave away from her. He was remarkably spry, considering he looked like a bundle of twigs held together with seaweed and canvas. Eldry followed more slowly. Her head throbbed.

"There!" The Scavenger crowed, throwing his arms wide as she reached the mouth of the cave. "See!"

Eldry stared at him for a moment, uncomprehending. Then she turned her gaze to the world outside the cave.

And she did see.

She could see the currents of air as they flowed over the

sand, carrying tiny grains with them, creating dunes and creeping the beach ever-so-slowly across the land. She could see the rhythm of the waves rolling into land. She could see the play of the currents in the water. And when she lifted her gaze to the clouds overhead, she could see that this one would be a storm tomorrow, and that one wouldn't be a storm until the next day. There was no rain in these clouds for this beach.

Her heart jumped in her chest and began pounding so hard she panted. She could see the *weather*.

"What did you do to me?" she repeated, her voice barely loud enough for her to hear herself. "What did you do to me?" she screamed.

The Scavenger held up his hands, a mirror between them. "I fixed you," he said, his voice full of glee.

Eldry stared at her reflection in horror.

Her right eye was gone. It had been replaced by an almost-round piece of seaglass, wintry blue-white and cradled in a cage of fine, copper filigree. The filigree was held in place by a leather strap, perhaps as wide as her thumb, that crossed her forehead and fastened behind her head.

And worst of all—her hair, which had only begun to streak with the silver that marked her as a stormwitch, had gone completely white.

"He has a plan for you, my dear," said the Scavenger. He was sorting through the contents of a barnacle-encrusted apothecary's chest. "He tells me things, whispers to me. He led me to you, after all."

Eldry ignored him. She told herself she didn't care what was in the chest or what plans the mysterious *he* might have for her.

She knew she was lying to herself. Every time the Scavenger dragged her out of the cave, she cowered from the sight of the weather swirling through the air. She didn't want this. But she couldn't escape it, either.

Rhys had been hurt because of her. Possibly lost because of her. It still ached in her chest, a worse pain than losing her eye.

"He rewards those who serve him well," the Scavenger went on. "He's sustained me all these years."

And just look at you, Eldry wanted to say. *Living all alone out here, ragged and skinny as a ferret, mad from solitude.*

She didn't look up. She cupped her hand around her sea glass eye, rocking in place. *Rhys, Rhys, Rhys,* groaned her heart.

It was like losing part of her own self. She should have ignored the captain's orders before letting Rhys be hurt.

But I didn't know it would happen, pleaded a part of her mind.

It didn't matter. She should have known. She should have suspected. Hadn't she wondered why she felt no fear when he was so terrified?

She would make it up to him. If she couldn't find Rhys, she could do her penance. It wouldn't be the same as actual wergild, but it would at least show the gods how sorry she was.

"You cannot lose yourself, girl!" snapped the Scavenger. "You are here, you survived, and you will serve his purpose!"

In the days she had been here, he had never yelled at her. He had been cheerful, rambling on at length about any thought that entered his head, and he had cackled madly at his own jokes, but he had never been harsh.

Eldry lifted her head and glared at him with her good eye. She kept the sea glass eye covered. There was no weather to see here in the cave, but she didn't want to give him the pleasure of seeing his work. He was so proud of his work that it turned her stomach.

"Then find Rhys for me," she snapped.

"Don't give me that look." His voice was still sharp, but not as loud. "He has chosen *you.* You are honored."

"I don't feel honored," she said. Eldry knew her voice

sounded sullen. She didn't care. "I don't care about anything but finding Rhys."

The Scavenger huffed and turned to face her. "Rhys doesn't matter. Your task is all that matters. The storm-witches have gone astray. They have lost their way. And he has chosen you to redirect them. You will guide them to a new era of glory."

"I'm not a stormwitch anymore." Eldry looked back down at the cave floor and pressed the back of her hand against a sharp ridge.

"You can't just stop being what the gods made you," he replied. "And they made you a stormwitch."

"I won't use it." Eldry wrapped her arms around herself. "The academy wouldn't have me back if they knew what had happened. I should have protected Rhys somehow."

"Eh." The Scavenger clattered something inside the chest.

"If you don't help me find Rhys, I won't do anything for you," Eldry insisted, glaring at him again.

The Scavenger hitched his shoulders.

"The lightning struck Rhys!" Eldry snapped. "I have to see if he washed overboard with me. I have to find him. He could be hurt."

"Eh." The Scavenger shrugged his skinny shoulders again.

"I hate you," Eldry spat. She stood up and stalked to the mouth of the cave. She crouched there, covering her seaglass eye so she could look out safely.

The sky and the sea were a flat gray, hard and dull like the color of a sword. She scraped the back of her hand against the cave wall, actively hating everything around her, and hating herself most of all.

***

The Scavenger's snores filled the cave, almost loud

enough to drown out the sound of the waves. Eldry got up, holding her breath, and crept carefully to the mouth of the cave. Her magical eye didn't let her see in the dark, exactly, but it did show her the air currents that teased their way into the cave. She was able to deduce the location of any obstacle by watching the air flow around it.

Once she was standing outside the cave in the light of the waxing gibbous moon, she found the dagger and water flask she'd hidden earlier in the day. She had a firestarter and two candles in her bag, along with a flask she thought held the pain potion the Scavenger had been dosing her with.

If he wouldn't help her find Rhys, she would find Rhys on her own.

She had no idea where the Scavenger had found her, so she walked until she reached the wet sand and then she turned north. The *Elana Bey* had been sailing for the capital of Tamnen, and that was in the north part of the kingdom. She didn't know how far off course the storm had blown them, but she thought it had probably pushed them south.

As she skirted the waves, Eldry thought about Rhys. They had been friends all their lives—almost twenty-four years now—and as close as siblings for twenty of those years. Her parents had both died before she was five. Her mother she remembered not at all; she had died of a blood sickness when Eldry was three.

Her father had left her with Rhys' family when he was drafted into the Shroud War, when the Shroudlings had come from behind the veil of clouds, fog, and mountains, and attacked Amethirian traders. Most of her generation had lost a parent or grandparent in the war. Rhys hadn't, because his father had been the village blacksmith and too valuable to draft, and his mother had been too ill.

When Eldry was five, word had come that her father had been killed in battle. She had lost count of how many nights since then she had crawled into Rhys' bed and snuggled against him, desperate to feel someone next to her that wouldn't leave her. He had never complained, even during the years she wet their pallet because she was too afraid the Shroudlings would get her if she went to the privy out back.

Pain twisted her gut and she doubled over, clutching at her stomach. She had repaid such love and loyalty by waiting this long to go looking for him.

"I suppose you think you're meant to be some sort of hero." The voice startled her out of her reverie. Eldry swung around, snatching at the dagger in her belt. She only half relaxed when she realized the voice belonged to the Scavenger.

She squinted at him, shielding her eyes from the glare of the lantern in his hand. She hadn't seen him coming because he'd had it shuttered until then.

"Why are you following me?"

"Because he told me to find you and fix you, and I'm not about to let you get away, my witchy lass." The Scavenger cackled, but his eyes sparkled oddly. "He has a task for you, and I'm to see that you complete it."

"Well, you can tell him for me that I'm not completing anything unless we find Rhys." Eldry might have been a poor friend to Rhys in the week since the storm, but she was done letting the Scavenger push her around.

The Scavenger heaved a tremendous sigh. "Yes, yes, you already said that a dozen times. And lucky for you, he seems to agree. He woke me out of a sound sleep to follow you and help you." He snorted. "You have no idea how honored you are, girl. He's determined to have you."

"Well, he can have whatever he wants, if he'll save Rhys," Eldry said.

The moment the words passed her lips, she felt the world shift under her. She flung out her arms, trying to keep her balance, and only just kept from tumbling to the sand. Heart racing and mouth dry, she stared at the Scavenger.

He barked a laugh. "Done!" he cried. "Well. You're going the right way, at least. Clever thing that you are. Let's go. We've nearly reached him."

Eldry stayed where she was as he seemed to dance

along the shoreline. She felt a sudden searing regret for her words. That had been a rash promise to make, and it seemed the Scavenger's god had taken her seriously.

She had a very bad feeling that she would live to regret it.

3

They found Rhys just as the sun was lifting from the eastern horizon. Eldry had pushed ahead of the Scavenger and stayed in the lead. She was determined to be the one who found Rhys. The Scavenger kept muttering to himself and cackling from time to time, but he didn't protest.

Eldry's legs ached from walking so far through the loose sand. She had started yawning uncontrollably some time back, her good eye watering every time she yawned. The right side of her head throbbed. But she would not give up.

The sky had been lightening for the past half hour. Sanderlings and plovers were running ahead of them, taking to the air whenever Eldry got too near. As she lifted her gaze to follow the erratic flight of the birds, Eldry's attention was caught by an unnatural-looking lump huddled on the water side of a dingy-sized chunk of driftwood.

As she watched, a gull skimmed in from the sea and landed on the lump—which moved. Eldry's heart leapt into her throat.

"Rhys!" she cried, her voice strangled. Ignoring the protest from her legs, she darted forward, the sand making her pace awkward.

The Scavenger exclaimed something behind her, but she didn't catch the words. Maybe he was just talking to his god. Either way, she didn't care.

The gull flapped up, screeching in offense as she dropped to her knees beside the lump. Whoever it was moaned. Eldry rested a hand on what she thought was a shoulder.

It wasn't a shoulder.

The man screamed, a hoarse, dry scream that trailed off into a strangled sob. Eldry jerked her hand back, her fingers wet with something dark and tacky. Blood. Gulping, she looked closer and realized she had touched what used to be a leg, but was now a crushed mass of flesh.

"I'm sorry!" she gasped. "Rhys?"

The man's sob faded into a whine and then disappeared entirely. His breathing rasped in his chest. "El…"

It *was* Rhys! She shifted around until she found his head. He was lying on his side, his back to her, but he turned his head until she could see the week's worth of stubble covering sun-blistered skin.

"Scavenger!" she screamed over her shoulder. "Come now!" She bent low over Rhys' face. "I'm so sorry," she whispered. "I should have found you sooner."

"Water?" Rhys' voice was paper-dry.

"I have water," she said, fumbling her flask from her belt. "Here. Not too fast, though."

He ignored her, gulping some of the water through chapped lips and then pouring it over his face and hair. It couldn't be at all cool, but he sighed as if it had been the sweetest, coldest drink he'd ever had in his life.

"He's dying." The Scavenger's voice was stark.

Eldry rounded on him, glaring up at him as fiercely as she could from her knees. "He *isn't*. And if you want me to help you at all, you'll save him."

The Scavenger heaved a huge sigh and sat on his heels next to her. "You'd better be worth this, boy," he muttered.

To her surprise, Rhys crackled a laugh. "I am." His voice wasn't much stronger. "She means it." He gasped as the Scavenger reached down and pulled blood-soaked cloth away from the mangled leg.

"Gently," Eldry snapped at the Scavenger. She reached up and stroked Rhys' wet hair away from his face. "Sleeping gods, I'm so sorry, Rhys." Her throat felt thick.

"Not…" He shook his head. "Not y'r fault."

"You wouldn't have left Maron if I hadn't insisted," she said miserably.

"Might've." Rhys shook his head and lifted the flask to drain the rest of the water.

"He doesn't have the energy to argue with you, missy," the Scavenger said. "If you want him to live, make yourself useful. Give him some of the sleepwater. It's best he doesn't feel what I have to do next."

"Are you going to fix his leg?"

Rhys tensed. "Eldry. Your face."

She looked back at him, realizing that in her worry she'd forgotten about her new eye. "My eye was ruined in the wreck. The Scavenger fixed it."

Rhys squinted at her. His face seemed hard suddenly. "Fixed."

Eldry shrugged. "I can see the weather now, without having to strain for it. I can see the magic."

"Did well enough without." Rhys turned his gaze down to what the Scavenger was doing.

The old man had set his bag down and was pulling out long lengths of cloth. He was humming as he did so. When he saw them both looking at him, he said, "Sleepwater. It's in that metal flask. He'll need it for us to get him back home."

Eldry took the flask and lifted it for Rhys to drink, but he pushed it away. "Don't fix me like her."

Eldry recoiled, staring at him. Would he rather she be blinded? Disfigured? She swallowed the angry words she wanted to spit at him. He was weak and hurting. He didn't understand.

Rhys lifted his gaze back to meet hers. "Don't, El. You'd still be beautiful without that eye. I didn't mean that."

Eldry glared down at him but didn't answer.

The Scavenger snorted. "No fixing to be done yet, boy. I have to get you home and see just how bad the damage is first. But it'll have to be straightened and bandaged, and you don't want to be awake for that."

Rhys looked suspiciously at the Scavenger for several heartbeats, then finally nodded.

"Good. Drink up, lad. It'll be a long way back, and we don't want you waking on the way."

4

Captain Arama Dzornaea, known as the Storm Petrel, had spent half her life as a privateer and half her life on a merchant ship, and she'd been through plenty of storms in that time. But she'd only been shipwrecked once, and it had been the worst night of her life. That was the only reason she hadn't torn up her letter of marque and killed the messenger bird that brought her latest assignment.

Well, that and the fact that she was in love with the prince's best friend, which would make it awkward for her to turn pirate again after all these years. Damned inconvenient, falling in love.

"Search and rescue?" Her first mate was staring at her, his dark eyes squinted. Beside him, the second mate, a sunburned lad named Zek, looked horrified. Carig coughed. "But we're pi—fighters, mum."

"Aye, Mister Carig." Carig would be easy to convince; he was devout. It was the rest of her crew she wasn't so sure of. They would follow her orders, but she didn't like sailing with an unhappy crew. And her crew had signed up to fight, not search for lost ships. "Have you forgotten," she said, matching Carig's gaze with a hard one of her own, "that Sea Lord Antos had mercy on us once?"

That was all it took. His sun-browned face flushed and he turned his squint out to sea.

"No, mum, that I haven't. T'would be ungrateful for me to deny another the chance of rescue."

"It would." Arama would never claim to be devout, but she was more than happy to indulge Carig's offerings to the sea god. Antos, it was said, slept more lightly than the other gods, and was more likely to hear the pleas of those who lived on the ocean.

Carig sighed. "You're a hard one, Captain."

"It gets worse, I'm afraid." Arama pushed a hand through her hair, tucking it behind her ear. "The missing ship's the *Elana Bey*."

"A trader?" The dismay in Carig's voice was clear.

"With a stormwitch posted on board."

"A noble's trader?" Zek blurted, his green eyes wide.

Arama smirked. "I told you it got worse." She was none too happy about the prospect of taking a stormwitch on her own ship, when it came down to it. There had been a witch on board the *Bounder* when it went down, and that had done them little good. In the end, Arama was certain Carig's faithful offerings to the sealord had done more to save them than all of Stormwitch Lijka's pushing and pulling with the magic.

"Aye, mum. That you did." Carig sighed and rubbed a hand over his head. "I suppose she was trying to beat storm season home."

"With a load of saltpeter bound for Tamnen, or Tamnese cotton and silk on the return. Either way, it's not a cargo the crown wants to lose. And the fact is, if the Strid took her, we're the best ship to give chase."

"That we are." Carig slapped his hands together and rubbed them briskly. "Right, then. We'd best get on with it, eh? What orders?"

Arama glanced at the sun and slid her compass out of her pocket for a bearing. They were in international waters— just—but they weren't that far off the Tamnese Coast. "There's no word yet if the *Elana Bey* reached Tamnen City at all. The ambassador there will let us know. So knowing the Strid as we do, Mister Zek, what do you suppose happened?"

Zek straightened, chewing his lip. "We know the word's leaked out that we're trading saltpeter to the Tamnese. They won't want Tamnen to have more guns than them, even if the guns aren't much good for the kind of fighting they're doing in the Kreyden."

Or much good at all, artillery aside, Arama thought, nodding. Her pistols looked ferocious, and the mere thought of being shot had made more than one adversary back down, but the fact was, they were damned heavy and hard to aim outside a few paces. She'd still rather rely on her cutlass in a fight.

"We know the Tamnese have lost more ships than we have, this past year and a half," Zek continued. "So my guess is the Strid are focusing on the saltpeter ships. If they know the *Elana Bey*'s one…"

Arama nodded. "They'll have been shadowing her from the moment she left Amethirian waters, and as soon as they had a favorable wind, they'd be on her."

"Those seacaves along the coast south of the Kreyden?" Zek was poised on the balls of his feet, ready for her order.

"Aye, Zek. Set course for the Kreyden, and look sharp for Strid vessels. Let's not provoke an international incident." Arama paused and grinned at his look of disbelief. "At least, one we can't win."

"Aye, mum!" Zek threw her a salute and trotted off to pass the orders.

"And you," she said, mock-scowling at Carig. "Get to your bunk for some rest. We'll have full watch through the night."

"Aye, mum." Carig ducked his head and went belowdecks.

Arama tucked a finger inside the pocket of her waistcoat, letting it brush against the soft edges of the paper inside. There were some advantages to being the king's favorite privateer. Regular service by the messenger birds, for instance. Suppressing a smile, she strode back toward the quarterdeck.

Once she had a little privacy, she pulled the letter out of her pocket. It was already creased and worn from rereading, though it had just come by bird two weeks past.

My dear Arama, Lozarr had written.

I write with news that has confounded our prince, but will probably please you as it does me. Princess Azmei has sent a letter to Vistaren, saying she is coming to Amethir. You have probably heard more than we have of the rumors out of her kingdom—her brother Razem is king, after their father was struck down by an assassin. We have also heard rumors of insurrection, but there are few details, and the princess gave none in her letter.

Arama smiled, but it was a grim expression. She had, indeed, heard more than that. The insurrection had been Razem and Azmei's cousin making a play for the throne. He had been the one who attempted Azmei's assassination three and a half years ago, and only the barest chance had kept him from winning the throne.

She didn't credit the rumors of dragons and necromancers, of course. There were always those who would see magic and malevolence where it wasn't. And why would dragons get involved in an insurrection, anyway? She shook her head.

Vistaren, as you can imagine, is beset with doubts. It is difficult to comfort him, but what little I can do, I will do. It would be well if you were with us in Maron when the princess arrives. Vistaren has spoken of you often since her letter arrived three days ago. I think he could do with your counsel.

That line made Arama grimace every time she read it. What advice did Lo think she could she give the prince that would help him? She still struggled with her feelings for Lozarr, though they had been sharing a bed for the past three and a half years, whenever they both found themselves in the same place. It didn't happen often—he was a general in the king's army, and she spent most of her time on the high seas—but every time they parted, she felt like she was losing part of herself.

She hated it.

I am in the capital for the time being, and expect to remain here at least through Azmei's arrival. It will be good to see her again, though not as good as it would be to see you again. I hope you are well.

Yours always, Lo

She sighed. "Yours always," she whispered, and folded the letter to replace it in her pocket.

She gazed at the ship's wake, letting her eyes unfocus just slightly. Lo had no trouble admitting that he loved her. Arama was the one who had difficulty accepting that love. Loving Lozarr was easy. Being loved in return…that was the hard part, somehow.

Thunder rumbled low across the ocean, and Arama jerked her head up to stare at the sky. She hadn't noticed them building, but the sky astern was full of roiling black clouds.

"Zek!" she shouted, and the mate came running.

"I've got the hands reefing sails, Captain," he reported.

"Good. When did the clouds come up?"

He shook his head. "They came up fast, mum. We caught the wind and were steering full and by, and just as we were really making headway, we saw the clouds building."

Arama frowned. That smacked of witchery, though she certainly didn't have a stormwitch on board. Could this have something to do with the king's missing ship? She allowed herself a moment of speculation, then pushed the thought away. The approaching storm was a more pressing problem.

She studied the wind direction, considered their position, and made a decision. "We'll scud under foresail. Move the shot forward to alter the trim. Then all non-essential personnel belowdecks. No sense getting the whole crew soaked. Oh, and Zek—get Mister Carig up here." She wanted her best helmsman on the wheel.

"Aye, Captain." Zek dashed off, already shouting orders.

Arama scowled at the clouds, offering a silent prayer to the Sea Lord. She had no intentions of being wrecked again, if the god granted.

Carig's heavy footfalls thudded up to the quarterdeck, making Arama realize how silent everything had gone. "Storm, mum?" he asked.

Arama jerked a thumb over her shoulder, scanning the crew's activity through the deepening gloom. She could see them shouting to one another, but the wind was carrying the noise away from her.

"You're relieved, Wirda," Carig told the helmsman. "Go on below. I'll keep on over watch."

Thunder cracked abaft and Carig swore. "It'll be a wild night."

Arama grunted. She turned to watch the storm. It was coming fast. She hoped the crew would have time to get the sails set properly before it hit. If they weren't carrying enough sail, the wind could sweep the sea over the stern and they'd be pooped. If that happened, the ocean would sweep the decks clean—of sailors as well as anything else that wasn't properly tied down.

"You want us running directly before the storm, Captain?" Carig was lashing himself to the wheel. He'd never been one for bravado; he'd rather have a firm grip on the wheel and confidence than worry about appearing stalwart.

"That's your call, Mister Carig," Arama said. "You know this ship, and you know your helm. I trust your judgment."

"Aye, Captain."

Arama nodded and turned again to watch the approaching storm. Thunder boomed almost as soon as the lightning flashed. The wind made her eyes water. She ducked her head, her gaze falling to the surface just astern of the *Dawn Star*, and cold speared down her spine. She'd seen a flash of silvery scales that was all too familiar.

She pressed her lips together and drew in a long, slow breath, trying to calm her suddenly pounding heart. There were sirens shadowing the *Dawn Star*. And in a following sea with a gale blowing up, that could be a recipe for disaster.

"Sirens teeth," she whispered, and sent another prayer winging to Sea Lord Antos. It would be a long, wild night indeed. She hoped they all lived to see the end of it.

***

"I said I don't want to be fixed!"

Rhys was still in pain, Eldry could see that, but his voice was much stronger after sleep, water, and food. And he was just as stubborn as ever.

"Rhys, your leg is crushed," Eldry said. Her stomach was still flopping inside her from the way the bones of his shin had poked out through the skin, the squishy way his ankle joint moved when the Scavenger poked at it.

"So it is. And many a fellow's had worse. Just wrap it as best you can and give me boneset. I don't need any fancy rigmaroles like what he's put on you."

The pang of hurt shouldn't have surprised her, but it did. "I can see the weather with this," she said. "And he did a good job of it, at least. I don't look so hideous, do I?"

Rhys' expression didn't soften. "You could never look hideous. But you'd be more fair without that seaglass contraption."

"It'll give me more power," she said, and she hated the wheedling note in her voice. She hadn't even wanted it when the Scavenger did it. She resented what the Scavenger had done. Why was she so intent on talking Rhys into letting the Scavenger do the same to him?

Off-key singing told them the Scavenger was coming back into the cave. Eldry didn't want the old man to hear her defending him or his work. She leaned in.

"You'll never live a normal life with that crushed leg," she hissed.

"What's normal?" Rhys said. "What part of our lives so far have been normal? You losing your kin to the war, us choosing each other as family that no one else understands, your magic, me following you?"

"But your leg!" she protested. Her throat felt thick.

"So I'll limp. So what. I'm a baker and cook. The leg doesn't stop me from doing that. I'm not *broken*, Eldry." There was a bitterness to Rhys' voice she couldn't remember ever hearing before.

"But…" she whispered, but the Scavenger was back, and she couldn't bring herself to argue anymore.

"Now then." The Scavenger's voice was gloating. "We have a broken bit of mast that might do well for the basis. And I have gears and cogs that should make a good knee. Plus there's a good leather harness I can remake to hold everything in place. He's sent all that I need to fix you."

"No." Rhys' voice was firm. "You've *fixed* enough. I won't let you do more than set the leg as best you can and let it heal."

The Scavenger sank back on his heels, studying Rhys' face. "You're a hard one."

No, he wasn't, Eldry wanted to say, but Rhys' face *did* look hard just then. He was the kindest, gentlest person she knew. But his expression was implacable.

"He won't change his mind," she said dully. "You might as well do as he says."

The Scavenger snorted. "It'll make traveling harder, if you're not able to walk."

Eldry swallowed and straightened her back. She ought to stand up for Rhys, even if he didn't agree with her. "Your god should have thought of that before he let Rhys be hurt," she said. "If he wants me to go anywhere, he'll just have to provide a way of traveling that works for Rhys, too."

She didn't miss the look of surprised gratitude Rhys flashed her. It warmed her a little, even though she still felt cold inside at how much Rhys loathed her new eye.

The Scavenger huffed, but after a moment he shrugged. "Have it your way. Though you may live to regret it."

Rhys settled back on his elbows. "I doubt that very much."

****

"Get up! Get up! It's time to go."

Eldry rolled over and yawned. She looked around the

cave and didn't see Rhys. He'd been hobbling around using a twisted piece of driftwood whenever he had to pass water. Perhaps he'd gone to do that.

"I said get up! Your body is healed, and the boy's body is healing, and your minds will just have to catch up along the way." The Scavenger sounded more lucid than usual. That was strange.

Eldry looked up at him. He was wrapped in an odd robe made of sail canvas, and he had strange rope sandals on his feet.

"Are you—going somewhere?" she asked.

"We all are. He is sending us to the river mouth. We have a task, and then you'll have to go on. I have clothes set out for you. I've sorted all the seaglass I have, and sewn you a bandolier to carry it. He will give us provisions when we get there."

"Get where?" Eldry choked out. She got slowly to her knees and looked around for the clothes.

"Wherever he is sending us," the Scavenger said. He huffed. "Get dressed. I'll wait for you outside."

"How will Rhys go with us?" she demanded before he could leave.

He didn't bother looking back. "A pony and cart came wandering along just when we needed them. That's how I know he's ready for us to move." He walked away. "We're both just waiting on you now."

Eldry scowled down at the scarlet dress that was spread on the low table. She didn't like red. It didn't go with her complexion, and the color would attract attention that she didn't want.

All the same, the dress she had been wearing stank of fish and sweat, and the scarlet dress looked clean. She sighed and stripped off her clothes, taking a minute to wash using water from the natural basin at the end of the cave. When she tugged the dress over her head, it was a little loose, but not baggy.

Her boots were still in good condition, though the salt

water had stiffened them. She tugged them on and sighed. She didn't want to leave. She didn't want to stay, either, but staying would take less effort than leaving.

Scowling, she walked out to the beach. Rhys was settled in a small trap, his unfixed leg propped on several packs and bedrolls. He looked like he was asleep. The Scavenger had his back to her, head tilted back a little, hands held out a little from his sides, palms up. He must have heard her footsteps.

"We'll go to the river," he said. "You will study the weather as we walk."

"I don't want to," she said.

The Scavenger opened his eyes. "It doesn't matter. You will."

Eldry wasn't sure why she had bothered to argue. What was the point of arguing? She'd agreed to do whatever the Scavenger's delusions demanded of her, as the price for healing Rhys. She wouldn't go back on that. She shrugged and uncovered her seaglass eye to study the wind that was pushing north along the coast.

The wind carried heat with it and was full of moisture. It would mean rain for whatever land was half a day's journey north of them. The air held a tantalizing scent that she couldn't place, but her eye told her it was the faintest strain of magic; someone had worked this weather. Or else a weather worker had stood in this wind. Eldry wasn't sure which.

"Well?" the Scavenger demanded. "Tell me what you see!" He seized the pony's halter and began dragging at it. The pony offered no complaint; it just began walking. Rhys' head rolled a little to one side. He *was* asleep.

Eldry told him, though part of her just wanted to stare at the beautiful swirls of blues and whites and greens that made up her vision in that eye. She felt she could lose herself in it if she didn't take care.

"And no rain today?"

Eldry tripped over a piece of driftwood and reluctantly dragged her gaze from the weather. The Scavenger steered the pony trap around the driftwood. Eldry clenched her fists so tightly her nails pressed into her palms.

"No rain today," she confirmed. "Not here. North of here by at least half a day."

"How certain are you?"

Eldry glanced back at the weather, trying not to get caught by it a second time. "Almost certain."

"Huh." He didn't sound impressed. Eldry tried to bristle, couldn't be bothered, and instead focused on putting one foot in front of the other.

They walked in silence for several moments, and then the Scavenger said "Huh," again.

"Huh what?" Eldry snapped. Why did he have to be so cryptic?

"Ohh…" He drew out the word. "I had just hoped you would be more certain. You do realize what a good piece of work I did, don't you?"

She didn't want to think about it. The seaglass eye forced the swirls and dips of stormwitchery into her vision, whether she wanted it or not. It hadn't been like that when she was a normal stormwitch. Then she had to reach for it, the not-sight that let her envision the weather magic. She wished it were still that difficult.

"I know you meddled where you weren't wanted," she said.

"Pff." The Scavenger hastened his steps. "You're feeling sorry for yourself again, and it's unattractive. On top of that, it's useless. He has a plan for you, and whatever it is, he'll make certain it happens. If you try to thwart him, you'll only end up regretting it."

Eldry kept up with him, resenting him but curious. "Have you tried thwarting him before?" she asked. She wasn't entirely clear on what god the Scavenger thought he was talking to, but it seemed like a good idea to learn more, just in case.

"We-e-ll, not *thwart* exactly," the Scavenger hedged. "But he's not patient with folk as drag their feet when he's given instructions." He darted a sharp look at her and Eldry huffed, looking away.

"I don't care." Her gaze wandered up to the sky again, taking in the swirls of the breeze as it played laughingly past. She *was* certain there would be no rain today. She had no doubt that whatever he'd done had enhanced her vision of the magic, whether or not it had enhanced her actual magic, but she wouldn't give the Scavenger the satisfaction of saying so.

They walked without conversing for a time, though she could hear the Scavenger muttering to himself or his god under his breath. She didn't try to hear what he was saying. She was too interested in watching the thermals that carried a gull aloft over her.

"Can't take your eyes off it, can you?" The Scavenger cackled. "You'll see I was right."

Eldry didn't bother replying.

They camped on the beach that night, bedrolls snugged up against a low bluff held in place by beach grass. The wind off the ocean was cool, but the Scavenger built a fire and brewed a thick fish soup. They sat across the fire from one another, none of them speaking. Rhys dozed off; whatever the Scavenger was giving him for the pain was making him sleep a lot.

Even the Scavenger's conversation with his god had died down during the last hour before sunset. Eldry wondered if whatever the Scavenger had expected to find had failed to materialize. She wasn't curious enough to ask, though.

Instead she looped her arms around her knees and let her good eye fall mostly closed. If she let her hair fall across the seaglass eye, she could almost pretend everything was normal.

No you can't, you idiot, she thought to herself. *Trying to pretend things are normal! What a stupid idea. Nothing's normal. Rhys is crippled. You failed your assignment to get the ship to Tamnen and back safely. Your eye was injured and that madman scraped it out and replaced it with seaglass—and the worst of it is that it worked.*

Anger surged through her. None of this would have happened if they hadn't assigned her to the *Elana Bey*. She had wanted a posting in the capital, close to the center of power and the bustling excitement of the city. Instead they'd stuck her on a fat, slow merchant ship. This was all the Stormwitch Council's fault. Councilwoman Lijka Ardelis had taken a disliking to Eldry for her ambition and talent. She had probably been the one who decided to relegate Eldry to an out-of-the-way posting.

Eldry lifted a hand to her face, making a cage of her fingers to cup her missing eye. If Lijka Ardelis had wanted to stop Eldry gaining power, her plan had twisted on her. Eldry could *see* the weather now. Lijka couldn't claim that ability. Eldry straightened slowly. She *would* return to Amethir. She would show Lijka how badly her plan had gone awry.

"You see your path." The Scavenger's voice was low and frighteningly sane. He watched her with unblinking eyes that glittered darkly in the firelight. Eldry didn't think she'd seen him so still in the whole time she'd been with him.

"I'm going back to the academy," she said.

"You'll show them how much more powerful you are." The Scavenger's gaze hadn't wavered from hers. "You'll show them that your power is not just that of a calmer or shielder. You're a storm*weapon* now."

Some part of Eldry knew she should be afraid of this sudden change in the Scavenger. But she just nodded. "A stormweapon," she repeated. "And I will show them all."

***

Eldry caught her breath when she saw the ship at the dock of the tiny coastal village. So *that* was what the Scavenger had been leading her to. A single-masted sloop, it looked lithe and quick, and she knew at a glance she could fill its sails with wind all the way to Amethir.

"That is mine," she whispered.

The Scavenger threw her a quick glance and then cackled. "So it is, my dear. He brings everything I need in good time. And now he has brought you a ship. A ship to carry you home."

Eldry shook her head, watching two crew members coiling rope. She didn't know much about sailing aside from how the wind and waves should treat the ship. She would need the crew along with the ship. They would have to answer to her, though. She would need to bring them to heel quickly. There could not be a repeat of the *Elana Bey*.

She was glad they had left Rhys with his cart at what passed for a public house. He wouldn't like what she was about to do. But he would accept it if he didn't have to see it.

"I will take the ship," she said. "And the crew. And I will be their goddess."

The Scavenger's hand flashed out so quickly she only realized he had slapped her when her cheek started stinging. "Not their *goddess*," he hissed. "Never their goddess. If you say that again, he'll take you to the bottom of the sea next time."

Eldry stared at him, rubbing her cheek. He'd said he was talking to his god, hadn't he? A shiver ran through her. What she'd said was perilously close to blasphemy, and was certainly impiety. "Their queen, then," she said, keeping her tone haughty. She wouldn't apologize to the Scavenger, even if she hadn't meant blasphemy. She certainly wouldn't apologize to a man who had just struck her.

And instantly the Scavenger was beaming at her again. "Their queen, yes. Their queen of air and water. That you shall be."

Eldry nodded. "And the ship shall be my *Revenge*."

The sailors didn't even see her coming. They were too busy with their dock duties, tying things and loading things and going about their business. The village folk were timid people, reliant perhaps on the sailors, but unwilling to place themselves in any danger. When they saw Eldry walking down the single street of their village, cradling lightning in both her hands, her silver-white hair crackling around her head, they faded away as if they'd never been there. No one raised a cry to alert the sailors.

Eldry had watched long enough to have identified their captain. He would be the one most likely to offer any resistance. She waited until he was standing on the quarter-deck, far enough from the others that no one could reach him. Then she drew back one arm and hurled the lightning at him. It struck him squarely in the back, and Eldry *felt* his reaction.

He arched backwards, his back curved like a figurehead. Screaming, he flailed his arms and jerked his legs in a horrible parody of a dance. Then Eldry clenched her teeth and forced more power along the arcing lightning. His scream choked off and he fell to the deck, unmoving.

The rest of the crew had jumped to help him, but it was too late. It had been too late for him the moment Eldry chose him as her target. One of them shouted, "He's dead!" The others were staring at her, mouths hanging open.

If it hadn't been so horrible, Eldry would have laughed at their bafflement. As it was, she couldn't help shuddering from both the pleasure and the horror of having killed again. She had to do it; she knew she must eliminate the captain if they were to take her as their queen. But she remembered how Rhys' body had looked on the deck of the *Elana Bey*, she remembered the emptiness in the pit of her stomach, and she felt the captain's death nestle in next to Rhys'.

I will be damned for this, she thought. *But I will damn the entire academy along with me.*

"I am Eldry," she called, channeling the wind to carry her voice to them. "I am your new queen."

Her shocking entrance had the desired effect; none of them laughed at her pronouncement as they would have just five minutes ago. Eldry surveyed them, satisfied.

"Who will speak for you?" She had stopped walking well out of the distance, she thought, of whatever firearms they might have. If one of them made as if to harm her, she would make an example of him, but she hoped the captain had been example enough.

The men shuffled their feet and muttered among themselves, then a tall, balding man took a reluctant step forward. "Might as well be me." His voice wasn't as reluctant as his posture implied. Eldry had known men like that at the academy. He would play the ignorant yokel, but he thought highly of himself. She cursed her hurry; if she had observed them a bit longer, she might have chosen him instead of the captain.

"Your name?"

He seemed to fight a smirk. "They call me Black Miry."

Eldry sniffed and lifted her chin. "I shall call you *dead* if you don't show me proper respect, dog." She made her voice cold, mimicking the way Pralith Menever talked to those he felt were beneath his notice.

The other sailors ooooohed and laughed. One of them slapped Black Miry on the shoulder. Eldry wasn't sure if it was meant to be a congratulatory slap or a quelling one. Miry seemed to take it as encouragement; he let the smirk escape.

"You must be one of them pagan weather witches," he said, and the arrogance in his voice curdled her mood.

She jerked her hand forward, snapping her fingers, and he howled as lightning crackled against his wrist. Eldry stepped forward slowly as he rubbed his skin.

"I will brook no insolence, Black Miry. I will tolerate no disrespect." She stood an arm's-length higher than he did, thanks to the slope of the land toward the dock. She looked down her nose at him, relishing the difference in height. "My orders will be followed to the letter, and they will be followed at once. Is that understood? I will take on whatever crew will agree to these terms." She paused, letting them consider her words for several heartbeats, then she added, "And I will kill whatever man refuses them."

There was a small silence as the sailors all stared at her, and then the Scavenger cackled. "Now you've got their attention, missy!" he crowed.

Eldry fought the temptation to throw lightning at him. Whatever god of his had set them on this path, it didn't seem prudent to strike the Scavenger down—yet. But she would do it the moment she saw her way clear without him.

The crazy old man's words didn't seem to impact how the sailors saw her, though. One by one, they dropped to their knees in front of her. Eldry called lightning to dance in the palm of her hand, relishing the fear she saw in their eyes.

"I am a pagan weather witch," she said. "I am Storm-witch Eldry, your queen, and I name this ship the *Revenge*. You shall be my crew, and I will reward faithful labor with riches and glory—but I will pay back failure with vengeance."

A biting glee spread through her as—one by one—the sailors pledged to serve her.

And through it all, the Scavenger giggled to himself behind her.

5

Prince Vistaren doth'Mara of Amethir trotted along the hall, puffing slightly. He was late; his practice session had run long, and he'd spent too long in the bath cleaning up. He hoped his first appointment of the afternoon would be late too. He didn't want to be rude, even unintentionally, to a powerful stormwitch. The woman who was scheduled to lunch with him was just that, and had become something of a friend as well.

The door to his quarters opened ahead of him and his secretary Beyas met him, bowing. "Highness, Stormwitch Lijka Ardelis is expected any moment to join you for—"

"Yes, I know," Vistaren interrupted, heading for his dressing chamber. "Have Isden get me a better tunic. This one is too tight."

Vistaren shouldn't feel as grumpy as he did about this meeting. He liked Lijka and her wife Kinnet, who had saved his life three years ago. But in her letter requesting the appointment, Lijka had given him no indication what it was about, except a 'matter of concern'—a term too vague for him to interpret. He knew there was some feud between her wife Kinnet and the king's own stormwitch, but neither Kinnet nor Lijka had ever used her friendship with the prince to political advantage before.

And he had his own concerns. Lijka's letter had arrived just a day before *The Letter*, the one that sent Vistaren's life sideways once again. He'd known this day was coming, of course. He had no excuse for being so confused about it. But he still had no answers to the question of Azmei Corrone.

"Highness." Isden's deft hands helped him out of his tunic and into a fresh one, mercifully looser. Vistaren frowned down at the blue cloth. He'd grown even pudgier than the last time he'd seen Azmei. What if she was embarrassed by him? He was embarrassed by himself. He was no glutton, nor did he shun physical activity—there *was* muscle under the layer of fat—but he would never be a finely sculpted figure of a man.

"You look sour enough to curdle milk," Isden observed. "I thought you liked Mistress Lijka."

Vistaren shook himself. "I do. It's just—" He paused. He didn't really want to go into it. "It's just hot out there."

It was a few weeks past Longday—the height of the dry season, when all the crops were stretching higher into the sky and the merchants were making good time along the roads. Vistaren loved the Longday celebrations and all the feasting and feats of arms that went along with it. The hot, dry weather was ideal for long horseback rides in the countryside, and game was usually abundant for the hunt.

His servant knew quite well how much Vistaren liked the heat. Isden tilted his head quizzically at Vistaren, but didn't question him further. Isden was friend and confidant as well as servant, but he knew when to stop pushing.

There was a tap on the door. "Highness," Beyas said, leaning his head in the room. "Stormwitch Ardelis has arrived."

Vistaren nodded and crossed to the dining room door. He took a deep breath, then strode into the dining room, stretching a smile of welcome across his face.

"Stormwitch Ardelis, welcome to the palace," he said, smiling. "It is a pleasure to see you after so long."

Lijka Ardelis was older than he was, but not as old as his parents. She was tall and lithe, with short, pure silver hair that proclaimed how long she had been practicing weather magic. She had been the king's own stormwitch once, many years ago, though Vistaren knew there was some shroud of sorrow over that time in her life. Her smile today was strained, on a face that didn't look like it smiled often, but it was genuine. She curtsied deeply. As she rose, she said, "Thank you for seeing me, Prince Vistaren."

"Please, sit," he said, and gestured at the place to the left of his. "How was your journey?"

Over the first course, they exchanged pleasantries and discussed her short voyage in from the light at the mouth of the harbor sheltering Amethir's capital city. While the servants cleared away the appetizers and poured them a second glass of wine, Vistaren took the opportunity to study Lijka.

There were new lines of strain in her face, and a restlessness he wasn't used to seeing in her bearing. Since he met her two years ago, he'd thought Lijka a self-contained woman—quiet, yes, but sure of herself. But now her fingers tapped and slid across the table, her lips pressed thin when she wasn't eating.

Once the servants had retreated, Vistaren broached the subject. "Your letter indicated that you had a, hmm…a matter of concern. Please tell me what troubles you."

The expression that flickered across Lijka's face was a mixture of relief, confusion, and…what? Frustration, perhaps. She set her fork down and leaned closer.

"I will try to explain it…clearly." She frowned. "Highness, how much do you understand of stormwitchery? Of how it works?"

Vistaren took a sip of wine and set his glass down. "Not much, really. As a stormwitch, you can sense the weather and touch it somehow. Influence it. Start rain or stop it. Redirect storms. But as for how it actually works?" He shook his head. "I have no idea."

"Well enough. You know that stormwitches usually have specialties? That some are actually better with springs and rivers, and others can always find water, no matter where they are?" When Vistaren nodded, she said, "I am good with storms especially. Calling them, calming them, diverting them. Some do better with gentle rain or streams, and some are wind witches, but I am a true stormwitch."

Her eyes flashed as she spoke.

"I understand so far," Vistaren said. But why did this matter, he wondered.

"It is not storm season yet," Lijka replied.

"Not for weeks," Vistaren agreed. He counted mentally. It was nearly three weeks after Longday. That meant roughly six weeks until storm season began.

"It stormed last week," she said. "It came in from the sea and turned south along the southeast coast." Her expression went bleak. "I felt it hit Anderly."

Vistaren frowned. Storms out of season weren't entirely unheard-of. He'd experienced it himself, three years ago. That summer storm had been called by a stormsinger who was seeking companionship. It caught Vistaren, Lijka's wife Kinnet, and everyone else on the ship with them. But that had worked out to everyone's good, he thought. Kinnet had befriended the stormsinger and learned from him secrets no human had known for centuries.

"Why has no other stormwitch announced this?" he asked. "Pralith—"

"Pralith Menever is a fool!" Lijka's voice was harsh. Vistaren blinked and glanced over at his secretary, who was standing by the door and pretending not to hear anything.

Lijka drew herself up, straightening her shoulders. She clasped her hands in her lap. When she spoke next, her voice was so soft he had to strain to hear. "Pralith doesn't scorn me the way…the way he does Kinnet." A line formed between her brows. Her gaze was on the table, not on Vistaren. "I didn't agree with his appointment, but I don't hold with Kinnet's feud, either. I've seen what can happen when a stormwitch's pride is hurt." She faltered and picked up her wine glass. She lifted it to her lips and lowered it back to the table with a shaking hand. "She didn't want me to come to you, but I can no longer be silent."

"No longer…" Vistaren let his words trail off, and Lijka took the opening.

"I have been noticing small anomalies. Rain that lasted

too long at the end of the season, not in one area, but in several. Breezes that always shift in the late afternoon, when the sea is heated by the sun and the wind blows in to shore—and yet they are shifting earlier, barely after midday. Casting that comes more slowly, with more effort."

"How long?" Vistaren said, and then immediately answered himself. "Since the end of the rainy season. That's only six weeks. Is that time to see a pattern forming?"

"Longer than the rainy season." Lijka's voice held a bleak note he didn't like. "Kinnet and I have been arguing about it since the end of the rainy season, but I first noticed these anomalies while you and she were sailing to Ranarr." Her lips twisted. "I felt nothing of your encounter with the stormsinger, though I should have. But I did notice that far to the west, it was raining out of season."

"Why wasn't that reported?"

"The magic is powerful, but we often choose to let nature have its course, if we think it will do more harm to change it. Just so, we have certain…" She paused. "Allowable percentages of error."

"Then the magic isn't perfect."

Lijka's gaze was coolly amused. "It has never been perfect, Your Highness."

Vistaren considered this. At least, he *tried* to consider it. It was too big to grasp, the notion that something might be wrong with the weather magic. Without stormwitchery, Amethir was just another kingdom, having to fight the elements as well as other vagaries of life. Stormwitchery had built Amethir into a powerful grain and fish exporter. Stormwitchery made it possible for the folk of the Gehb River Valley to farm without worrying about the cycle of flooding and drought.

After a while he realized he had been sitting motionless, holding his fork in the air, for far too long. "Please explain." He set his fork down.

Lijka sucked in a long breath. "Stormwitches always feel the weather energy around us," she said slowly. "We are aware of the weather always, to some degree. But we must channel to see it, to touch it and work it. You know about seaglass augmenting and refining our magic?" She touched her pendant, made of frosted white seaglass wrapped in silver wire.

"Yes."

"From here, I can feel the weather patterns most of the way to the Sandswamp, if I channel through seaglass."

Vistaren stared at her. The Sandswamp was a good three weeks away by horseback. "I thought stormwitches had to be closer—"

"They do." That was the second time she'd interrupted him. "I tell you this so you will know how powerful I am. I cannot *change* weather so far from here, but I can feel it."

"This still doesn't tell me how something is wrong."

She shook her left wrist. Vistaren watched a bracelet full of seaglass charms slide down her arm. "It doesn't take much effort for me to monitor the weather almost constantly. With a light touch only, just an awareness, but even now I can feel the breeze across our lighthouse point. So you see that I am…" She paused, searching. "Attuned to the weather."

"Go on." Vistaren hoped his face didn't give away his confusion—or his growing concern. Lijka was being cagier than was her wont, and he didn't think that could possibly bode well for whatever news she had come to share.

Lijka looked away. "I told you Kinnet and I argued about this for months. She kept saying she wanted to learn more from the stormsinger, but he's been absent since the autumn. We feel others of his kind passing, but never him. And after the rainy season—" She broke off and lifted a hand to touch her cheek, then dropped it again.

Vistaren waited in silence.

"I wrote a letter to Pralith." She sighed. "At the end of the rainy season. As I said, it rained later than it should have in some parts of the kingdom. There are allowances to be made, but the foothills where the Gehb originates saw rain for more than a month past the Spring Evener. Other places, like the Sandswamp, it stopped raining too early, just days past the Evener."

"You told Pralith that?"

"I didn't have to. He knew it as well as I. He receives reports from the academy."

Vistaren nodded. The academy posted stormwitches to every part of the kingdom. A large city like Maron had dozens of stormwitches, while a single stormwitch might be responsible for a rural region with a dozen villages, but there was no part of the kingdom that did not have stormwitches. It made sense they would have reporting in place.

Lijka made a noise that almost sounded like a growl. "I have felt wildness brewing in the deeps. I have sensed winds from places that are usually still. I tried to tell him that something is wrong with the currents of the world. But he tells me I am imagining things. He writes that I should stay at my light and attend to my wife. As if I didn't once hold his high position myself, and understand it better." She tossed her head.

Vistaren arched an eyebrow. Pralith was certainly skilled in the witchery, to have been chosen to serve as king's own stormwitch, but he was a little too overbearing for Vistaren's taste. It was like him to condescend to Lijka. "I don't imagine you appreciated that."

Lijka's smile was small and fierce. "I finally came to see him."

"And so when you brought your concerns to him in person…" he prompted.

"Pralith told me I was creating a flood from a single raindrop." She bit each word out like it hurt her. "He told me to stop imagining problems where none existed. The academy would deal with anomalies as they always have."

Vistaren frowned. While it was true that the king didn't interfere with the academy's policies, for the most part, it seemed only courteous for the academy to have informed the king about any such anomalies. "How often do these anomalies occur?" Perhaps his father already knew about this, but he never said anything about it to Vistaren.

Lijka took a long time to answer. She looked away from him, across the room, and Vistaren got the feeling she was staring at a different place—or time—altogether.

"There was one fifteen years ago," she said, her voice cracking. "When the *Bounder* sank off Swordfish Island. And there was one last week. I fear the town of Anderly must be in ruins."

***

With a thunderous *crack* the musket jerked in Vistaren's grip. He swore, ears ringing, and checked the target he had been shooting at. If he had been shooting a bow, he would have been at least near the center. With the musket, he had barely hit the edge of the target.

"You tense up. When you hold it." General Lozarr Algot, Vistaren's dearest friend and mentor, was leaning against a waist-high wall meant to keep unobservant passersby from straying onto the musket range. Lo's arms were folded loosely across his chest. His face was expressionless.

"You try holding the blasted thing," Vistaren muttered. "It weighs as much as a goat, and holding it out at arms' length to shoot with it—"

"When was the last time you held a goat?" Lo asked, amusement coloring his voice.

Vistaren huffed. "You know what I mean."

"I know they aren't light. And I also know that you are well-built and muscled enough to handle it, if you would just relax a bit."

"I don't like guns," Vistaren muttered.

"I don't care for them much myself," Lo said. "But they're remarkably useful in a fight, as long as you have heavy cavalry and pikes to protect the musketeers."

Vistaren scowled and set to cleaning the powder from the barrel, then reloading. "I'm not sure why I'm even doing this. It certainly isn't as if Azmei needs impressing."

"You haven't suddenly decided you want her to fall in love with you, have you?" Lo asked. "Then I would say no, as your friend and betrothed, who is completely aware that you are unable to love women as you do men, she requires no impressing." He coughed. "Not by you, at least. Your father's court could do worse than to attempt it."

Vistaren snorted. "They're surprised enough to hear she's alive. I expect she'll be the seven weeks' wonder and then some before they're truly comfortable with her." It also didn't help that he had never particularly hidden the fact that he didn't love women. The court must be confused—but they couldn't be more confused than he was himself.

"She is a fine young woman," Lo said, his voice soothing. He watched as Vistaren lifted the musket again. "She esteemed you highly, I judged, while we were in Ranarr together."

"That was three years ago."

Lo reached out and placed his hands around Vistaren's, adjusting his grip on the musket. Three years ago that touch would have sent a thrill through Vistaren, before he had realized Lo was incapable of loving anyone but Arama Dzornaea. "Yes, it was. But the basics of the situation haven't changed since then. You are in need of a queen to produce heirs. She needs to formalize her brother's alliance with us by treaty. A marriage seems a useful compromise."

Vistaren let out a slow breath and gently squeezed the trigger. It took more effort than he thought it should, but finally the gun roared in his hands. He blinked hard to clear his eyes of the gunpowder smoke, but when he looked at the target, there was a neat hole in the second-smallest circle.

"Much better," Lozarr said. "Now keep that up for another half a glass."

"I hate you," Vistaren mumbled, but he dutifully began preparing to load another shot. "Is it fair to her? I can't ever give her what she deserves."

Lo cast a caustic look at him. "And can she give you

what *you* deserve? No? Then perhaps it is time, as I said, for a useful compromise."

Vistaren gave up on trying to explain his misgivings. He wasn't even certain he understood them. He didn't like the thought of marrying a woman like Azmei, doing his duty by her enough to get heirs on her, and then taking a lover to satisfy his own desires. It felt dirty somehow. And how would she like it, knowing the whole time that Vistaren didn't desire her as a man should desire his wife?

"You're thinking about it too much. Perhaps Azmei has come up with a solution herself. Best not to worry about it until she gets here." Lozarr gave him a smile that was far too cheery for Vistaren's taste. "Besides, the more things you're thinking about, the worse you're going to shoot."

Vistaren squeezed the trigger, watched a hole blossom on the very edge of the target, and swore.

6

Azmei let out a long breath as she left the stink of the sickroom behind her. She stretched, pressing her hands against the small of her back, and looked across the water to the orange western sky. Destar's wound hadn't killed him yet. He was fighting fever and infection, but he had periods of lucidity. He also had increasingly long periods of restless sleep.

She thought with longing of the soft-cushioned bunk set aside for her use. She wanted nothing more than to sleep, but the healer had stepped away to rest just an hour ago, and he needed the sleep worse than Azmei did.

Large hands settled gently on her shoulders. Azmei tensed. She hadn't even heard Hawk approaching. But he squeezed her shoulders and Azmei couldn't help but relax into his touch. She loved how easily Hawk could soothe her, without even speaking.

Seeing Destar on his sickbed like this was as bad as losing Master Tanvel all over again. Her first teacher had died trying to save her father's life. She hadn't been there, but she had known he believed he was going to his death when he left her. Ultimately he hadn't even saved the king; he had merely prolonged the king's life until Razem could return from the desert.

She took a long breath. That had been enough. It had given Razem the chance to uncover their cousin's treachery.

"You need to talk to Yar," Hawk said. His voice was a low rumble.

"What now?" Azmei asked, her voice dull. She couldn't bring herself to turn around while Hawk was rubbing her shoulders.

"He's been upset ever since the fight with the seadragon."

Azmei pushed down a flash of anger. "Haven't we all." In the days since the fight, she had been spelling the healer during his rounds. The ship's mate had taken command of the ship, but everyone feared for their captain.

"This is different and you know it. He's upset because the dragons are upset. That could be important."

Azmei let out a long sigh. She was so tired. She didn't look away from the orange-gold glow of the sunset.

"He might be able to shed light on what happened," Hawk prompted.

"Can he save Destar?" Azmei regretted the words as soon as she spoke them. Hawk didn't deserve her ire. He was right; whatever was bothering Yar might be important. She could feel Hawk's reproachful look boring between her shoulder blades.

She huffed. "Fine." But to show him she wasn't really angry, she turned and stood on her toes to brush her lips against his before she went looking for Yar. It earned her a brief smile that only emphasized how tired Hawk looked.

She found Yar sitting in the bow of the ship. He had his knees drawn up and his arms folded over them. He was rocking in place. Hawk hadn't been exaggerating how upset Yar was.

Azmei lowered herself to the deck next to him, folding her legs and resting her hands on her knees. She looked out to sea, back to the east, to whatever distant point held Yar's attention. She tried to pray to the god of peace, but found herself fighting yawns. She was on the verge of dozing off when Yar shifted in place. Just a little, but it got her attention.

"It was wrong."

Azmei blinked herself back to alertness. Remembering, she said, "You said that then."

"Something forced it to attack us. Forced it to chase the orca."

"How do you know?"

Yar's shoulders jerked in a resentful shrug. "It told me. It was in pain." He sighed. "Forced. It wasn't right."

"You can talk to seadragons, too?" Azmei wasn't sure why that surprised her. Maybe because the seadragon had attacked them in such seeming mindlessness, while the dragons were so keenly intelligent.

"Not as well. It's distant. Like hearing an echo." Yar sighed again. "But it made me understand. It didn't want us, not really. I'd almost convinced it. And then…" He trailed off and pressed his lips together. A single tear slid down his cheek.

"And then they shot it while you were talking," Azmei finished.

"They *used* me. To distract it."

Azmei nodded. "I'm sorry." She spoke quietly, wondering as she did if she was telling the truth. She certainly wasn't sorry the seadragon hadn't killed them all. But there had been a majestic, frightening beauty to the creature, and she couldn't help thinking the world was a poorer place without it. "They didn't know you could communicate with it."

Yar was frowning. "The seadragon was in pain. Even before they shot it. Something…" He shook his head, opened his mouth, and shook his head again. Finally he said, "I saw it wrapped in something that twisted. Around it? Or twisted it. I couldn't tell. But it was like a thorn twisting into your palm."

Azmei took that in. She wondered if the seadragon had died. It had looked like it was badly injured. But perhaps they could heal themselves. "I'll tell the crew to let you talk if another seadragon turns up."

Yar gave a bitter laugh but didn't otherwise respond.

"What does Xellax say?" Azmei asked slowly. She wasn't sure if she truly wanted to know what the dragon said about their killing—possibly killing—a seadragon. But if anyone could make Yar feel better, it was his dragon half.

"She mourns." His voice was stark. "Too much pain. Too much death. Too many." He put his head down on his folded arms and went back to rocking in place.

Azmei sat with him for a while longer, until she was sure he had said all he wished to. Then she stood, let her hand hover in the air just above his shoulder, and went back to Destar's cabin.

Hawk had dozed off propped on the deck against the cabin wall. Whether he had been waiting for her to return or had just decided that was as good a place as any for a nap, Azmei couldn't say. She tiptoed around him. He had only slept a little more than she had. He could use the rest.

She took one last breath of fresh air and stepped back into the stink.

Destar lay still on the bunk. The thick layers of bandage over his face made him look dead already. She pushed aside the thought as ill-speaking and focused on tidying things up. The chamberpot hadn't been emptied since they'd had to clean Destar up earlier. She was tempted to throw pot, soiled rags, excrement, and all out the porthole, but she wasn't sure that wouldn't count as an attack on any unsuspecting seadragon that might be happening by.

Instead she carried it down to the bilge. She emptied the pot, draped the soiled rags over a nearby railing, and went back to Destar's cabin.

This time when she went inside, he was awake.

"Y'ought to rest, lass." His voice was a mumble through the bandages. She could tell it hurt him to talk, though his lips barely moved.

"I'll rest soon." She smiled at him and settled on the stool next to his bunk.

"Look done in." His eyes were bright, and she feared fever, but he seemed alert.

Azmei nodded. "We've finished repairs to the ship. The navigator says we'll soon be able to see the Maron light. Just another day or so."

"We're late as 'tis." He blinked a few times. "Hope they didn't plan you a celebration."

Azmei forced a laugh. "I'm not worried about that." For that matter, she wasn't certain of her welcome with Vistaren. Every time she reminded herself that he'd promised not to marry another, she thought of how unfair it was to force him into a marriage that wouldn't give him what he needed.

She shoved the thoughts away. There was no use brooding on it, and she had other things to worry about in the meantime.

"Yar doesn't think that seadragon wanted to attack us."

Destar grunted. "Never heard of one doin' it." The one eyebrow she could see lowered. "Tied to y'r mission."

"I don't know." She held his gaze for several heartbeats. "I wondered that myself. Yar says something twisted it, forced it to hurt us. Something that was hurting the dragon."

"Maybe your prince'll make sense 'f'it."

Azmei bit her lip. "I hope so," she said softly. Even if she feared Vistaren would be just as puzzled by all of this as she was.

7

Arama fingered the soft edges of the letter from Lozarr. She ought to write him back, but her letters never seemed quite satisfactory to her. Lo had the knack of being tender without being utterly annoying, but any time Arama tried to write something sentimental she just ended up feeling like an idiot.

My dear, she wrote, and then she swore and dropped her pen on the table. That seemed forced. She tore a strip from the top of the paper and picked up her pen again. She held it poised over the paper for several moments, then swore and shoved a hand through her hair.

Dear Lo, she wrote, and it felt not tender enough, but better than too tender.

Dawn Star ran afoul of a sudden storm yesterday while we searched for the Elana Bey. Not sure where the merchant ship ended up, but I'm assuming it ran afoul of the same storm we did. I chose to scud ahead of the storm, but a ship like the Bey probably hove to somewhere. We haven't seen a ship since the storm, though, and I'm afraid the king has sent pirates on a rescue mission. Not the most natural choice.

She considered that for a moment, crossed out *pirates* and replaced it with *privateers,* and then chewed the end of her pen idly.

We've spent today repairing sails and making other repairs. I would swear I saw sirens in the water during the storm. Not an unusual thing, if we were closer to land, but we're in deep water still, and they don't usually venture so far out. It makes me wonder what devilry is afoot.

She paused again. She always had trouble deciding how

vulnerable to be in her letters. Lozarr shared so much with her she occasionally blushed—not because of his love talk, but from embarrassment at how open he was with her.

It wasn't even that she had secrets she wanted to keep from him. She couldn't think of anything she would be unwilling to tell him—in person, at least. But committing such confidences to ink and paper…that was, frankly, frightening.

I miss you. I hope to find the Elana Bey—or what's left of her crew—soon so I may return to Maron. If the search takes us much further south, however, we'll likely have to resupply at Anderly before sailing around the head to the capital.

She was almost at the bottom of the page. The birds were fast, but they couldn't carry heavy correspondence, so she usually tried to keep her letters to a single sheet of paper. And there was no way she would write outside the seal, where anyone might read it. Arama nibbled her pen again, wondering if she had anything else to add.

Footsteps thumped across the deck outside her cabin. "Ship off the port bow!" someone shouted.

Thank the gods. Arama could use a distraction from romance, and blowing up a Strid ship would answer well. She folded the letter and tucked it into her pocket. Then she left her cabin, dashed up the deck to the bow, and raised her spyglass.

She couldn't see it yet, but she didn't doubt it was there. They were sailing at a good clip; it would take less than a quarter of an hour for her to see whatever the lookout had spotted from his high perch.

"Ready the guns!" she called over her shoulder. It wasn't likely to be the missing merchant ship; if the *Dawn Star* had taken this much damage in the storm, the *Elana Bey* had to be in worse shape yet. If it was a Strid ship, what she was doing was considered an act of war. Then again, the Strid had enough to worry about in their twenty-year-long war with Tamnen. The king of Strid wouldn't kick up too much of a fuss if Arama took one of his ships this close to the embattled Kreyden District. Besides, she might not leave any witnesses, and Tamnen could have the credit—at least until some Strid sailor recognized the rechristened ship sailing under Amethirian flag.

Before too long, the ship was in view of her spyglass. It flew the Strid flag, a blue field with a gold crown and bars. Zek joined her at the bow.

"Will we fight, Captain?" he asked.

She tucked her finger into her pocket again, rubbing her unfinished letter. "Mister Zek, when have you ever known me to back down from a fight?"

He grinned at her. "Never, mum!" And he was off, issuing orders to the crew. Arama checked her pistol to make certain it was primed and ready. She loosened her saber in its sheath. Usually it only took a shot or two from the cannons to get them to stand to for boarding, but there were no guarantees in life.

The Strid vessel came on. Arama glanced up to be sure her men were manning the fighting top. One of them saluted when he saw her looking. The bow gunners were at their posts, keen gazes fixed on the approaching enemy.

"Hoist the colors!" she shouted.

"Hoisting colors, aye!" came back, and she watched in satisfaction as her personal flag—a field of black with a white storm petrel soaring across it—rose just below the Amethirian colors. She'd never been one to lure other ships in by flying a false flag. Indeed, there had been times when the mere act of hoisting the storm petrel had convinced a ship to heave to and prepare for boarding.

Arama tested the wind. The *Dawn Star* held the weather gage, standing upwind of the Strid ship. That gave them a tactical advantage, though the Strid captain didn't seem to care. Arama folded her arms across her chest. Good. Let him be overconfident. She'd show him the error of his ways.

"Gunners ready!" she shouted. They were close. The Strid ship was a tidy ketch with no bow guns. The captain must be crazy. She could see guns on the sterncastle, but he'd have a blind spot dead ahead. Arama didn't have that disadvantage. Her opponent was mad if he thought he could take her.

"Fire!" The order rang out across the deck, and in answer, the guns roared from bow and fighting top.

Arama's gunners were the best in the business. The first shot tore through the main topsail of the Strid vessel, and the second through the jib. The gun crew wasn't wasting time watching their shot, though; they were already cleaning and reloading their cannon.

The Strid ship began to turn. Arama didn't want to give him time to fire back at her. She knew *Dawn Star* could take it, but prolonged battles weren't efficient.

"Swivel guns!" she called.

"Swivel guns, aye!" came the reply, and soon one of the gunners was loading the smaller guns with grapeshot. It wouldn't damage the Strid vessel, but it would definitely damage the Strid sailors as they approached.

"Prepare for a broadsides!"

As the ships came alongside each other, *Dawn Star*'s guns fired broadsides. Arama didn't have a chance to see what damage her own gunners had inflicted. The Strid's sterncastle guns fired at almost the same time. She dodged to avoid the splinters that flew up from the deck.

She heard the smaller bang of the swivel guns and gave Zek a fierce grin as several members of the Strid crew toppled. The topgunners had fired with the broadsides and were already reloaded. They fired again and more Strid sailors fell.

"One more barrage and they'll raise the white," Arama told Zek.

"Aye, mum!" he shouted, his voice thickening with excitement. He was young, and this was only his second or third battle. She could see the courage and battle-lust rising in him. Good things in a privateer, but she would have to watch to make sure he didn't go too far when they boarded the Strid ship.

She felt the ship lurch under her feet. It wasn't the recoil of the guns, nor the impact of a cannonball. It was the peculiar lurch *Dawn Star* gave when the hand at the tiller was too light. Arama twisted to look at the quarterdeck. Carig was hunched over the tiller, a hand clutching his shoulder.

"Zek!" she shouted. "Relieve Mister Carig! Surgeon! Tend the helmsman!"

Zek and the short, dark-skinned surgeon were both dashing for the quarterdeck before Arama had finished shouting. She cast a final worried glance at the injured helmsman, then turned her attention back to the battle.

Dawn Star had fired twice more and the enemy ship was listing, the mizzenmast sheared off a third of the way from the top. As Arama watched, the Strid ship struck their colors. She bared her teeth in a grin of victory.

"Prepare for boarding!" she shouted.

Arama crossed with the first wave, saber in hand. She watched the Strid crew, ready to defend herself, but the fight had gone out of most of them. Arama's crew mopped up the last few defiants while she strode to the sterncastle to parlay with the captain. Six of her crew followed her.

"Storm Petrel!" the captain spat when he saw her.

Arama grinned. "You can boast you required a third round of shot from the Storm Petrel. You'll drink free on that story for a year."

"No one will believe it," he said in heavily accented Common. "Damn you."

"Nonsense. One look at your ship will convince any-one."

He winced and then caught himself. Glaring at her, he drew himself up. "What are your terms?"

"We'll take your cargo and gold. Leave you water and hardtack enough, and put you adrift in the longboats to get home. If there are slaves on your ship, they'll come with us." Arama didn't bother to hide her distaste. Strid was the last of the civilized nations to employ slavery. Amethir had out-lawed it generations ago, and it was their policy to free all slaves on any vessel they took.

The Strid captain pursed his lips and hurled a gobbet of spit at her. "You won't be able to keep that pretty head attached to your shoulders much longer, Storm Petrel," he muttered. "The fleet will take you."

Arama's laugh rang out. "I'll sleep when the sea god takes me, and not before," she informed him. She turned her back and strode away, knowing her men would restrain the captain until the pillaging was finished.

On deck, she discovered her victory over the Strid had brought her more than riches. It yielded information about the very merchant ship she'd been seeking—specifically, what was left of that ship's crew.

"The *Elana Bey*?" she repeated, staring at the peach-skinned man who stood before her. One eye was swollen mostly shut and his lips were cracked.

He nodded. "Went down a week back after a storm." His good eye darkened. "T'wasn't the stormwitch's fault. She were brave as anything, and ran out to try to protect our crew. She pushed the storm aside, and we would've been fine, but we got pooped. Lost the witch and her man, and our mate was killed under the mast." He shook his head. "As t'was, nearly half my mates died in that storm, and t'other half were taken slaves by yon Strid dog."

Arama pulled her water flask from her belt and held it out to him. "You lost the stormwitch?"

He drank. "She were young, not above twenty-five summers, and her hair were only streaky. She were a good one. Her man what came along, though, he wasn't much of a sailor. Scared easy, and he wouldn't leave her alone to do her work. I reckon he was why she got swept overboard."

"Any idea where you were when that happened?" Arama frowned. She wasn't fond of stormwitches. She hadn't been, since a stormwitch failed to save her first ship from sinking all those years ago. But for all her dislike of them, she wouldn't want to see one die. They were servants of the kingdom, for one thing. They always studied at the academy, and even though they couldn't be nobles, they were certainly well compensated for their trouble.

"Off the Kreyden shore, mum." The man drained her flask and handed it back to her. "Captain was worried we'd be drove aground in Strid-claimed territory." He shook his head. "Not that it mattered, in the end."

Arama hummed thoughtfully. "What's your name, sailor?"

"Vetch, mum. I were second mate on the *Elana Bey.*"

She nodded. "Well, you're safe now. The king sent us to look for you when your owner reported you past due. Now we've found you, we'll head back to Amethir."

"Many thanks, mum. And praises to Lord Antos."

Arama grinned at him. "Talk to my first mate. He'll have offerings you can sacrifice in thanks." Only then did she remember that Carig had been in trouble. Had he been shot? She kept her expression easy until she turned away from Vetch.

Once the Strid ship was cleared of valuables and rum, half of Arama's crew returned to the *Dawn Star.* The other half would sail their prize in tandem with the *Dawn Star* at least until they reached Anderly for resupply. At that point she would evaluate the situation and decide whether or not to send the ship on to Maron or leave it at Anderly for the time being.

She was shocked when her first mate joined her near her cabin door. He had a bloody bandage tied around his upper arm. He grinned at her expression.

"How then, Carig?"

"Sixty bales of cotton, ready for the spinners. Forty barrels of saltpeter. Two chests of mixed currency. One hand lost, two wounded but not mortal. As you can see," he added, gesturing to his arm.

Arama frowned. "Who was lost?"

"Wirda, mum."

Damn it all. Wirda had a wife and three babes at home. She sighed. "Set aside his fair portion of this take, and then double it before you portion the take out to the others."

"Yes, mum." Carig shifted on his feet. His teeth worried at his lower lip.

Arama folded her arms across her chest. "Out with it, whatever you're keeping back."

He sighed and held out a rolled paper. "We found this in the captain's chamber, mum. The Strid have placed a bounty on your head and on the *Dawn Star*."

That wasn't news. The Strid had good reason to hate her. Then Arama unrolled the paper.

In flourishy handwriting it read, "Wanted for crimes against Strid: Arama Dzornaea, the Storm Petrel, Captain of *Dawn Star*. For information leading to her, one thousand gold crowns. For her head, two thousand gold crowns."

It said nothing about taking her alive.

8

General Lozarr Algot surveyed what was left of Anderly village with a sinking in his stomach. "The gods witness," he muttered.

Anmeir, his aide, nudged his horse up alongside Lozarr's. "Beg pardon, sir?"

Lozarr shook his head. "There's nothing left," he said. He couldn't take his eyes from the scene before them.

Anderly had been a tidy village of limed cottages, most of them built on a cliff two hundred feet above the ocean on Comar Head. There had been some six or seven hundred souls in this town, many of them fisherfolk. It was the seat of the fisher lord Faran Ebb, Count of Comar, whose sprawling white manor at the high point of the head spoke of Ebb's wealth. The village had boasted three inns, half a dozen public houses, and a decent-sized market. Down a steep set of steps carved into the cliff had been the Anderly Docks, where the fisherfolk tied up their crafts and the boatbuilders plied their trade.

Anderly today was gone. Lozarr stared at a shamble of buildings whose walls had fallen in after the entire cliff crumbled into the ocean. He couldn't see the docks from the road, but he had no doubt they were buried under the remains of what had been Anderly village.

"Lord Antos have mercy," Anmeir said, staring around them.

Lozarr's lips twisted. "I don't suppose you should let the villagers hear you say that," he said, sweeping his arm at the ruin. "This appears to be the quality of Lord Antos' mercy." He saw his aide crook his fingers at his waist in a holy gesture, but Lozarr didn't have the stomach for false piety today. Not when all that was left of Anderly village was Ebb Manor, one pub, perhaps a dozen houses, and the temple of Antos.

Lozarr sighed. "I had hoped Stormwitch Ardelis was wrong," he admitted. "Well. No sense all of us riding into the village. Give the order to set up camp here. I'll go down with some of the surgeons and the quartermaster. We'll see what aid we can render."

"Yes, sir." Anmeir rode off to make arrangements while Lozarr set his horse at the manor house. He would have to find out how many had survived, and how many of the survivors were wounded. He would need to set up healing tents and food tents. Vistaren had sent them with plenty of surplus; the prince had obviously had faith in the stormwitch. Lozarr hadn't really doubted her, though; he knew Kinnet Ardelis. She wasn't given to exaggeration.

Lozarr had only crossed half the distance before he heard his men trotting to catch up with him. "General," said the surgeon, saluting. Lozarr nodded for him to report. "Sir, my surgeons are preparing their supplies for a crush of wounded. The soldiers have set up the tents for us. Lieutenant Anmeir said the quartermaster would be ready to distribute food and blankets to any who needed it within the hour."

"Very good. Let's see if we can find Count Faran at home."

The wind tugged at their hair and clothes as it gusted across the headland. Lozarr was a Sterr. He'd grown up far from the sea in the heart of Amethir, and he would never be used to the constant wind off the ocean. Comar Head was beautiful, with a rugged, harsh, windswept beauty, but he thought with sudden longing of his home in the rocky interior.

The village and its manor had looked all but deserted, but someone in the manor was apparently paying attention. Lozarr's party was still a hundred paces from the manor when a handful of foot soldiers issued from the house and approached them at the double-time. Lozarr reined in his horse and they waited.

"I am General Algot of His Majesty's Army," he greeted the men when they reached him. "His majesty had word of an…aberration that hit Anderly, and sent aid as soon as could be. Is the count within?"

The soldiers looked at each other, then one of them stepped forward. "Aye, he is. Your business here is to aid us?"

"As I said," Lozarr confirmed, frowning in puzzlement. Surely Faran didn't believe anyone would move against him in such dire circumstances. While the king ruled at the consent of his nobles, there were strict traditions concerning warfare among the nobles.

The soldier gave a sharp nod. "The count will see you, sir. Just you and one other, please," he added as they prepared to move.

Lozarr's eyebrows shot up, but he glanced over at the chief surgeon, who nodded. "The rest of you, return to the camp," Lozarr ordered. "We'll send word soon."

As they followed the foot soldiers into the manor courtyard, Lozarr wondered what had happened to make Faran so chary. He had always been a stalwart supporter of the king and his policies. For his house guard to be suspicious of King Rekel's soldiers was a foreboding indication that something very bad had happened.

He dismounted and turned his horse over to a gawky teenaged girl, who smiled at him. Her welcome drove home how unfriendly the soldiers had been. Lozarr exchanged glances with the chief surgeon and followed the guard inside.

The manor interior, in contrast to its bright white exterior, was dark and gloomy. All the windows were covered, and the house was wreathed in silence. Footsteps echoing, Lozarr followed the guard to a practical office, where he realized what had happened to change so much.

Faran Ebb was no longer the count.

A young man of fewer than thirty years sat behind the

desk. His eyes were red and swollen, his full lips pressed together. When Lozarr came in, the man stood, but his posture did not convey respect. There was tension in every line of his body, from his broad shoulders down to his hands, which clenched into fists as he saw Lozarr's uniform. The man's gray eyes were hard when they met Lozarr's.

"Did your stormwitches send this?" he demanded.

Lozarr widened his eyes, more at the belligerent tone of voice than at the question. "They sent *me*," he said. "To render aid as I could, and to report back. The stormwitches didn't cause this storm, but they felt it, and reported it to his majesty as soon as they could."

He felt a twinge of guilt as he said it. That was probably a falsehood. Vistaren had been unable to learn whether or not the stormwitches had hidden news of the anomaly that hit Anderly from his father. But the end result was the same; King Rekel had agreed that the crown must send aid.

"My father was always a friend to the crown," the young man said, and Lozarr finally remembered his name. Kedar. Faran's oldest son, but there was another, and three girls. "I am glad to see that meant *something* to the king."

"Be careful of your words, sir," Lozarr said quietly. "My heart breaks for you and your people, but I can brook nothing that sounds of treason."

"Treason!" Kedar Ebb slapped his hand against his desk. "Treason is a breaking of faith. But there can be no breaking of faith if it is already broken. My father is *dead*, general. The king and his stormwitches gave us no warning. We had no time to prepare. So my father was down at the docks when the storm hit, helping our folk secure their boats and their catches."

"I am so sorry," Lozarr said, holding Kedar's gaze. "But there is little his majesty could have done. The stormwitches felt it hit, but did not feel it ahead of time. Or if they did, they did not report it to the king. He sent me as soon as he was aware of Anderly's peril."

"It wasn't soon enough for my father!" Kedar shouted.

Lozarr drew himself up. He felt a terrible sympathy for Kedar and his folk, but there was no sense in attempting to lay blame before he had done all he could to alleviate their suffering. "My lord count, I have come with surgeons and supplies. We are setting up camp west of the village. We will serve Anderly as best we can."

Faran Ebb had been a stolid, unflappable man in his mid-sixties. His son favored him in looks, but didn't have his temperament. Or perhaps it was simply the grief speaking when he said, "Do whatever you will, and may the gods grant you forgiveness."

Lozarr issued a shallow bow and turned on his heel. He heard the surgeon's footsteps hurrying to keep up with him. As they approached the entry hall, a young woman who looked too much like Kedar Ebb not to be his sister appeared from a side room and curtsied.

"General, my brother is grief-stricken, as are we all. But I am not so blinded by my grief that I cannot recognize the king's generosity. I beg you not to think ill of Kedar."

Lozarr took in her swollen eyes and chapped lips, and felt himself moved by pity. Barely out of childhood, and Faran Ebb's daughter was bearing up with better grace than her much-older brother. "My lady, it is not my place to think well or ill of your brother. I am simply here as an instrument of the king's grace." He took the hand she extended to him and bowed over it. "But it is my pleasure to serve House Coman and Anderly."

As he straightened, he saw her lift her chin in a nod. Her shoulders straightened, and the smile she offered him was more genuine than he had expected. "Thank you, general."

Lozarr nodded and took his leave. As their horses carried them out of the courtyard, the surgeon murmured, "That was well done."

"She will grow to be a lady of grace," Lozarr agreed, and the surgeon chuckled.

"I meant your actions, general, but as you say."

Lozarr looked over at him. The chief surgeon was a man with iron gray hair and eyes, with a square jaw that made him look more like a soldier than a life-giver. He was new to Lozarr's command, and to Lozarr's chagrin, he couldn't remember the man's name. He would have to learn it. "Let's do the best damn job we can for these people, eh?"

The chief surgeon gave him a grave smile in reply.

***

When they got back to the camp, Lozarr was surprised at the frenetic activity in the healing tent. He had expected there would be injuries, but a journeyman surgeon dashed up to the chief as they arrived.

"Master Uisden, they've been calling for you. Please, can you come quickly?"

Uisden exchanged a worried look with Lozarr, who gestured for him to go on. He would need a report eventually, but he would trust the chief surgeon to know the best time for that. Pushing down his curiosity, Lozarr went instead to find Lieutenant Anmeir.

"Sir! How was the count, sir?"

"Faran is dead. Kedar Ebb is count now. And he is not…well." It was a stretch, but Lozarr didn't want word getting out about the new count's belligerence. It might be a product of his grief that would fade as he dealt with the loss of his father. If not…time enough later to deal with it.

"There will be dispatches to send to Maron, when I have time. Make certain the messenger birds are ready."

"Yes, sir. The quartermaster reports that few villagers have come to partake of the bounty. When he detailed troops to convey our mission to the village leaders, he discovered there's been a huge number of them taken ill."

"Is it contagious?"

"I have few details, sir, but surely the chief surgeon will report soon."

Lozarr rubbed his forehead. Disease on top of tragedy,

yes, that would make any man distraught. "What has been done for these people so far?"

As Anmeir reported, they walked through the camp toward the command tent, which would house both Lozarr's sleeping area and his meeting space. Some villagers *had* come for blankets and food, but most hadn't, which led the surgeons to speculate initially that the disease was virulent—only to discover there had been more fatalities than any of them had anticipated.

"The storm hit during the peak of their work hours, sir," Anmeir said. He looked drawn, and paler than he had when they arrived. Something about this tragedy had touched him. "There—there are whole families who fish together." His voice was hoarse. "Children, sir."

Of course. It was the same in the interior, where herding families taught their children to watch the goats and cattle from a young age. Lozarr went to his supply chest and poured a finger of whiskey for his aide. "Sit," he said, and pressed the glass into Anmeir's hand.

Anmeir gulped the drink and exhaled shakily. "I'm sorry, sir. I—I'm used to fighting, and that's grown men, not children."

Lozarr nodded and took the glass back. He filled it a second time, but with water instead of whiskey. "When was the last census? We'll have to compare those who survive against the village rolls."

"I, uh. I think it was three years ago." Anmeir's voice turned up at the end, making it more of a question. "I'll check at once, of course."

Lozarr rested a hand on his shoulder. "No, sit here for a bit. I have initial reports to send. When I've finished writing them out, you may take them to the birds. That will be soon enough for you to check on the census."

He sat at his field desk and inked a pen, then frowned at the paper. He would send his report to the king, of course, but he would also report to Vistaren. He thought longingly of another letter he wished he could write, but there wouldn't be time for that. Not yet.

He composed the report to Vistaren first, because they were friends. He could be more free with his thoughts and emotions in a letter to the prince. It helped him compose his thoughts well enough to write a succinct, business-like missive to the king. Lozarr sealed both letters with wax and glanced over at his aide.

Anmeir had recovered his composure and came to attention when he saw Lozarr's glance. Lozarr knew better than to think the man entirely recovered, but he was capable of doing his duty. That would do for now. And after supper tonight, Lozarr would allow him a bit more drink and offer a chance to decompress a bit. Anmeir was keen, but Lozarr had seen soldiers with that same edge burn out before, or snap under the strain of what they saw. He didn't want to see that happen to Anmeir.

9

Eldry wasn't sure if she would ever grow to enjoy sailing.

The *Revenge* wasn't as nice a ship as the *Elana Bey* had been, though it was faster. The crew followed her orders without protest. She often caught Black Miry watching her, but he seemed cowed for now. She would have to come up with an effective solution to that problem soon, but for now he was still cowed by her power.

She had claimed a spot amidships, where she could lean against the mast and stare out at the air and water currents flowing past. It was as the Scavenger had said—she couldn't stop watching the weather, now that it was constantly in her sight. She had spent the past two days experimenting. She would close her eyes and call her power, extending it in the way she had learned at the academy. Then she would open her eyes.

Every time, there was a single instant where she could see her mental image superimposed over what her physical eyes—eye—showed her. Then she let her magical awareness fade as she was caught in the wonder of seeing it herself, something she had only imagined now visible to her eye.

She heard the drag-thump of Rhys' slow approach. Eldry took in a long breath, wishing he wouldn't disturb her. She knew he was in pain, and that he disliked sailing even more than she did. He was, in fact, terrified. But what good would it do to listen to him tell her that yet again? It wouldn't make them get to Amethir any faster.

She waited until he'd groaned to a seated position on the hatch cover behind her. She glanced over at him and felt a sudden pang at the agony etched across his face. He slumped sideways, letting his arm press against hers, and Eldry didn't shift away.

"What are we doing?" he asked.

"Getting back to Maron." She closed her eyes, relishing his warmth. He was afraid and in pain. She should have asked if he wanted to share her bunk. They were used to sharing, after all. Perhaps he would rest better.

"These men are scared of you," he said, his voice taut.

Eldry hitched her shoulder in a tiny shrug she knew he would feel. "Wise of them."

Rhys let out a huff. "I don't…" He trailed off and shook his head. "You aren't the same. He did something to you with that eye."

Eldry thought of the Scavenger, then of her rash words on the beach. *He can have whatever he wants, if he'll save Rhys,* she'd said. It had been rash and unthinking, but the Scavenger's god had obviously taken her seriously. "Yes, he *did* do something to me," she said. "He gave me power and resolve."

"Eldry, he—" Rhys broke off and lowered his voice to a whisper. "He's mad."

She shook her head. "He talks to a god. He says it's the maker god, but I don't know for sure which one it is. Not the healer."

"The gods are all asleep." Rhys' voice stayed low. "They have been for centuries."

"I don't know," Eldry said. She thought of the way most of her new crew had cut their arms and dripped blood over the bow of the ship before they set sail. "The sailors sacrifice to Antos. Why would they bother if he's asleep?"

Rhys was silent for so long that she turned to look at him. He was staring at her. "You don't believe him. El. You don't." He kept staring at her, and she almost heard the *Do you?* he didn't say aloud.

She gestured up at her face. "I know he has power from somewhere. He gave me my sight back. He gave me *more* than my sight back."

"And he infected you with his madness." Rhys' voice was bitter.

"Shut up," she said, annoyance beginning to outweigh her pity. "Either let me work or go away."

She regretted the words after they left her lips. She had just been thinking how she should help Rhys, how he was frightened. This wasn't any way to treat a frightened friend. But something held her back from apologizing.

She watched as Rhys heaved himself laboriously to standing, taking no weight on his injured leg. The Scavenger had, of course, fashioned a crutch for Rhys, though Rhys hadn't bothered to even thank him.

Eldry watched Rhys' slow progress toward the hatch to go below, pity swelling up inside her again. Why did Rhys have to pick at her so? If he would just let her follow her plan, everything would be fine. She would get him back to Maron safely and he could begin mending. And then… and then she would begin.

She settled back into her practice, extending her weather awareness around her. She stroked her thumb against a large, green chunk of seaglass as she did. The Scavenger had given her a bandolier full of seaglass, some pieces as large as her palm, some just barely larger than grains of sand.

She had never had seaglass respond to her with as much intensity before the new eye. She thought there was something in her that was attuned with the seaglass now. She let her awareness slip across the waves, soaring as easily as an albatross. Her magic slipped without trouble through the air currents and clouds that were building.

From afar she sensed the clockwise motion of air that indicated a storm was building. Eldry paused, fixing the spot in her thoughts, and then pushed her conscious closer to it. She took her bearings, gauged the wind and water, and gave the budding storm a tiny push. Gloating, she indulged in a moment's fantasy of arriving on the winds of the storm.

That wouldn't happen. The storm was too far ahead of

them, and Eldry wasn't truly keen to sail through ill weather again. But it did make for a nice image.

Dragging herself away from the storm, Eldry curled her fingers around the seaglass. Her stomach growled, stealing a fraction of her attention back to her body. She was just about to give up practicing for the evening when her power brushed against something immense and resonant.

It was unlike her power, but it was strong and wild. It appealed to Eldry on a gut level. She quested after it, trying to figure out what sort of person—or creature—could cause a power signature like that.

All through supper Eldry kept a tiny thread of attention on the strange power. She felt it swim in circles and then dive deep. She felt it hunger for orca and took a moment to be grateful she'd already eaten.

At last she realized what the power must be. She knew the feel of sirens and orca, of fish and little sea creatures. But she had heard the stories and folklore passed down over the years.

The power, she thought, was a seadragon. And with that realization came the instant desire to control that power. She would watch it, she decided. Watch it, tie a little bit of her awareness to it, and when the time was right, she would call the seadragon to her.

10

Yar leaned against the ship's railing, staring out at the sea. If he looked over his shoulder, he knew he would see the towering cliffs and the Maron Harbor lights. He could feel power gathered in the light south of the harbor mouth, though he wasn't sure what it meant. There were no dragons in Amethir, he knew that, but he hadn't known about seadragons, so what other creatures of power might there be?

He sighed and looked down at the water, wishing he could trail his fingers in it. He'd always liked water, though where he'd grown up it was tamed into canals and fountains. Something about the ocean felt more real to him.

What troubles you, loved one? came a gentle thought in his mind.

Yar closed his eyes, smiling faintly. He couldn't hide anything from Xellax, even though she was farther from him than she'd ever been. "The seadragon," he whispered softly, knowing she would hear. "It was so scared."

Neither of them spoke for a long time. Yar thought of the terror that had swamped him, overwhelming his own awareness of the battle, making his own heart race, his own lungs feel tight. He'd been on the verge of panic despite knowing the seadragon wasn't there to hurt him. Finally he added, "I understand being afraid. I know how it feels to lose control."

Xellax didn't answer in words, but he felt a deep sense of shame and regret from her.

"No," he said quickly. "I didn't mean that as a reproach. I just…" He shook his head, searching for words.

"I've felt that. I want to stop whoever made a creature as powerful as the seadragon afraid."

They aren't quite like us, you know, Xellax said. *We were once as they, but we left the sea and learned from men and from gods, and became more than men and less than gods.*

"They aren't as intelligent as you?"

Nor quite as aware of the world around them. She paused, and he felt affection in her. *It is not a criticism. What need have they, deep in their sea caves, to know about the world around them?*

"What need had you, far out in your desert palace?" Yar teased, and he was gratified to feel her chuckle thrum through him.

Well said, loved one. But let us say only that we have a different purpose than our cousins.

Yar thought about that, feeling his brows pull down into a frown so deep it hurt. "But that doesn't excuse anyone—or anything—hurting and scaring your cousins. I want to know who did that. I want to stop them."

Why do you think we have sent you to be our Voice to the human kingdoms?

Yar sucked in a breath. "Is this part of that?"

For a long time there was no answer. He felt his awareness of Xellax grow thin, as if she had turned her attention to something outside herself. Then for just a moment he had a flash of the old Voices.

HE SEEKS TO KNOW. THEN SHOW HIM.

But we cannot help—

IT MATTERS NOT. SHOW HIM.

And that was all the warning he got before he was plunged into—

Darkness. Darkness so thick he could feel it pressing against his skin. He opened his mouth to cry out and the darkness slipped in, choking him. He wanted to scream.

Then the darkness faded just enough, to a deep blue light, so weak he could barely see. He was under the water, in a cavern with rough walls, walls that glittered in the light as it grew stronger. He turned his head to look and felt thorns prick his cheek. He winced and held still, hoping not to get hurt again.

But the thorns were pressing in, coming at him, twisting around him, twisting him, his body, creeping into his mind. They pricked at him, at his thoughts, at his hopes. His fear ballooned inside him, somehow not punctured by the thorns but increased by them.

He saw a white-haired girl with one eye. Her arms were uplifted, a light of ecstasy on her face. She looked away from him, but he could feel power crackling around her.

A man in ragged robes stood behind her, drawn back into shadow so he couldn't be seen clearly. He urged the girl on.

Then the light was strong enough he could see seadragons, swarms of seadragons, roaring, bellowing in pain, writhing around on themselves. The girl shouted something and the seadragons all screamed as one.

High, thin laughter rose from a dark, misshapen figure standing high above them all, watching the cavern, ruling it. He spurred them on, relishing the seadragons' screams, and he laughed through it all.

Someone was calling his name, low and urgent. Yar realized he was stretched flat on the deck of the ship. Azmei knelt over him, her gaze on his face, but she didn't touch him. He felt a sudden flash of love for her, that she respected how he didn't like to be touched. Then he saw Hawk standing over her, one blade half-drawn before his gaze met Yar's.

They had thought he was in danger. And perhaps he was—at least, they *all* were, he was sure of that. But he wasn't certain it was anything that could be answered with a blade.

"Are you yourself again?" Azmei asked softly.

Yar coughed and nodded. He licked his lips, wished for a cup of tea, and croaked, "Twister of Worlds."

Azmei and Hawk exchanged a wide-eyed look, and then they both stared at Yar.

He coughed again and said, "We fight the Twister of Worlds."

***

Azmei shifted her weight from foot to foot, watching the sailors prepare for docking. She knew it could go no faster, but she desperately wanted to talk to Vistaren. She'd sent a bird ahead of them as soon as they'd crossed the bar into Maron Harbor. Surely Vistaren would meet her at the dock.

Beside her, Hawk pressed gentle fingers against her elbow. "You aren't going to make the ship go any faster by dancing," he murmured.

"Shut up."

He snorted.

Azmei looked up at him. "Aren't you terrified?" Her mouth was so dry she could barely get the words out.

"Not much more than I already was," he said wryly. "We knew the gods were waking. Just our luck that we got the worst of the lot."

Azmei glared for a moment, but his solid unflappableness was reassuring. As he probably meant it to be. She took a deep breath and settled onto the balls of her feet, turning her gaze to the harbor.

The city of Maron was built up the side of the harbor, climbing in a gentle rise to where the palace was built on top of a bluff overlooking the whole harbor. It was a pleasant-looking harbor. Ships of all sizes docked there, including one flying the Ranarri standard. Azmei felt a pang of nostalgia as she saw the White Stone on its banner. She might have been dead to the rest of the world, but her time in Ranarr had made the city feel like home.

The sailors doubled their speed and Azmei realized the shouted orders were those of docking. She straightened and smoothed her clothes automatically. She had abandoned the practical breeches and tunics she'd worn on the ship in favor of a lovely gown with split skirts, still too practical to be appropriate court dress, but something that a typical royal would wear on board ship.

"You're lovely," Hawk murmured in her ear, and then

he stepped away from her to a proper distance for a body-guard. Azmei shivered at the loss of his warmth beside her.

On the dock stood an elegant coach bearing the royal crest, door open, while a matching set of grays pranced in place in the traces. Beside the coach stood a tall man, almost skeletal in his thinness, with the olive skin and blue-black hair indicative of Crelin ethnicity.

Azmei's heart sank. No Vistaren. And she didn't recognize the man who stood there. It wasn't General Algot, who had come with Vistaren to their meeting on Ranarr three years ago. It certainly couldn't be the king; aside from the coloring, he looked nothing like Vistaren.

She drew a deep breath, glanced to either side of her to summon Hawk and Yar to follow her, and headed down the gangway.

The man bowed deeply. "Greetings, Princess Azmei. I am Chancellor Itotia Avidius." He gestured to the waiting coach. "His majesty is pleased you have arrived. He sent me to assure you are made very comfortable during your stay here."

Azmei nodded in acknowledgment of his bow. "Thank you, Chancellor Avidius. We feel most welcome." She paused. She was out of practice with court manners, though she'd made sure never to forget them. "This is my guard, General Hawk." Gesturing to her right, she added, "Our companion Yarrax."

Avidius blinked at them both for a moment. "Be welcome," he said when Azmei didn't elaborate. "Have you any others who will travel to the palace with you?"

"Admiral Destar Thorne, who captained our ship, was injured at sea," Azmei said. "It is why we are late in our arrival. Have you healers ready at hand?"

"The Surgeon School is hard by the palace, Your Highness. I will order our second carriage to convey him to the surgeons, if you do not mind waiting while your trunks are loaded on our carriage."

Azmei relaxed a little. "It is well," she said. "Admiral

Thorne has been treated as well as our healer was able, but our supplies were running low."

Avidius nodded. "We will have your healer also attend the admiral, if you wish it."

"Please do." Azmei stood near the carriage while Avidius made the arrangements. She didn't want to get inside the carriage until she had to. The air was warm and sticky, and the sea breeze hadn't followed them to the dock.

Azmei waited until Destar had been carried out, sweaty and pale, but looking heartier than he had that morning. She went to stand by him, taking his hand. "I will call on you as soon as I am able, Destar," she promised.

"Bless you, lady," he whispered, and smiled up at her, squeezing her hand.

When Destar's carriage had gone, Chancellor Avidius bustled back to them. "I am certain you wish to get settled in the palace," he said. "I have arranged for our carriage to take a route that will show you some of the splendors our city has to offer, but I did not take the longest route, in case you were tired. Shall I change my orders to the driver?"

"No, Chancellor Avidius, you have done well, thank you. I do look forward to seeing the palace." Azmei allowed him to hand her up into the carriage. Hawk followed, sitting between her and the door. Yar opted to ride on the top with the driver, for which Azmei was grateful.

Avidius settled into the backward chair facing her. He had thin lips and bright eyes, his gaze keen on Azmei's face. This was an intelligent man, she thought, and perhaps a dangerous one. If he saw too clearly what her situation with Hawk was, he could cause trouble. She made sure she was not touching Hawk in any way.

"I hope their Majesties are well," Azmei said as the carriage lurched into motion.

"Indeed, very well. They look forward to your visit."

"And Prince Vistaren?" She held in that she had hoped he would meet her. Vistaren had said his preference for men wasn't unknown here, and she didn't think she would be able to fool this Avidius into thinking her desperately in love with Vistaren.

"I regret that the prince is very busy. The king required him to deal with a matter involving the army, and he was called away for the afternoon."

"Ah." Azmei wondered if that had been done intentionally, or if they had just given up on her arriving. She couldn't expect Vistaren to sit around doing nothing while waiting for her, after all. "Very well. I look forward to meeting everyone."

Avidius nodded. "Indeed, Your Highness. The formal reception is set for tomorrow. His majesty assumed that, after such a journey as you have had, you would wish to dine in quarters and retire early."

Azmei pushed aside her annoyance and schooled her expression carefully. "Of course." She smiled. "His majesty is very gracious."

Hawk had been looking out the window while they drove. The road they took to the palace was steep and wound its way past warehouses, inns, and public houses before making a sharp curve. After the curve, they climbed another incline and saw the public bath complex, rich merchant houses, and upscale artisan shops.

Avidius, seeing his interest, boasted about the luxurious baths and said his majesty would be pleased to provide them with entry chits. Azmei was careful to neither accept nor decline. She merely lifted one eyebrow in acknowledgment and turned her gaze to the pale, white columns on the other side of the road.

"The public library," Avidius supplied. His tone dipped just enough to indicate his displeasure at the notion of a library for the filthy masses to pillage. "Beyond the tall wall we are approaching is the palace grounds. The stormwitch academy is located on the palace grounds, as well as the surgeon's school." He pointed to each of the famous institutions as they passed. Then they were pulling up before a massive palace built of marble in gray, white, and rose.

"I do hope you will like the rooms chosen for you," Avidius said as he led them into the main building. "Prince Vistaren was particular about choosing them, and there will be rooms for your guard and staff, of course. We were uncertain if you would bring your own maids. Of course her majesty will assign a lady-in-waiting, if you require."

"Thank you," Azmei said. "I will be fine for tonight. More arrangements can be made tomorrow."

She refrained from telling the chancellor that she had been dressing herself for several years now; the court dresses she had brought, after all, might require help with laces, and certainly she would need a maid to do something with her hair.

After showing them about a richly-appointed suite of seven rooms, Avidius took his leave with a bow, promising to send dinner up.

Azmei looked around the sitting room, annoyed and restless and worried. "Well," she said. "Welcome to Amethir."

11

Azmei smoothed her skirts and watched Yar anxiously from under half-lowered eyelids. Wanting to appear as official and proper as possible, she had had a special outfit made for her before they came to Amethir. Three years ago, the idea of wearing such a gown would have infuriated her. Now, though, she would use every advantage to be pleasing to the people of Amethir. She didn't know what her errand would demand of her, but she feared it would not be palatable to King Rekel.

"Stop fidgeting," Hawk said, capturing one hand in his. "You will dazzle them all." There was a light of appreciation in his gaze, though his expression was carefully blank. The chancellor should arrive at any moment to convey them from their quarters to the court, and they could not be caught in impropriety.

Azmei smiled at him. "I wish you were coming with us. I feel stronger with you at my side."

"You are strong enough for all of us," Hawk replied. He squeezed her hand and stepped back. "The gold suits you. You look like a conquering queen."

That made her laugh. "And yet here I come as a petitioner, attempting to win back my alliance with this empire so I may convey a message the king will certainly not wish to hear."

"Why *isn't* he going with you?" Yar asked.

Azmei gave him a gentle smile, hoping her anxiety didn't show. "Hawk will be presented later, but we must be careful not to dilute the message you carry with too many introductions." It was part of the truth, at least.

Hawk gave her an impatient look and stepped closer to Yar. "And no one here must know that I love the princess," he said, his voice low. "You know she is still formally betrothed to their prince. My presence would be an insult."

Yar frowned. "That makes more sense," he said, and glared at Azmei. "You can't keep shielding things from me. I have to *learn.* I have to be useful to the dragons."

Azmei felt a pang in her chest and looked away. He was right. She knew he was. She was used to thinking of him as a young boy, but that had been a byproduct of the way he had been trapped inside his own mind when they first met. Since his bonding with Xellax, he had changed considerably. He still disappeared inside himself often, and he still disliked being touched, but he was more cognizant of things around him.

"You're right," she said, looking back at him. "I'm sorry." She started to smooth her dress again, then clasped her hands together.

Yar nodded. He wasn't one to hold a grudge, which Azmei admired. She couldn't seem to let things go, herself. She still held a grudge against his sister, who had been dead three years now.

Azmei took a deep breath, wishing she weren't so nervous. She had faced down insurrectionists and dragons before now. Surely she could handle the court of Amethir. "I…I wish we could have seen Vistaren before the presentation. It would be good to know the mood of the court before I walk into it."

Hawk didn't reply to that. Azmei was still getting used to talking about Vistaren in front of Hawk. She didn't like the situation they were in, but she saw no good solution. She only hoped Vistaren would have better ideas than she did.

"It'll be all right," Yar said, when Hawk remained silent. "We can—"

He stopped talking as someone knocked on the door. It opened a moment later, and Chancellor Avidius stepped inside. He swept Azmei a bow. "Your Highness, the King, the Queen, and their court formally request you join them."

She stepped forward. "I am ready."

Avidius straightened. "His majesty sent me to accompany you to the receiving room, with his gracious thanks for your patience. Your guard may await you here. I swear to you that no harm shall come to you."

"Thank you," Azmei said, and the chancellor turned and led the way out of the room.

The walk to the king's audience chamber was silent. Avidius didn't make any attempt at pleasantries, and Azmei had no interest in conversation. She listened to their footsteps echo on the pale marble floors and studied the people who passed them in the halls. Did all go as planned, these people would one day be *her* people. What were they like? What did they care about?

"A moment, your highness," Avidius murmured, stopping outside a tall set of double doors. He spoke to the guard, who stepped inside and announced Azmei's name loudly enough for it to echo through the room.

Azmei walked a dozen paces into the room, then sank into a deep curtsy. She heard voices whispering, though she didn't take her eyes from the floor. Barely a heartbeat passed before a man's voice spoke heartily.

"Welcome, Princess Azmei. Come, dear cousin, sit with us, and we shall talk."

Azmei straightened, her gaze finding an olive-skinned, gray-eyed man with Vistaren's nose. King Rekel was handsome, his face stretched into a broad smile. At his side, a plump, beautiful woman studied Azmei's face intently. She was obviously Vistaren's mother.

"I thank your majesties for the welcome," Azmei said, walking forward. As planned, Yar remained where he was, motionless in a deep bow.

"We have much to discuss." Rekel's gaze was keen on Azmei. "Have you come to finalize our treaty with Tamnen? Despite the unfortunate circumstances that stalled our negotiations three years ago, we do hope yet to reach an accord."

At that moment, there was a disruption at a side door. Footsteps shuffled as people moved away from the door, murmuring. Vistaren strode into the room, dressed in navy and scarlet. He had gained weight since she saw him last, and there was something tired in the way he carried himself, but his face was as pleasant as ever. Azmei's heart leapt to see her friend, and when his gaze found her, she was almost certain his expression lightened.

"Vistaren," Rekel said, his voice clipped. "You are late." As Vistaren opened his mouth to answer, the king waved a hand. "Well enough, you are already acquainted with our guest. If she is not offended, I am not."

Both men looked at Azmei, who widened her eyes as if the thought of being offended had not occurred to her. "Of course not, my lord prince," she said, smiling at him as she swept into a low curtsy. "Well met, highness."

Vistaren's hands closed on hers as soon as she straightened. "Welcome, indeed, Princess Azmei," he said, and his genuine smile warmed her. "I cannot tell you how pleased I am to see you," he murmured.

Azmei smiled at him, pleased that their friendship was still intact. "And I you," she said. Having his hands clasping hers made her wonder why she had questioned her decision to come to Amethir. She loved Hawk, of course, but she also loved Vistaren, even if there was no romance between them. It *was* good to see him.

"The princess had just arrived," the king said. There was a reproach in his voice, and Azmei tried to remember if it was improper of her to touch the prince. But she could think of nothing in Amethirian etiquette that prevented it, particularly as she and Vistaren were technically betrothed.

Vistaren dropped her hands at his father's words, though. He stepped back with a bow.

The king turned to the woman at his side. "I present to you my Queen, Kahrin."

Azmei curtsied again, though this time she knew not to wait for permission to rise. "My lady queen," she murmured.

Kahrin rose and came down off the dais to meet her. She was taller than Azmei, and she stooped to kiss both of Azmei's cheeks. "Welcome to Amethir, my dear. We heard of your difficulties on the sea. I hope there was no lasting harm."

Azmei gave her an honest smile. "Admiral Thorne was injured, but your surgeons have treated him marvelous well. More than pleased, I am impressed."

"Very good." Queen Kahrin stepped back, urging Azmei to come with her. "And your suite is all as you wish?"

"All I could wish and more, gracious majesty."

Rekel cleared his throat. It was a quiet noise, but it caught Azmei's attention as well as the queen's. "My question stands, Princess Azmei: Do you intend to finalize our treaty?"

Azmei's gaze found Vistaren's. She was certain she wasn't imagining the trepidation in his gray eyes. Nevertheless, he nodded, and Azmei took a breath. "I will put pen to parchment this afternoon if it will assure your majesty of my good will," she said, her voice clear and carrying.

The slight relaxation the set of Vistaren's shoulders told her, more than Rekel's chuckle, that she had spoken well. "Oh, not necessary, my dear," the king said. "But I am pleased."

"As am I," Kahrin put in. "I look forward to getting to know you." She was beaming at Azmei.

Vistaren bowed. "I am also pleased," he said quietly. Azmei didn't think she was imagining the way his father's gaze sharpened, but the expression was gone in an instant.

Rekel clapped his hands. "Enough ceremony!" he cried. "Let us sit together and talk." He gestured at a gallery overlooking the hall. "Musicians!"

A soft, pleasing ripple of music filled the air, and it was as if an enchantment had been broken. All around the room, the carefully arranged groups of courtiers began to mill about. Voices rarely rose loud enough for her to discern any words, the music acting to dampen the noise.

Azmei let Vistaren guide her to a chair next to his mother's. To her disappointment, he took the chair on the other side of his father, so they were nearly opposite one another. She wished this were all over. She wanted to be able to speak freely with Vistaren, to tell him of her errand and introduce him to Hawk and Yar.

The king asked for more about the seadragon attack, and Azmei obliged, telling the story as if she had been more terrified than she was, as if she had been no part of the action, just an observer. She left out Yar's strange dialogue with the seadragon. That could wait until she explained more about Yar's errand here.

The king and queen were an appreciative audience, murmuring astonishment and exclamations at all the right moments. Azmei couldn't help noticing, as she spoke, that Chancellor Avidius interacted with several of the groups but never left his position between the courtiers and the dais. At one point, just as she was finishing her retelling, she saw a nobleman with pale skin walk a line directly for the dais. Avidius smoothly intercepted him, and Azmei thought there were some heated words, at least on the other man's part. But he walked away again.

She glanced over at Vistaren and found him watching her. He nodded slightly. "That must have been terribly frightening for you, princess," he said. His voice was obliging and overly solicitous, not like him at all. Azmei had to suppress the urge to make a face at him. He was playing a role in front of his parents. She had expected to do that, but she had not expected their own son would do the same.

Queen Kahrin clucked at her in a pleasantly mothering sort of way. For another kind of princess, it would have been appropriate, so Azmei smiled at her as if she appreciated it. For that matter, it would have been an appropriate response for the princess Azmei had been just four years ago. At that thought, Azmei's smile warmed.

Kahrin responded to the genuine good will Azmei felt, even if she didn't realize why. She leaned in and asked Azmei what she knew about Amethir, and if she missed her home terribly.

"I miss my brother," Azmei said honestly. "But he has his duty, and I have mine. I am grateful to be well enough finally to fulfill it." She smiled at Vistaren. "And I am obliged to you, my lord, for waiting for my full recovery."

Vistaren's expression was unreadable as he inclined his torso slightly from his seated position. "I swore to you that I would, and I am more than happy to have kept my word."

Azmei didn't miss the glance Rekel and Kahrin passed between them. She wished even more that she had been able to talk to Vistaren before she met his parents. There were things she didn't know, and she hoped she wasn't doing him harm in his parents' eyes.

Vistaren didn't seem troubled, though. They made small talk for another quarter glass before the king finally straightened in his chair.

"I fear I must take my leave. We have a council meeting scheduled directly after lunch, and I must review certain documents before the meeting."

Azmei, Vistaren, and the queen all rose as Rekel did. Azmei sank into a deep curtsy, though she noticed Vistaren and his mother only bowed their heads. Rekel's hand closed on her shoulder and he drew her upright.

"Make yourself free of our palace and our city, Princess Azmei," he said, smiling at her. "We are pleased to have you with us." He glanced over at Vistaren. "I must withdraw, but I insist that Prince Vistaren clear his schedule. You two must renew your acquaintance."

Vistaren did bow then, and Azmei thought it a curt gesture. "I had already cleared my schedule for her, my lord. Lady, I am at your service."

Azmei nodded graciously at him and took the arm he extended to her. They both stayed where they were until the king had departed. Then Azmei looked up at Vistaren just as he drew a breath and looked down at her.

Their gazes met, and Azmei knew he could see the

mirth in hers, just as she could see amusement in his.

"Come, Princess. We will take lunch and…renew our acquaintance."

***

"By the seven," Vistaren muttered as soon as they were free of the audience hall. "I think he's hoping I'll fall into bed with you and stop eyeing handsome guardsmen."

Azmei's laughter was clear and unaffected. It soothed Vistaren's tumbling stomach somewhat. At least she had not changed her expectations of him, it seemed.

"But handsome guardsmen are so plentiful," she said, grinning at him. "And so worth eyeing."

Vistaren raised his eyebrows. "Minx," he said, delighted. She seemed much more self-assured than she had the day they met. He found it appealing, though he couldn't deny it was also somewhat intimidating. What would she make of the changes in him?

"It is good to see you," Azmei said, as if she could read his mind—or, more likely, the tension he was showing, he thought ruefully. "So much has changed in the past three years, but one thing has not changed—I value our friendship. I hope we can be open with one another."

He looked at her in surprise. "Of course."

Azmei nodded. "I do look forward to spending time, ah, 'renewing our acquaintance,' as it were," she said, and flashed him a mischievous look. "But I would request that my companions Hawk and Yarrax join us at lunch."

Vistaren was puzzled by the request—hadn't he heard that General Hawk was Azmei's bodyguard? But surely she couldn't honestly need a bodyguard. And why would she think she needed him here? Hadn't she ended the threat against her life? Wasn't that why she had returned to the world of the living?

But he simply nodded. He would have to trust that she had her reasons.

When Azmei and Vistaren reached his apartments, his manservant Isden opened the door, bowing as Vistaren and the others swept through it. Beyas looked up from the small secretarial desk where he sat, made a noise of surprise, and stood.

"My lord prince, I did not expect you back so soon. My apologies—" He broke off as Vistaren held up a hand.

"Beyas, wait. Isden. Go you to the princess' apartments and bring her bodyguard Hawk to her here."

Isden bowed and vanished.

"Beyas, we will dine here, and we are not to be interrupted."

Beyas nodded. "Is there anything else, highness?"

"No, please make lunch arrangements, and send someone in with drinks. The seven know I need one." Beyas slipped out of the room.

Vistaren finally turned to look at Azmei, who was standing in the middle of the room, her hands clasped together. She looked entirely composed until she lifted her gaze to meet his. Then he saw that her outward stillness hid a world of anxiety.

Vistaren's shoulders relaxed as their eyes met. He smiled at her and opened his arms in welcome, and to his relief, Azmei threw herself into them, hugging him tightly.

"By the seven, it's good to see you," he breathed, and he felt her laugh.

"And you," she whispered. She kissed his cheek, just a dry touch of lips, and then buried her face against his shoulder.

Vistaren couldn't believe how much better he felt just having her here. What a relief that they were still friends, and what deep comfort that she trusted him so much still. He breathed in the sandalwood scent of her hair and held in a sigh. And what a disappointment that he still felt no stirring of desire at the feel of her body against his.

He set her away from him finally, smiling down at her. She was thinner than when they had first met, he thought, and more muscular, less a young lady of books and letters and more a warrior princess. He had liked her well enough before, but thought the change suited her. As she beamed up at him, Vistaren could sense her strength despite her worry, her sense of self, and an iron determination.

Yes, regardless of his complete inability to love her as she deserved, she would make an excellent queen for Amethir, if she still wished it. Vistaren knew he would find no better partner than Azmei, as long as she were still willing to accommodate his particular situation.

"Well," he sighed finally. "You made quite an impression."

"I take it your parents liked me?" Azmei's cheek dimpled prettily as she grinned at him, though when Vistaren looked closer, he saw that it wasn't a dimple—it was a scar from the night Orya had tried to kill them both.

"They certainly did. I had a time of it trying to convince them I would consider no other princess or lady besides you." He made a face. "Well, trying to convince Father. Mother, I am certain, is much more willing to see me happy than dutiful."

It was a shame he couldn't be both. He had set his aim at dutiful and would thank the gods if some happiness managed to come his way in spite of it.

"I take it your father believes I will somehow change you?" Azmei's snort told him what she thought of that.

Vistaren sighed and nodded. "Well. We might as well sit down. I for one need a glass of wine while we talk."

He led the way to the seating area and settled into his favorite chair. Azmei took the seat next to his, smoothing her skirts automatically as she tucked one leg under her to face him. She seemed so much more self-possessed than the princess he had met three years and more ago.

Vistaren roused himself from studying her again and smiled faintly. "My dear friend, I am so glad to see you here and well."

To his relief, Azmei smiled back at him. "And you. I

knew I could at least count on your understanding."

"You have such faith in me?" Vistaren asked. It pleased him, but he hadn't entirely expected it. They had corresponded for a time before they met, but they had only spent a few weeks getting to know one another. Then again, those few weeks had been filled with experiences that taught people a great deal about one another.

"You did save my life," she pointed out. "And we are friends, if naught else." Her voice was warm, and Vistaren's stomach flipped as he realized what he needed to do. They couldn't work out whatever obstacles they faced with this tension between them. He sucked in a breath.

"This is neither the time nor the place, but…Azmei, are you truly still…of the same mind, regarding our prior arrangements?"

Azmei took a slow breath, but the warmth in her expression didn't fade. "There is much to discuss," she said, "but…yes, I do still desire an alliance. Are you—"

"I fear I am very much unchanged." Vistaren coughed and glanced aside. "In every way."

When he looked back at Azmei, he was surprised to see her smiling again. "That's a relief, actually," she said, and for a moment she sounded very much like the girl he had first met. "I actually…er…" She bit her lip and glanced toward the door, which had opened.

Isden stepped inside, followed by a man with ochre skin and a limp. His neatly-trimmed beard was sprinkled with white, though his dark, shoulder-length hair had only a single lock of white. He was dressed in practical but fine clothing, and his gaze was not on the prince, but on Azmei.

"Your highness, I have brought General Hawk," Isden said quietly.

Vistaren looked from Hawk to Azmei, and the expression on her face told him what she'd been unable to say aloud. When Vistaren looked back at Hawk, the man bowed, an abashed look on his face.

"Oh, good," Vistaren said, and laughed awkwardly.

"Well. Somewhat good. Anyway. Now we all know, and we'll work that out later. Welcome, General Hawk."

Hawk straightened, his expression guarded but cordial. As he looked at Vistaren, though, the guardedness gave way to something bewildered. After a moment, he nodded.

"Come, sit down. There's no need for us to stand on formality." As awkward as it might be later, Vistaren couldn't help but be glad Azmei had someone who could look at her like that, since Vistaren never could. And if Azmei trusted Hawk, Vistaren could too.

"Isden," Vistaren called, "Come pour for us. We'll likely be here a while."

***

Eldry held awareness of the seadragon in the back of her mind all the time now. They had been at sea for over a week, and she was beginning to dream of what the seadragon was doing. She hadn't attempted more than awareness, not yet. She would know when the time was right to bring the seadragon to her.

She swayed with the movement of the deck, wishing the Scavenger hadn't insisted on coming with them to Amethir. She would do better without his constant harping and muttering. Still, she supposed she owed him something. She wouldn't be a stormweapon without him. He had showed her the direction she needed to go.

"And so your plan is simply to walk into the academy?" he asked. He was tinkering with a small box, not looking at her.

"I will go back to the academy and show them how I have changed. What I have learned."

The Scavenger muttered under his breath, but the only words she caught were the last ones. "But she knows them there."

Eldry looked at him, and when he didn't say anything else, she said, "What is it?"

The Scavenger hitched a shoulder, "Oh, he isn't certain you'll be safe there. Says they'll lock you up if they suspect anything."

Eldry snorted. "Not if I do it properly. If Mistress Lijka were there, certainly she'd be suspicious, and my task might be harder. But she doesn't live at the Academy. She only comes in for important meetings and things."

She thought of the haughty Lijka, former King's Stormwitch and still head of the academy's Council. She thought she knew everything, and she looked askance at any witch who seemed to enjoy their power too much. The only odd thing was that it didn't seem to be bitterness on behalf of her wife, who lost out to Menever.

Menever, who would be the perfect stormwitch to use.

"So I'll make certain Lijka isn't there, and that Pralith Menever is," she went on. "Pralith is the one we want. He's ambitious. He needs to prove he deserves his title instead of Stormwitch Kinnet. So I'll go to him, show him my new powers, whisper in his ear." She smiled slowly, thinking of how easily his greed for power could be turned to her use. "And then…"

The Scavenger cackled loudly. "Oh, yes, and then!"

"And then what?" demanded Rhys' voice from behind her. She hadn't heard him approach, so involved had she been in her plans. She blinked, dismissing the visions of the white marble corridors of the academy. "What exactly is it that you've set out to do, Eldry? Do you know how you sound, planning to twist and manipulate everyone? And to do what? To prove some horrible point?"

Eldry turned to glare resentfully at him. She didn't have a good response, that was the problem. It probably wasn't noble of her to want revenge on them for posting her on the *Elana Bey* or abandoning her to the storm that sank her. But it felt good to think of correcting the academy council. They were so used to thinking they were special, that they had all the answers. That no one among the lower echelons of the stormwitches could have good ideas. She would show them otherwise.

Before she could think of a good retort, the Scavenger had climbed to his feet. Eldry watched in surprise as he squared off against Rhys, hands on his bony hips.

"Oh, no, my lad. You shan't speak to her so. If it weren't for the miss, you'd be food for the gulls right now."

Rhys stared at the Scavenger, mouth open.

"Oh, yes. He chose *her*, and you were her price. So here you are. But don't suppose he won't let you be eaten by a siren if you try to interfere in the mission he's chosen her for."

Eldry sighed. "Enough. I gave my word, Scavenger. If he really is a god, he ought to know I'll keep it." He ought to know Eldry *wanted* to keep her word by now.

"Wait, you—El, you made a vow to a god?"

The Scavenger cackled. "And he's awake and watching. Be sure he'll keep an eye on *you*, lad, to make sure you don't misbehave."

"You…" Rhys stared at Eldry, comprehension dawning on his face. "You didn't speak true when you told me they hired you to call the wind."

Eldry felt a fierce grin tugging at her lips. Why not let him see her as she was now? Let him see what he had refused. "No, Rhys, I didn't. I took this ship like the Storm Petrel takes Strid ships all the time. If she can be celebrated for that, why not me?"

His eyes were wide. "Because stormwitches aren't supposed to take ships! You're supposed to divert storms and call rains for the crops and—"

"Why?" she demanded. "Why only that? Why not call lightning to hand like the weapon it is? Why not use it to cow the other nations? Why not use it to cow my enemies?"

Rhys shook his head slowly. "I didn't know you had enemies, Eldry." His voice was soft.

She narrowed her eyes. "I do now. And if they get in my way, they'll find I've grown. I'm not the foolish, biddable girl I used to be."

Rhys' throat bobbed as he swallowed. "No, you're…you're not at all the girl I used to know."

Eldry watched as he turned awkwardly and made his slow, painful way along the deck. She was angry, but her throat ached as if she were going to cry. How dare he judge her? She'd been ill used. She was due some turnabout.

"Don't worry," the Scavenger said. "He'll come around. Or if he don't, *he* will deal with him." His words sounded sane, which made the thin cackle that followed them sound even madder.

Eldry shivered.

12

"We need to go now," Yar blurted. They were the first words he'd spoken in over an hour. Azmei looked over at him.

He was sitting bolt upright on the edge of a velvet-upholstered chair outside the council chambers, looking finer than she had ever seen him. Dressed in rich brown trousers and a bright green tunic, he looked the part of a bold young lord. When he looked up at her, his dark hair fell into his eyes, which were a swirling silver color that matched the eyes of his dragon partner, Xellax. But despite his new-found confidence, there was still so much he didn't understand.

"We can't," she reminded him. "We have an appointment with the king, and we must wait until he calls us."

He sighed. "You said that. But the longer we wait—"

"I know," she said. "It will be soon."

They had all been chafing at the delay. It had been two days since her formal reception with the court, and Yar had been growing more and more impatient. He kept insisting that their message was urgent, and nothing Azmei said could convince him that their message was so urgent they needed to handle it properly and present it to the king right.

"Remember what we talked about?" she said. "Every-thing we practiced."

"I know how to bow properly," Yar said. "If I could do it on the deck of a ship, I can manage it on dry land. And you've had me practicing all morning."

"And how to speak to him? King Rekel is not like my brother."

Yar drew himself up, his lips curling in a proud smile. "Xellax will speak through me."

"Not until you're presented and the king allows it, though," Azmei said.

"I know!"

"You've been over it enough, Az," Vistaren said. His tone was gentle. "I think I could bow properly to the king now."

She rolled her eyes at him, but she took his point. Her badgering was only going to make Yar more impatient.

Finally the great oak doors opened and the chancellor stepped out. "Princess Azmei, the king and council will hear your…petition."

She knew this must look strange, that she was petitioning the council over a matter she had said she couldn't discuss beforehand. Perhaps she should have, but Vistaren had urged her to approach the whole council.

"My father's a fair man," he said, "but I'm afraid things are being hidden from him." He had frowned and then added, "Or else *he's* hiding things. Best make certain this is brought to light before everyone."

Azmei led the way into the chamber, flanked by Vistaren and Yar. She stopped and curtsied in front of the council table, waiting until the king spoke.

"Princess Azmei, we are pleased to see you again. Rise and tell us what troubles you."

She straightened. "Your majesty, I came to Amethir partly to resolve the matter of our treaty. I also came to Amethir to accompany this man, Yarrax, who has an important errand to your court."

Rekel's eyebrows went up. "Carry on, then. I welcome you, Yarrax. Come, join your princess."

Azmei glanced over her shoulder at Yar, who was still bowing, though she could see the fingers of one hand tapping against his thumb. "Your majesties of Amethir," Azmei said, raising her voice to address the whole council, "Prince Vistaren, counselors and ministers of state and stormwitches,

I request now the honor of presenting to you Yarrax, Voice of Dragons."

There was a long silence. Someone shuffled their feet. Next to her, Vistaren took a couple of loud breaths. Finally, someone coughed.

Chancellor Avidius, from his seat next to the king, said, "Did you say *dragons*?" There was polite disbelief in his expression, as if he were just waiting for someone to finish the joke.

Someone tittered, which burst the dam on general laughter that rippled throughout the council chamber. Voices rose in commentary and exclamations. Azmei looked across at Vistaren, who was watching her gravely.

Rekel held up a hand, silencing the laughter. He nodded to Azmei. "Pray forgive the interruption," he said.

Feeling suddenly very grim, Azmei took a breath. "Your majesty, Yarrax was called by the dragons, chosen at a young age to speak for them. I have met these dragons. I have heard some of their concerns."

"Then you do claim that dragons are still alive?" The king was leaning forward in his seat. He seemed to be intrigued, at least.

"They are. After the Godwars, they withdrew from humans, to a valley deep in the desert of Tamnen. But they called to Yarrax from their valley, and we found them. They have come forth to aid humans once again." She wished she could lick her lips, but she didn't want to appear nervous. "There are dragons protecting my brother's palace even now."

The king sat back, his gaze going to Yar. "Why does the Voice of Dragons not answer for himself?"

Yar straightened, lifting his chin high. "I waited your permission to speak, majesty." His voice was clear and unwavering. Azmei felt a brief upswelling of fondness.

"Very well," Rekel said. "Speak, and await no further permission. What is your mission here?"

"I have come bringing a message of dire urgency. A

portent of danger and darkness." Here he paused and glanced at Azmei. It wasn't part of what they'd rehearsed; she could sense his sudden nervousness.

Rekel had noticed the glance. "And so? Princess Azmei, do you know his message?"

Azmei did lick her lips then. "I know the main of it, sire. I…fear great change is in store." She paused, heart thumping harder in her chest. "Not all who hear the dragons' Voice will be pleased." As warnings went, it wasn't strong enough, but it was the best she could do without stealing Yar's thunder.

King Rekel sat back all the way in his seat, his gaze wandering slowly from face to face at the table. Azmei could read the faces as easily as he must. They were still obviously uncomfortable with the thought of dragons. They didn't want to take Yar seriously; he was still a boy, and he was very different from them. Those swirling silver eyes were alarming, and they didn't have Azmei's knowledge that his eyes matched those of his bonded dragon Xellax.

But Rekel is intrigued, she thought, surprised. *Is it that he is aware something is wrong? Or just because Yar is so different?* She glanced over at Vistaren, who was also appraising his father's reaction. *Or is it because he trusts Vistaren, and Vistaren trusts me, and I take Yar seriously?*

Whatever the reason for his interest, Rekel came to a decision. He gestured for Yar to continue.

She saw Yar's shoulders move as he took a deep breath. "Your majesty, the dragons urge repentance."

There followed a deep, shocked silence. Azmei sensed the council's discomfort and bit back a grim smile. If this shocked them, wait until they heard the whole message.

"Repent…" Rekel mused. "Of what?"

Yar bowed slightly. "I am not given to know. My bondmate Xellax, who is not the least of the dragons, gives me words to speak to you. This is what she says: REPENT. TURN ASIDE FROM YOUR PATH OF GREED. THE GODS MOVE IN THEIR SLUMBER."

Azmei's throat tightened with sudden pride. Yar was doing so well. It was a hard message to bring, but Yar was managing to convey humility with confidence. She wasn't sure she would do as well as he was.

While the king mulled over Xellax's words, the councilors shifted in their seats. Two or three shuffled papers. Others exchanged glances. Someone coughed.

"Yarrax," Rekel said finally. "What does this message mean?"

Yar bowed. "As I said, I am not—"

"Given to know, yes," Rekel said dryly. "Are you given to *guess?*"

Azmei's cheeks grew hot. She knew Yar was being mocked, even if Yar didn't pick up on it. It was gentle, but nonetheless, Rekel had slipped into treating Yar like a young man, rather than a prophet.

"My task is that of messenger only," Yar said. "But I will try to elaborate where I may. Xellax and her kin speak to me with words, but they also send me images, scents…impressions. I have had visions of sleeping mountains shaking. Of the earth splitting open and the sky raining fire." He paused, his voice growing bleaker. "My dreams are filled with death."

Azmei felt the sudden sting of pity. She hadn't realized his dreams were so dark. She knew he had benefitted from his bonding with Xellax, but she hoped the good outweighed the bad.

Rekel hummed thoughtfully. "But what is it I have done, that I must repent? If I am not told the cause of my offense, how may I repair it?" He tapped his fingers against the arm of his chair. "For that matter, whom have I offended? The dragons? The gods?"

Chancellor Avidius could take no more. "Majesty," he broke in, "surely you don't credit this!"

Rekel turned a sober look on him. "Chancellor, Yarrax comes to us with a serious message. We would not only be discourteous but also unwise to dismiss it out of hand."

Azmei took a slow, quiet breath. Rekel's reaction so far had been much better than she had feared it might be. And she didn't think, judging by his reaction, that Vistaren's fear of his father hiding something was a valid one.

"If it's a matter of repentance, why not call in a priest?" asked a woman sitting at the far side of the table.

"Wouldn't the priests have seen this already? Why haven't they said anything?"

"Perhaps they have seen it," Rekel said. "Perhaps they have not."

Yar's body went taut. He lifted his head. "THE GODS WILL WAKE. ONE AT LEAST DREAMS VIVIDLY ENOUGH TO AFFECT THE WAKING. TWISTER OF WORLDS."

The entire room gasped as one. Azmei saw several hands twitch in gestures to ward off evil. She even heard Vistaren suck in a breath, and he had known what was coming.

Rekel said, his voice grave, "We do not speak that one's name, Voice of Dragons."

"You might not," Yar replied. "But I speak for the dragons, and they *do* name him." He paused for a moment and a note of humor entered his voice. "I have found that they are rarely so clear, and we must grasp on tightly whenever they are."

The room filled with a babble of angry voices. Azmei, glancing around, got the feeling Yar had done something blasphemous by naming the Twister of Worlds. She wasn't sure how else you were supposed to be clear about who exactly you were speaking of, if you couldn't say his name. Yar was clearly untroubled by the reaction he was getting.

At the far corner of the room, a man with shoulder-length silver hair slipped out of the room. Azmei made a mental note to ask Vistaren later who he was.

The king stood, his chair scraping back loudly on the stone floor. "You will speak of this to no one," he ordered, looking around at each person in turn. "We must consider all that has been said. We will discuss this further after the noon meal."

***

Vistaren led Azmei and Yarrax to his apartments. He wanted a chance to discuss the council meeting with them while they lunched. He had been pleasantly surprised by his father's reaction to the warning Yarrax brought, and he felt guilty now for having doubted him. But Lijka and Kinnet's concerns pressed at the back of his thoughts. Perhaps Pralith Menever and the other stormwitches had been hiding this from the king.

What would that mean, Vistaren wondered suddenly, if the stormwitches were keeping secrets from the king? Did they have some long plan that was suddenly coming to fruition? Were they making a play for power? Or had they been controlling things secretly for much longer than even Vistaren suspected?

"You're far away," Azmei observed. She settled into her chair with the grace of a queen. It struck him again how much she had changed.

"They should listen," Yar blurted, cutting off whatever Vistaren would have said. The prophet sounded upset but not petulant. It was almost as if he couldn't believe the council had doubted him. "They'll regret not listening."

"I know, Yar," Azmei said. Her tone was quiet and firm. Vistaren would have expected her to soothe the boy, but she spoke to him as an equal. "We'll keep trying to convince them."

Vistaren cleared his throat. "My father didn't dismiss it all out of hand," he said, as if Yarrax cared one way or the other what his opinion was. So far, Vistaren hadn't seen much evidence that he did. "That's a good sign."

Yarrax blinked at Vistaren, then at Azmei. After a few moments, he looked down at the table. "I have to talk to Xellax," he announced, and abruptly his eyes, though still open, seemed almost blank of any life.

Vistaren eyed Yarrax, wondering if the boy were still aware of what was being said around him, or if he had shut himself off entirely. What did a Voice of Dragons do, anyway? He still hadn't grasped that concept, though he knew Yarrax spoke for the dragons, who were somehow aware of things on a level that humans couldn't be.

"It's all right," Azmei said comfortably. "This used to happen with no warning. It's much nicer now he can choose when to talk to her."

Vistaren looked away from Yarrax with some relief. Azmei was smiling fondly at the boy, her expression almost sisterly.

"Once he fell off his horse in front of me, before his Joining," she said. "That was magnitudes more alarming than this is."

"I'll take your word for it." Vistaren shifted in his seat, hoping Isden would arrive soon with their ordered lunch. "I, ah, I'm sorry things haven't gone as you'd hoped."

He wasn't even certain what he meant by that. He didn't know what she'd hoped for. He didn't even know if he was talking about the council meeting or about the three years they'd spent apart or the fact that her father had been murdered and her brother now ruled Tamnen. She had always had that ability, to throw him off balance and make him unsure of what to say or think or expect.

Azmei gave him a crooked smile. Her hair was still short, curling just under her jaw. It suited her far more than the long, fancy braids had. "I'm not sure *what* I hoped. When you're up against the—"

Vistaren twitched. Azmei shifted her words so smoothly he almost questioned if she'd changed what she intended to say.

"—that god, what *can* you hope for?"

She must have picked up from what his father said that speaking the Twister of Worlds' title was a strongly-held taboo. All the same, she didn't seem to feel the same fear of the name that Vistaren's folk did. His lips twisted wryly.

"You've changed," he said, smiling so she would know it wasn't a complaint. "I'm certain the princess I met three years ago would be daunted by what we face. Yet here you are, prepared to defy a god."

To his surprise, Azmei blushed. "I..." She hesitated as if weighing her words. "I don't serve the gods of my homeland anymore. Becoming a disciple of the god of peace..."

"And an accomplished Silent Diplomat," Vistaren interjected.

"No," she said. "I'm not that." She frowned at him for a moment. "I couldn't make those vows. It would have taken me from Tamnen *and* from Amethir if I had. I am an assassin. An accomplished one, even. But I am not a Diplomat."

"That's just semantics," Vistaren said, but Azmei shook her head.

Isden entered the room then, his soft footfalls barely registering, but enough to keep her from continuing. Isden was followed by two kitchen boys carrying trays laden with food. As they transferred the lunch from tray to table, Isden poured red wine from the decanter he carried. When the transfer was complete, Isden shooed the boys away with a soft, silent gesture, but he took up his place next to the door.

"No," Azmei said at last. She curled her fingers around the stem of her wine goblet, not meeting Vistaren's gaze. "I chose my own future. *My own*, not that of the Diplomatic Council. I should have made my vows once I killed Orya's grandfather and beat my cousin, did I intend to be a Diplomat."

Her brows were drawn tight, her jaw set. This was important for him to understand, he could see; or at least it was important to Azmei, which meant he should want to understand.

"I trust you that there's a distinction I'm missing," he said. "But it sounds like you think you chose selfishly, and I can't believe that."

She tilted her head, her gaze trailing over his face. He'd

surprised her, he thought, but he wasn't sure how. Was she surprised that he didn't understand? Or that he was willing to take her word for it? But why should that surprise her? He trusted her completely. More, he realized suddenly, than he trusted his own father. And wasn't that the complete opposite to how it should be?

"Not *selfish*, necessarily," she said finally. "But…but not the Diplomat's path. My master, Tanvel, told me that I could be a great Diplomat, but he also said I could accomplish much as Queen." She bit her lip, dropping her gaze to the food Isden had placed in front of them. "I hope he was right."

Vistaren served himself from the plates. Isden would have had one of the royal food tasters sample all the food before bringing it here, but there was no way for Azmei to know that, so Vistaren demonstrated that it was safe.

"I'm sorry about all you've been through," he ventured after a long silence. He had liked Azmei a great deal, even loved her as he would a friend, three years ago. He still liked her, but he wasn't entirely certain of how to be with her now, after all that had passed.

The past three years for him had been spent studying the science of ruling and the art of warfare. For her, the past three years…well, he didn't know what they had been like, but they must have been very different.

Azmei lifted one shoulder in an elegant shrug. "I don't know. What I went through has shaped me, but…. It isn't necessarily good or bad. It just is."

Vistaren nodded. He glanced at Yarrax, who seemed entirely unaware that lunch had presented itself before him. Would the boy spend the entire recess communing with his dragon? For that matter, did the Voice of Dragons have mundane needs like food and chamber pots? Perhaps he wasn't truly a creature of flesh.

Azmei was watching him, her lips quirked in a tiny smile. When he saw her looking, Vistaren gave her a crooked smile of his own. She grinned openly then and turned her attention to her lunch. He took that as a sign to do likewise, and it was some time before either of them spoke again.

"Do you know why the gods are waking?" he asked finally.

He hadn't received a satisfactory answer to that question the day she arrived, and he could tell, from the look of frustration on her face, that he wasn't destined to receive that answer now.

"I'm not even sure what we're supposed to do about it," she said acerbically. "The dragons—well, Darixu, actually—just told me to come to you."

"To Amethir?" he asked.

"No, Vis," Azmei said, and the warm intimacy in her voice made his breath catch. "To *you*."

He looked at her in sudden alarm. Why would dragons talk about him? Why would they care about him? He wasn't anything special, just the heir to Amethir's throne—and one that wouldn't please half the lords in the kingdom, if he was any judge.

Yarrax spoke into the taut silence. "Xellax likes you. She says you are soft in the proper places and strong in the others. And your heart is right."

Vistaren stared at the boy. He was slender, almost *too* slender, as if he'd been chronically underfed for most of his life. His dark hair flopped into his face. He was almost pretty, but Vistaren got the sense Yarrax would be offended if someone pointed that out to him. The way the boy—no, young man, he thought—held himself, it was almost as if Yarrax were above matters of attraction and desire.

Yarrax shrugged. "She was curious about you," he said. He shoved a piece of meat into his mouth; it was bigger than he could chew, but he talked through it. "They know *about* you, but it isn't the same as *knowing* you."

Vistaren looked at Azmei. To his relief, she was looking back at him with a similar expression of bewilderment.

"Does Xellax have any advice for me?" he asked Yarrax.

"Follow the path you know is true," Yarrax said. He took a long gulp of wine.

Vistaren opened his mouth to ask for clarification, but at that moment he heard a commotion from his study. A moment later, Beyas appeared, carrying a falcon with a message tube on its leg.

"Highness," Beyas said. "A letter. It bears General Algot's seal."

***

Vistaren took the letter and unrolled it. His gaze scanned it, and then Azmei saw him pale. "She was right," he whispered. The paper trembled in his hand.

"Vistaren?" she asked.

He shook his head. "I told you that Lijka Ardelis had sensed a storm hit Anderly?" When she nodded, his lips twisted. "The village is gone. I sent Lo there to look into it, and his report…" He trailed off and handed it over.

As she read, Azmei's stomach began churning. She handed the letter to Yar and then looked at Vistaren. "Your father needs to know this," she said. "Do you know if he got the letter Lo mentions?"

Vistaren stood. "He may not see it before council resumes. We might as well head back to the council chamber."

Yar trailed along behind them as they walked through the corridors. Azmei liked how people in the palace responded to Vistaren. They smiled when they saw him coming and many were openly friendly with him. He spoke pleasantly to everyone in return, not showing anything of the shock he must be feeling.

Some of the council members were already in their seats again, and more filed in after Azmei, Vistaren, and Yar. Many of them were conversing in low tones, but Azmei and her companions sat in silence. She kept glancing at Yar, but his expression was turned inward. She didn't want to interrupt if he was talking to Xellax, but she hoped he had conveyed what the letter said.

Finally King Rekel entered the room, trailed by a brown-skinned man with gray eyes. The man's silver hair was cut short in back, but it fell down artfully across his forehead. Azmei guessed he was probably around forty years old. He was clearly a stormwitch.

Beside her, Vistaren groaned softly. "Pralith Menever," he muttered. "King's Stormwitch. The position is given to the one chosen to interact with and advise the king most closely. He's a…" Vistaren trailed off, but Azmei could fill in what he didn't say.

"I have asked Stormwitch Menever to join us and comment on the news from the dragons," Rekel said before he sat. The room quieted instantly. "I have also brought the high cleric of Sea Lord Antos to speak with us."

He sat. Pralith Menever did not. His gaze sharpened as he found Azmei and bowed to her. "It does you credit, princess," he said, "that already you are concerned for Amethir. Anyone can see you care for the kingdom you seek to join yourself to." His expression was respectful, but she could hear a smirk in his voice. "I am uncertain how you got the notion stormwitches are to be feared, though."

"That isn't what—" Azmei began.

Yar spoke at the same time. "Not stormwitches."

Pralith chuckled. "There's no need to fear storms, either."

Azmei lifted an eyebrow. "When the storms are driven by a god, I think there may be need, Stormwitch Menever."

He smiled indulgently at her. "I assure you, we monitor the seasons closely. No danger could come to anyone here."

"Perhaps not here in the capital," Vistaren said, his voice mild. "But I fear the Count of Anderly might take exception."

Azmei didn't miss the stormwitch's flinch, though he covered it by brushing his hair off his forehead. She felt Vistaren tense next to her.

"What is this?" Rekel asked.

Vistaren stood. "Father, I had a letter from General Algot. It arrived while we were at table. He arrived at Anderly, as he was ordered, and his report is that the town of Anderly was destroyed by a storm more than a week ago." He paused, then added heavily, "Six weeks before storm season was set to begin."

The room burst into chaos as everyone began talking over one another. Pralith Menever stood very still, gazing at Vistaren. Azmei could almost see how fast he was thinking, trying to come up with an excuse or explanation.

King Rekel rapped an empty goblet hard against the table, and slowly the voices subsided.

"What explanation, Pralith?" Rekel asked.

Pralith turned to face him, bowing. "My king, you know Prince Vistaren informed us of his concerns. We went through all our dispatches and reports. We had received nothing to cause concern."

"Then why did you not know of this?" Rekel demanded.

Pralith cleared his throat delicately. "Could it be that Count Faran—"

"Faran is dead," Vistaren interrupted. "His son Kedar has inherited."

Another eruption of sound followed this announcement, and this time it was slower to die down.

"But surely the boy has exaggerated, then," Pralith said. "His grief would explain why the loss seems so much more than it surely is."

Vistaren took the letter from his pocket. "I shall quote General Algot's letter. 'Anderly as we have known it is gone. Most of the village was washed into the sea. Count Faran was killed, and his son is much grieved. Disease is rampant. We have set up a tent city to shelter the villagers. Our surgeons do what they may. I fear more aid will be needed. This was a disaster.'"

The council's shouted reaction took several minutes to calm after Vistaren finished reading. Pralith's gray eyes narrowed as he looked from Vistaren to Azmei and then to Yar at Azmei's left. Did he know who Yar was? But he must not, for his gaze traveled back to Vistaren's face.

This time Rekel let the council's shock burn itself out. He waited until everyone had fallen silent, and then he stood. "So then," he said heavily. "Anderly is destroyed, Faran dead. It is well we sent Algot to investigate these concerns. Pralith? What explanation?"

The stormwitch cleared his throat again, and this time Azmei could tell it was genuine fear clogging his throat rather than artifice. "Majesty, it must have been an anomaly," he said. "We *have* seen them before. They are not unheard of."

"They aren't exactly common," Vistaren said dryly.

"No, but there are times nature is stronger even than magic. There is a price for witchery, highness. The occasional anomaly is that price. But they are called *anomalies* because they are exceedingly rare. The last anomaly anyone experienced was fifteen years ago."

"Let us ask Arama Dzornaea how she feels about that anomaly," Vistaren suggested. "Or perhaps we should ask Lijka Ardelis—Stormwitch Ardelis was the one who alerted me to the event that killed Anderly village."

Pralith let out a high-pitched laugh. "Lijka Ardelis? But your highness, she is no longer the king's stormwitch. She has retired to her wife's lighthouse, has she not?"

Vistaren's hand slowly clenched into a fist. "I am not here to debate politics or academy policy, Pralith," he said evenly. "I am here to discuss a very real danger to Amethir."

"Certainly, your highness. But Lijka Ardelis was much changed by her experience on the *Bounder*. I fear the trauma made her…timid…about our powers."

"Perhaps. But I defy anyone to call Arama Dzornaea timid."

"Oh, that pirate," Pralith said, his voice dismissive, and Azmei felt her own hand clench into a fist.

"Captain Dzornaea is our most honored privateer," Rekel said. His voice was calm, and Azmei took a slow breath, reminding her it wasn't her place to be angry if the king was not. Beside her, Vistaren sat abruptly.

"Certainly, majesty," Pralith said hastily. "But aren't all sailors prone to exaggeration?"

Azmei cleared her throat. "How, then, do you account for my own ship being attacked by a seadragon while we were en route here with our warning?"

Pralith flashed her a poisonous look but quickly smoothed his expression out. "I know nothing of seadragons," he said, his voice stiff.

There was a brief silence. Azmei didn't feel the storm-witch had countered anything very credibly, but she could see a few faces around the table looking gratefully at him. Rekel, at least, didn't seem satisfied, and she knew Vistaren wasn't.

"Well," the king said at last. "Perhaps the Sea Lord's chosen can offer some insight into this situation?"

A short, slender man stood and bowed. "Majesty. Honored as I am to be consulted, I fear I can offer no explanation. The temple makes the monthly offerings as is our custom, but we have noticed nothing out of the ordinary. We have seen nothing untoward."

Azmei wondered what clerics would do all day if their gods were truly sleeping. Did they mumble prayers they knew wouldn't be heard, then go about the same business as merchants and craftsmen? Did they consider sleep a form of worship? She bit her lip against a sudden desire to giggle.

"We have searched the teachings and found nothing that would give us any pause," the man added. "I am truly sorry I can be of no further help." He bowed and sat.

At least he wasn't as self-important as Pralith, Azmei thought. That was a point in his favor.

The king sighed. "Well. We shall consider this. We must turn our attention to the practical matter of what aid shall be best rendered to Anderly, now that we know the village requires it." He stood. "I will have the minister of finance and the minister of agriculture with me. The rest of you are dismissed."

Two men followed him out of the council chambers. Azmei looked over at Vistaren, who had slumped back in his seat.

"What now?" she asked.

He shrugged. "We wait. I'm to have breakfast with Father tomorrow. I'll sound him out then."

"But tomorrow—" Yar began, but he subsided when Vistaren held up a hand.

"If I push him too hard today, Yarrax, he will be less inclined to listen. If I respect his wish to think about it, perhaps he will see his own way clear to believing you. Either way, it will do no good to attempt to force his hand."

Yar clasped his hands together. "I...see. Yes. Thank you."

Vistaren shook his head. "You have precious little to thank me for, Voice of Dragons. I will do my best, but even I cannot promise my father will listen."

Yar surprised Azmei by smiling at the prince. "I am glad you believe me, Prince Vistaren. Remember, it was your name the dragons spoke. Not your father's."

He stood and walked out of the room briskly, Azmei and Vistaren staring after him.

13

"Anderly Point in sight!" called the lookout.

Arama climbed a few feet up the rigging and peered to the west, squinting against the lowering sun. She'd hoped to be closer to Anderly by now, but the tide would carry them in to harbor. Or…

"Sirens teeth," she muttered, and skimmed up to the crow's nest. "Glass," she ordered, hauling herself inside.

Gratt, who was on his third signing with her crew, looked unsurprised at her presence as he handed her his glass. "It don't look right, mum."

Arama lifted the glass to her eye and peered at the coast. "It certainly don't," she agreed. She caught the tip of her tongue between her teeth. Not only did Anderly Point look wrong, it looked…missing.

"The harbor's been wrecked," she said. "Did you see any other ships?"

"No, mum. Not even little fishing boats, which is odd for Anderly."

Arama hummed a thoughtful noise as she scanned the coastline with her glass. "There—there's a tent village up on the head. Too regular to be anything but the army." Her heart gave a treacherous little jump at the thought it might be Lozarr's division. She shoved the thought aside.

"D'you think they was attacked?"

"Mm. The Strid sailing around behind us to slip in and hit Anderly? It seems daring for them—but perhaps they were emboldened by the bounty on my head?" Arama considered it. She'd fought more than one determined Strid captain who might have the stones to do such a thing, but somehow she didn't think that was what happened.

She straightened and handed the glass back to Gratt. "I don't know. We'll hoist the colors and have the cannon primed and ready, just in case. I'll have prize ship stand off until we signal them in. You keep a sharp eye."

She descended to the deck and started issuing orders. If Anderly had been hit by a surprise attack, Arama would not let herself be similarly surprised.

When they came near enough to get a good look at what was left of Anderly Harbor, the first thing she saw was a uniformed soldier waving the flag of the Amethirian army, and her hope proved true—it was Lozarr's division. She found herself smiling and bit at the corner of her mouth to fight it.

"Gunners, stand down," she called. "Prepare to come in to dock."

It wasn't an easy docking. The lookout kept crying out the location of debris in the water, including several sunken fishing boats.

"Lord Antos preserve, what happened here?" Arama whispered to herself. She kept her expression impassive, not wanting to rattle her crew, but the first thing she would do upon landing would be to find Lozarr and demand explanations.

As it turned out, Lozarr found her first.

Arama went back to her cabin, shrugged into her captain's frock coat, and slung her sword belt around her hips. She tugged her boots on with a grimace. Then she thumped along the gangway to where a tall, olive-skinned man was waiting for her, hands on his hips. He had a broad smile on his handsome face.

"Storm Petrel," he greeted her, and clasped her hand familiarly but without undue intimacy. Arama looked approvingly at him; it had taken them some practice and missteps, but they'd found a balance they could live with in public.

"General," she said, giving him a brief smile before gesturing up at the head. "What happened here?"

Lo's smile slid off. He ran a hand through his spiky, black hair and glanced over her shoulder to the ship. "We should discuss it in private, I think," he said.

Arama frowned up at him. "All right. That's your tent city up there, I assume."

"It is. Your cabin's closer." There was a strain in his voice that made Arama's stomach jump. Her frown deepened but she turned to lead the way.

She paused as she reached Carig. "Make us fast and check in up top with—"

She glanced at Lo, who interjected, "Lieutenant Anmeir."

"—Lieutenant Anmeir to see if they need anything we can provide. Then have him pitch a tent for the two of us up near their headquarters. We'll berth here at least tonight, maybe tomorrow night. Oh, and have someone guide the prize ship in. We'll tie her up next to *Dawn Star*, and we might just leave her moored here for the moment."

Carig threw her a snappy salute and turned to start bellowing orders at the sailors, most of whom were already doing what he ordered them to.

When Arama and Lo were in her cabin with the door shut firmly behind them, she turned to really look at him.

Lo's spiky hair was untidy and he had at least two days of stubble on his jaw. There were shadows under his eyes, and a tightness around them that made her chest feel like it was being squeezed. Part of her still hated that he could make her feel this way.

She stepped close and wrapped her arms around him. "You look done in," she murmured as Lo's strong arms closed around her.

"Mm. Better now though." His chin rested on the top of her head. She felt him draw in a deep breath and then sigh.

"You're ridiculous," she informed him, and lifted her

face for a kiss. There was no way her presence could possibly make him less tired.

"You lift a weight from my shoulders, just being here," he murmured against her lips. He kissed her properly and then sighed again and set her gently away from him.

"So what happened?" she demanded again.

"A rogue storm." Lo's voice was bleak, his gaze steady on hers.

Arama stared at him for a moment and then fumbled behind her for her chair as her knees started to shake. "What kind of storm could destroy Anderly Head?" she whispered.

Lo wet his lips. "A storm like the one that sank *Bounder*. The stormwitch called it an anomaly."

Arama locked her knees and stayed upright. "What stormwitch?"

Lo held her gaze and didn't answer.

"What stormwitch?"

"You know what stormwitch."

"And suddenly we believe Lijka Ardelis? Just because she had the good sense to marry a talented stormwitch—"

"Arama." Lo's voice was quietly reproving.

Arama huffed and crossed her arms over her chest, turning her back on him to pace the cabin. She hated the loud thump of her boot heels on the wooden deck. She ought to have kept more of those fancy rugs from that Strid ship bound for the Long Coast last month.

"I thought you'd made your peace with Lijka." Lo's voice sounded tired again, and Arama felt a surge of irrational anger that the stormwitch who had ruined her life was now causing a fight with her lover. She snorted and didn't answer.

"She said she'd discussed it with Kinnet."

Arama rolled her eyes and didn't look at him. Kinnet might have saved the *Dawn Star* from a confused stormsinger, but that didn't mean she knew everything there was to know about stormwitchery.

"Will you at least look at me if you're going to roll your

eyes at me?" Lo sounded resigned, but there was a hint of amusement in his voice. From anyone else that hint of amusement would have been the spark to Arama's temper, but somehow from him it just felt like he was accepting her anger.

In the face of that, how could she stay angry?

Arama sighed and let her arms fall to her sides. She turned to look at him, knowing her gaze was baleful and yet somehow affectionate. *How* did he do this to her? Every time.

"I love you, you know," Lo said, his lips quirking up at the edges.

"Damn you," Arama replied, and went to kiss him again.

***

All the way up the cliffside road to the remnants of Anderly, Lo kept glancing sideways at Arama. He understood her feelings about Lijka, though he didn't agree with them. It had been fifteen years, after all, and it hadn't been Lijka who caused the storm. She had just been the one who couldn't avert it.

Lo knew men who had lost their entire companies during the war with the Shrouded Realm. He himself had benefited from it, indirectly. He'd been a nineteen-year-old corporal when the war broke out, and the devastation among the Amethirian ranks had been part of the reason for his swift climb up through the ranks. But soldiers were used to losses, or at least they knew to expect them, even if they never really got used to them.

Arama had been a privateer most of her life, it was true, but she'd been cocksure at eighteen, and the loss of her mentor, her crew, and her ship all at once had been hard on her. Lo had always regretted that he was unable to be there for her as she dealt with the loss. He didn't think she blamed him, but he blamed himself.

He glanced over at her again.

"Will you stop that?" she snapped. "I'm not going to fall to pieces like a seashell dropped by a child!"

Lo held in a sigh. Her prickliness was part of what made him love her so much, he reminded himself. "I don't think you're going to fall to pieces," he said calmly. "I've never seen you fall to pieces. I just—Well, is it so bad that I like to look at you?"

He suppressed a grin at the way her brown cheeks darkened with a blush at his words. She might be a hard-bitten sailor who knew more bawdy songs than any soldier, but when it came to romance, he might as well be speaking a foreign tongue.

"That isn't what I meant," she muttered.

"I know." He couldn't help teasing her sometimes. It had taken her so long to give in to what they had between them, he sometimes had to gloat just a little.

"So this sickness. What is it?"

Lo relented, letting her change the subject. "Fever and chills, with a deep cough," he said. "The surgeon gave it a name, but I've forgotten. Nothing we usually see run through army camps, though. They have it mostly under control at this point. It's just that their livelihood has been destroyed, and we'll need fishing boats here soon if we want Anderly to be able to recover economically."

"That I can take care of," she said. "Or at least, I can carry any healthy sailors who want to come on to Maron, where we can arrange for ships. And we'll leave the prize ship here, if they want to strip her down to rebuild their own." Fishing boats were generally smaller than the Strid ship, but there were plenty of supplies that would help the fisherfolk.

"Providing the king agrees to supply them," Lozarr said. "Vistaren's last message to me wasn't encouraging. Apparently Princess Azmei came to the capital and—" He paused. Vistaren hadn't come right out and say the princess had made a fool of herself, but reading between the lines, Lo thought that's what had happened.

"And what?"

Lo paused as they reached the top of the cliff. He was fairly fit, but even he was breathing a little hard, and he could tell Arama was winded. She was fit herself, in her way, but sailing didn't require the same kind of stamina as hiking a quarter-mile uphill did.

"Well, she brought some sort of prophet with her, it sounds like. The king and his council didn't exactly receive the fellow happily." He shrugged. "He didn't go into detail, but it sounds as if Vistaren and his father are at odds, perhaps over this."

"Over Anderly?"

Lo hitched his shoulder again. "Or the prophet, or Azmei, or all three."

Arama huffed. "Well. All the more reason for me to get on to Maron and find out what's happening there. We'll stay two nights and leave with the tide day after tomorrow. The men will see to resupplying the *Dawn Star* with fresh water."

Lo glanced around to be sure no one could overhear, then murmured, "Only two nights."

She met his gaze and let her lips quirk up at the edges. "We'll have to make the most of them."

Later that evening, Arama lounged on his camp bed, wrapped only in a thin blanket, and watched as Lozarr penned a letter to the prince. He didn't dare trust all of his concerns to a messenger bird, but Arama would guard his letter with her life.

I will approach the new Count Ebb in the morning to see if he is willing to accompany Arama to Maron. If he can modulate his tone, the king might be more inspired toward charity by an appeal from the nobility. I half fear the man will prove to be a rebel, though. He's lost a lot. He wasn't prepared for it. I hope his majesty will be merciful.

He glanced over at Arama, who smiled at him. Her eyelids were half closed and she looked sated and sleepy. "I like the way your forehead crinkles when you're concentrating," she murmured.

Lo huffed a laugh. "It doesn't make me look like I'm getting old?"

"If you are, so am I," she replied. "But no. It makes you look serious and smart, and maybe a little tired. But not old."

And that was apparently the end of the romantic talk. Lo bit back a grin. Another thing he loved about Arama was how practical she was. She had no use for romance the traditional way, which he thought was part of why she'd resisted having a real relationship with him for so long.

"Let me finish my letter," he said, smiling at her. "Then I can come back to bed and prove I'm not tired."

Arama's laughter made him write faster.

***

Arama had never met the old Count of Coman, but she had always heard he was respected by his fellow noblemen as well as his tenants. Lozarr had told her the new count was grieving, but she wasn't sure that was a strong enough word.

She stood beside Lozarr and his aide Anmeir and watched the count's party approach. A young woman rode a gray palfrey next to Kedar Ebb's rangy brown. On Kedar's other side was a white-haired man who carried a thick book against his chest. Four armed guards completed the party.

"That's the sister, Mirzana," Lo murmured. "The other man is the count's administrator. We've compared the names of the living with our last official census, but the administrator said they'd done their own census with the tax payments last autumn."

Arama nodded, studying the count.

Kedar Ebb had the muscled shoulders and tanned skin of a man who had spent countless hours rowing, hauling sails, or pulling in fishing nets. The broad shoulders were slumped, though, and dark smudges looked like bruises under his eyes. The count looked to be twenty-five or so; Arama had lost her mentor when she was eighteen, and had been an orphan for more than half her life at twenty-five. Still, she remembered the fear and anger and desperation well enough.

Kedar reined his horse in several paces away from them. His sister and administrator did likewise. The guards arrayed themselves in a loose box formation around the count.

"They said a ship had come in." Kedar's voice was dismissive, but his gray eyes were on Arama's face.

"My lord count, this is Captain Arama Dzornaea," Lo said. He bowed as he spoke, so Arama took her cue from him and bowed too. "Her ship, *Dawn Star*, was underway for Maron when she noticed the damage to Anderly. They came in to investigate and found us. The captain has volunteered to convey you—or an appointed representative—to the capital, if such is your pleasure."

"Can the king bring my father back from the sea?" Kedar said. "Then why should I go with her to the capital?"

Arama took a swift breath, but in her peripheral vision she saw Lo shift. She bit back on her annoyance.

"My lord, your people are in sore need. I came without knowing your specific needs, but the king would gladly provide succor, if Anderly appealed to him."

"Would that he had provided warning of the storm so readily." Kedar's voice was harsh. His sister placed a hand on his arm. Arama's gut clenched in pity. The girl looked to be sixteen or so, and yet she was comforting her brother.

After several awkward moments of silence, the white-haired man cleared his throat. "General Algot, you asked for our administrative records. I have brought our last tax roll for your staff to reference."

Lozarr stepped forward to receive the tome. It looked heavy. Arama wondered if it served the same purpose as a ship's log. What would a nobleman's log have in it?

"Thank you, Master Pennal. I will have my staff copy the list and return this to you as quickly as possible."

Master Pennal bowed and stepped back. The interlude

had apparently given Kedar time to compose himself. He stood with his head bowed, and his voice was low when he spoke next.

"Captain, I will come to Maron with you. The general is correct when he reminds me that I owe my people a duty I cannot currently fulfill."

Arama swallowed. What the blazes was she supposed to say in response to that? "It is my honor to convey you to the capital, my lord count," she said after a moment. Hells. She was no courtier. She'd grown too used to being informal with Prince Vistaren, and it made her unsure of herself with other nobles.

Kedar nodded without looking up. "When do we sail?"

She cleared her throat. "I had intended to sail with the evening tide tomorrow, my lord."

"Very well. I am needed in the village, but I will be at the docks with time to spare."

He turned on his heel and went back to his mount. She saw his shoulders slump as he reached the horse. Then he swung himself into the saddle with a move that didn't seem quite as graceful as she had expected.

Then again, he is a fisher lord, she reminded herself. *If the stories are true, they spend as much time on the sea as on land.*

"That was harrowing," she muttered as Kedar urged his horse away from them in the direction of Anderly. His administrator followed, as did two of the guards. The sister and other guards made their way back towards the manor.

"His grief is raw," Lo said. "But you handled him well."

"Did I?" She looked askance at him. "And now I'm stuck handling him until we reach Maron. At least it's a short trip."

Lo gave her a wry smile. "Sail quickly."

14

Vistaren arrived early to his breakfast appointment with his father, hoping it would put his father in a good frame of mind. He had slept poorly, and he hoped his father wouldn't notice how red his eyes were and blame it on drink.

Then again, he might be pleased to think Vistaren hadn't slept well, if he thought it was Azmei's influence. Vistaren's parents loved him, he knew, but he wasn't entirely certain they understood that he felt no attraction whatever to women. The seven knew he had tried, but it left him feeling uninterested at best and disgusted—with himself or the girl, he was never certain—at worst.

The breakfast room was empty. Vistaren took his seat and helped himself to a steaming mug of coffee. It would be rude to begin eating before his father arrived, but there was nothing to say he couldn't have some of his energizing drink.

His father arrived soon after Vistaren had taken his first sip of coffee. Rekel smiled at him, eyes crinkling warmly at the edges. Vistaren stood, smiling back at him. One thing Vistaren had never doubted was his father's love, even when the king had to be strict or even harsh.

"Good morning, Father."

"And to you." Rekel eyed him. "Though I am not certain you wouldn't rather still be abed."

Vistaren waved a hand. "I was wakeful last night. A trifling thing. Nothing coffee won't cure."

His father laughed. "Well, then." He sat down opposite Vistaren. As soon as the servants heard his father's voice they had come to the door bearing trays of food. Vistaren grinned at the smell of bacon and egg pies. His father knew his favorite breakfast, and always made sure to serve it when they broke their fast together.

Visitors from other courts had remarked on the peculiarity of his father's breakfast habits. It was apparently unusual for the king to be so informal, but Vistaren knew his father felt sharpest first thing in the morning, and he liked the opportunity to visit with members of his court and family over the early meal. It could be disadvantageous for those members of court who preferred to stay up late into the night, but there was something cozy about their mornings, and Vistaren had always enjoyed it.

"How was your sleep, sir?" Vistaren asked politely as a servant loaded his plate.

"Sound." Rekel sighed. "More than it probably should have been. Your lady mother was troubled by recent events, I think, but one of Yarrax's dragons could have landed on my head and not woken me, I believe."

Vistaren snorted a laugh and then coughed.

"You are supposed to swallow your food, not inhale it," his father remarked.

"When I am king," Vistaren said loftily, "I shall instate a rule that no one shall say something funny while the royal personage is eating or drinking."

Rekel snorted at him.

Vistaren wanted to follow up on his father's broaching of the subject of dragons, but he wasn't quite that brave before he'd had an entire mugful of coffee. He took a bite of eggs and chewed carefully before asking, "Was your meeting with the ministers productive?"

"Quite. We agreed upon initial supplies to send to Anderly. General Algot's report on the situation was disheartening."

"I don't understand how this could have happened," Vistaren admitted. "Lijka told me she felt the storm hit Anderly. If she could feel it at the light, why couldn't anyone here feel it coming?"

"Why didn't Lijka feel it coming? Why did she only feel

it when it hit?" Rekel countered. He sighed. "I don't know, son. I will not lie, I am concerned. But I cannot begin to mistrust my stormwitch. He says it was an anomaly. I must believe him."

"But, Father, the Voice of Dragons—his arrival at just the same time, that can't be a coincidence."

Rekel raised an eyebrow. "The timing is hardly suspect. The reports are that King Razem of Tamnen just put down a rebellion, and his sister helped him. As soon as she was finished, she made her way here. We were told that she had falsified her death to draw the traitors out. Is that not so?"

Vistaren, mouth full of bacon, just nodded.

"Well, then. As soon as she had no need to hide her survival, she came to you. The Voice of Dragons, if he truly is such, traveled with her, and the timing of his arrival was determined by hers. Not by some message about the gods."

"But, Father—"

"Enough," Rekel snapped. "Are we here to breakfast or to argue?"

There had been many times when his father did both, Vistaren thought mulishly, but he held his tongue. The servants brought in more food—flaky breaded fish cakes that Vistaren had always loved. He opted to eat two before speaking again.

Before he had finished the second one, his father spoke.

"I am curious. How do you feel about the treaty we began with Tamnen?"

Vistaren looked up at him. His father was watching him, one hand curled around his cup. "I am content with it, Father." He took a deliberate sip of his coffee. "As I was three years ago."

"You are content with this Tamnese girl?"

He would be more content with a Tamnese boy, but Vistaren didn't see any point in saying so. The royal blood had to be preserved. "Azmei is my friend," he said carefully. "I like her a great deal. Many marriages have worse cause."

"True." Rekel was silent for some time, focused on the sausage-and-grain pudding he favored for breakfast.

Vistaren kept waiting for him to say something else that would hint at his reasons for asking, but he just kept eating. Vistaren couldn't imagine what had prompted the question, though. There was nothing to be done. Vistaren liked men, but he was the only prince. Most people in Amethir had the luxury to marry whomever they loved, as Lijka and Kinnet had, but there were expectations of a noble, let alone a royal. Vistaren wanted to know love, but first and foremost he would do his duty.

Finally he could take the silent waiting no longer. "Do you mean not to sign it?" he burst out. "Or else why ask me these questions?"

Rekel traced a finger around the lip of his mug. "I do wish for you to be happy, Vistaren," he said. His voice was thick with sadness.

Vistaren's throat tightened as well. "Yes, sir." He smiled at his father, loving him the more because he cared about it, whether or not there was no answer. "I am as happy as I could wish," he said finally. *As long as the gods don't destroy us first.*

Rekel nodded. "Very well. I am content. Your mother may require more reassurance. Perhaps you and your princess should take tea with her this afternoon."

"Yes, sir."

"And in the meantime, I will issue an announcement that we will have a betrothal feast in three days. Take that time to court your princess."

"Sir." Vistaren considered the last fish pie and decided, regretfully, that he would be uncomfortable if he ate anything more. "And…the Voice of Dragons?" he ventured.

"Bedamned!" Rekel glared at him. "The boy is addled. We'll send him to the academy and let them deal with him."

Vistaren frowned. "Azmei won't like that."

"Then *she* may deal with him. I shall not. Pralith Men-ever says all is well, and so all shall be well." Vistaren opened his mouth to protest, but his father cut him off with a curt gesture. "No. Take the boy to the academy—and your princess as well, if she insists—but that is the end of it."

Vistaren rose to his feet, his chair scraping harshly against the stone floor. He bowed curtly, wishing he could hide his anger better. "Sir," he said, and strode out the door. He wasn't looking forward to sharing this information with Azmei, but he supposed the sooner the better.

***

Three years ago, Azmei had been worried she would hate Amethir. She remembered wondering if she would miss the plaintive sound of doves cooing in the morning. She had feared she would miss snow.

Sitting on the balcony of her suites in Maron Palace, Hawk silent in the chair beside hers, the scent of coffee tickling her nose, Azmei found herself strangely content in Amethir.

"You're pensive this morning," Hawk murmured. It was as if he were afraid to disrupt the silence. Azmei smiled at him.

"I'm not sure why; I slept poorly," she said. "But something about the sun rising over the ocean makes me feel nothing will destroy us utterly."

"It's a pleasant thing to think," Hawk agreed. He didn't sound convinced, though.

Azmei leaned her head back against the chair, which was oversized and extremely comfortable. "The council doesn't believe Yar. I could tell. I'm not sure if the king does, either. But Vistaren believes him. And as Yar pointed out, Vistaren is the one the dragons named."

"What does that mean?" Hawk's voice was neutral. Azmei had been unable to determine how Hawk felt about Vistaren. He was always courteous to the prince, but she had expected nothing else. Vistaren treated Hawk with extreme courtesy as well. She thought perhaps they were both being very careful of one another. But that couldn't last forever.

She knew it was idealistic to hope that they would all become great friends. But they couldn't change their situation, so their only option was to change their attitude about the situation. Surely that wasn't too much to ask?

"I don't know why the dragons mentioned Vistaren specifically," she said at last. "I hope it means that he will somehow come up with the solution to whatever is causing the gods to wake." She paused. "I assume we are hoping that the gods will fall back into a deeper slumber."

"For that matter," Hawk said, "we haven't really discussed what our object is. The dragons say the gods are waking. They say the gods are angry. But…what do they advise us to do?"

She looked sideways at Hawk. "That's a question for Yar, not me."

Hawk narrowed his eyes slightly. "I have not forgotten that you understood their speech more than once, Princess Azmei Corrone, who carries the blood of dragons in her veins."

Her stomach did an odd flip. She wanted to forget about that herself. The dragon Rexiel had hinted at that, when Yar told her he believed the dragons possessed shapeshifting abilities. *They can be shaped like us,* Yar had said, and Rexiel had added, *How else could we have our stake in the royal line?*

The hallmark of the Corrone bloodline was golden eyes. She had never seen that color eyes in anyone besides her father, brother, and cousins—but the gold of her brother's eyes matched exactly the gold color of Rexiel's eyes. She wondered if Rexiel himself was her forefather. She wasn't certain how long dragons could live, but she knew it was a very, very long time.

Azmei sipped her coffee. "I can't really read the king yet. I think he worries about the things Yar has said, but he doesn't want to believe them."

Hawk allowed her to deflect. "Rulers rarely appreciate a

disruption in the status quo."

"I daresay." Azmei's voice was tart. "But my status quo has been an endless disruption for three years now. I feel no compunction about Rekel's."

Hawk flashed white teeth at her in a grin. "I love how fierce you are, my princess."

Azmei couldn't help but smile at him. "And I love that you are so gentle, my warrior," she replied fondly. He could fight better than she, who had been trained as an assassin; but there was no bloodlust in Hawk. He was a warrior, yes, but he was one who understood when a peaceful answer was better than a violent one. She supposed it was something he had learned during his six years of captivity among the Strid, but there were some things she was still too shy to ask him.

She reached over, curling her fingers around his. "You know that, no matter what happens, I have no wish to be parted from you?" she asked.

He was silent for a long time, though his fingers tightened around hers. Finally he said, "I know you wish that." She could hear the doubt in his voice.

"Vistaren isn't a cruel man. And I want to see him happy, which I know can't happen with me." She took a quick breath. "I mean to look away from whoever catches his fancy, and I believe he will do the same for me."

Hawk's lips twisted in an unhappy smile. "There are different standards for a queen than there are for a king," he said.

"And well I know it, having lived those standards myself," she retorted. Then she softened her tone. "No, I am well aware I must give Amethir her heirs before I can pursue any happiness of my own. And I mean for there to be two at least. I do not wish to force my children into the decision Vistaren has been forced to make."

"The gods don't always allow..." Hawk's voice trailed off.

"I know." She swallowed against a tightening in her throat. "But I want you to know that I count you in my plans, Jacin Hawk. You cannot get away so easily, now that I have found you."

His smile was wistful, and Azmei couldn't help but lean across the space between them to press her lips against his. Stubble scratched against her lips. She lifted her free hand to cup his cheek. "I love you," she whispered against his mouth.

"And I you, Az. With all my heart."

She didn't like how sad his voice was, but she pushed it from her mind and kissed him again, letting her lips part in invitation. She was tempting them both further along a path they hadn't dared follow yet, but she didn't care. She wanted to erase that sadness from his voice.

That, of course, was when the door to the balcony slammed open so hard it bounced against the wall with a crash.

Azmei and Hawk jerked apart. Azmei leapt all the way to her feet, a knife half drawn before she realized it was a red-faced Vistaren who stood in the doorway. Hawk melted from his chair to kneel in front of it—a posture Azmei thought was overkill, since Vistaren wasn't the king.

"Gods above and below," Vistaren blurted. "I apologize. I shouldn't have just—"

"Stop," Azmei said. She shoved her dagger home in its sheath. Her face was blazingly hot, but she supposed this was as good a time as any to address the strangeness of their situation. "We'll probably have a lot of these moments, so we might as well get used to them."

She folded her arms across her chest and leaned back against the balcony, facing Vistaren squarely. "And get up, Hawk. He isn't your king. You didn't even kneel to my brother like that."

Vistaren and Hawk exchanged a startled look, and then Vistaren leaned forward, extending a hand to pull Hawk to his feet. Azmei felt a small swelling of pride as Hawk accepted the hand and stood.

"There," she said. "This is how it is. I am in love with

Hawk. He is in love with me. I mean for us not to be parted. But I also mean to marry you, Vistaren. Besides that, I mean for you to find happiness in some way of your own choosing. We must marry and have heirs, yes, but what I emphatically do *not* want is for us to all be awkward with one another."

Vistaren sighed and then laughed. "You're braver than I am, Az. But your solution is just about the best one I've thought of. So we might as well all agree to go on with it." He checked himself and added, "That is, as long as you agree, General Hawk?"

Hawk rolled his eyes, and Azmei saw that he had chosen to push the awkwardness aside too. "You might as well call me Jacin, your highness. Or Hawk. Most call me Hawk." He glanced sideways at Azmei. "Even the princess."

Vistaren's laugh wasn't entirely comfortable, but Azmei gave him credit for the attempt. "Very well. Then you should call me Vistaren, at least when we're in private. I suppose it wouldn't do for the princess' bodyguard to be on a first-name basis with me in public."

Hawk tilted his head.

"Just so," Azmei said. She retrieved her coffee mug from the balcony floor, where she had dropped it. At least it hadn't broken, though she couldn't help but mourn the spilled coffee. "Now that that's out of the way, perhaps you'll tell us how breakfast went." She smiled so Vistaren would know she wasn't really angry.

Vistaren sighed. "You won't like it," he warned. "And neither will Yarrax. Though I suppose my father is right in one aspect, at least. We *should* take Yarrax to the academy. He will want to see it."

Azmei arched an eyebrow. "What exactly did your father say?"

She wasn't terribly surprised at what Vistaren related about his argument with his father. Yar had seemed to believe Xellax's word enough for anyone else to believe, but Azmei had always feared their message would be ill received.

She was grateful that King Rekel had at least not demanded Vistaren and Azmei put Yar on the first ship back to Tamnen. If he was willing to let Yar wander around the stormwitch academy asking questions and talking about repentance, that was more than she had expected.

"Well," she sighed, when Vistaren was done, "we'll just have to take Yar to the academy and see what happens. You *will* go with us, won't you?"

Vistaren looked surprised. "I hadn't thought…but of course, that's a good idea. I can introduce him to Lijka and Kinnet. He ought to meet them anyway, they're likely to listen to him. And perhaps he can learn more about what we should be looking for."

"In the meantime, it sounds like you and I have a betrothal to get underway," Azmei said. She looked deliberately at Hawk as she said it. "I have little patience for social activities, but one thing I have learned from the Diplomats is that even things that seem pointless at the time may produce results."

Vistaren grinned. "I hope someday you'll tell me all about your Ranarri training," he said. "In the meantime, I suggest we act as if we're both happy about the betrothal."

"Aren't we?" Azmei murmured, but he talked over her.

"It might not be perfect for either of us, but we've agreed to make it work, and the general public doesn't need to know that we aren't dazzlingly in love with each other, whatever rumors they may have heard."

"I'll defer to your opinion on this," Azmei said. "You know your people, and I do not, though I look forward to getting to know them."

Vistaren shrugged. "Well. It wouldn't look right at first if you joined me without your bodyguard. I suppose I ought to find someone to act as mine, for that matter. And when we go in public, we should have at least a ten-unit nearby, just to be safe."

Azmei nodded. "Good. So what do we do first?"

"My father suggested, before we argued, that Mother

might need a bit more reassurance about how happy we are to be together," Vistaren said. "For that, I think, Hawk only need come to the door of Mother's day room, and wait outside. But I warn you, there will be talk of gardening, which is Mother's passion. I hope flowers don't make you sneeze."

Azmei grinned at him. "I don't know about Amethirian flowers, but Tamnese and Ranarri flowers never have. Your mother seems like a dear. I'm afraid I don't know much about mothers in general, since mine died when I was so young. Guira was the closest I had to a mother, but, of course, she wasn't a queen."

"Don't worry too much. Treat Mother as you would Guira, and I think you'll get along quite well."

"Very well. Then what is our plan?" Azmei asked.

"Afternoon tea. I'll come to get you, if you'd like time alone. Or…" Vistaren paused, looking almost shy for a moment. "I haven't any obligations for the day. I had thought about a horseback ride in the countryside. If that would interest you."

Azmei perked up. She loved horses, and anything would be better than sitting idle in the palace. "Yes, please. Hawk will go with us, of course?"

"Of course. He's your bodyguard." Vistaren grinned at her.

For the first time in many months, Azmei began to wonder if everything might just work out after all.

15

The sun was lowering in the west when Count Kedar Ebb arrived at the *Dawn Star*. He wore a pack on his back and carried a modest-sized leather trunk. Arama couldn't help but be pleased that the count was a punctual man. She'd known far too many nobles who believed they were to be waited on, regardless of how it inconvenienced others. On more than one occasion she had had to point out that the tide would wait for no one, be he stormwitch, sea captain, or landed gentry.

"Captain," Ebb said, nodding to her. "No formalities," he added as she began to bow. "On deck, the captain is lord."

Arama's lips quirked. His eyes were deeply shadowed and he obviously hadn't shaved in days, but he would insist on proper shipboard protocol? She couldn't find much fault with him, despite Lo's misgivings about the man.

"Very good, sir," she said.

"Where should I stow my gear, captain?"

"I thought you'd be most comfortable in my quarters," she began, leading the way up the gangway.

"No," he said. "General quarters, please. I'm not accustomed to luxury. I fish with my people, Captain Dzornaea, and I can tie off a line as well as anyone born to it. Just give me a hammock in the crew's berth."

Arama eyed him askance. She wasn't certain he knew what he was asking. *Dawn Star* wasn't the largest ship in the king's fleet, but she was crewed by more than three-score sailors, and the crew's berth was tight with hammocks. There were times the crew had hot-bunked, one rolling out for watch just before the next slung herself into the same hammock. Surely a count, fisher lord though he be, would want more than that.

But she led the way to the general quarters without a word of protest. She could see he knew his way around a ship; he ducked automatically when going through doorways, and the slight roll of the deck didn't bother him at all.

When they got belowdecks, he looked around for a moment and then nodded. "Very tidy," he said. "Is there an unclaimed hammock anywhere?"

She gestured to Wirda's rig. He wouldn't need it, after all, she thought, her throat tightening a little. She hadn't been close to Wirda, but she'd known him for a good man, and she'd relied on him, as she relied on all of her crew.

"Very good," Ebb said, stowing his trunk under the hammock. He dropped his pack in the hammock itself. Then he ran a hand through his black hair. Arama watched as he pressed full lips together so tightly they thinned.

"You took a fine prize from the Strid ship, I understand," he said. His voice sounded casual; if she hadn't just seen how much it cost him to make small talk, she wouldn't have believed it.

"Aye," she agreed. "Some of it cargo they took from the *Elana Bey* before she sank. Cotton, rum, a fine haul of saltpeter. Not to mention the gold. I'm leaving the prize ship here, so your folk can strip her down." She paused. "I left some of the rum, too, in care of the surgeons."

He nodded, but that was apparently the extent of his casual conversation. He glanced around the hold, then headed back the way they had come. Arama followed him, studying the slump of his shoulders. She found herself curiously drawn to this young man, despite his anger and despair.

Or, perhaps, because of it.

When they were on deck once more, Ebb stopped walking and watched the crew in their preparations to get underway. Arama could see him gauging their experience and skill. She knew he wouldn't find them wanting, but it was interesting that he had such a keen eye for it.

"My lord," she said slowly, wondering if she was a fool to speak out of turn. "I am very sorry for your loss." She cleared her throat. "I wasn't much younger than you when I lost the man who raised me."

She saw his shoulders tense. "I don't need your pity, captain."

"That's well enough," she said, making her tone acerbic, "for I have none." She gentled her next words. "I only wanted to tell you that I grieve with you."

He glanced over at her. "Did you know my father?"

"Not to speak to, no," she said.

"Then why do you grieve?"

Arama shrugged. "Because I've known loss. That's all."

They stood in silence for a while. Arama found herself missing Lozarr keenly. They had made their farewells earlier in his tent, and they'd agreed he wouldn't come down to the ship with her. But he was the one who was skilled in gentle words. He was the encourager, the one who looked beyond a person's prickles to see the fear behind it.

Finally she took a breath. "You might be old enough to remember the storm, fifteen years ago. When *Bounder* sank off Swordfish Island." Her mouth felt dry, but a rush of saliva made her wonder if she was going to throw up.

Slowly Ebb turned his head to blink at her. "I…yes. I was eleven." He sucked in a breath. "My father's people told him the ship had gone down. They found the debris and bodies."

Arama nodded. "I was mate on that voyage. My captain, a fine man who taught me all I ever knew of sailing, was killed by the sirens."

Ebb's brows drew together. "Didn't you have a stormwitch?"

"Mm. The King's Stormwitch, in fact; we were on a special mission for the crown. But she didn't feel it coming in time." Arama shrugged. "Couldn't stop it." She heard the bitterness seeping into her voice and forced it away. She had to be honest with him if her story were to do any good. "She almost died trying to save us," she added.

He snorted. "Damned stormwitches."

"Aye," Arama agreed. "That's what I always thought." Her heart was thumping in her chest. She could still hear the eerie singing of the sirens, feel the cold water creeping into every part of her. She could still feel the throb of her cut hand. "Fact is, I was scared of them after that. Stormwitches. Blamed her for my loss, and never had a witch aboard any ship I captained, save once, at the king's command."

"So what?" Some of the belligerence crept back into Ebb's voice. "Why tell me all this?"

"Because." Arama shoved her hands in her pockets and trained her gaze on the deck. "It was that same witch, Lijka Ardelis, who felt the storm hit Anderly this month. She was the one who took the trouble to go to the capital and tell the prince. And he listened to her and sent Lozarr—General Algot—to investigate."

Ebb's shrug was almost violent. He didn't want to hear it. Arama could understand. There were plenty of truths she hadn't wanted to accept over the course of her life.

"I'm not saying I'm keen on witchery now," she said. "But seems to me she did what she could to make up for not knowing ahead of time." Sleeping gods, wouldn't Lo laugh if he could hear her now? But what he'd said about Lijka two days ago had stuck with her, and she couldn't forget the way the woman had changed over the past few years, since she married Kinnet.

Ebb sighed. "I'll think about what you've said."

Arama bit back a smile. He wouldn't appreciate it. "All I can ask," she said. "And for what it's worth, I *am* sorry about your father. He sent some of his folk with them that rescued us, all those years ago. I've never forgotten." She did smile then. "He was a good man."

"Yes." Ebb's voice cracked. "Yes, he was."

***

As she walked with Vistaren through the crowded Scholar's Market, Azmei couldn't help but think back three years to what she still remembered as one of the best days in her life. Guira, the maid who had practically raised her, was still alive. Azmei had been nervous about her future, but she had still thought it held nothing more frightening than marrying a stranger. Assassination attempts, rebellions, dragons—they were the furthest things from her mind.

But still, she couldn't be too wistful. She missed Guira, and always would, but the years since that day had made Azmei more self-reliant, more confident. And this last year had given her Hawk.

"You're pensive this morning," Vistaren said, his voice quiet. Azmei was dressed like a noble and holding Vistaren's arm. They looked like nothing so much as a happily devoted couple. That was exactly as she intended.

"Just thinking about how different we both are from the scared children who met three years ago," she said, smiling up at him.

He huffed a laugh. "Are we both? I hardly feel I've changed at all." Azmei thought he sounded sad.

"You've grown up, just like I have," she said. "You're more confident. More decisive. I can see that."

"I'm glad you think so," he said. "Though I fear I have you fooled."

Azmei lifted her chin. "I'll have you know I'm a fine judge of character these days," she said loftily. "All that time observing people during my training."

He grinned at her, which made Azmei feel better. Vistaren had been courteous all morning, but she could tell he was preoccupied. She thought the visit with his mother the day before had gone well, so she could only assume he was worried about the situation with the storms and the dragons and the gods.

Well. She was worried about all that, too, but until there was something she could do about it, she would focus on the things she *could* control. And right now, that was making Vistaren look good in front of his father's court and his people. The first step in that was to be seen publicly with him, and while Azmei refused to play the simpering maiden for anyone, she could certainly be seen as a devoted companion.

"You're complimenting me and I haven't even taken you to the library yet," Vistaren said.

"If I promise more compliments, will you take me there next?"

He laughed. "We're almost there. The Scholar's Market caters to the library users. Oh, here, I especially wanted you to see this one."

He guided her into a shop filled with paper, pens, ink, and books. "I treasure the book you translated for me, you know," he said softly. "It was such a thoughtful gift, so much more than mine to you—"

"Not really," Azmei said. "I have to think highly of any man who gives me a knife." She nudged his arm.

Behind her, Hawk coughed. Azmei's expression froze, and then she felt heat sweep through her cheeks. Did he think she was flirting? But she was just talking to Vistaren as she would her brother. They could tease each other without it being flirtatious, couldn't they?

Vistaren glanced past her, then ducked his head. "It was just a cough, Az. By the seven, do you think he doesn't trust you? He came here with you, knowing…all this."

Azmei's cheeks grew hotter. "You see right through me," she murmured. "I just…" She bit her lip and lowered her voice even more. "You and I were born to this. We're raised expecting it. I…I worry that I'm unfair to him…"

"No." Vistaren's voice was firm. He touched her chin with one finger and held her gaze for a moment, then smiled. "Come and see the pens they have. I think you'll like the artistry of them."

She *was* impressed. The craftswoman sold pens of fancy woods turned on a lathe and pens made of glass, as well as pens from more mundane materials. Though Azmei couldn't help stroking one finger along the handle of the glass pen, she ended up selecting a pen made of smooth bloodwood. The craftswoman tucked it into a special leather sheath along with an extra nib.

"My compliments to you, princess," she said when she handed it to Azmei. She smiled warmly at both Azmei and Vistaren as they made their farewells and left the shop.

After their stop at a stationer's, Azmei found herself wishing she'd engaged a palace servant to carry things for her. She didn't really mind carrying her own things, but she was uncomfortable unless she had at least one hand free for her knife.

I've lived too long away from the niceties of court, she thought. *Too long away from safety. But is it possible to go back to those careless years?*

They walked through the library, with its strict guardians and heavy tomes chained in place. Azmei decided she would have to visit again when she had an entire afternoon to lose among the shelves. Surely they wouldn't refuse a princess the right to spend as much time as she wanted, even if most scholars were only allowed a glass at a time with the books.

From the library they passed through another smaller market on their way to the stormwitch academy. Luthiers and harp-makers occupied spots next to a woman whose shop was full of hand drums of various sizes.

As they walked past a stall where a man sat playing a flute, Vistaren's steps dragged. Azmei slowed as well, listening. It was a haunting melody, beginning low on the scale, then slowly rising in pitch. Vistaren was whisper-singing along with it, but she couldn't catch many of the words. It was a song about Fann and Rona and Aevver, she could tell that much.

When he caught her looking at him, he flushed and walked a little faster.

"Do you play?" she asked.

"No." He gave her a crooked smile. "Always wanted to. But I was never patient enough to learn. I love the whistles and flutes, though. And I like to sing, even though most people probably don't want to hear me at it."

She smiled. "I couldn't judge; you weren't singing loud enough."

"Heh. Thank your guardian spirits for small mercies."

Azmei snorted. "I should have learned music like a proper noblewoman, but I'd rather read back then. My cousin Ilzi plays the lute very well."

"I love to listen, though," Vistaren said as they approached the wide steps leading up to the academy's main building. "I'll have our court bard play for you. She's good."

"Will you have her play that song you were just singing?" Azmei asked, pausing a few steps from the top. "I'd like to hear it."

Vistaren smiled again. "Did you ever read the Four Daughters—"

"—of the Storm?" Azmei finished with him. "Yes. In both Tamnese and Amethirian, in fact. Master Tanvel offered to find me a copy in Ranarri, but I didn't think I was fluent enough in it to do the story justice."

Vistaren gave a tiny laugh. "Well, I'm certain I can have our bard sing at least one or two of the Rona and Fann cycle. Though really, you'd be better off with the Daughteriad. It's a connected cycle about Aevver and all her sisters."

Azmei was grinning as she mounted the top of the steps and saw the tall marble columns of the stormwitch academy. Her grin slowly faded as she realized how magnificent the edifice was. She was impressed in spite of herself. She'd seen plenty of mansions, fortresses, and palaces, but few of them had matched the stormwitch academy for opulence.

She had known they were important to Amethir's economy, of course. Any nation that could control the weather to ensure good crops every year was bound to be a wealthy one, and the stormwitches could not only guarantee good plant harvests, but also safe fish harvesting for more of the year than most other countries. But somehow that theoretical knowledge hadn't translated to a realization of just how dependent Amethir was on the stormwitches—and how much the stormwitches received in return.

Vistaren stuck his hands behind his back and rocked onto his heels. "It is impressive, isn't it?" he said, turning his head to look up at the building. "It's been around for a long time. Longer than the palace, in fact. The kings and queens of Amethir used to rule from further inland."

Azmei nodded slowly. "It…it is impressive." She had realized that Pralith Menever was important. She hadn't realized just how very important he was.

"Ugh," Vistaren breathed, and Azmei looked over at him, then followed his gaze.

Speak of the jackal and he came to feast, she thought. "That's your father's stormwitch, isn't it?" she asked, though she knew very well the identity of the silver-haired man approaching them. He was dressed in robes of dramatic dark purple. He probably thought he looked like a stormcloud; Azmei thought he looked like a bruise.

"Pralith, what a pleasant surprise," Vistaren said, smiling at the man. He seemed all that was affable and genuine. Azmei could feel the way he'd tensed, though.

Pralith Menever bowed more deeply than a prince's rank required. Azmei pressed her lips together to keep them from curling. "Your Highnesses," he said, his voice unctuous. "You do us a great honor."

Azmei glanced sideways at Vistaren. "I had hoped you would favor me with a tour of the academy, Stormwitch Menever," she said. "I have only met one or two stormwitches in my life. I confess, I am curious about it all."

"I would be pleased to answer any questions," he said. "Perhaps you would like to see the rooms where we practice our meditations and rituals?"

"Yes, please," Azmei said, after a glance to confirm Vistaren agreed. "How does it work? In general, I mean. I'm certain it's impossible for someone who hasn't the talent to truly understand." She smiled at Pralith, who puffed up a little.

"You are keenly perceptive, princess," he said. "But I will do my best to explain it in simple terms. You know that we are able to affect the weather, of course. Are you aware that we do not all have the same talents?"

Azmei nodded, following him as he turned and walked down a long colonnade. "I know that some are more powerful than others, and that someone who is highly skilled in one area might not be able to do anything outside that specialization."

"Very good." Pralith's exaggerated praise made her want to roll her eyes. "Some are skilled at stormcalling, while others may divert a storm. Some are able to make rain, and others call water up to the surface in a new well. Most stormwitches are able to channel, to some extent—to touch lightning. Powerful stormwitches can even direct the lightning, though there's little practical purpose to that."

Azmei thought that calling lightning to hand would be a tremendously useful weapon, if a bit flashy. But then, she'd never heard of Amethirians weaponizing the stormwitchery—for all the good it did, since economic dominance was just as effective as a sword or musket.

"It all sounds very useful," she said. Their footsteps echoed along the passage. "Can stormwitchery work everywhere?"

"It can be done anywhere," Vistaren put in. "Remember how Kinnet frosted a glass for you in Ranarr?" Azmei smiled at him.

Pralith, however, looked put out. "It *can* be done anywhere, but it is not polite to do so outside our own borders."

Azmei nodded, thinking that no one had taken any offense at Kinnet's minor working in Ranarr. Then again, Amethir's borders had expanded several times in the past few generations. She knew better than to point that out, but it occurred to her that there were probably places where stormwitchery was practiced today but had been unknown fifty years ago.

"There is a council that oversees the academy," Vistaren said. "The crown doesn't interfere." He smiled at Azmei. "We rely on the stormwitches, of course, both for information and for their talents, but we do not command it."

Pralith bowed. "It is true. Each stormwitch makes vows to serve Amethir with his power—or hers," he added.

Azmei tilted her head. "Are all witches bound to the academy?"

"Of course!" Pralith said, chuckling. "We can't allow untrained witches to wander around unsupervised."

"I see." Azmei nodded slowly. She was trying to follow all this to the logical conclusion, but she wasn't certain she liked where it was taking her. "So what happens if someone doesn't want to be a stormwitch? Someone who has the talent, I mean?"

Next to her, Vistaren hesitated enough that her next step took her past him. Pralith, however, didn't pause.

"We would persuade them, of course," he said smoothly. "The gods give us our gifts for the greater good of our people. That is why stormwitches have rules regulating our behavior and practice. And why we vow to use our power only to serve."

Azmei could hear voices coming from some of the rooms they passed. They had the tone of rote instruction, or perhaps guided practice. She wondered if learning magic was anything like learning a weapon or learning to pray. "Then you mean an unwilling stormwitch would be unable to leave," she clarified.

Pralith spluttered.

"Well," Vistaren said, "I can't imagine someone wanting to leave. They're compensated well for their services." He waved a hand to indicate the elegance of the hall. "It is in the best interest of the crown and kingdom to ensure stormwitches are happy."

Pralith straightened. "Oh dear. Please excuse me, your

highnesses. I see Councilor Bernays is beckoning to me." He hurried off, ducking into one of the classrooms. Azmei smirked at his retreating back, though she felt little mirth regarding the topic of conversation.

"This smacks of a draft," she murmured. *Or slavery.* Something Amethir had outlawed a century ago, at least in name.

"It isn't quite like that," Vistaren said. He shifted his weight and then curled his fingers gently around her arm to urge her back into motion. Azmei didn't resist, mostly because she could tell he would give in if she did.

"How is it, then?"

"Well—there," he said, pointing to two women who were approaching them. "Like Lijka Ardelis. She was King's Own Stormwitch at one point, but after the *Bounder* sank, she left the service herself."

Azmei eyed him askance. "She's here now."

"Yes, well…she came back." Vistaren shrugged. "Well, I should let her tell it. You need to meet her, anyway. She'll want to talk to Yarrax."

"Will she?" Azmei asked, surprised.

"Lijka's the one who came to me about the storm hitting Anderly." Vistaren, catching Lijka's eye, smiled broadly and waved her over. He lowered his voice. "She is very powerful, and very concerned about the situation. She felt the anomaly, even if she couldn't predict it. She'll absolutely be interested in what Yarrax has to tell her."

"So you think she's more likely to listen than Pralith Menever?" Azmei felt her lips twist a little as she spoke the man's name. There was nothing really wrong with him, except that he felt a little too needy. He wanted people to see how important he was.

"Doubtless. Her wife Kinnet is the stormwitch who frosted the glass for you in Ranarr. They both have more experience than others with strange happenings. I think they're both more open-minded about such things."

The woman had changed course and was striding to

meet them. She was probably close to Pralith's age and generously curved, but she carried herself like a tall woman. Her hair was short and pure silver, swept back from her face.

"Good." Azmei gave a decisive nod. "I wouldn't mind having a stormwitch willing to listen to us."

The woman reached them and swept a correct—if somewhat perfunctory—curtsy. She was wearing close-fitting trousers with a knee-length tunic over them. Green seaglass bobbed at her earlobes and the base of her throat.

"Your highness," she murmured.

"Princess, this is Stormwitch Lijka Ardelis," Vistaren said. "Lijka, I present Her Royal Highness, Princess Azmei Corrone of Tamnen—my betrothed."

Azmei was certain she hadn't imagined the swift glance Lijka darted at Vistaren, but the woman curtsied again, a bit more deeply this time. It didn't feel disingenuous the way Pralith's bow had, though; this felt appropriate for her first meeting, whereas her greeting to Vistaren was clearly a greeting between friends.

Azmei nodded. "Stormwitch Lijka, I am pleased to meet you," she said. "I have heard good things of you, and I am eager to learn more of stormwitchery."

"Lijka and her wife Kinnet are the lightkeepers of Maron Harbor," Vistaren told her. "They live at the east light and ensure the safety of all who travel to and from the capital."

"You live in the lighthouse?" Azmei said, smiling. "I remember seeing it on our way in to the harbor. It must be a lovely place to live."

Lijka smiled. "It can be lonely for those who like the company of other humans. But Kin and I do all right with each other and the gulls for company, highness."

The woman's smile transformed her face from stern, almost hard, to friendly. It was a startling difference. Azmei found herself instinctively drawn to this woman, whom Vistaren seemed to respect so highly.

"Is it a long journey from the lighthouse to here?"

Azmei asked.

"Not so long. And we had Council business to attend to. Kin left a journeywoman tending the light, and we'll go back in the morning."

Azmei glanced over at Vistaren. "I would greatly like to meet your wife and learn more about you both," she told Lijka. "We're set to dine privately tonight, aren't we, Vis?"

Vistaren nodded, as she'd known he would. He smiled at her.

"Come dine with us at the palace tonight," Azmei urged. "Please. I am so curious about stormwitchery. And I can see that Vistaren thinks highly of you and Kinnet, and so I would like to know more of you as well."

"Of course," Lijka said. "We would be pleased." She looked like she genuinely meant it.

"We shouldn't take up more of your time now," Vistaren said. "Pralith had begun showing us around, but I believe Azmei's questions were too pointed for him." He grinned at her.

Azmei had noticed they seemed a little too pointed for Vistaren as well, but she grinned back at him. No point in making it uncomfortable just now.

"Pralith isn't really used to dealing with discomfort," Lijka said acerbically. "I assure you, highness, we aren't all like him."

Azmei let her grin include Lijka as well. "I am certain of that, Stormwitch Lijka. I can't believe anyone as desperate for public accolade as he is would willingly live in a spot isolated from constant human companionship, regardless of how imperative the lighthouse service is."

Lijka snorted a laugh. "Perceptive as well as beautiful," she observed. "I can see you and Vistaren are well suited."

The words pleased Azmei. If nothing else, Lijka seemed to think she and Vistaren could be friends. She glanced over at Vistaren, who was watching her in amusement. Then her gaze wandered past Vistaren to Hawk.

He stood straight, his gaze roaming the area around

them. Feeling her eyes on him, he met her gaze and smiled slightly. Apparently he also approved of how she was doing. Sleeping gods, she hoped he did. She gave him a small smile back, as soon as she was certain Lijka wasn't watching.

"Very well," Vistaren said. "We shall expect the two of you at the seventh hour. Nothing formal. As Azmei said, we are dining privately, with only our intimate staff."

Lijka curtsied. "I look forward to it."

16

By the time the *Revenge* passed between the familiar lighthouses of Maron Harbor, Rhys and Eldry were barely speaking to one another. She had done everything she could to make him happy and comfortable, taking him boneset tea and trying to explain that she'd made a vow that couldn't be broken to the Scavenger's god. No matter what she did, though, Rhys kept withdrawing deeper into himself—or perhaps he was simply withdrawing from *Eldry*. The crew seemed to like him well enough, and they spent time showing him how to do some of their work, the tasks that could be done sitting, at least. They'd even set up a nice little pallet on the deck for him, padded as soft as could be, because he got claustrophobic belowdecks.

Eldry had tried to snuggle next to Rhys on the pallet last night, and he had rebuffed her. He'd *never* done that, not even when they'd been in the most uncomfortable stages of growing up. She had considered faking a nightmare, but she couldn't bring herself to do it. She wouldn't force her company on Rhys, even if her actions had saved his life. If she hadn't insisted the Scavenger look for him, if she hadn't taken that vow, Rhys would have died on the beach.

But she didn't want him to talk to her out of gratitude. If more than twenty years of friendship weren't enough to salvage...

She pushed the thought aside as a curious feeling quested into the back of her mind.

It's all right, love, she told the seadragon. *I'm not unhappy with you.*

She wouldn't pretend she could understand the

seadragon's thoughts—if it had something you would call thoughts at all—but she could sense its emotions, just as it seemed to sense hers. Just now it could tell she was unhappy, and she felt that it worried it had done something wrong.

She sent it feelings of acceptance and pride, of belonging. *I'll call for you soon, but not yet. For now, eat and rest.*

"We're almost ready to dock, majesty," said one of the sailors. It wasn't Black Miry. She hadn't bothered to learn all their names; she wouldn't need them once she reached the academy.

"Very good," she said. "Two men will need to assist Rhys until I get a carriage. Then you may all choose a captain from among you." She paused and glanced at Black Miry. "Not Miry. He's coming with me."

The sailor bowed, which made Eldry smile. "Go on about your duties," she told him gently. She liked that they were afraid of her. People *should* fear stormwitches.

She could hear the Scavenger giggling as he approached her. She propped her fists on her hips, turning to watch him.

"You like it," he said. "This mission of yours. It suits you. And you like it."

Eldry lifted one shoulder in a shrug. She couldn't really argue with him. She knew some part of her hadn't wanted to do this. She remembered that. But she no longer hesitated. The more time she spent watching the weather and communing with the seadragon, the more she realized that the Scavenger and his god were correct.

You begin to listen for me, hissed a cold voice in her head.

Eldry's eyes widened and the Scavenger giggled again. "Yes!" he crowed. "Yes! You hear him, don't you? I can tell you do. His voice is too big for us to really take in. You'll get used to it though."

She wasn't certain she believed that. The voice had sent prickles down her spine and set her stomach roiling. It wasn't a comfortable voice at all, not the sort of voice she'd expected of a god who made things. She could still feel her skin crawling.

You swore a vow, the voice hissed. It was insidious, pervasive. She knew there was no place she could hide from that voice.

"I did," she said aloud. It would serve to answer both the Scavenger and the god. She shivered She had liked it better when the god spoke through the Scavenger.

You will take us to the academy.

"I will," she agreed.

She folded her arms across her chest as the sailors took the *Revenge* up to the harbor. They maneuvered the ship expertly into an empty slip. Before Black Miry could leave the ship, Eldry went up behind him and touched his elbow.

"You will come with us," she said. "Your time on the ship is over."

He blenched but didn't argue, and Eldry gave him credit for having learned from his mistakes.

"Go get my things from my cabin," she told him. "You will carry them for me."

He bowed and hurried off, returning quickly with her possessions in his arms.

"Come," she said loudly. "We will go to the academy."

Rhys was waiting by the railing, propped awkwardly on his makeshift crutches. "I'm not going with you, El." His voice was quiet and calm. "I won't be a part of whatever it is you have planned."

"You already are," she said. "You're the reason I'm sworn to it."

"I can't help it. I didn't make you swear any oaths. You should have just looked for me on your own instead of swearing to follow some god whose name you don't even know."

Twister of Worlds flashed through her mind and was gone. Eldry was shaken to her core.

She must have paled. Rhys narrowed his eyes at her and he opened his mouth to speak. Eldry should interrupt him. She should cut him off. But she knew, with a desperate certainty, that the hissing voice had spoken truly. It was not the

Maker god the Scavenger served, no matter what the old man thought. It was the Twister. The one they didn't name. The one who had caused the Godwars.

"You *do* know his name." Rhys' voice was barely more than a whisper. "You know what you're doing is wrong. Eldry, don't go to the academy. Come with me to the surgeons' school. We'll find a priest who can help you. We can—"

"I am sworn, Rhys." Eldry had never imagined she could speak so coldly to him. "I will do as I am sworn."

His expression froze and then he dropped his head. "Then that's it," he said. "Goodbye, El. I'll…I'll make offerings for you. I'll pray for you. I don't know if it'll do any good, but I can at least do that."

She narrowed her eyes.

"You'll always have my love," Rhys said. "But I won't be a part of this."

She felt a sudden urge, as he turned his back on her and stumped away, to call lightning to her hand and smite him with it. She shoved the thought down. She had loved Rhys almost all of her life. He was closer than a brother to her. She didn't want to hurt him!

But deep down inside, some little voice assured her that she did.

She shook the feeling off and turned away from him. She wouldn't be able to hurt him if she didn't watch him go. Instead she stared off across the harbor, watching the little fishing boats maneuvering nimbly between the larger craft. She looked for the Storm Petrel's ship, *Dawn Star*, but didn't see it. She had seen it when *Elana Bey* left Maron, but apparently the privateer had somewhere else to be.

"Majesty," Black Miry said. "There's a carriage ready."

Eldry turned back, fixing her eyes on him and not looking for Rhys. "Good," she said. "We'll go."

The ride to the academy was a short one. She closed her eyes, feeling a little odd in the carriage after so many days on the ocean. She wondered if she should have had the carriage take her to the baths first, so she could make a good presentation when she arrived.

But no, she wanted to arrive just as she was. Let the other stormwitches see what the academy had let happen to her. Let them see that she had come through it on her own, without any help from them. She smoothed her hands over her knees, feeling the thin fabric of the dress.

She didn't like the red. It didn't suit her. She would rather have arrived in clothes that matched her seaglass eye. But she'd been cast adrift on the ocean, and she would return home in the clothes the sea had given her.

The carriage jolted to a halt and Eldry opened her eyes. The Scavenger was perched on the edge of his seat, eyes bright on her face.

"You see the academy in all its glory," she told him, her voice dull, and climbed out of the carriage without waiting for someone to open the door.

She recognized a few of the journeymen she saw in the courtyard, but none of them were friends of hers. She had only been friendly with a few of her fellow journeymen, and most of them had received better postings than she had.

She did, however, see the one man she had hoped to see upon her return. There was Pralith Menever, standing and talking with two of the instructors at the academy. Eldry straightened and gestured for the Scavenger and Black Miry to follow her as she strode across the yard.

"Stormwitch Menever," she called, channeling a little wind to strengthen and magnify her voice. It was so easy to do when she could see the threads of power in the air around her.

He broke off his conversation, looking annoyed. Eldry could see the moment he realized who she was; his eyes widened and his mouth dropped open. The two men he was speaking with turned to see what had shocked him and they ended up gaping at her.

"I have returned," she said simply. She would look humble for now. She would act as if there had been no question of her return. Let him think she had never feared for her life.

"Eldry Karayan!" he cried. "We've been so worried! We sent the Storm Petrel to look for you as soon as the *Elana Bey* was reported missing."

Eldry lifted her chin. "I didn't need her," she said. "I made my own way back. With the help of this loyal fellow." She gestured at the Scavenger, who bobbed and tugged his forelock, grinning at Pralith. "I'm afraid he won't hear of being parted from me now."

"No indeed." The Scavenger cackled. "I must watch over you."

Pralith blinked at them for several heartbeats. "Highly irregular."

"I'm afraid I made him a promise," Eldry said, trying to look apologetic. "Do let him stay by me." She honestly didn't care whether or not the Scavenger stayed. She just wanted to have Pralith grant her first request in order to pave the way for many more.

She could see him wavering. His gaze traveled down to the stained skirt of her dress. "Well..." He drew out the word. "You have been through so much. How could I tear you away from the man who saved you?"

Saved me? she thought with scorn. *I wouldn't have died.* But she only smiled at him. "I knew you would understand."

"Do you need a healer or surgeon?" Pralith asked. "I will have servants freshen your rooms at once."

"Thank you," Eldry said, giving him a small smile. Before she could say anything more, a woman's voice interrupted.

"Eldry? Sweet seven, I am glad to see you!"

Holding in a groan, Eldry fixed her smile in place and turned to face Lijka Ardelis.

***

Lijka could hardly credit her eyes. She and Kinnet had

just finished up their business at the academy and had been on their way to the palace for dinner when she saw her lost journeywoman standing in the courtyard in a bedraggled red dress.

"Eldry? Sweet seven, I am glad to see you!" she had blurted. Then Eldry turned, a smile on her face, and Lijka sucked in an involuntary breath. Eldry's right eye was gone, replaced with a contraption that seemed to be half eye-patch and half…seaglass? Yes, it was a round piece of seaglass, ice pale and trapped in a cage of leather and copper. It was beautiful, in its own way, but Lijka felt a spasm of guilt that Eldry had been so hurt.

Eldry's smile looked a bit ragged, but she clasped her hands in front of her and said, "Good evening, Councilor Ardelis, Stormwitch Ardelis."

"We had begun to fear the worst," Kinnet said, her atonal voice a little louder than it needed to be. Lijka's wife had been born profoundly deaf, though she had learned to speak as a child. Thanks to Kinnet, Lijka knew better than most that a disability didn't have to be a disadvantage; still, she grieved that Eldry had been injured.

"You can see that I am well," Eldry said.

Lijka nodded slowly. "Did Pralith tell you we asked the Storm Petrel to look for *Elana Bey*? We had heard she was overdue and feared lost. I cannot begin to say how pleased I am you are safe."

Eldry's smile thinned a bit. "I am. We were caught in a terrible storm. The captain told me not to do anything, and it was my understanding that I was to defer to the captain's preferences. So I did nothing, and yet the storm worsened and worsened, until…" She bowed her head. "I fear the *Elana Bey* must be lost. The captain finally allowed me to nudge the storm aside, but they lost the mast right after, and then I was swept overboard."

Lijka's gut tightened. She remembered how the sea closed in over your head, the cold water blocking the sound of the storm, blocking anything but the strange groaning of the ship as it died. Kinnet's hand curled around Lijka's, and Lijka squeezed gratefully.

"I am so sorry, Eldry. How came you back to Maron?"

Eldry tipped one shoulder in a shrug. "I was fortunate enough to wash up on the shore, and the Scavenger found me." She indicated the ragged, mad-looking old man grinning behind her. He bobbed a strange bow at them and giggled.

"Thank the seven he did," Lijka said. "I…I cannot begin to tell you how sorry—" She broke off and shook her head.

"He knows a little of healing," Eldry continued, "and over the years he has collected many pieces of seaglass. When he learned how important it is to us, he made me a present of some." She gestured at her face. "As you can see, the Scavenger is very creative with the things he finds."

"I see that," Kinnet said. She had been following the conversation avidly by lip-reading. "I hope the eye does not pain you."

Eldry shrugged again. "Not much now."

Lijka felt Kinnet's hand tighten on hers. Lijka cleared her throat and said, "Well. We will set aside time tomorrow for a formal report. I will have the kitchens prepare a celebratory meal, but we must wait until the day after tomorrow. The prince's betrothal feast takes precedence." She gave Eldry a smile that felt forced. "I am very glad to have you back with us, Eldry."

Eldry's smile and murmured thanks were demure, but there was some gleam in her remaining eye that Lijka didn't like for some reason. She didn't like leaving Eldry in Pralith's company, either. She knew Pralith was a strong stormwitch, but he grasped after power in a way that left him open to unwise influence, in Lijka's opinion.

Nevertheless, she and Kinnet made their farewells and headed for the palace. She let Kinnet set the pace as they walked. It wasn't far to go, and they both liked walking around Maron when they were in the city; it made up for the days trapped on their cramped headland, where there was little room for walking.

She felt a weight off her shoulders that Eldry had come back, and mostly unharmed at that. But the uneasiness that had dogged her since she felt the storm hit Anderly had in no way lessened with the knowledge that the anomaly hadn't claimed her journeywoman's life. After all, there had still been plenty of death to go around.

Kinnet tugged at her hand, making Lijka look up at her. *You're thinking hard*, Kinnet signed. She didn't use her finger language with most people, but it was easier when it was just her and Lijka. Kinnet's throat hurt when she spoke too much and Lijka didn't like to strain her.

"I am," Lijka said, a smile tickling the corners of her mouth. She had been with Kinnet for two years now, after spending a lifetime thinking she would be alone. Her stomach still swooped pleasantly when she looked at Kinnet and found her wife watching her with so much love. "Sorry. I'm glad Eldry is back."

But? Kinnet raised her eyebrows, watching her.

"But the timing is…odd. And that Scavenger. And the seaglass eye."

The eye is very odd. Kinnet shrugged. *You'll puzzle it out. Learn more tomorrow after her report.*

"I hope so." Lijka shook herself slightly and laughed. "You'll have to kick me if I'm preoccupied during dinner with the prince and his friends."

Kinnet gave her a sly grin. *You know I will.*

***

Yar had never met so many people in so short a time. His head spun when he thought of all the sailors and nobles and soldiers and royals and witches he had met in the past few weeks. He liked himself better now that he was mostly able to control his own thoughts (most of the time), but there were times when he missed the walled house he'd grown up in. There he had been able to hide in his rooms when there were too many people in the house.

But you didn't truly know me then, dear one, Xellax crooned in his voice. *You feared me then.*

"I didn't like you at all," Yar murmured. He knew he shouldn't speak aloud to her; there were servants nearby who might hear. But then, everyone here seemed to know he was the Voice of Dragons. Some people seemed to think that title made him mad—or a liar—but at least Azmei and Vistaren knew better. What did it matter if the rest of them thought he was mad?

They won't respect what you say? Xellax suggested.

"But aren't prophets always thought mad?" he asked her. "Maybe I ought to be making myself look even madder. I should stop shaving or cutting my fingernails."

He was rewarded by a dry, slithery chuckle in the back of his mind. He was still grinning when Azmei came out into the front room of their suites.

"Oh, good, you're ready," she said. She looked distracted and a little unhappy. Yar thought it probably had something to do with Hawk. He was of the opinion that they were all making things too complicated, but he supposed etiquette probably demanded it. He knew etiquette was important. He just didn't understand most of it because it was too much fuss.

He stood up. "Xellax told me to wear my nice clothes."

Azmei's golden eyes flicked over his face. "Yes. You look good." Her smile was a half-beat late, as if she'd had to drag her thoughts back from somewhere else.

Since Yar could relate, he decided to act as if she weren't distracted. "You said we're dining with the prince and meeting other people."

"Yes." Azmei led the way out of their suites. Hawk was waiting outside; he fell in behind Yar. "Lijka and Kinnet. They are both stormwitches. They're married. They—" She broke off and gave Yar one of those assessing looks she gave him when she wasn't sure how much he would understand.

It didn't bother Yar, because he knew he *had* been sheltered in a lot of odd ways. He knew Azmei was just concerned about not making him uncomfortable.

"What is it?" he asked.

"Lijka and Kinnet. They're women. Both of them, I mean. Here in Amethir, two women are allowed to marry each other."

"They aren't allowed in Tamnen?" he asked, scrunching his nose.

Azmei shook her head. "Not in any formal way. I suppose there are women who live together as spouses, but it wouldn't be recognized."

"Why does it matter?"

The blunt question made her laugh, though it sounded sad. "It shouldn't. Doesn't, I suppose, not really. But some people seem to think it does." She frowned. "I ought to have said something to Razem about it, though."

"Your brother has larger issues facing him than social ones," Hawk murmured, his voice barely loud enough to hear.

Azmei's frown deepened. "That doesn't mean he can't fix the broken social issues as well."

Fortunately for Yar's peace of mind—he hated it when Azmei and Hawk were at odds—they arrived outside the prince's rooms just then. Hawk strode past them to knock on the door and they were admitted barely a moment later.

Yar followed Azmei inside. He had crossed half the room before he remembered that he ought to bow. His steps stuttered to a stop and he almost fell over trying to execute the bow Azmei had taught him. He felt his cheeks heat as a man laughed, but then the man said, "That isn't necessary here, Yarrax. I only invite my friends to dine with me here."

Yar lifted his head to find Vistaren crossing the room to meet him. The prince reached out and clasped Yar's hand, just the way a buyer might have clasped Orya's hand when she negotiated a contract.

"At least, I hope we are friends," Vistaren said.

"Yes, sir," Yar blurted. "I hope so too."

Vistaren gave a crisp nod and released Yar's hand, turning away to indicate two women who had already risen to meet them.

Yar liked the tall, skinny woman as soon as he saw her. She had wavy silver hair that touched her shoulders, and her light gray eyes had a strange light in them that reminded him of himself. Her hands were clasped, one hand twisting a ring on the other hand.

The woman next to her was plump and curvy with pale skin and the shortest hair he'd ever seen on a woman. It was even purer silver than the tall woman, and her eyes were bright green and looked like they saw everything. Yar felt a little bit afraid of her, but she smiled at him.

"These are my friends Kinnet—" Vistaren indicated the tall woman, his face turned to look at her the whole time he was speaking — "and Lijka Ardelis. I present to you Yarrax, Voice of Dragons."

Kinnet didn't smile at him. Her expression was solemn. "Voice of Dragons. You caused a stir at the academy." Her voice was almost a sing-song and it was a little too loud.

"I'm sorry." Yar wanted her to like him, but this didn't seem like a good way to start out.

"Please look directly at me when you speak," Kinnet said. "I must see your mouth to understand what you say."

"Oh." He lifted his face so she could see it better. "I'm sorry."

She cannot hear you, Xellax said in his mind. *If we lived in Amethir, we might have called to her instead of you, though.*

Kinnet gave him a startled look and Yar realized she could hear what Xellax said. He grinned at Kinnet. "Voice of Dragons," he said.

Kinnet's laugh was a pleasant sound. Even more pleasant was the warm look it kindled in Lijka's green eyes. Yar thought he was still a little afraid of Lijka, but he found that he liked her anyway, because she looked at Kinnet like that.

"Let us sit, friends," Vistaren said. "There is wine and

food awaiting us."

Yar didn't miss the fact that Hawk stood straight-backed beside the door while the rest of them went into the dining area. Hawk was here as the princess' bodyguard. Lijka and Kinnet weren't to know the truth about him, then. Yar filed that away so he wouldn't accidentally tell them.

They are trustworthy, Xellax said. *Kinnet at least understands making compromises to get through life.* Yar sent back a questioning thought and Xellax said, *No, she doesn't have to hear what I say to you. I only did that so she would realize what you say is true. Easier to prove it true than earn her belief.*

That Yar could understand. He turned his attention outward again in time to see Azmei turn to face Kinnet.

"I am pleased to finally meet you, Kinnet," she said. "You did me a kindness three years ago that I have never forgotten. During a ball I grew overly warm and you frosted a glass for me."

Kinnet's eyes crinkled a little. "It's a small favor for a princess to remember."

"It was appreciated." Azmei didn't elaborate, but her gaze went to Vistaren's, and the prince was smiling faintly.

"I am sorry we didn't meet then," Kinnet said.

"You said Yarrax had caused a stir at the academy," Vistaren said once the servants had withdrawn. "Does that mean you've heard about the last council session?"

Lijka had just taken a sip of wine. She shrugged.

"I know it maddened Pralith, and so I approve," Kinnet said. Her lips were curved in a smirk. Yar found himself grinning back at her.

"I am concerned that the matters you brought to me are connected to Yarrax's mission."

"You believe the dragons' warning is about witchery?" Lijka's voice was sharp.

Yar sent the question to Xellax and felt her musing on it.

"You yourself told me that you have been seeing changes in the magic for three years now." Vistaren's voice was calm and rang with certainty. "You said the seasons have been pulling awry, raining longer in some places, or not enough in others. You said that casting your magic is harder of late."

Lijka's thin shoulders slumped as Kinnet turned and gave her a hard look. "Did you tell him about what Pralith said to you?"

Lijka nodded.

Kinnet rounded on Vistaren. "He was insulting to her. He implied she had passed her prime, that she had better leave the work to him."

"I know all that." Vistaren's tone was soothing, even though Kinnet couldn't hear it. Perhaps he knew she would read his expression too.

"He is—" Kinnet broke off. Lijka had moved, only a little, but to Yar it looked a lot like when Orya had kicked him under the table.

"I know there is bad blood between you," Vistaren said. "I don't know all the details—" He held up a hand when Kinnet would have spoken. "And I don't need to know. The Crown does its best not to interfere with how the academy governs itself. Stormwitchery is complicated enough without bringing politics into it."

Kinnet snorted, but she didn't attempt to speak again.

"You have been concerned," Vistaren said, "both of you, about how you didn't feel the anomaly before it hit Anderly—that in conjunction with all these small anomalies, the harder magic, the shifting patterns, it could mean something more."

There was a pause. To Yar it looked like the storm-witches and Azmei were all holding their breath. Were they afraid of what Vistaren would say next? Then he realized that Vistaren hadn't said it—that Vistaren seemed to be holding his breath, too.

Yar said, "Could there be something wrong with the magic?"

He heard them all whoosh out a breath. Maybe he

shouldn't have spoken, but—

You spoke rightly, beloved, Xellax said in his mind. *I mean, in the right time. I do not know it is their magic that is at fault. I know that things are being twisted, made wrong. To us it seems that Amethir is at the center of it. What is it that makes Amethir special?*

The magic. That was all Yar could think of. But maybe they would have some other explanation.

Azmei sighed. "What Yar isn't telling you is that his last vision before we arrived here—it was a powerful one. It took him away from us entirely, the way it hasn't done in a while. When he came back, he said he'd seen—"

She paused and glanced at Vistaren, who said, "The god we don't name."

Lijka went paler than she already had been. She turned wide eyes on Yar, who felt obliquely guilty, even though he'd had nothing to do with the content of the vision. He swallowed, grateful for the reassurance Xellax sent flooding their connection.

Finally Kinnet looked at him. "Does your dragon say that one touches our magic?"

Xellax answered as soon as the question was spoken, and Yar relayed her words to Kinnet. "Not that he…touches it directly. I would tell you if we felt that. Er, she would tell me. And I would tell you." He frowned. "Something warps things. They have seen that Amethir is important. That Vistaren is important. What makes Amethir special? Is there anything besides the stormwitchery? If there is, the dragons don't know it."

"Your dragon isn't very specific." Lijka's voice was sour, but Yar could tell it was because she was afraid. He could see the fear glinting in her green eyes.

"We should feel grateful she bothers to speak with us at all," he told her, trying to smooth the edge from his voice. "She could keep her knowledge to herself and let us all die."

"I imagine even dragons might suffer if the world ends," Vistaren said mildly.

Yar felt a stupid surge of liking for the prince. He was

so *kind* about disagreeing without making you feel stupid or unworthy. It wasn't something Yar had seen much in his life, before he met Azmei and Hawk, and Vistaren was even better at it than they were.

"How do we stop it?" Kinnet demanded. Her voice was much too loud and shrill. "What do we do?"

Yar looked down at his plate. He knew Xellax had heard the question. He could feel that her attention was mostly directed away from him. She must be consulting with the others. He wondered how long that would take. They could consult for hours or even days without coming to agreement, if the problem was serious enough. For that matter, it had taken them almost seventeen years to decide to call him to them to become their Voice.

He lifted his eyes without moving his head, glancing around at the others. They were all staring down at the table except Kinnet, whose gaze darted from face to face. Lijka's brows were drawn together. Azmei was tracing a finger around the lip of her wine glass. Vistaren was rubbing his jaw with one finger. Yar shifted in his seat and Kinnet's gaze flew to meet his. But he didn't know what to tell her that he hadn't already said. The dragons weren't sure, but they would speak when they were.

Xellax was growing annoyed. He could feel it, could picture her twitching her long green tail in agitation. There was a pressure building in his head. Yar's throat tightened. He hoped he wasn't going to have a vision right now at the dinner table. He knew he looked like an idiot when he was in a vision. He didn't want his new friends to see that.

What happened was both better and worse than a full vision. Instead his eyes went wide, the sight of the room obscured by silver swirls. His jaw locked and then opened and Yar said, "WE MUST CONSULT WITH THE FOLK OF THE STORM. BRING OUR VOICE TO A STORMSINGER. BRING OUR VOICE TO A SEADRAGON. OUR VOICE SPEAKS FOR US."

Xellax let him go and Yar slumped back in his chair,

drained of all strength. He felt his mouth hanging slack but didn't have the energy to close it. He felt a thin line of drool trickle from the corner of his mouth. Then his sight cleared and he straightened, scrubbing the back of his hand across his mouth.

"That was clearly your dragon companion speaking through you." Vistaren's voice was gentle. "Should we give you a moment of privacy?"

Yar coughed and took a gulp of his wine. His hand trembled when he lowered the glass. "No, thank you. I will be well in a moment."

He could see Lijka and Kinnet having some sort of flurried exchange. Their fingers were moving, their facial expressions changing oddly. Then Kinnet turned to face them again. Her shoulders were set.

"I will see this done if I am able. But my stormsinger friend is late this year. Usually he has passed by our light with his mate and this year's calf. I will call to him and see if he will answer. It…it may be dangerous." She paused and straightened. "We may have to borrow a ship."

Lijka's face drained of all color again. Her gaze turned away from them and Yar could tell she was turning inward somehow. He tried to send her reassurance, the way Xellax sent it to him, but if she felt it, she didn't show it.

Azmei cleared her throat and Yar looked over at her. "What happens after they consult?"

Yar shrugged. "I only know what Xellax said. She didn't say anything else. She usually withdraws for awhile after one of those speakings. It takes a toll on us both."

There was a general silence, and Yar could tell he had annoyed them. He couldn't help it, though. He wasn't anything more than he'd told them—just the Voice of Dragons. And if the dragons spoke and the people didn't like it, that wasn't his fault. And if the dragons spoke and the people didn't listen…well, perhaps that was sometimes his fault. But not this time.

"Well," Vistaren said, and his voice sounded strange.

Resigned but hopeful, Yar thought. "We cannot make it happen by wishing. May I suggest Yarrax travel with the two of you to your light? I know you have simple rooms for guests and journeymen, and it seems best to have him near you if your stormsinger friend makes contact."

Kinnet nodded.

"I fear Azmei and I are unable to travel with you, much as we might prefer it." Vistaren and Azmei exchanged a glance and Yar felt a lessening of the tension as they made almost identical faces at each other. "My father has planned a party tomorrow that she and I are, unfortunately, unable to miss."

"That would be good," Kinnet said. She had her gaze on Lijka's face, but she was clearly talking to Vistaren. "We will be able to show Yarrax the stormwitchery. Perhaps if the dragons observe it through him, they will learn more."

"Yarrax? Is this plan acceptable to you?" Vistaren turned to look at him.

Yar didn't really want to be parted from Azmei, but he could see the sense in it. He shrugged and nodded. "I am curious," he said. "I should learn as much as I can. The more I understand, the more Xellax and the others will understand."

"And the more we understand, the closer we are to knowing how to stop it," Azmei said in satisfaction.

Lijka seemed to shake herself back to being present with them. "If that is settled, what if we eat?" she asked. Her voice was bright and she smiled brittlely at Yar. He felt a sudden pang of pity for her.

"I'm starving," he said, and was rewarded by a tiny easing of her smile. "And maybe another glass of wine."

To his relief, Azmei and Vistaren both laughed at his suggestion, and the air in the room seemed to relax even more.

17

Before Eldry's return, Pralith had begun to fear perhaps there was something to Lijka Ardelis' concerns. Not that he thought that Voice of Dragons fellow had the right of it, but that stormwitchery was perhaps becoming more difficult. That perhaps the seasons were shifting. That perhaps stormwitches were losing some of their skill.

He looked around the academy's council room and smiled. Eldry's return had proven to him that was incorrect. She was here, and if she wasn't entirely as she had been when she left, she was obviously still a stormwitch.

Lijka met his smile with an irritated glare. She still wasn't ready to believe Eldry, that much was clear. Her arms were folded across her chest, her eyes narrowed. Mezika, a pretty, young Sterr stormwitch who represented the journeymen to the council, was watching Eldry, her grey eyes wide. Mezika's hair was still mostly black, with just a few swathes of silver, showing how little time she had been channeling the weather. She had been a good choice as journeyman representative, though; she was eager to please, but was loyal to her fellow journeymen.

The third stormwitch on the council was Bernays, an older man who had been channeling longer than Pralith had been alive. He was humble, from fisherfolk, and a gifted teacher at the academy. He also had the commendable habit of deferring to whatever Pralith thought was best, which made him invaluable on the council. The fourth councilor was Denae, a middle-aged woman who wore her hair plaited around her head and dressed in drab clothes. She was another instructor at the academy, overseeing the new arrivals, who often came to the academy stunned at their own talents.

The last person in the room was Eldry, who sat across the room from the councilors. Her hands were clasped in her lap, her face composed. She looked, Pralith thought, as if she had survived some harrowing experience without any harm to her spirit. He hadn't known much about Eldry before she went missing, but he found himself drawn to her now. She seemed to have handled herself well.

Lijka coughed and then cleared her throat. Pralith refused to look at her. She probably wanted him to hurry. Well and good, but he was in charge of the council, not Lijka. She had given up her position as King's Stormwitch years ago, and Pralith's selection might have been against her recommendation, but she had to live with it.

Pralith waited another minute just to make the point that he wouldn't be hurried. Then he smiled at Eldry. "Well. Journeywoman Eldry, will you please tell us what happened?"

She lifted her chin. "As you know, I was given little choice about my posting. I was either to return to my hometown in the mountains or go to sea on a merchant ship."

"Journeymen are often sent wherever there is need." Lijka was not frowning, exactly, but her expression was stern. Pralith got the idea she didn't approve of Eldry's impertinence.

"True, but we allow choice as often as possible," Bernays said. "It is as it has always been."

Eldry bowed her head. "I did not say that to complain," she said softly. "Merely to point out that I am from the mountains, and had little experience with sailing before my posting. Perhaps you will think it is my own fault that I went overboard. Because of my lack of experience."

"Even experienced sailors have accidents," Pralith said. "After all, even the Storm Petrel has lost a ship."

It was unkind of him, throwing that in Lijka's face. From the corner of his eye, he saw her go rigid in her seat.

All the same, it was a good reminder to her that Lijka had also lost a ship. *Think of how the Bounder went down,* he thought at her, *and be kind to this girl.*

Eldry's lips curved up just a little. "Thank you, Master Pralith. I liked sailing. The crew of the *Elana Bey* were skilled, certainly, and they seemed to have every expectation of arriving home before storm season. We were almost to our destination when a storm blew up very quickly. I had little warning of it, but I told the captain, and he said he would prefer that I not tamper with it, as we were outside Amethirian waters."

"There is no law that says stormwitches cannot use their witchery outside Amethir," Mezika said.

"No, but there is courtesy." Lijka's voice was tight. Had his remark about the *Bounder* so unsettled her? "It would be unkind to deflect a storm from our ship, only to have it run a trading partner's ship off course, or flood an ally's crops."

Mezika's expression cleared and she nodded.

"I put my faith in the captain," Eldry went on. "I thought he knew best. But the storm kept getting worse, and finally the mast broke. It killed the ship's mate, and the captain asked me to save us." She closed her eyes for a moment. "So I did. Or at least, I did deflect the storm. But I was swept overboard, and from that point I don't know what happened to the *Elana Bey.*"

"It is still missing, as far as I know," Pralith said. "The Storm Petrel was looking for it, trying to find you."

"You said so yesterday, Master Pralith." Eldry blinked her good eye and widened it as she looked at him. "Why were you looking for me?"

"Because your ship had been reported late," Lijka snapped. Pralith could almost heard the unspoken *fool girl* at the end of her sentence.

Eldry's eye narrowed as she looked at Lijka. Pralith made a soothing noise to distract her.

"We are always concerned when a stormwitch's ship is not on time," he said. "It could mean trouble—and this time, it obviously *did* mean trouble."

Eldry sighed. "Yes, well." She lifted one hand and brushed at her cheek. Pralith hoped she wouldn't cry. He didn't like seeing people cry. It was so messy.

"Take your time, child," Denae said. Her voice was gentle and full. She was good at soothing frightened apprentices, but Eldry was no apprentice. The tone must have caught her attention. She straightened in her chair and shook her hair back, eye flashing.

"When next I was aware, I was lying on a beach and my eye was gone." She continued her story dispassionately, explaining how the Scavenger had found her and healed her, devising the seaglass eye-patch to adorn her face. She talked about the old man's kindness—despite his oddity—and that he had volunteered to travel with her so she wouldn't be afraid to sail again. She finished her story with her return to Maron.

"It all seems straightforward," Mezika said. She was watching Eldry with sympathy in her gaze.

Pralith realized he was frowning slightly. It was *too* straightforward. The narrative was smooth and unemotional for the most part. It was as if she had rehearsed it before arriving home.

"You said the Scavenger healed you," Pralith said. "Why the seaglass?"

Eldry's brows drew together. "I told you yesterday, Master Pralith. We were talking, and I explained a little of stormwitchery to him, and he found out that we use seaglass to augment our talents. He calls himself the Scavenger because he lives off everything he finds washed up on the shore. He has found much seaglass over the years. He used it for my eye because it is important to us."

He was still frowning at her. He tried to smooth away the expression when he saw a similar one on Lijka's face. He didn't usually agree with Lijka about things. "And how did the Scavenger come to know healing?"

Eldry's lower lip pooched out a little. "Master Pralith,

you sound as if you doubt me."

"No," Pralith said slowly. He exchanged a glance with Lijka, who looked equal parts doubtful and surprised. "But I feel sure, Eldry, that there is something you aren't telling us."

She sighed, letting her shoulders slump. "That is true." Her voice was very small. After a long moment she lifted her head and smiled thinly at him. She raised a hand to her side and opened it, palm up. Lightning crackled in her palm.

Pralith jerked back, some part of him registering that the others were also recoiling. They weren't in the observation tower; they were deep inside the academy building. There was no access to the outside. She shouldn't be able to call lightning to hand like this so far inside the building.

He stared at her, watching the blue-white light crackle around her fingers. It arced from fingertip to fingertip, dancing on her skin without harming her. He'd never seen anything like it. It made his mouth water.

"I know the skills of each I train." Lijka's voice was loud, cutting through the hubbub of raised voices from the rest of the academy council. "You were not this strong when you left."

Denae was quick to object. "She's too old to develop more talent. No matter the age when it first shows, we don't see them get stronger years after they end their apprenticeship."

Eldry was watching Pralith. Her lips had curled to one side in a smile that seemed to be just for him. Pralith wanted to smile back, but he wasn't sure what this was, what this meant. "There...are no records of it," he said, trying to sound as if he agreed with Denae. He wasn't sure if he did.

"There is oral history telling us talent can be granted," Lijka said. Her voice had lost some of its volume, taken on a softer, considering tone. Pralith should look at her to gauge her attitude, but he couldn't drag his eyes from the flickering light reflected in Eldry's eye.

"Yes," Mezika said eagerly. "As the stormsingers did for Amethir in the beginning."

"Fables," Bernays scoffed. Pralith tore his gaze from Eldry's to look hard at Bernays. The man had been channeling longer than most of them, but that sometimes made him hidebound. He had not been one of those interested in Kinnet Ardelis' encounter with the stormsinger three years ago.

Pralith *had* been interested. He had been sick with envy, for that matter, and angry that the king insisted on keeping him in Maron and sending Kinnet instead.

Bernays's expression was implacable. Pralith glanced at Lijka and saw her roll her eyes; when she saw that he'd noticed, she gave him a wry look.

"Council members, why do you argue among yourselves?" Eldry's voice was soft. It dragged all eyes back to her. "Ask me what happened."

"True," Pralith said quickly. "Eldry lived through it. What is your explanation, my dear?"

Eldry's smile widened a little and Pralith wondered if he had misspoken. Perhaps he'd been too ingratiating, too insincere. She let the lightning go and it hissed into nothingness.

"My eye," she said simply. "The Scavenger felt I should have seaglass to replace it, as I told you. When I woke after he did this, I had more power. I could access the magic more easily and quickly. I could attune myself to it with little effort."

"We've known for generations that seaglass augments power," Bernays grated. He was sitting back in his chair, eyes half-lidded. Pralith suspected the man wanted his afternoon nap.

"Yes," Eldry said. "Worn or held. But this—this is fused to me. I am now *one* with the magic."

"So do you propose we all remove one eye and replace it with seaglass?" Mezika's voice was skeptical. "The surgeons might protest."

Eldry laughed. "No, not that. But there must be some way to harness this. My casting is so much easier. So much quicker. I don't need to meditate."

"And is meditation such a bad thing?" Lijka's voice was dry. "When we are about to shift the weather, should we not *wish* to meditate on the consequences of our actions?"

"But if I hadn't needed to meditate, I might not have gone overboard. Could we not save many lives if we could act so quickly?" Eldry leaned forward, gaze earnest on Pralith's face.

"We could have saved Anderly," Lijka said softly.

Pralith felt a surge of irritation. He huffed a sigh. "That was an anomaly, Lijka," he snapped. *But what if it hadn't been?* "No one felt it coming until it was too late to avert it or warn anyone."

"What if I could have felt it?" Eldry said. "What if there were some way to make all the stormwitches able to feel anomalies as well as normal weather?"

Pralith didn't have an answer. He looked at Lijka and then Mezika. The journeywoman was leaning forward in her chair, her expression rapt.

"As if we need any more power than we already have." Denae's voice was amused and easy. "However we got this power, whether it was the gods or the stormsingers or what, we already have so much power it frightens everyone the first time they cast. If you've forgotten how terrified you were when you first arrived from that mountain town of yours, Eldry, I haven't." She was smiling at Eldry, but there was no softness in her attitude. "Killed one of the Shroud-lings, hadn't you? Calling lightning to hand like you just did, but in panic and desperation that you would be raped or killed for being in the wrong place at the wrong time. I re-member that brother of yours, too, the way he had to half drag you in to see me."

Pralith glanced at Eldry in time to see a flicker of pain or grief cross her face. But she lifted her chin and shrugged. "So what? You quickly set me right, and once I understood everything, I was fine."

"Yet you think we need more power? You think *you* needed more power?" Denae's tone was still gentle, but she had that way about her; she seemed kind and mild, but she always got the answers she needed. "What would you do with that power, girl?"

"Save people!" Mezika blurted, and then blushed. "I'm sorry, I shouldn't have interrupted—"

"We don't need more power. I don't know as we can really have more power. P'raps the trauma of losing the eye was enough to unlock more in you, as the threat from the Shroudling was enough to unlock it the first time. But nothing says it could happen to anyone else." Bernays's jaw was set. He was done with this conversation.

"I certainly think that any further discussion of this should be expanded to all of the master stormwitches in residence," Lijka said. "We will have to conduct study, see if anyone else has experienced an increase in power after a trauma."

"Did you?" Eldry asked coolly.

Lijka froze for a bare instant. By chance she had been looking at Pralith, and he saw the stark grief in her eyes. Then she shuttered her expression and straightened in her chair. "I did not, Journeywoman Karayan." She stood, pushing her chair back. "I am afraid I have other obligations this afternoon. I cannot spend the entire day debating this issue."

"I suggest we table the discussion for now," Mezika said quickly. Pralith had noticed before that she was eager to please Lijka more than the rest of them. Pralith couldn't argue that Lijka had no talent; despite the loss of the *Bounder*, she was still one of the most powerful and skilled stormwitches Pralith had ever met. And she did have a certain mystique to her, having survived the wreck and returned as a semi-recluse. Then her marriage a few years ago to Kinnet, the aloof lightkeeper who had almost become King's Stormwitch, had added to Lijka's image.

"If you do not have the courage to—" Eldry began, but Pralith gestured sharply at her, hoping the motion was hidden from the others by the table.

"We will table this discussion until such time as we may

bring it before a larger assembly. Perhaps the senior masters at first." He mustered a bland smile and directed it around the room. "I thank you all for your attention this afternoon."

Lijka was the first out the door, the heels of her boots ringing against the stone floor. Bernays wasn't far behind her, though he was moving at his usual shamble. Mezika lingered briefly, eyeing Eldry, but Pralith gave her a hard look and she scurried off after the others.

Denae was the last to rise from her chair. "I am truly glad to have you back with us, child," she said, her gaze warm on Eldry's face. "If you will take the advice of someone who has decades of experience with new witches, I think you should seek rest and solitude for the next fortnight. Take time to reacquaint yourself with meditation and the ways of the academy. Let your inner mind realize that you are safe."

Pralith saw Eldry's expression harden just before she lowered her head in what was almost a curtsy to the Apprentice Mistress. "Thank you, Mistress Denae," she said, her voice soft. "Your advice is invaluable, as it always has been."

Denae gave Pralith a comforting smile: *There, see? The child only needed a bit of guidance.* And then she finally walked out of the room, leaving Pralith and Eldry alone at last.

***

Eldry could tell Pralith wanted more. The pompous, power-hungry fool. She would give him more. She would give him more than he could handle, he or any of the other arrogant, condescending academy council. Only Mezika, of all of them, had been willing to hear what Eldry could do. She made a mental note to seek out Mezika later, once there were fewer eyes watching her.

She finally raised her head and saw Pralith watching her, head tilted to one side.

"Master Pralith?" She tried to make herself sound innocent, vulnerable. She didn't think Pralith was truly a predator, but she knew it would appeal to him anyway.

He tapped a finger slowly against his chin. "What else can you do that you shouldn't be able to?" he asked softly.

Eldry let herself smile a little. She called lightning to hand and cast it instantly at a jug of water in the center of the table. The jug exploded and the water sizzled, evaporating so quickly a fog hung in the air.

Pralith ducked and then shoved his chair back, eyes widening. He stared at the shards of the water jug and then lifted his gaze to meet hers. "That almost felt like a weapon."

"Why not?" she whispered.

"We have never used it so," he protested.

"Haven't we?" Eldry's smile slipped into a smirk. "When we choose who shall receive rain and who shall not? When we divert a storm from a populous region to one with fewer people? There are, as Lijka so thoughtfully pointed out, consequences to every action we take. A good reason to meditate, I suppose. Or a good reason to truly consider when and how we should use our power."

Pralith was still tapping that finger against his chin. "I suspect Lijka and Denae wouldn't particularly approve of such talk." He gave her a small smile. "And that Bernays wouldn't see any reason to, since his father and his father's father never had such power to hand."

Eldry giggled, as she knew she was supposed to. She had learned a great deal from Bernays, but she would not accuse the man of having an inquisitive mind or great curiosity. "I feel like you understand the potential, Pralith," she said, leaning forward in her chair. "It is too bad you are the only one who can truly see."

"What we could do with this new power…" he whispered. He gazed into blank space, presumably picturing himself controlling a storm or being lauded for saving thousands of lives.

"We could change everything," Eldry said. She wanted Pralith to be the first to suggest a possible use. If she were the one who championed the notion of weaponizing storm-witchery, it would probably work; Pralith was hungry, after all. But so much better if it were Pralith's own idea. She had observed over the years that when someone thought it was his idea, he would fight harder for it. He would remain so dedicated to the idea, even when it turned horribly and bit him, that he would go down fighting for that idea.

Eldry's task was to weaponize stormwitchery and destroy the academy from the inside out. But how much more delicious if Pralith were the one who started it.

"We could station the most powerful stormcallers at the borders," Pralith said. "We could use storms as a defense, to keep our enemies at bay."

Eldry wondered if that would have worked when the Shroudlings came down out of their mountain kingdom and attacked. Certainly they had been as susceptible to lightning as anyone else, whatever their mystical powers. "Yes," she breathed, looking with admiration at Pralith. "And if the king had a rebellious nobleman, we could withhold rain from the noble's holding. Dry up the streams until he agreed to the king's terms."

Pralith raised his eyebrows, but he nodded slowly. "Not so very far from what we already do, is it?" he said. "We call rain when the crops need it, we lull rains when the crops are flooded. Who would be able to stop us if we also used the rain as incentive?"

Eldry nodded, eyes wide. It almost sickened her how easy Pralith was to guide. How easily he took her little hints and turned them into something he could take full credit for. "We could train others to call lightning to hand at will," she suggested. It was something almost every stormwitch had done once in their life—generally the way one found out she was a stormwitch, in fact. Many could never master it again, despite that initial call. Eldry herself had been unable to call lightning to hand after she used it to kill the Shroudling that had her backed into the dead-end alley in Stony Lonesome. Denae had suggested it was trauma remnants, but had also said it wasn't important, because, after all, stormwitches weren't in the business of attracting lightning. They had other more important things to focus on.

Pralith picked up a shard of the jug she had exploded and turned it over in his fingers. "To see it wielded with such precision," he mused. "I called lightning myself, the first time I channeled. I was angry at my father and ran away from home, and it was the rainy season. I got caught out in it, and I blamed my father for that, too, and worked myself into a real temper tantrum." He gave her a rueful smile. Eldry wondered if telling this humiliating little story was how he had convinced himself he wasn't an arrogant peacock.

"What happened?" she asked.

"Oh, I was shouting about the unfairness of it all, the usual stupid things a half-grown man gets angry about, and at the peak of my ranting, lightning struck the ruined tower where I'd taken shelter." Pralith chuckled. "As the crumbled rocks rained down around me, I had the fit that sometimes takes you after a first casting. Fell to the ground, my limbs shaking, and I remember thinking, *This will teach Father.*" He snorted. "Teach him what, I have no idea. When I recovered, I was frightened and shaking, of course. I went sniveling home to him and told him what had happened, and he packed me off here."

Eldry wondered if anyone had ever come eagerly to the academy. She certainly hadn't, and it sounded as if Pralith hadn't, either. Were there people who had sought the magic? Were there people who rejoiced at it? Who strove for it and expected it and celebrated when the casting finally came?

"I think you are right," she said at last. "We could teach others to wield the lightning with precision. It could be a useful tool."

Tool, she called it. Not weapon. Let Pralith think of that word on his own.

Pralith nodded slowly. "Of course, if Prince Vistaren and this Voice of Dragons have their way, we probably won't be allowed to explore this at all. We should be careful about how the prince learns of your new talent."

"Voice of Dragons?" Eldry frowned. The Scavenger

hadn't said anything about dragons.

"That's right, you wouldn't know about that," Pralith said. "You arrived the same day he did, or near enough." He snorted. "You remember that Prince Vistaren agreed to a treaty betrothal with Princess Azmei of Tamnen?"

Eldry frowned. "Wasn't she assassinated by some fanatic in Ranarr?"

"That's what everyone thought," Pralith said. He was smiling; Eldry suspected he enjoyed knowing something she didn't know. "Or everyone but Vistaren, at least. As it happens, she survived the assassination attempt and has spent the last three years in hiding. But she finally came to Amethir this week, and she brought a skinny boy with her. He claims he's the Voice of Dragons."

Eldry was probably supposed to scoff at the idea of dragons. How could she, though, when she had spent the past fortnight sharing her thoughts with a seadragon? There must be dragons who lived on land, too. "What does that mean?" she asked instead.

"He says he's a prophet." Pralith snorted. "Says the gods are waking, and that the dragons have felt it. They want us to stop using stormwitchery, apparently. Of course, if the witchery is truly a gift from the gods, it doesn't make sense they would want us to stop."

Eldry frowned. "But I thought Mistress Kinnet had met a stormsinger. Didn't everyone decide then that the old stories were true, that the stormsingers had taught us the magic?"

Pralith shrugged. "Some people believe that happened before the Godwars, and others think it was after. No one quite knows for sure."

"King Rona had a stormwitch, didn't he?" Eldry couldn't quite remember.

"The stories don't agree." Pralith shrugged. "Some of the stories suggest one of the Daughters of the Storm was, in fact, the first stormwitch. Others suggest that was added later to make it seem so. I'm no scholar of history, though, so I can't tell you for certain."

Eldry fought to keep from scowling. She didn't like this. Any of this. "We must not let this Voice of Dragons stand in our way, no matter what." She looked up at Pralith and saw that his expression was suddenly doubtful. She smoothed away her scowl and leaned closer. "We could do so much good. Pralith, you have the king's ear. He will listen to you." She smiled. "We won't have to worry about Prince Vistaren and his prophet."

She knew, when Pralith smiled back at her, that she had won.

18

Arama was on the quarterdeck, watching the Maron East Light retreat abeam on their port, when the wind began whistling. When she noticed it, she realized the sound had been tickling at her ears for some little time already, and it had just now reached her awareness. She cursed inwardly and turned to squint astern. She'd been inattentive, and that wasn't a luxury she could afford, even this close to home.

"Cap'n?" Carig was on the tiller. He was looking at her in confusion, and Arama pointed at her ear. Only then did his expression clear. "Seven hells," he muttered in sudden understanding.

"Yes," she said, and turned to glare at the dark, sharp-edged cloud behind them. "Storm incoming, fine on the weather quarter, Mister Carig." She didn't like the timing of it. Another half glass and they would be docked and safe. She didn't want to luff up this close to home.

"Bear away," she told him. They could beat it, she hoped, as long as there were no fallwinds associated with it. She gave an apprehensive glance at the landward light, built high on the cliffs that rose over the harbor. They couldn't count on no fallwinds, not with the cliffs as high as they were.

"Aye, mum."

Footsteps thumped on the deck beside her. Kedar Ebb, whom she had said was welcome on the quarterdeck any time. He was pale underneath his tan, and sweat stood out on his forehead.

"It'll eat us." His voice was ragged and raw.

Arama glanced sideways at him, not sure what to say to

that. He might be right.

"The storm," he said, as if she needed clarification. "That thing's a monster. Almost as bad as the one that ate my father."

Arama's mouth went dry. He was stormshocked, no question about that, and no wonder, with all he'd lost in the storm. But that didn't mean he was wrong about the size of it.

"Pray Lord Antos has mercy, lad," Carig said from his place at the tiller.

"Mercy?" Kedar's voice cracked. "What mercy did he show my people?"

Arama stirred, her eyes back on the approaching storm. "Prince Vistaren's got a prophet says the gods are waking. Maybe your Lord Antos is only merciful in his dreams, Carig."

"Blasphemy, mum!" Carig sounded shocked. Arama had stopped giving him grief over his devotion fifteen years ago, when his sacrifice to Antos might have been what saved their lives. Still…

"Is it?" she asked seriously. "What do we truly know of the gods? They've been sleeping so long." She often wondered how the priests stayed so faithful. How did people worship a god that was silent and sleeping? How did people care about a deity that obviously didn't care about them?

"We know enough to hate them," Kedar said, low and vicious.

Carig groaned.

Arama glanced back at him, wondering if the groan was for Kedar's words or for the tiller fighting back. The wind was stronger now. If they didn't outrun the storm, Arama wasn't certain they would make it home intact. Still…better to take in the sails now than try to do it once the storm hit.

"Hands by the lee sheets!" she shouted, and heard Zek repeat the command from the main deck. "Bring in the topgallant!"

She listened for Zek's orders as he had the studdingsails, royals, upper staysails, and mainsail brought in. He was a good officer—and more than that, he was a good sailor. Arama gave a quick glance astern to the East Light; she hoped Kinnet was safe there. Would she get warning to Maron in time?

"Do you think the gods will destroy the world once they're awake?" Kedar asked. His voice was remote. He was watching the storm come, dread and eagerness mixed in his face.

Arama gave him a long, silent look. What did you say to a question like that?

She had come to like Kedar in the two days they'd been sailing together. She understood his grief and anger, and she understood also why he cycled so quickly between the two. She hadn't let his flares of temper bother her, and she'd seen him sink back into grief again almost as soon as his temper was spent. It made her chest ache; she had been through this herself, fifteen years ago.

He had a good head on his shoulders, even if he did let emotion rule him more than he should. And she could tell he knew the sea well. He'd been all over *Dawn Star*, from the crow's nest aloft to the deepest hold. He'd never sailed a ship so large, he'd told her, but he knew a fine vessel when he saw one. That alone would have endeared him to Arama, even if she hadn't seen so much of herself in him.

"I suppose if they do destroy the world," she said finally, "a storm's as good a way to do it as any. At least I know what to do with storms."

"Captain!" It was Zek's voice, accompanied by pounding feet on the quarterdeck. "Look!" She looked at Zek, startled, and saw he was pointing abaft.

She and Kedar both turned. Arama searched the storm and then the horizon for whatever had caught Zek's attention. Then her gaze finally lit on the East Light. A tall figure stood on the walk that surrounded the top of the light. Her silver hair whipped around her face in the wind, but Arama recognized the figure of Kinnet Ardelis, keeper of the light.

Her heart leapt. Kinnet was home and fighting the storm. Thank the gods!

A moment later a second figure joined her, plump with generous curves, and Arama pushed down the automatic distaste. Lijka was there as well. Pray the gods she did better with this storm than she had fifteen years ago.

Not fair, said a voice in the back of her mind. It sounded suspiciously like Lozarr's. *She was as wounded as you by that storm, and you told Kedar as much not three days gone.*

"Well spotted, Mister Zek," she said heartily. "At least we aren't wholly alone. If they can deflect it—or even delay…"

"Pray Lord Antos forgives your blasphemy," Carig put in.

Beside her, Kedar stiffened. He darted a single glance at Arama and then marched away, his back straight.

Arama sighed. "The boy lost near everyone he loves, Carig. Don't force religion down his throat whilst he's angry at the gods."

Carig harrumphed. "If not when he's astray, then when?" he demanded.

"Sir," Zek ventured, "I think the time to talk of religion to someone is when *they* want it, not when someone else thinks they need it."

Arama glanced at him, surprised by how astute the boy was. "Well said, Mister Zek."

Carig harrumphed again but said nothing else.

Arama turned back to the storm. It was closer now, the ragged edges of the dark cloud reaching for them like grasping fingers. A shiver ran down Arama's spine. It truly was massive, and it would be on them in a short time. It didn't take long for a storm to wreck a ship. They wouldn't be caught aback, and she could be grateful for that, but she didn't want to see them pooped again, and with the wind in the weather quarter, that was a very real possibility.

"Get us home, Mister Carig," Arama ordered. "We'll visit Antos' temple together if we make it back to Maron."

She had given Carig more leeway than anyone else in her crew since *Bounder* sank. She wasn't going to stop doing that just because they disagreed. But she also wasn't going to spend time debating religion when they were in the teeth of a storm.

"Aye, mum!" Carig agreed.

Zek had ordered the crew capably, and the sails had all been shortened to Arama's satisfaction. As she surveyed the top, the wind pushed so hard that she staggered to keep her footing. A moment later she heard a scream from aloft and someone dropped to the deck, thudding hard. Arama heard the bone snap from the quarterdeck.

She was running forward as soon as she realized the woman was falling. She and Zek met over the woman's writhing form. Aside from the one scream, the woman was silent, though her face was frozen in a rictus of pain. She'd had the breath knocked out of her by her landing, Arama thought.

"Tynni," Arama said, crouching beside the fallen woman.

Tynni sucked in a loud, ragged breath and looked up at her. "My ankle, Captain, no worse," she panted. Tears streamed down her face, but Arama knew she was brave and determined. Arama gripped her shoulder. "Zek, have someone get her some easeall."

"Yes, mum!" He darted off, already shouting orders. Arama clasped Tynni's hand in hers.

"We'll see you healed, no fear, Tynni," she promised.

"I know, Captain." Tynni's gaze was confident despite the tear tracks on her cheeks. Arama felt a moment's gratitude that she'd earned such devotion from her crew.

"Captain!" It was Carig, and he sounded worried. Arama squeezed Tynni's hand and pulled away to return to the quarterdeck.

She saw at once what had caught his attention: a waterspout rose from the ocean's surface some hundred yards abaft the *Dawn Star*. It danced across the water, light as a bird but menacing as a siren.

"All hands out of the rigging!" Arama screamed. "Secure hatches!"

The waterspout danced closer. She could hardly drag her gaze away, it was so graceful. It wasn't right that something so deadly should be so beautiful. Arama shielded her eyes, knowing the deck was about to be deluged.

It was probably a futile hope, but she shouted, "Gunners, ready shot!" She had heard of cannon shot breaking a waterspout, though she wasn't sure she believed it. Thank the gods the waterspout was abaft and not abeam. There was still a chance they might outrun it.

Arama found herself wishing she believed as strongly as Carig in Sea Lord Antos. For herself, she had always liked the idea of the gods, until recent news of Vistaren's prophet spoiled that. But she had never seen the need to make sacrifices to deities who were sleeping at best, or dead at worst. She had never mocked Carig's beliefs, though she had teased him for them a bit. But she wondered now if his faith wasn't what kept him struggling in the face of the storm.

What keeps you struggling? asked a voice in her head.

"Lozarr," she whispered, thinking of his quick laugh and gentle nature. Whatever else happened, she would live as long as possible for Lozarr.

The stern cannon boomed, the shot going wide of the waterspout. With much swearing, the gunners began the laborious process of swabbing the barrel, worming, and reloading.

"Come on, come on," Arama whispered. Her gunners were fast, but they weren't pulling away from the waterspout quickly enough.

"Nearly there, mum!" Carig called to her.

The cannon roared again, and this time they hit their mark. The cannonball tore through the waterspout, breaking the twisting column of water. Arama breathed a sigh of relief as she saw it dissipate. She'd never tried that before, though she'd been told it would work.

"There!" Carig shouted. "We've reached Maron, mum!"

Thank all the gods, they had. Arama shouted orders to prepare for docking. She kept an eye on the oncoming storm as she went to stand by Carig's shoulder. She was happy to keep her word about the sea lord's temple, if it meant they would arrive safely. She hoped Carig wouldn't insist on it being right away. Arama knew how Kedar chafed to be before the king.

She knew, also, how much Lozarr feared Kedar wouldn't hold his tongue. She intended to follow Count Kedar wherever he went until he had seen King Rekel. She didn't have any illusions about the king's favor; it would change with the wind, as she well knew. But if she could use his goodwill for her to protect Kedar, she would.

"We'll go straight to the palace," she told Carig. "They'll need to be warned of the storm. It must be bad if it's still coming so fast."

"Aye, even if the witches know about it, they're not doing aught about it," Carig agreed.

"You and Zek make *Dawn Star* as ready as possible, and get yourselves and the crew to shelter. Understood?"

"Aye, mum."

"And after the storm passes, I'll see you to Antos' temple myself."

***

Azmei walked out to the front room of her suites, both hoping and fearing that Hawk would be waiting for her. He was, of course. Thank the seven that Yar wasn't there. She had thought she was used to Yar's keen vision and lack of tact, but that was before he'd made several observations about her relationship with Hawk—and her relationship with Vistaren.

She missed Yar, of course she did. But let Lijka and Kinnet show him their stormwitchery for a few days, and Azmei would happily enjoy time without his astute—and entirely aromantic—commentary on her love life, such as it was.

Hawk was dressed in nondescript formal attire, as befitted the princess' bodyguard. His face lit up when he saw her. Azmei's heart fluttered as she smiled tentatively at him.

You are a princess and accomplished assassin, she told herself. *Have faith in yourself. You have earned his devotion.*

It didn't stop her from feeling grateful that Hawk thought so highly of her.

"You look lovely," he told her, stepping close to her. She was glad she'd dismissed her chambermaid. Regardless of what Vistaren knew about her feelings for Hawk, it wouldn't do for the servants to know—none but the most trusted, and Azmei hadn't spent enough time with her chambermaid to be certain of her.

"Thank you," she murmured, smiling up at him. She loved Vistaren, even if it was in a very different way, but she couldn't help wishing she could be on Hawk's arm when she arrived at the betrothal ball.

The corners of his eyes crinkled as he lifted a hand to brush her cheek. "Make them love you as I do," he whispered, and leaned down to kiss her. "It won't be difficult."

Azmei laughed awkwardly. She still wasn't certain Hawk's faith in her was deserved, but she would never do anything to discourage it. "I hope I can live up to what you see in me."

His smile widened. "Why do you think I fell in love with you in the first place?"

Azmei grinned back at him, though she still wasn't sure she had earned it. She looped an arm around his neck and kissed him heartily, then pulled away. "We cannot be late," she said. Then she cleared her throat and sighed. "*I* cannot be late."

Hawk's smile faded, though it didn't disappear entirely, and he nodded. "After you, princess," he murmured.

She arrived at the betrothal ball on Vistaren's arm, her golden dress making an attractive contrast to Vistaren's dark blue jacket and trousers. She couldn't help but imagine how they must look as a couple. Dark blue suited Vistaren's olive complexion, and she had long known that gold was flattering on her. If Vistaren's court were at all inclined to approve of this marriage, they would fall in love at the sight of them.

When the court herald announced them and the doors to the ball room were thrown open, Azmei knew she had been right. A cheer rose from the court at the first moment they saw their prince arm-in-arm with Azmei. A cynical part of her couldn't help wondering if they were merely happy to see him with a woman, but she couldn't resist the thought that some of them must wish their prince happy, even if it meant there would be no queen.

"You are beautiful, and everyone sees it." Vistaren's voice was low in her ear. "My family is pleased." He smiled down at her, though she couldn't help seeing the sadness in his eyes. "The entire court is pleased."

"I hope so," Azmei said, though she wanted to hug him tightly and promise she would see him happy regardless of their treaty.

Vistaren led her out onto the dance floor as the royal orchestra struck up a slow, traditional love song. It was one she knew even in Tamnen, though she knew the words were different in Amethir. Azmei melted into Vistaren's touch, letting everyone around them see nothing more than a woman besotted with the man she danced with.

"I feel as though I should let Hawk dance with you," Vistaren murmured. "Poor fellow. Bodyguard was a good assignment for him. He can't take his eyes off you."

Azmei bit her lip to keep from making a face at him. It was so unfair to all of them—all three of them, and whatever man was lucky enough to catch Vistaren's eye at some future time. "Is there no way for you to persuade your father to let you marry as you please?" she asked, lifting her face so she could speak in his ear. "If Lijka and Kinnet can be together, why can't you be with someone you honestly love?"

Vistaren's smile was sad. "Love isn't what's needed for

a king. Heirs are."

Azmei shook her head. "Could you not choose one? Why must it be an heir of the body?" She thought of her cousin Arisanat, who would have inherited the throne if both Azmei and her brother Razem were dead. He had been a traitor, but the law, in general, was a solid one.

"That is our law." Vistaren's voice cracked, but his tone was implacable. He had grown up knowing what was expected of him, Azmei realized, and he couldn't easily turn his back on it, even if it meant he would be miserable.

Couldn't she understand that?

She licked her lips. "What good is a king if he can't change the law to suit him?"

Vistaren shook his head. "What good is a king if he thinks himself above the law?"

Azmei stared at him for several steps of the dance. "Damn it."

He smiled at her, the expression surprisingly warm despite the topic of conversation. "Not to state the obvious, Az," he said, his voice gentle, "but I've been wrestling with this longer than you have." He took advantage of a pause in the music to press his lips to her forehead. "I love you for wanting me happy, but there are no loopholes."

Her eyes stung, but she nodded. She had heard the collective intake of breath—or was it a sentimental *awwwww?*—at the brush of Vistaren's lips to her skin. How could a people be so willfully blind to their future sovereign's wellbeing?

And yet... Hadn't her people allowed her to contract herself to a foreign prince in exchange for the promise of peace?

It was the lot of royalty, perhaps, to choose duty above happiness. But were commoners truly free to choose happiness? Azmei wondered if there were any people who were able to choose what would make them happy. Perhaps everyone in the world toiled without hope of joy or pleasure. The thought made her throat tighten.

She was almost glad when the song drew to an end and

the orchestra flourished a fanfare. Her steps stuttered to a halt and she and Vistaren turned to look at King Rekel, who stood on the dais, arms raised, a smile on his face.

"My people, I am glad to have you all with us tonight as we celebrate my son's betrothal." He beamed out at them. "My son Vistaren will take Azmei of Tamnen to wife!"

The room erupted into cheers. Azmei glanced around at them, forcing herself to smile. Did they truly think this was cause for celebration? Was it because they loved Vistaren and thought he wanted this? Or were they celebrating the stability a royal wedding represented? She looked up at Vistaren, who was smiling down at her.

"Service and duty come from love, Az," he murmured, and finally she nodded.

The king was talking about unity and new alliances, and how pleased they were that King Razem had chosen to honor the treaty embarked upon by his father. The people of Amethir, the king said, grieved with Azmei at the loss of her father, but celebrated her return to them.

Azmei did her best to nod and smile graciously even as her throat tightened. She shouldn't have let herself grow accustomed to the freedom of the past three years. Her heart fluttered in her chest. She had grown more capable than she had ever thought she would—and now she would be trapped in a golden cage.

"Azmei, Vistaren," Rekel said, his voice warm. "Stand by me and greet our people."

Vistaren took Azmei's hand and led her forward, standing aside to let her mount the dais first. She couldn't help but warm at the courtesy he was showing her in front of everyone. Bless him, he was trying to make this as easy for her as possible. She faced the courtiers and smiled at the cheer that rose once again.

Vistaren stepped up beside her. "My friends." He was smiling easily at them, as if he believed they *were* all his friends. "I am so grateful to be among you as we celebrate this wonderful night. Many of you know that we mourned—

I mourned—when we believed Azmei lost. You saw me dressed in black and I know you all hoped and prayed that I would one day be happy. I am glad to tell you, now, that your prayers and hopes for me have been realized. Azmei was not lost. She is with us now. Join me in celebrating that!"

More cheering. Azmei's cheeks hurt from smiling. Her heart was pounding in her chest now. She knew this feeling—it was the one she'd had on many a rooftop when she was first beginning to go out on assignments alone. She had long gotten past that feeling when she was shadowing a target.

How did you get past it? You prayed, she told herself, and took a long breath, letting it out slow. *God of peace, touch my fearful heart. Help me embrace this new part of my life with your peace. Let me see that I am doing the work of peace. That I am here to—*

"Azmei," Vistaren said, and she jerked her attention back to him. He was smiling at her. "Will you greet my people?"

Her heart settled just a bit. She could do this. She was Azmei of Tamnen, and she was also Aevver Balearic, and she would now be Azmei of Amethir. *I am doing the work of peace.*

"Nay, Vistaren," she said, and felt those around her inhale with shock. She waited a beat, letting Vistaren's surprise make the point she wished. Then she smiled. "I will greet *our* people." She turned to look out at the assembled dancers and courtiers and minsters. "For as I said to you three years ago, I shall become Azmei of Amethir. And I shall love your people just as my own."

It was the right thing to say. The room erupted again into cheers. She felt Vistaren's hand tighten on hers ever so slightly. She smiled up at him and then looked beyond him to King Rekel, who was watching his son and future daughter-in-law with benevolent amusement.

After that came the ritual greetings as each person of importance came forward to meet her, pay his or her respects, and curtsy or kiss her hand. Azmei tried to remember all the names and positions they held in the government, but she knew it was hopeless. She would have to ask Vistaren for a list she could study later.

After the greetings there was more dancing, and Azmei liked that better than the greetings, though she was only allowed one more dance with Vistaren before she was expected to dance with the king, the dukes, the earls, the counts… She lost track of everyone she danced with, but when she was finally able to extricate herself from the crush, pleading the heat, she thought she had acquitted herself well enough.

She managed to find a quiet corner where she could fan herself and sip at a glass of chilled fruit wine. Her head was aching. The music seemed strangely loud, especially the deep drums used to emphasize the cadence. She trailed along the wall, thinking wistfully of her last ball—their first betrothal ball, in Ranarr, where the ballroom had tall, arching windows and doors that led out to a balcony overlooking the sea.

The drums crashed again and Azmei frowned. The percussionist was off-cadence. She turned to look at him, but as she watched, he beat the cadence again, and she saw clearly that he was correct. So what—

Another crash, again off-cadence. Azmei turned toward the ballroom doors. That was not the sound of drums. Were they being attacked? She thought of the sound of the cannons on the *Victorious*.

Then the doors flew open and a man about her age strode in without waiting to be announced. He was followed by a short, wiry woman with blue-black hair. The woman was barefoot, and Azmei recognized her. Arama!

Who was the man with her? Not General Algot. He had the same coloring, though, with his brown skin, black hair, and angry gray eyes. He was not dressed for a ball—though Arama wasn't, either. They must have just come off the *Dawn Star*.

Azmei hurried to intercept them. "Arama," she called in

a voice pitched to carry to the seacaptain without alerting those around them.

Arama turned. Her expression was grim. It didn't lighten when she saw Azmei. "Princess," she said, but kept following the young man.

Azmei caught up with her. "What is—who—"

"That is Kedar Ebb, and he is about to make a scene," Arama said. "I can't stop him. We need to get everyone here to safety, anyway, so maybe it won't matter. Much."

"Safety? What—we're being attacked, aren't we? I heard the noise."

"Attacked?" Arama barked a sharp laugh that held no mirth. "I suppose you could say that, if it's the gods that are attacking us. There's a storm bearing down on Maron. We barely made it to dock ahead of it, and that only because Kinnet and Lijka are trying to quell it or slow it."

The news was bitten out as Arama continued trotting after Kedar Ebb. Azmei understood suddenly—this was the Count of Coman, who had lost his village and his father to a storm out of season—and they had just sailed into Maron Harbor in the teeth of another out-season storm.

"King Rekel!" Kedar was shouting. "King of Amethir! King of Amethir!"

"Siren's teeth," Arama hissed, covering her face with a palm. Then she darted forward and seized Kedar's elbow. She stuck her face up into his, though she had to stand on her toes to do it, and talked furiously at him.

Azmei froze for a single instant. Then she pushed aside Azmei and drew Aevver into herself. She scanned the ballroom and found Vistaren thankfully near. She slid through the crowd like an assassin rather than a princess, finding space to move without making people notice her. She cut into the dance with a smile for Vistaren's partner and led him back to where Kedar was no longer shouting, but was arguing loudly with Arama.

She felt Vistaren stiffen when he saw Arama, and then he rushed forward. "What is this?" he asked.

Kedar turned to glare at him. "I leave my village in ruins and come to the palace and find people dancing and drinking and laughing while my people die!" he snarled. "What is *this?*"

"Your highness," Arama threw in hastily.

Azmei bit back an inappropriate laugh; Arama knew damn well that Vistaren didn't care about your highnesses. She was just trying to keep Kedar from making a fool of himself by not recognizing the prince.

"Your highness," Kedar bit out. He was still glaring at Vistaren, who looked…

Azmei looked closer. Vistaren looked like he'd been punched. His eyes were wide, his mouth half-open to answer. She kicked gently at his foot and he closed his mouth. He glanced at her, then looked back at Kedar.

"You are Count Kedar, of course," he said. He still seemed stunned. What was wrong with him? "By the gods, I wish I'd known you were coming. We would have delayed the betrothal ball."

"Betrothal ball," Kedar scoffed. "There's a storm headed straight for your precious betrothal ball. If you don't get everyone to safety, this will be the last ball they have."

"What?" Vistaren snapped suddenly to attention "Storm? But it's four weeks—"

"Tell that to my people, *your highness.*"

Vistaren shook his head. "You're right, of course. Yarrax warned us." He exchanged a rueful glance with Azmei. "I'll take you to my father."

19

Eldry had been listening to the thunder approach for a quarter of a glass.

She had nearly finished dressing for the demonstration. Her underdress was a soft sea-green, worn under a dark blue overdress with a laced bodice. The skirt of her overdress parted in front to display the sea-green. Eldry was pleased with the effect; she looked as though she were dressed in seaglass.

She had ropes of seaglass at her throat and wrists, and of course her seaglass eye completed the effect. She smiled at her reflection. She would make quite an impression when she went to the palace to save everyone.

Brisk, erratic knocking at her door heralded the Scavenger's arrival. Eldry wrapped her belt around her waist and jerked open the door.

"I am ready," she told him, and stepped out into the hall.

She didn't bother looking at him as she passed him. She merely began walking down the passage. She heard him spluttering at her and then there was a moment of silence, followed by a burst of cackled laughter.

When he caught up with her, he was wiping his streaming eyes. "Oh, he chose well, there's no doubt of that. What a surprise you have in store for them!"

Pralith wouldn't like what she was about to do. Eldry knew that quite clearly. But the god—*the Twisted One*, whispered a nasty little voice in her mind—had been clear about what she must do. He had sent the storm. It was too big and strong for the stormwitches to divert, even those who were well versed in working in concert with others. The storm-witches would struggle against it and give up in despair. But Eldry was no longer a stormwitch.

She was a stormweapon.

Smiling to herself, she strode out of the academy complex towards the palace. The storm was nearly on them. The sky should have been light still, but only a thin line of light at the west still lingered. The dark clouds roiled overhead, thunder rumbling almost constantly. The sky flickered madly with lightning—blue and white and even red as the storm kicked up dust in the air.

Eldry paused on the stone terrace and threw her head back, spreading her arms wide. She saw the wind eddying around, swirling and swirling. Soon it would spin itself into a waterspout, unless it made landfall too soon. Mouth open, she gulped at the salt tang on the wind. Her fingers itched with the urge to call it to her, to take the power into herself and hurl it as far as she could—just to see how far it would go.

"Not yet!" The Scavenger was almost shouting in her ear to be heard over the thunder. "You have to save the king first!"

"I know!" Eldry drew herself back in and turned on her heel. The guards would believe she had entry to the ball; stormwitches were not members of the court or nobility, but they were highly regarded in society. She would be equated with the nobility for an event such as this.

Did they realize the danger they were in yet? Had they heard the thunder over the noise of their music and chatter? Silly, soft nobles—had they any idea that Eldry was the only thing standing between them and utter destruction?

"Faster!" the Scavenger urged.

He wouldn't be allowed into the ballroom, Eldry was certain. Well enough. She must take credit for this all herself. No one could be allowed to think the Scavenger was any part of her magic. He might have altered her, augmenting her magic in the process, but *she* was the stormwielder. *She* was the stormweapon. *She* would be the one who saved them.

Her heels clicked along the marble halls of the palace, which were strangely empty of people. A servant girl rushed around a corner into the passage and squeaked when she saw Eldry. She dropped to her knees and hid her face in her apron. "Save us, stormwitch," she quavered.

Eldry checked her steps. This was exactly what she needed. She changed direction and brushed her hand gently over the girl's hair. "Never fear, child," she said, though the servant was probably the same age as her. "I will save you all."

The girl dropped her apron and looked up at Eldry, the fear in her tear-streaked face slowly transforming to hope and even awe. She nodded.

"Get up," Eldry said. "Wipe your face. And then go tell everyone that the Stormweapon will be your shield this night."

The girl scrambled to her feet, staring at her. Then she scrubbed at her face with her apron and darted off the way she had come.

The Scavenger coughed as Eldry resumed her path to the ballroom. A moment later he was by her side again, surprising her once more with how spry and quick he was. Perhaps he was younger than the weather and his lifestyle had made him look.

"That was surprising," he said. From the pitch, Eldry thought it was aimed at his god, but she answered anyway.

"I am their salvation. Who better to ensure everyone knows it than the servants? They see everything, and they gossip among themselves." She smiled. "By this time tomorrow, they will all know that the king and his court cowered in the palace, while Eldry the Stormweapon took action."

They had reached the ballroom doors, which were still guarded. Eldry looked sharply at one of the guards, who quickly threw open the doors. She didn't wait for anyone to announce her. She stopped in the middle of the doorway and put her hands on her hips.

The cowards! They were huddled in bunches around the room, spouses and lovers clinging to each other. Did they think perhaps they would be safe here because there were no windows? Eldry knew better. This storm would flatten everything in its path—even stone. It was a godstorm. The other stormwitches might call it an anomaly, though this one was ten times stronger than anything these small-minded fools might have seen.

"What is this?" King Rekel was standing in front of his dais. He looked at Eldry, his brows drawn together.

"It—It's Eldry Karayan, your majesty." Pralith's voice was stunned. "A journeywoman." He was standing behind the king. He took advantage of that to make a face at Eldry that was clearly meant to tell her to shut up and go away. Then he cleared his throat. "Have you news from the academy, Journeywoman Karayan?"

Eldry threw her head back and laughed. It felt good. Pralith had seemed intrigued with her abilities, but he was too cautious. Well, after tonight he would answer to her.

"I am no journeywoman, Pralith. I am Eldry. Storm-weapon. And your salvation." She grinned at him, hoping it looked more friendly than fierce. "Come. Bring anyone who is brave enough and I will show you more of what power I have gained."

She swept a challenging look across the room, seeing Prince Vistaren next to a short, pretty woman who must be Princess Azmei. Past Pralith and the king was the Storm Petrel, and next to her a young man Eldry didn't recognize. He was well-muscled and handsome, with full lips, but he looked furious. At the interruption? No matter. Eldry looked back at Pralith, sharpening her gaze, and then she spun on her heel and strode back out of the room.

She knew they would follow. How could they not? They had to know what she would do.

Oh, not everyone. There would be plenty who were too cowardly to leave what they thought of as shelter. But the king would certainly send someone close to him, even if he refused to leave his spot of safety. The prince would come, she thought. And perhaps that princess as well. And Captain Dzornaea—everyone knew what the Storm Petrel thought of stormwitches. She would come watch, if only to catch Eldry in a mistake.

She led the others down a side passage leading to a terrace where fair weather events were often held. Eldry herself had attended a party there once. It was perfect for what she intended.

Is all in readiness? she queried. She bit her lip. Would the god answer her instead of speaking through the Scavenger? He had begun to hint at it. But she was gambling on it now.

He couldn't let her be seen as a fool, though. He spoke, as she had known—almost known—he would.

Call lightning to your hands, whispered that horrible voice in her mind. *Speak with the wind in your voice. You will know what to do. I will do the rest.*

Eldry sensed people at her back as she threw her head up again, lifting her arms to embrace the storm. They wouldn't dare touch her. They were watching. They were hoping she would save them.

It was difficult to stand against the buffeting of the wind. Eldry wondered how much harder it would be for those who couldn't see the wind as it came at them. She spread her fingers wide and called the lightning to hand.

Those behind her gasped and shouted. Eldry let the lightning dance along her fingers and up her wrists until she was wreathed in lightning to her elbows. She opened her mouth and shouted, "Storm! I push you away!"

Only it didn't come out as words in the common tongue. It came out as a rushing, howling wind, first keening high and then dropping to a low, throbbing moan. She saw the winds slow in their spinning. She shouted again, paying less attention to the words and more to the power in them, and the winds began to shift.

"Eldry! Wait, Eldry, what are you doing?" Pralith was

beside her, shouting over the wind and thunder.

"I am saving Maron," she told him, and had to say it twice to make her voice come out as Eldry's voice and not as the wind's.

"But how?"

She exerted a little power to channel the wind around them; the air stilled around them so everyone could hear her. "I will send it south of the city. There are only little fishing camps there."

"Little fishing camps!" That was a voice she didn't recognize, ugly with rage. "Those are people's lives! Those are our sustenance!"

Eldry shrugged. "They are in the way of the storm."

"So *this* is how the crown protects itself!" It was the man who had been standing by the Storm Petrel, she realized. "Nevermind the fisherfolk who feed you—strike *them* with storm after storm as long as the palace still stands!"

"There—there are far fewer souls living in the fishing settlements," Pralith wavered. "Surely the folk of Jorey and Harkenerth will have already fled the storm."

"Is *this* your idea of mercy, King of Amethir?" the man raged.

"I hear your anger, Count Ebb." By the gods, it was better than Eldry had realized. King Rekel himself had come to observe her! "But I do not know what to say to you. Would you rather the entire population of this city—who are fisherfolk as well as merchants and blacksmiths and shipbuilders—be destroyed? This storm is terrible, and the death of any man or woman is a tragedy. But what would you do in our place?"

The king's voice was calm, rational. Calculating. Eldry smiled grimly. This was exactly why Amethir needed to be destroyed. They allowed the destruction of a village like Stony Lonesome because it was deep in the mountains, close to the Shrouded Realm. They allowed the destruction of a village like—Jorey and Harkenerth, was it? because they were better dead than Maron, the seat of Amethir's power.

"Damn you to the seven hells!" Count Ebb was going to get himself executed for treason if he wasn't careful.

Eldry darted a glance at Pralith. He looked frightened, but also avid in some way. She turned to look at Ebb and then at the king. The king was looking at Ebb, his expression sad, but when he saw Eldry looking at him, he nodded to her.

"Do what you can to save us, stormwitch," he said.

Stormweapon, Eldry corrected him, but she merely smiled at him and turned back to the storm.

"Father, you can't—"

"I can, and I will. We cannot rule the kingdom if there is no capital."

Soon enough you will have no kingdom to rule, Eldry thought, and hurled the storm away from Maron. She would save the capital. She was here for bigger things. She was here to destroy Amethir itself.

****

Azmei looked around the nearly empty ballroom. This wasn't exactly how she'd imagined the betrothal ball going—but then again, her life had never been as she had imagined, so why start now? The king was speaking urgently with Chancellor Avidius and Stormwitch Menever. Vistaren had spent the past hour issuing orders to those whose task it was to respond to the emergencies in the city. Azmei had mostly tried to stay out of the way, helping when she could.

Everyone she saw walked with slumped shoulders, clearly exhausted. Her own back ached so badly from bending down to help people that she wasn't sure she could walk upright if she tried. Her ball gown had torn twice; the elegant, sweeping hem was tattered now. What she wouldn't give for a nice, close-fitting suit of black clothes and a roof to climb.

Since that alternative was unavailable to her, she opted for coffee.

Her estimation of Vistaren's servant, Isden, had already been a high one, but it had risen sharply when he appeared shortly after the storm passed, bearing a heavy carafe of coffee. Two other servants had followed him, each carrying a similar load.

Azmei found Isden, who looked almost asleep on his feet, and directed a questioning look at the carafe. He straightened sheepishly and poured two steaming cups. Azmei accepted them with a smile.

"Thank you, Isden," she said. "If it isn't presumptuous of me, I think you should turn this task over to someone else. Go back to Vistaren's chambers and be ready to help him. I'm going to try to get him to rest."

Isden arched an eyebrow just the tiniest bit. "Good luck, highness," he said with a bow. He didn't question her, though. Instead he handed the carafe to a nearby young woman and did as he was instructed.

Azmei carried the cups over to where Vistaren had just slumped into a poufy chair designed for a woman with flouncy skirts. She fought a smile at the sight. "You'll never sleep after all this," she told him. All the same, she held out the coffee.

He stifled a yawn and smiled at her. "You didn't have to stay."

"Yes, I did." Azmei plopped down on the chair next to him. "I'm a part of this now."

Vistaren slid an arm around her shoulders and squeezed once. "I need to talk to him about this, Az, but I'm still so…so fuddled about it."

She followed his gaze to where King Rekel and Chancellor Avidius were talking. Pralith Menever had disappeared, presumably back to the academy to fulfill whatever duties he had there. Azmei made a mental note to discover what those were, then dragged her sluggish thoughts back to the matter at hand. "Fuddled about it because Eldry doomed those two fishing villages? It's damned awful poor Count Ebb had to witness that."

"Don't I know it." Vistaren's arm tightened slightly around her. "Don't I know it. *Blast.* Here I was trying to convince him that my father's a good man who cares about his people. And then Father turns around and…" He trailed off and then shook his head. "I mean, I don't like what happened, but…" Sitting back, he let his arm fall from around her shoulders. "What do *you* think he should have done?"

Azmei thought of the chill that had settled in her stomach when Eldry so casually pointed out that the villages were in the way. "I don't know," she admitted. "What's north of the city, besides all the cliffs?"

"There's a village on the headland. Do you think the cliffs would have blunted the storm's force?" Vistaren gulped his coffee and hissed. Azmei tested her own and found it still too hot to drink.

"I don't know," she said again, and sighed. "I wish there had been more time. Aren't your stormwitches meant to predict these things sooner?"

"Usually." Vistaren's voice was bitter. "Pralith said this was another anomaly. Which—I don't like *that.* The last anomaly was fifteen years ago and set off a major search effort for those affected, and then we have two in a month? That points even more to your Voice of Dragons having the right of it."

Azmei stiffened. Yar had gone with Lijka and Kinnet to the lighthouse—right in the path of the storm! What if he had been hurt? Her breath tightened and she pushed the thought aside. If he had been hurt, there was nothing she could do about it this moment, and worrying wouldn't help him.

"I asked Arama to check on him," Vistaren said softly. "I knew you would worry."

Azmei let out a sigh that sounded a little too much like the beginnings of a sob for her liking. She was exhausted and wanted her bed, but that was no excuse for giving in to her emotions. She leaned against Vistaren's shoulder. "Thank you," she whispered. When she thought she had her voice under control again, she said, "What else did Arama tell you?"

"Eh, that she saw Lijka and Kinnet out fighting the storm. They were at the light, working to protect the ship." He lowered his voice. "And that's rare enough, that Arama would be fair about a stormwitch. She hasn't liked them since the *Bounder*, Lo says. Lijka in particular."

"But she agreed to go to the light for me?"

"She wanted to make certain *Dawn Star* was sound. Anyway, she's not one to shy away from her debts—even if they are to a stormwitch, I suppose." He smiled faintly at Azmei, and she found it in her to smile back.

"So Arama is gone," Azmei mused aloud. She looked around the room. "Did she take Count Ebb with her?"

She felt Vistaren go still for a moment. When she looked at him, she thought his cheeks were darkening. "I told Isden to make certain the count had somewhere comfortable to sleep. I know he's angry with us—rightfully so—but he deserves every courtesy."

"Yes." Azmei looked thoughtfully across the room, wishing her head didn't feel so fuzzy from exhaustion. "I think you should write to Lozarr about this." She nodded her head in the direction of the balcony where Eldry had banished the storm. "All of this."

Vistaren nodded too. "He needs to know. Az, my father won't forget what Kedar said. He didn't like it. A king probably shouldn't overlook something like that said in public, but..."

Azmei straightened, glancing across the room at the king, who seemed impatient to be rid of Avidius. "A king who doesn't take offense easily is stronger than one who does, my father always says," she mused. "Said." She paused, waiting for the pang of grief. It came and she let it run its course. Then she smiled wryly. "Of course, he was talking about the king of Strid when he said that, but the point stands."

Vistaren's gaze was gentle on hers. "Aye. I need to talk

to my father about all this."

Azmei's smile strengthened. "You said that already," she said, feeling ridiculously fond of Vistaren just then.

"Do I let him sleep on it or get to him tonight?"

Azmei shrugged. "If you mean to get to him tonight, you'd best hurry. It looks like Chancellor Avidius is taking his leave."

Vistaren straightened. "What do I say?"

"You know him better, but I would say to speak from the heart." Azmei gave him an encouraging look.

Vistaren made a face. "All right. Go to bed, Az. But have brunch with me tomorrow, yes? Later today?"

Azmei nodded and took her leave.

***

Vistaren watched Azmei walk out of the ballroom, knowing he was stalling. He couldn't help but admire how composed she was after everything that had happened. He sighed and got to his feet. He needed to talk to his father. His thoughts kept swirling from the events of the ball to Kedar Ebb's angry face to Eldry Karayan's strange powers and back to Kedar's face…

He shoved the thought aside and crossed the room to his father. His feet were killing him. He didn't have the energy to be more than barely polite when he spoke. "Father."

Rekel turned, though Vistaren was certain his father had known he was coming. "There you are. I've just finished deciding, with Pralith and Itotia's help, how we shall honor the stormwitch, Eldry."

Vistaren blinked. "Honor?" he repeated stupidly. "Father—"

His father cut him off. "She saved us, Vistaren."

Vistaren blinked some more. "At what cost?" He took a quick breath and held it, trying to keep a firm grip on his temper.

"Her own health, among other factors." Rekel's voice

was dry. "Such loyalty is to be commended, that she thought first of the crown, and sacrificed so much to protect us."

Vistaren thought about Kedar Ebb's grief-stricken eyes, the full lips twisted in scorn. "Are we worth so much more than fisherfolk?" he asked his father.

Rekel straightened. He was a tall, thin man; Vistaren took after his mother, and regretted it most whenever he disagreed with his father about something. It was hard to argue with a man taller than you. "It is the price we must pay for the responsibility and privilege of royal blood," Rekel said, his voice thin and cool. "Sometimes we must take the guilt in order to continue our service of the greater good of Amethir."

"If I thought what that stormwitch did was in the greater good, I might agree," Vistaren replied.

"What would you, Vistaren? Do you wish that we had all died, then?" His father was angry, but Vistaren didn't care; he was angry too.

"We have stone walls to protect us," he pointed out. "The fisherfolk do not."

"Pralith assures me that even stone walls could not have withstood this storm. We are most fortunate Eldry Karayan was here to save us. In a rare show of humility, Pralith told me openly that even he could not have moved that storm as she did."

"How would he know?" Vistaren's words felt thick in his throat. "He didn't even feel it coming."

"Enough." Rekel's voice was sharp. "Why do you recriminate with me over a thing that is already done?"

Vistaren drew himself up and inhaled slowly. Calm. He would be calm. He could do no good by arguing with his father. "Very well," he said, schooling his voice to even tones. "What will we do to make reparations to those who lost houses, families, or livelihoods? To what shall I turn my attention first in the morning?"

"Reparations?"

"What will you tell Kedar Ebb, who came all the way

from Anderly to seek justice for his people?"

He knew as soon as he spoke the count's name that it had been a tactical error. His father's brows lowered, his eyes narrowing. "Kedar Ebb," he said, his voice quiet and dangerous. "Kedar Ebb, who spoke treason openly to me?"

"Not treason, Father. Criticism. Justified criticism."

Rekel snorted and Vistaren felt his face getting hot. He wished he could pretend he was interested only in justice for Ebb's people. But he couldn't lie to himself. He wanted to wipe the anger from the count's expression. He wanted to make Kedar Ebb admire his fairness and compassion.

"Justified. Criticism." His father repeated the words as if he were trying to make sense of them. Vistaren swallowed. He and his father often disagreed about things, but they rarely argued like this. It was usually a reasonable discussion. He had never known his father's pride to be so piqued by Vistaren's questioning before now. "Justified criticism." Rekel lifted his chin. "Kedar Ebb may consider himself lucky I allowed him to crawl back to whence he came."

Vistaren thought of Ebb, installed by Isden in rooms not too far from Vistaren's, and wondered if he had made a grave miscalculation. "And the folk of Jorey and Harkenerth?" he pressed, hoping to divert his father's thoughts from Kedar Ebb.

"We will assist them in the morning. What has gotten into you, Vistaren? Cease your harping on a tired issue. Get you to bed." *Preferably with that Tamnese princess of yours,* his gaze added, though Vistaren knew that was probably just his imagination.

"But—" he tried once more.

"I said *enough!*" Rekel's voice rang out loudly enough to get the attention of the servants still cleaning the ballroom.

Vistaren's face felt like it was on fire. He was seized with the sudden mad desire to strike his father. Instead he turned on his heel and stalked out of the ballroom. He wanted something stronger than coffee to drink.

20

Arama forced herself not to fidget or order Zek to row faster. *Dawn Star* was at anchor off the Maron Light, but she couldn't get in too close to the headland, so she'd tasked Zek with manning the oars of her launch.

"You said the women who live here are stormwitches, mum?" Zek was younger than she was; he wasn't even out of breath from straining at the oars.

"Yes. They were working to keep the storm from catching us. They're probably resting." Arama wished she'd had a chance for rest. She'd taken to her bunk for a brief nap, but she'd been too keyed up to sleep well.

She wasn't looking forward to this, but she couldn't refuse Vistaren when he asked her a favor, especially when she could see that things in the capital were strained. Vistaren hadn't specifically said so, but he's been angry at his father, and the look on his face when he realized who Kedar was had spoken volumes. Much safer to be on the high seas with a prophet and a stormwitch than to be in the capital while dissent was brewing.

The launch's hull scraped over the rocky beach and Arama surged to her feet, jumping lightly over the edge. "Wait here, Mister Zek. I'll be back shortly—probably with a couple of passengers."

"Aye, mum."

She was grateful for her boots as she climbed the rough path up to the light. The round tower was built of light gray limestone and loomed several levels into the sky. Arama had never been inside the light, though it had stood there all the years she'd been sailing. A balustraded terrace surrounded the main floor of the tower, guiding her to the entrance.

She hammered on the rough wooden door with the side of her fist. It took several minutes of pounding to raise anyone, as she'd expected. Finally, a sleep-rumpled Lijka jerked the door open, her face scrunched against the lantern Arama held.

"Storm Petrel," she rasped. Without another word she turned and led the way inside the tower. Arama shrugged and followed. Just inside the vestibule was a tidy living area, its furnishings simple but comfortable-looking. Lijka knelt to coax the banked fire back to life.

Footsteps shuffled down the stone stairs that clung to the outside of the room. Kinnet was wrapping a robe around herself as she came down the steps. Her eyes were painted with deep shadows underneath them.

"I never thought to see you here, Storm Petrel," Lijka said. She set a kettle heating over the fire and then went to stand next to Kinnet.

Kinnet nudged her. "We saw you sailing in the storm last night."

"And we saw the two of you working to save our asses," Arama said.

Lijka's eyebrows went up. "A visit *and* gratitude? What do you want?"

Kinnet smacked her arm.

Arama gave them a rueful smile. "I can't say I ever thought I'd be doing this myself. But we might not have made it to port without you. And when we got there, this slip of a girl calling herself Stormweapon Eldry turned the storm."

Lijka frowned. "Stormweapon?"

"She *turned* it?" Kinnet demanded, her voice loud. "It was all we could do to slow it, working together."

Arama shrugged, careful to keep her face turned to Kinnet. "She seems to think she's our salvation. Sent the storm into the fishing camps instead of letting it hit Maron. Didn't please Vistaren—or Kedar Ebb, who I've just brought in from Anderly."

She saw the comprehension dawn on Lijka's face. "Sleeping gods..." the stormwitch whispered.

More footsteps scuffed down the stairs. Arama looked up to see a tall, skinny lad with the same complexion as Princess Azmei. This must be Yarrax. Arama gave him a swift smile of greeting but turned back to Kinnet.

"Prince Vistaren wanted me to check on you. He also said I might have work to do, aiding the Voice of Dragons, as long as you are all well."

Kinnet looked over her shoulder to Yar and then back at Arama. "Correct. We are well. This is Yarrax, Voice of Dragons. He needs a stormsinger." She smiled oddly at Arama. "I can't think of anyone better to help us find one."

Arama smiled back, thinking of the mission, three years ago, when they had been on *Dawn Star* and first encountered the stormsingers.

"Kin, no." Lijka clutched at Kinnet's arm. "Please," she whispered.

Kinnet leveled a gaze at her wife. Arama saw love and duty both in that look, and she averted her eyes. This wasn't her business. "You know we must," Kinnet said. "Yarrax cannot speak to the stormsingers, so I must interpret for him."

Lijka didn't make any reply Arama could hear. Either she'd switched to their hand language or she wasn't speaking. Either way, Arama felt like she was intruding. She turned to Yarrax.

"I'm glad to meet you, Voice of Dragons. My name is Arama Dzornaea. Some call me the Storm Petrel."

The boy's smile transformed his face. "I've heard of you. My friend Azmei admires you. I'm glad we got to meet."

Arama couldn't help but smile back at him. "I admire your friend Azmei, for that matter. Will you sail on *Dawn Star* with me, sir?"

Yarrax studied her, holding her gaze with his own. Arama gulped at the focus of those swirly silver eyes. She felt like he could see through her.

"Yar is fine," he said. "And yes, I will sail with you. The dragons must speak with a singer. Kinnet said she met one while sailing with you before."

Arama nodded toward the fire. "Let's have some tea out on the terrace and give these two a chance to speak privately, eh?" she suggested, gesturing to the kettle over the fire.

****

Lijka ignored Arama and Yar as they poured themselves tea and went back outside. She was clinging to Kinnet, squeezing her eyes shut tight. She couldn't let Kinnet go out on that ship with Arama. Perhaps Arama was a fine sailor. Perhaps she was the best sailor. But the one time Lijka had sailed with her…

Kinnet's hand smoothed over Lijka's hair in slow, soothing movements. "You know I have to go, Lijka. I sailed with her three years ago and all was well. We need to find the stormsingers."

"I can't lose you," Lijka whispered. She made herself sit up and face Kinnet. "I can't lose you," she repeated. "You saved me. I was going about life out of duty, but you brought joy back to me."

Kinnet's smile was brilliant. "I know. And you have eased my loneliness." She leaned in and kissed Lijka softly. "You know I love you more than anything. But we were both sworn to Amethir before we swore to each other, my dearest." Her hand cupped Lijka's cheek. "We cannot shirk that duty."

Lijka didn't want to shirk her duty. She just didn't want to risk her wife. She closed her eyes, relishing Kinnet's touch. How many nights had Kinnet woken her from a nightmare of the *Bounder*'s sinking and soothed her like this? What would Lijka do if she had a nightmare while Kinnet was at sea?

"This is…it's too hard," she breathed. Her voice was barely audible, even to herself, but Kinnet needed only to read her lips. "The storms have been too much like that run on the *Bounder*. I…" She opened her eyes and met Kinnet's gaze. "I've been hearing sirens in my sleep."

There was no way to explain the siren song to Kinnet. How it began low and throbbing and then rose through the octaves until it was almost too high-pitched to hear. How they sang in a strange harmony with one another, drawing you in. How the song made you want to scrape your fingers against your skin until you bled.

Kinnet kissed her again. "I wish I could stay with you," she said. "If you dream while I am away, remember how I soothe you. Imagine my lips drying your tears and my arms around you. I won't be gone so long."

Lijka shivered, her chest tightening. "I…hope that is true, but…a foreboding fills me. I think…" She faltered, drinking in Kinnet's features. "I think great tragedy will befall us before you and I meet again." She swallowed and looked down, fear rising to choke her. But she couldn't let this sour their farewell. She took a deep breath and lifted her head to look back at her wife. "You must go," she said. "I do see that. Yar needs you." She managed a tremulous smile. "Maybe the whole world needs you."

Kinnet gave her a sad smile back. "My unique skill is with the stormsingers. They do not come to my call, and this is the first time in three years that has happened. What if they can't come, Lijka? What if they are bound? Kept away somehow?"

Lijka sighed. "You should have been King's Stormwitch."

"Yes." Kinnet lifted her chin. "But perhaps this is why I am not. So I have the freedom to go seeking them now." She paused. "I shall be the Prince's Stormwitch."

Lijka laughed shakily, tears flooding her eyes. "Sleeping gods, how I love you, Kin."

Kinnet hugged her, pulling her close and holding her tightly. "I love you."

***

Vistaren ran his hand through his hair and turned on his heel to pace back towards Azmei. She was sitting on a settee, her hands folded in her lap. She looked composed, which only made him feel more frazzled.

"It's wrong, Az," he said. "It's all wrong." He knew he looked awful. He was rumpled, he hadn't shaved this morning, and he was too unsettled to eat. He shouldn't have gone back to try to convince his father after the reports started trickling in. They'd argued again, and his father had only dug in his heels.

"What have you heard of the damage?" Azmei's voice was calm. Maybe she was trying to be so calm because he couldn't.

"Near three hundred dead. Countless fishing boats destroyed. Houses levelled. The water so stirred up by the storm that it's too thick to drink. And my father plans to honor Eldry!"

"Does he intend to make reparations?"

"He laughed at me this morning when I suggested it again." Vistaren scowled, thinking of his father's angry words. "And Faran…gods, Az, he's so angry at Faran. I've had Isden taking meals to the count. I asked him to stay put until I visit him."

Asked him—he hadn't asked him. He'd had Isden lock the count in his rooms. He'd have to go make explanations soon, but he hadn't wanted to risk Faran wandering the halls and running into someone who had witnessed what he'd said last night.

"Does the king not see that losing the fisherfolk hurts everyone?" Azmei asked. She was frowning at last. "How often do you eat what they catch?"

Vistaren swung around for another circuit around the

room. "Most meals! I don't understand his attitude. If we have no catch, we have no food and there will be no pearls or seastars for the artisans to craft into jewelry. It will make more work for the gamekeepers, putting meat on the table. We'll have to expand what we buy from other regions—or from Ranarr. Overall, it weakens us. How does he not see it?"

"Perhaps he's afraid of what it means," Azmei suggested. "You have long depended on the stormwitches to ensure safe fishing. It's a daunting thought, that it might be ending."

"Fishing—and good harvests," Vistaren said. "Siren's teeth! What if the next anomaly doesn't strike from the sea? What if our crops go next? We could all starve!"

Azmei nodded. "This is a grave situation." She curled one leg under her, watching his face. "What should be done, in your opinion?"

He wished he could read her face better. She'd learned to guard herself more over the past three years, and she spoke so neutrally that he couldn't tell what she was thinking.

"Repair what ships we can," he said slowly. "Rebuild homes. Build new ships. Thank Eldry, perhaps, but *quietly*, not celebrating her as a hero. Perhaps she saved Maron, but she did it at the cost of hundreds of lives. And perhaps she didn't save Maron at all—perhaps we would have been fine in our palace of stone."

Azmei nodded.

"And we should ask the academy to—well, to rein her in, I suppose. Keep her from rushing into another situation like that without the sanction of the academy council."

"Can this be done without the king's approval?" Azmei asked.

Vistaren sighed and plopped down in a chair. "He controls the treasury."

"Do you think he will do it?"

Vistaren frowned. "Until this morning, I'd have said yes. But Pralith's been talking about the new potential of witchery. Potential—as if we haven't already been exploiting that potential for generations!"

"What sort of new potential?" Azmei's voice was tense.

"Warfare." He spoke the word heavily. "Using lightning as weaponry. Setting a wall of storms against the border with the Shrouded Realm. Using the threat of a storm sent into enemy territory to blackmail an enemy into capitulation."

Every use uglier than the last. Vistaren had always thought Pralith enjoyed having authority and status, but he hadn't imagined the man was so power-hungry. He was advocating the use of stormwitchery—a magic that ultimately tied into the magic of the world itself—for killing.

Azmei shook her head. "Amethir is already strong. Ranarr's neutrality and independence are assured because you have pledged it so. My father came to you when our kingdom needed an ally against Strid. Why would Amethir need even more power?"

"To bully everyone around us," Vistaren muttered. It wasn't right. It wasn't what he wanted for his people.

"This," Azmei said, her voice muffled. Vistaren looked over at her. She had covered her face with her hand. "This is what the dragons feared."

They fell silent.

Had the dragons been warning them for what they had already done? Or were the dragons seeing in advance the arrival of Eldry and Pralith's call for weaponizing stormwitchery? Vistaren wondered suddenly if he should have urged Yarrax to wait until they had some sign that it was time to speak. Perhaps he had helped manufacture this crisis by preemptively telling his father that stormwitchery was faltering.

But how could he have anticipated that? The dragons sent their prophet to him, telling him the gods were waking and danger was upon them. Wouldn't it have been irresponsible to delay acting on the warning? For that matter, hadn't the storm that hit Anderly been a sign? Or the seadragon attack on the *Victorious*?

And what do I do now?

He was afraid he knew what he had to do. His father was always open to ideas if he came up with them himself. He was a good man, a kind man, in many ways. But he often couldn't see the merit in an idea someone else suggested. Vistaren had thought, since Azmei and Yarrax were there on a diplomatic mission, that his father would listen to them with a more open mind. He should have realized that wouldn't be the case.

There were ways of making his father believe something was his idea, of course. Vistaren knew it, as did the ministers of finance and trade. General Balahar was not quite as skilled in those methods, since Amethir had been largely at peace with her neighbors since the Shroud War nineteen years ago, but even he had begun learning the diplomatic art of making the king think an idea was his and his alone.

Vistaren hadn't made that happen. He'd been thoughtless in the way he reported Azmei and Yar's message to the king and council. At this point there was no convincing his father of anything other than the truth: Azmei had come to Amethir with a prophet, delivered a dire ultimatum, and blamed the one advantage that made Amethir more powerful than her rival nations.

Vistaren looked at her. She was frowning down at her hands, lying palm up in her lap. He wondered if she had learned to read the future in the lines of her palms, the way he'd heard some Strid mystics could do. She had come here trying to help him. She hadn't known what she was getting herself into.

"Azmei," Vistaren said slowly, "Azmei, I…I wonder if you and Hawk should just go home. This isn't what you agreed to."

Azmei glared at him. "Nor were three years of waiting for me what *you* agreed to," she snapped. "No. I am meant to be here, with you. We are friends, and I admire you. I think you will make a fine ruler for Amethir, and I want to help you. You won't get anywhere trying to send me home."

Vistaren half-laughed, half-sighed in his relief. "Well, I didn't *want* you to go," he admitted, "but it only seems fair to give you the opportunity, especially considering what I—"

He broke off and stood again, pacing away from her. He couldn't bring himself to speak it aloud. Vistaren knew his father. He wouldn't change his mind. He would dig in if he were challenged any further. He believed strongly in the right of nobility, but more strongly in those of royal blood. He chafed at any restrictions the aristocracy tried to place on the crown.

Vistaren thought again of Lozarr's letter after Anderly. *I half fear the man will prove to be a rebel, though,* he had written of Kedar Ebb. *He's lost a lot.* Just imagining everything Kedar had lost made Vistaren's throat tighten. Kedar had lost his father. Vistaren knew how desperately that must hurt.

After all, Vistaren loved his father.

If he left the palace, it would be treason. If he openly disagreed with his father, it would be treason. How could he do that?

"Vistaren?" Azmei's voice was gentle.

He just shook his head. How could he say what was on his mind? How could he even *think* it? And how would Azmei react if he told her? Would she be angry? Would she blame him?

He groaned. Why was this so difficult? For all that he was betrothed to Azmei, he wasn't in love with her. He didn't have to impress her. He didn't have to win her approval.

But none of that was true, was it? He glanced over his shoulder at the way she was watching him. She was still, so still, but her gaze was warm as she looked at him. Her hair fell across her cheek. There was no judgment in her gaze; just a willingness to understand.

He *did* want to have her approval. He wasn't *in* love with her, but he did *love* her. Azmei was someone who could be a true partner to him throughout their lives, and he didn't want to disappoint her.

He turned and paced away from her again. He shouldn't try to cushion what he planned in polite language. He should just blurt it out. Her reaction would be honest, and he knew he could trust her judgment—more, perhaps, than anyone else currently in Maron, with the exception of Isden. Vistaren took a deep breath and opened his mouth.

"You mean to break with your father." Azmei's voice was so low he could barely hear it.

He flinched. He turned, mouth still open, but found he didn't know what to say. He couldn't deny it.

She gazed wide-eyed at him. "Vistaren," she whispered. "That…that is war. Civil war."

He held her gaze. There didn't seem to be any condemnation in her golden eyes, but he could tell he had shocked her. After a moment, he made a face. "Treason, at the very least," he agreed. "I don't know if it will go so far as a war. I am certain General Balahar would not countenance joining a rebellion, even one led by the crown prince. General Orshard…I'm not sure. I don't know him as well, but I know his opinion has differed from Balahar's in the past." He tried to work up enough spit in his mouth to swallow. "Lo and Arama will back me."

I think they will back me. Sleeping gods help us all if they split over it.

He shrugged. "But it may not come to war."

Arama crossed her legs, sitting back into the settee. "If it does, you'll face witchery as a weapon. You know that, don't you?" When he nodded, she added, "What will you do?"

He shook his head. "I…don't know. But I don't see any alternative. We approached the council with Yarrax's message. I spoke to Father once privately before last night. Then Eldry—" He broke off, shaking his head again. "And this morning, Father was more determined than ever to ignore what's right in front of us. He just kept repeating what Pralith had said about weaponizing and the power and potential."

"But Vistaren," Azmei said. She tilted her head, gaze serious on his. "*War.* Could you depose and even kill your own father?"

A pang of sickness gripped his stomach. He couldn't. He knew he couldn't. And suddenly it all came back to him, what Azmei had just survived—the bloody coup attempt that nearly became civil war in Tamnen. The way assassins had come after her, her father, her brother. He thought of just how much Azmei had given up to end the war her kingdom had been fighting since she was a child. Shame washed over him.

"Az…gods, I'm sorry."

"Don't," she said fiercely. "Don't apologize to *me*. It's your father you'll be sinning against."

He jerked at her vehement tone. Was she judging him now? She'd acted like she wouldn't, but perhaps it was too painful for her. But if she didn't want him to apologize… He looked down at his fingers, clenched together so tightly his knuckles ached.

Sin. Would it be a sin, he wondered? Thann was the god of fire and death, sleeping or waking. Would he condemn someone who started a war? Then Vistaren remembered that Azmei had renounced the gods of her youth and served a god of peace now. *The* god of peace, she had called him.

He took a deep breath. "I could never kill my father. But if it comes to it, can't I just force his abdication?"

Azmei looked sadly at him and Vistaren sighed.

"All right. No. You're right. He—he would never abdicate. But what other choice do I have? What would your new god of peace tell me to do?"

She frowned down at her hands. "I wish I knew. You know your own laws better than I. If, as you say, everything hinges on your father's decision, then he must be convinced. Peacefully convinced, if at all possible."

Vistaren nodded. "And if it isn't? Possible?"

Her mouth turned down. "Vistaren, you met Master

Tanvel. I am not like him; I chose not to swear his vows. But he was a Diplomat, a *Shadow* Diplomat. Peace may…sometimes…be attained through a single death."

He didn't at first realize what she was suggesting. Then, as the full implication of her words hit him, he recoiled. Then he checked himself. "I—no," he said at last. Was she saying she thought he *should* ask her to assassinate his father? Or was this a test? And if so, what of? Of his reaction to her lethal past? Of his dedication to the cause he now proposed? Or of something else? "No," he said again heavily.

Azmei nodded, and he could tell she had known this would be his response. "Then," she said softly, "I think it must be war."

21

Vistaren held his breath as he knocked on Kedar Ebb's door. The count would be angry. He wondered if what Vistaren told him would make him angrier. Or maybe he would still be angry, but instead about how long it had taken Vistaren to figure out what to do?

His stomach roiled and he wondered if he were going to be sick.

The door rattled, and then muffled, through the heavy wood, "If you don't have a key, you might as well go away. I'm locked in."

"Shit," Vistaren muttered. He dug in his pocket for the key he'd gotten from Isden. He should have unlocked it before knocking. He inserted the key and twisted. As soon as the bolt clicked, the door jerked open, tearing the key from Vistaren's hands. "I'm sorry," he blurted, "I forgot."

Kedar Ebb stared at him. The throat of his shirt was open as if he'd had trouble breathing, and his eyes were red-rimmed. The past fortnight must have been so horrible for him. Vistaren's stomach twisted again. The count must *hate* him.

Kedar's heavy-lidded eyes opened wider as he looked at Vistaren, surprise chased from his face by another expression Vistaren didn't recognize, before finally settling into anger.

"Your highness. How good of you to call."

He turned his back on Vistaren in a deliberate insult and stalked away. Vistaren was too miserable to take offense. He stepped inside and shut the door behind him, bolting it from the inside this time so they wouldn't be interrupted.

"Am I to be imprisoned for speaking truth to your father?" Kedar asked.

Sleeping gods. Vistaren bit his lip. "My father...pray the

gods he doesn't realize you are still here." He wasn't sure what his father would do, but nothing good. With the temper his father was in, he might do something irreversible.

Kedar turned back to look at him. His gaze was assessing. He raked his eyes down Vistaren's form, then back up to his face.

Vistaren felt himself growing warmer. He wasn't as obviously muscular as Kedar, and his clothes were finer than the ones the count wore. He must look like a useless royal.

"So I haven't been a prisoner," Kedar said finally. "You've…been hiding me—from your father?" He frowned. "But the servant—"

"Isden is my man," Vistaren interrupted. "He's loyal to me."

Kedar's eyebrows rose. "Over your father?"

Vistaren folded his arms across his chest, comfortable in his trust in Isden. "Over anyone. We've been together for years. He's not just a servant. He's friend and confidant. His loyalty to me is unimpeachable."

Kedar's eyebrows rose further. "I…may have misjudged you, highness."

Vistaren gave him an unhappy smile. "I could hardly blame you. The court of Maron has not exactly shown itself well in the two days you have been here. Nor, for that matter, in our initial response to the tragedy in Anderly."

Kedar's lips tightened briefly, but this time, when he turned, it was not to shut Vistaren out. "Your man Isden brought me a very tasty liquor from Simiri. Will you drink with me, highness?" He led the way further into the suite to a comfortable sitting room.

"Gladly," Vistaren said, following him. His stomach was still jumping, but perhaps Simirian whiskey would settle it.

He watched as Kedar went to a side table and filled two cups from a decanter. He had strong hands and sinewy forearms. Many of the fisherlords worked the sea alongside their people, and Kedar was without question one of those who did. With Kedar's gaze on his task, Vistaren let his own gaze linger on the full down-turned lips, the count's handsome face that was shadowed with grief.

He couldn't help feeling he had failed Kedar Ebb.

"You must think we're horrible people here in the capital," he said as Kedar turned to him. "I am so sorry for all that you've suffered. And I'm sorry that we made it worse."

Kedar tilted his head slightly. "You say 'we.' Do you agree with your father's choices? Because I am certain I heard you protest last night."

"No!" Vistaren blurted. "But I was there, and I didn't stop it."

Kedar nodded once. "Aye. But you're here now." He held out one of the glasses, and when Vistaren took it, their fingers brushed.

Vistaren licked his lips, heart suddenly pounding for more than one reason. "Count Kedar, I am about to take a risk. I don't know you, after all. But I have come to some conclusions, some—decisions—and I believe I must share them with you, risk or no." He looked down at the glass of whiskey, hoping his hands didn't shake. Somehow this was more difficult than it had been with Azmei.

Kedar sipped his whiskey slowly, watching Vistaren over the rim of his cup. His gaze was coolly curious.

There was no other way to do this but state it baldly. Vistaren sucked in a breath. "I am about to start a war."

Kedar lowered his glass, eyes on Vistaren's.

"My father is wrong," he continued. "He will not see the signs or hear the prophecies. He ignores the suffering of his people and disregards all advice his son and councilors give him. And so I shall break with him."

"Treason—" Kedar whispered.

"Aye, perhaps," Vistaren said grimly. Now that he had begun, he felt better. It was too late to back out, the treason already committed by its mere utterance. "Treason against my father, certainly. But he has not kept faith with the people of Anderly or Jorey or Harkenerth."

Kedar took another sip of his whiskey and exhaled shakily. "Why…why tell me, highness?"

"Because you deserve to know." Vistaren pushed his hair back from his face. "You deserve a choice. If you will join me, I'll send you back to your home on the fastest horse I own."

Kedar licked his lips. "And if not?"

Vistaren shrugged. He hadn't actually thought that part through. If Kedar, who had lost the most, who had the most reason to want to rebel, wouldn't join him, what hope would Vistaren's rebellion have? "I suppose I'll have Isden keep you locked up in here long enough for me to put my plans in motion, and then I'll have him free you."

"To be hanged as a traitor when your father finds out!" Kedar exclaimed, glaring at him.

Vistaren smiled faintly. "No, he'll know you aren't with me. I'll make it clear, if that's your choice."

Kedar's gray eyes glittered icily. "You play a dangerous game, highness."

"No game." Vistaren's lips tightened. Gods above and below, he felt old suddenly. How had it come to this? And yet…he could think of no alternatives. "I know my father won't forgive me. This will end—*must* end—in either his death or mine." He swallowed hard. "And I love my father, Count Kedar. But I also love the people of Amethir."

Kedar was shaking his head slowly, gray gaze still fixed on Vistaren's face. "I had heard, my lord, that you were soft," he said, his words weighted as if he were choosing each one carefully. "Softer than some of the other fisher-lords would like. But I see now that you are anything but soft." He wet his lips. "You're gentle, as befits a man of power. But you can cut keener than a fish-knife if it's need-ed."

Vistaren's heart lurched and he exhaled shakily. He didn't know what to say in response to that. He just looked back at Kedar, hoping he deserved the count's good opinion. He felt, suddenly, as if he would like to cry.

Kedar finally broke the gaze and drained his glass. "I will join you, Prince Vistaren," he said decisively. "And win or lose, you shall always be my king."

Vistaren's throat tightened and he drained his own glass to hide the sudden rush of emotion. He lowered his glass and nodded. "Gather what you need and come with me now. We'll need to travel light."

"I am ready." Kedar stepped just inside the bedroom and hefted a leather pack. "I didn't bother unpacking last night." His lips twisted wryly. "I hadn't intended to stay, until I found myself locked in."

"Good." Vistaren walked back to the door. "We'll meet Azmei and Hawk in the barracks. Isden is waiting for us outside."

***

Azmei wasn't surprised to see Count Kedar follow Vistaren to their appointed meeting spot near the army barracks. Vistaren had reported that Lozarr thought Kedar ready to rebel with or without encouragement, and having the prince with the rebellion would certainly make it more likely to succeed. More nobles would rally around a royal figure than around a minor fisherlord.

She fell in beside Vistaren as Kedar dropped back, studying their group with a guarded look. She smiled in welcome at him and saw him relax a little, but she knew it was Vistaren who had earned his trust, not the rest of them.

Vistaren looked around at them. "Very well. We've come this far. There's no going back at this point. General Hawk, I thank you for your support as well as Azmei's."

Hawk merely nodded. He had probably seen this coming longer than Azmei. She knew he wasn't thrilled at the idea of fighting another war, but he had come to Amethir with her and Yar because he believed in the message they carried. And for Hawk, belief in something meant fighting for it—just as it did for Azmei.

Vistaren took a deep breath and led them into the building that housed the general officers. Azmei followed him into a central study, where desks and a large planning table took up most of the floor space. Bookshelves and weapons cabinets lined the walls. Two men were leaning over the central table.

A man with spiky, purple-brown hair looked up in surprise. "Your highness! How may I serve?" He bowed.

Azmei stared at him for a moment before turning her gaze away. He was clearly of Ranarri blood—no other ethnic group had that color hair—but his skin was a light tan, rather than the chalky-gray skin she was used to. He must have been born of Ranarri parents, but come to Amethir many years ago. The minerals of the White Stone leached into the water, creating trynen, which tinted their skin through prolonged exposure. She had no idea how long this man must have been away from Ranarr to not be so tinted.

"General Balahar. How goes the work in the fishing camps?" Vistaren asked.

Balahar made a face. "As well as might be imagined. Too many dead to count, and the men aren't used to this." He shrugged. "Death in battle, certainly, but not this…disaster." He looked at Vistaren's companions, obviously curious, but Vistaren ignored that.

"What are my father's orders?"

"He wants the dead buried quickly," Balahar said. "My men are grumbling about all the digging, to be honest. But we aren't to give the dead any chance to spoil the water."

Vistaren was frowning. "And what of the injured?"

Balahar hesitated. Azmei could tell he either didn't like what he was about to say or that he was afraid the prince wouldn't like it. Perhaps both. "He had the surgeon's school send some of their journeymen. Once we're sure it's safe— some of the rubble is unstable—they'll go to work."

"Who is coordinating the cleanup?" Vistaren asked.

The other man in the room spoke up. "That would be one of my captains, Harjan." He was a Crelin, with Vistaren's olive complexion and blue-black hair, but his hair was cut short. This must be General Orshard.

Vistaren nodded. "How many journeyman surgeons?"

Balahar and Orshard exchanged a glance, and then Orshard cleared his throat. "Four, highness."

"Four!" Vistaren's face twisted into a scowl.

"I'm sorry, highness," Balahar said. "Your father did not make it a priority."

Orshard coughed. "My company surgeon is also with them."

Vistaren turned to Kedar. "How many surgeons came to your county, my lord?" Azmei noticed that he was careful not to identify Kedar or the name of his holdings.

Kedar was frowning, too. "At least twelve. Maybe more." His lips pulled to one side. "I confess, I was not entirely…aware of all the details."

Vistaren nodded, more to himself than anyone else. He was thinking very hard, Azmei thought. She watched his face, wishing she could read his thoughts. "This is a test," he said softly.

Of course! Azmei blinked in dawning understanding and horror. The king was allowing a limited response, testing how devastating the stormweapon's attack had been. He was making an experiment of his own people!

"Highness?" Balahar asked.

Vistaren didn't answer, but looked at Azmei. He saw that she understood. His mouth was tight, grim lines framing his lips.

"But—his own people!" Kedar cried. Azmei looked over at him and realized he had also understood. She didn't have to look behind her to Hawk. She knew he would understand. He had seen the cruelty of war in many ways.

Vistaren shook his head. "This is wrong. All wrong."

Azmei saw Orshard nodding faintly. He had understood as well. The best generals didn't long for war, she knew. They wanted to fight only when they thought it was necessary, and when they could win. And they knew, too, that an unfriendly populace could make their job much more difficult. Besides, how many of his recruits came from fisherfolk, originally? How would they react to this, once they realized what was happening?

Balahar drew himself up. "You would countermand the king?" His voice was stiff.

"The king is *wrong*, Balahar!" Vistaren snapped.

Balahar gave him a hard look. "He is the *king*."

Vistaren nodded and sighed. "Very well. I dislike what I am about to do, but…" He drew his musket from its leather holster and leveled it at Balahar. "I must insist you stay here, Balahar. I cannot have you free to work against me, but I must present my case to General Orshard."

Orshard looked alarmed suddenly. He must not have intended to be so transparent. But Azmei was certain he could be made to see sense.

"Seven damn you!" Balahar spat. "Treason?"

"Pretty much, I suppose," Vistaren said. His tone was apologetic, which somehow fit him, Azmei thought. "My father has not kept faith with the people of Amethir, Balahar. We have clear warnings that we are on a doomed course. We must change or risk the gods' wrath."

"I'll see you in chains," Balahar raged.

Vistaren's voice was pleasant as he said, "I must ask you to *shut up*, General."

Balahar's face got very red, but he shut up.

The alarm on Orshard's face had transformed to thoughtful concern. "Princess," he said, "you agree with this? It was you who brought this prophet to Amethir."

Azmei sighed. "I would not have brought him if I didn't believe him. And I have faith in Prince Vistaren. I can see that he wants what is best for Amethir." Balahar made apoplectic grunts, but she ignored him. "I have seen firsthand how terrible war is. But I can also see the situation here is dire and growing more so. We must take action."

"I have done all I can to persuade my father through nonviolent means," Vistaren said. "I can see no other course forward. He must be convinced by force if necessary."

Orshard looked unhappy, but he did not shy away from it. "Speak plainly, highness. You would depose your father."

"Yes."

Orshard's frown deepened. "Why not wait? You are the only heir. You will be able to change things when you become king in the natural course of things."

"I have been content to wait until now," Vistaren said. "But we do not have time to wait longer. The warnings are clear: the gods are already waking. One has arrived who serves that god we do not name. There is no time, general."

Orshard paled. "You are certain of this?" Azmei watched him take in Vistaren's set face, Hawk's implacable one, Kedar's anger. He could see they were certain.

"This is an attempt by Tamnen to overthrow us!" Balahar burst out.

Azmei, to her own surprise, laughed at him. "General Balahar, Tamnen only just survived her own war. We have no designs of conquest. I am here because I pledged an oath to Amethir."

"An oath that means nothing!" Balahar retorted bitterly. "He won't thank you for it—he won't love you! He loves men!"

Azmei was suddenly aware that Count Kedar had shifted a little, his gaze on Vistaren's face. Thank the gods Vistaren didn't notice, she thought. He was looking calmly at Balahar. After a bare instant, Kedar shifted again, his expression thoughtful.

"This is not about love, Balahar," Azmei said coldly. "I pledged to become Amethir's queen and to aid Vistaren in protecting and governing Amethir. *That* is the vow I keep."

Kedar cleared his throat. "I am certainly not here because I wish Tamnen to rule us, Balahar," he said. "I am here because my village was devastated by a storm out of season. Vistaren sent aid. *Not* the king. Vistaren cares for my people. The king condemned two more villages after mine. I can see clearly which man truly loves my people. And I can assure you, I am not the only fisherlord who will see that."

Recognition dawned on Orshard's face. "Count of Coman." He looked at Vistaren. "You have Algot already."

Vistaren nodded. Azmei prayed that was so, but she had seen the love Lozarr had for Vistaren, and she believed that Vistaren's faith was not misplaced.

"And the fisherlords."

Vistaren's voice was wry. "One fisherlord, anyway."

Orshard straightened and gave a decisive nod. "My prince, command me."

Hawk tied up the protesting Balahar; they would have to guard him at least until they were out of the city. If he tried to interfere, Vistaren would have to kill him, and Azmei could tell he didn't want that. She couldn't bring herself to tell him it would be the wisest course. Balahar was by all accounts a competent commander, as well as loyal. It would be best for the Prince's chances of winning the war if they crippled the other side as much as possible when they left.

She exchanged a look with Hawk; he knew as well as she did that killing Balahar would be the best plan. But over the past weeks he'd taken Vistaren's measure, and Azmei knew that he liked the prince and respected him. She shook her head at Hawk and he shrugged.

"The men should know," Vistaren told Orshard. "I don't want anyone branded a traitor who does not choose it."

Hawk did speak up then. "It isn't a quick thing, getting a company ready to move out."

Orshard was nodding. "With your leave, sire, I say we mobilize my entire brigade and march it out to the plain under guise of an exercise. Once we're clear of the city, I'll explain to the commanders. They can tell the men, and at that point any who wish to leave will be free to return. Balahar will understand that they were only following orders until then."

Balahar glared at him, but they could all see the grudging acknowledgment of Orshard's point.

"Yes, I see." Vistaren paced across the room and looked down at the map of Amethir that was spread on the work table.

"I must go issue the orders if we are to be out of the city before nightfall," Orshard said. "Will you trust me for that?"

Azmei saw Vistaren open his mouth to agree, and she couldn't let him. Orshard seemed to be exactly who he presented himself as, but she had to protect Vistaren.

"I think General Hawk should go with you," she said quickly. "No offense, General Orshard, but this is, as you can see, a delicate matter."

Orshard bowed to her. "Of course, highness." There seemed to be no resentment in his tone. Hawk nodded to her and followed Orshard out the door.

***

Four hours later, the prince's army was on the road, marching out of Maron. Azmei rode a handsome dun gelding at Vistaren's side. She looked over her shoulder, concerned about the length of the column. There were a lot of men in Orshard's brigade. She was grateful for it, but it made it impossible to slip out of the city quietly. Townsfolk lined the side of the streets watching them go.

"How has your father not gotten wind of this?" she asked Vistaren softly.

"I sent him a message that I was showing you the countryside around Maron. He'll expect us to be gone all day. Orshard will have filed records of an exercise on the plain, so if Father notices the troop movements, there will be a clean explanation of it."

Azmei studied Vistaren's face doubtfully. "Will he believe it? That you're showing me the countryside? After last night's events, I mean."

He gave her a rueful look. "I often take to the countryside when I am upset by something. Frequently it is presaged by an argument with my father." His lips twisted. "I spent a whole week out there after the day he told me I was to marry some silly princess I'd never met."

Azmei grinned at him. "I hope I didn't turn out to be too silly."

Vistaren laughed, and she felt a breath of relief that she'd eased his worry a little. She'd seen the weight on his shoulders all day, and although taking action had lessened it somewhat, it had to have added to it in other ways, for other reasons.

Her gaze drifted past Vistaren to where Kedar rode with Hawk. He was watching Azmei and Vistaren, though, an assessing look on his face. Or was it intrigued? She wasn't entirely certain.

"You've earned that one's loyalty," she said, nodding her head in his direction. Kedar saw her looking and glanced away before Vistaren turned.

"I hope so." Vistaren's voice was speculative.

Azmei didn't miss the way his gaze lingered on Kedar's face. She wondered if perhaps he had earned more than Kedar's loyalty today. She hid a smile by leaning down to pat her horse's shoulder. Time would tell, she supposed. And there were more important things to think of right now.

22

Arama was still sitting on the terrace with Yar, watching the sky idly and listening to the raucous cries of the gulls, when Zek appeared, toiling up the path from the launch. Behind him was Carig. Arama frowned and stood, striding to meet them.

"Mister Carig? What's the meaning of this?" He was supposed to be on *Dawn Star* as officer of the watch.

"Beg pardon, mum, but we had a message bird, and it's sealed with red." Carig took off his hat and mopped his brow. With the other hand he held out the message cylinder.

A red seal meant it was urgent. It would have been sent with the fastest bird on hand, and the crew was under orders to get it to her at once. Arama took the cylinder with a muttered thanks and broke the seal.

Captain, I hope my message finds you well. I must make a great request of you. I have broken with my father. He refuses to acknowledge Yarrax's warning. Indeed, he has engaged the services of a weaponized stormwitch and is already gauging her ability to use witchery to kill. I have given up all attempts to persuade him back to the right.

Even now I am marching my army out of Maron. General Orshard's brigade has joined me. General Balahar is currently in our custody. I hope you will consent to be the admiral of my fleet. I have sent a similar message to General Algot, in hopes he will command my army.

If you have Kinnet and Yarrax on board, please take them as far to sea as possible. Keep them safe. Their mission must succeed.
Vistaren

Arama sucked in a breath. Could this be real? But why would anyone forge a message like this? She chewed her lower lip. Lo would join Vistaren, of course. There was no question. She wouldn't willingly side against Lo, but in this case, that wasn't at issue. She had long believed the storm-witches presented a greater danger than advantage. She would side with Vistaren.

She looked at Carig. "Well, Mister Carig. We have a tidy little predicament on our hands."

"Captain?"

"I have just learned that Prince Vistaren has broken with his father. He's raising an army to bring Rekel down."

"Mum!" Carig's exclamation gave no indication of his opinion on the right or wrong of it—just his shock.

Arama nodded. "He wants a navy, too."

Carig's expression cleared as he understood. "Captain, your decisions have always been good enough for me, so long as you honor Lord Antos."

"Good." She looked over at Zek. "And your thoughts?"

"Well, huzzah!" Zek said. "It's been too quiet with only the Strid to fight."

Arama snorted. "As if that wasn't your first battle a fortnight ago."

Zek was unabashed. "Well, captain, I hear talk. This crew's a good one, no doubt. But some of 'em chafe at civility and crown service. I reckon a good number would be happy to turn pirate again. And fighting for the prince will be piracy enough for most of 'em."

Arama nodded. "Best tell them, then." She watched as Carig hurried back down the path to the skiff he'd rowed over. She stayed just long enough to see him shove off, then headed back up the path to the lighthouse. She wasn't surprised when, a few minutes later, she heard a cheer go up from *Dawn Star*'s crew.

Back at the light, she outlined the change in plans for Lijka, Kinnet, and Yar.

Kinnet paled in reaction. "Civil War," she croaked.

Yar frowned. "Nothing civil about war."

"It's an expression, lad," Arama told him, and he shrugged. She looked at the others. "Here's what I'm thinking. His majesty'll know I'll side with Vistaren. He'll try to catch us still in harbor. I don't know how long the news has been out, but I can't take any chances." She propped a fist on her hip. "If you want to seek the stormsingers, we have to sail *now*."

Lijka looked stricken. She turned to look at her wife.

"If the king will not listen," Kinnet said, "we will serve the one who does. Vistaren has earned our aid."

"But treason—" Lijka began, but Kinnet cut her off.

"Yes."

Lijka shook her head. "We shouldn't get involved."

"We are already involved." Kinnet's voice was harsh and too loud. "He is doing this as much because of us as because of Yar."

"My message came after yours," Yar said helpfully.

Lijka had no response to that. She looked back and forth from Kinnet to Arama to Yar and back to Kinnet.

"I think Kinnet and Yar should come with me now. The king doesn't have to know about Kinnet siding with the prince. He won't suspect you, Lijka."

"He might! I should…" Lijka faltered and then looked up. "I should go too."

"No." Kinnet put a hand on Lijka's arm. "We've a duty to this light, and to the sailors who rely on us. Not all of them might side with the king, given the chance."

"And we'll need a spy," Arama put in. "You can keep us informed."

Lijka's expression wavered.

"You haven't time to dither over it," Arama snapped. "We must away."

Clearly not happy with the decision, Lijka nodded anyway. She went inside and fetched Kinnet's half-packed bags. She handed one to Arama and the other to Kinnet, then pressed her lips hard against Kinnet's.

"Come back to me," she said, just loud enough for Arama, already hurrying down the path to the launch, to hear.

Arama had only gone halfway when she met Zek coming up. "Captain, there's a crown ship coming from Maron!"

"Quick!" Arama called to the others, and moved faster down the path, her feet sliding on loose rocks. "Have they seen us?"

"Not sure, mum."

"We need to get away from the light, or we'll implicate Lijka. Run on down and signal *Dawn Star* to pull out and ready guns. We'll just have to row further to board."

"Rig a sail to the launch," Lijka said, following. "I can call wind to push you."

Arama didn't like the idea of relying on a stormwitch, particularly *this* stormwitch, but she nodded. "We'll do it."

****

The activity on *Dawn Star* was frenetic by the time Arama and her companions climbed aboard. Arama tossed Kinnet's bag to a crewman and gestured for him to take the other as well. Then she turned to face Kinnet, who looked surprisingly calm.

"Kinnet. Can you keep that ship from closing with us?"

Kinnet closed her eyes for a moment, lifting her hands palm up. "He's coming too fast," she said. "He has a stormwitch." She opened her eyes and looked at Arama again.

"Damn. All right. I'm not used to doing this with a stormwitch of my own anyway. Can you stay by me and tell me if there's ever anything you can do to help?"

Kinnet nodded.

"Yar," Arama said. "I want you belowdecks. Can't lose our prophet."

"I'm no prophet," Yar said.

"Close enough. Go on, get below."

He allowed himself to be shooed away with alacrity. Arama remembered what he'd told her about the battle with the seadragon. He'd hated it, all the booming and the pained screams of the seadragon echoing in his head. At least there were no seadragons this time, Arama thought.

She *hoped* there were no seadragons this time.

They got underway. There was enough of a breeze to fill the sails naturally, and Kinnet coaxed it along, just enough to make maneuvering easy. Arama saw Carig slip away to the stern and throw something over the railing; he must have prepared an offering as soon as he learned they were siding with Vistaren.

They had almost made it out of the harbor when the crown ship caught up with them. A single gun boomed, echoing across the surface. A plume of water spewed into the sky, well short of *Dawn Star*. She was signaling *Dawn Star* to heave to. Did she know Arama had turned her coat?

Arama sighed. "Damn. I'd hoped to avoid this." She lifted her spyglass to her eye, trying to make out the ship's paint.

"*Celerity*," she muttered, when she had it. "Captain Forcyte. He'll be aggressive, but he relies too much on speed and not enough on well-drilled gunners."

Beside her, Zek nodded.

"The crew was unanimous in supporting our defection to the prince?" she asked, not taking her gaze off *Celerity*.

"Yes, captain. One man expressed a bit of reluctance, but when I told him we'd set him ashore here and let him walk back, he said that wasn't what he'd meant."

"Who was it?" *Celerity* was still out of range. *Dawn Star's* gunners were ready to fire as soon as they could. She wanted them firing broadsides—the mental effect of having shot booming at you, all the enemy's cannons belching smoke at once, was nothing to be scoffed at. *Celerity's* crew might be good, but they were ships of the line, not privateers. They'd likely never seen action before.

"Gratt, mum. But he said he'd sail with you wherever you sail, and I think he meant it. He was just nervy."

Arama grunted. Gratt had an old mother at home that he supported. He'd worry about her, and what the crown would do if he turned traitor. She made a mental note to ask Vistaren to safeguard the old woman if possible.

She lowered her glass. "All right. Looks like *Celerity's* almost in range. Get the ship's carpenter below, ready to patch us up. I want the men firing broadsides. Aim for the sails first, but if we can get position on them, let's try to take out her rudder. I'll sink her if I have to, but it'd be a shame. She's a lovely lady."

"Aye, captain." Zek strode off, shouting orders. Arama slid her glass into its leather case at her hip and drew her pistol to check it. She already knew her cutlass was keen and ready.

Would Forcyte try to sink *Dawn Star* or just try to force her to heave to? He ought to know she wouldn't. Arama would take *Dawn Star* to the bottom of the harbor with her if necessary. She'd always expected the sea to kill her, after all.

Lo's brown, honest face flashed into her thoughts. "Siren's teeth," she growled. She couldn't die. Lo would never forgive her.

All the same, she'd be damned if she would surrender her ship. "Mister Zek!" she shouted. "Strike that Amethirian flag! I want my Storm Petrel the only banner flying!"

"Storm Petrel up, aye!" he shouted back, with such enthusiasm that Arama wondered if he'd been itching for piracy the whole time he'd been sailing with her.

The crew cheered as they saw the Amethirian flag slip down to the deck. As the black banner, a gray bird soaring across it, rose, Arama drew in a deep breath. Was she ready for this? Was her crew ready for this? Was she, gods help her, going to be firing the first shot of the war?

Too late to worry about that. She was a pirate, by the gods. She bared her teeth and sucked the wind through them. Then she shouted with all her strength.

"Fire!"

Six guns boomed in concert, smoke billowing from their muzzles. Her gunners were already wheeling the cannon back in place from the recoil, ready for swabbing and worming and reloading. Turning, Arama caught sight of Carig's face, stretched in a grin.

Celerity's fore-topsail groaned and toppled. Arama heard a cheer from someone in the fighting top, but a moment later it was drowned out by the roar of a second volley. Arama mentally calculated the distance from the mouth of Maron Harbor back to the city. The sound probably wouldn't travel so far, but some of the coastal villages would know about it.

"Fire at will!" Arama shouted, and heard Zek echo the order. Her crew had practiced with the guns until they could reload and fire in just over a minute, but she knew the process would take longer with each successive shot. Fatigue would set in, and they were operating at a small crew, so any injury would slow them further.

She was aware of wooden splinters pattering against the deck around her, of the acrid sting of gunpowder in her nostrils. She knew she was grinning manically, her eyes narrowed against the smoke. She knew she was firing against men who had, just a day ago—just a glass ago—had been her allies. Men who were still her countrymen.

In this moment, the only thing that mattered was seeing the *Celerity* strike her colors.

"Captain!" It took a moment for Arama to realize the voice shouting at her was Carig's. She turned slowly away from the action, only to see him gesturing emphatically at something fine on the starboard quarter. She swung around and realized they were being driven towards the Blades— sharp, deadly limestone shoals that rose like knives from the surface of the headland north of Maron Harbor. Any ship that found itself on the Blades was in for a watery grave.

"Hard to port!" Arama screamed, grabbing at a line for stability.

Dawn Star seemed to come about slowly, guns still firing. Arama's thoughts raced. Could she lure *Celerity* onto the Blades? Captain Forcyte's ship was good, but she knew him for a cautious sailor near the shoals. She'd taken *Dawn Star* in close dozens of times to make a fast run.

Her gunners were slowing. Arama straightened and crossed the quarterdeck to Carig. "We're going to push them on the Blades," she said. "Bring us about like we're preparing to run. I'll have Kinnet fill our sails."

She looked at the stormwitch, who stood near the tiller. Kinnet was watching Arama's face and nodded.

"I can do that."

Arama grinned. "Can you blow some of the smoke back at them while you're at it?"

Kinnet's brows drew together and she closed her eyes. She twisted one hand in the air and opened her eyes, nodding. "I can."

"Excellent. See to it, Mister Carig." She dashed along the deck to Zek.

"Captain?"

"Keep them firing. We're going to turn and lure them on."

His head swiveled as he took in their position. "Keep firing, aye," he repeated.

She could imagine the cheers that went up as *Dawn Star* began to turn. It hurt her pride to let anyone think they'd scared her off, but if this worked…

No. She could see almost at once that Forcyte had realized his peril. *Celerity* held back instead of giving chase. The guns redoubled their firing.

"Damn!" Running back to the quarterdeck, she waved for Kinnet to let the wind drop off. "He didn't fall for it. We'll have to swing back around and rake her again."

"Course he didn't fall for it, mum," Carig said, grinning at her as he pushed the tiller back amidships. "F'it was anyone else but you, mayhap, but the Storm Petrel doesn't turn tail after a fight this short."

Arama snorted, but she grinned back at him. By the gods, she shouldn't be enjoying this, should she? Those were Amethirian sailors in that ship. They might not even know why *Dawn Star* had attacked them, aside from the fact she had piracy in her blood. Had Vistaren even declared himself yet? Did the rest of the kingdom know they were at war?

"Captain!" Zek was at the ladder to the quarterdeck. "I think they've struck their colors."

Arama jerked her glass up and strained to see through the smoke. "No," she decided. "They've been shot away, that's all. Don't ease up."

"Aye, Captain!"

The next volley sent a cannonball skipping across *Celerity*'s deck, tearing through the personnel manning her guns. Arama thought she could hear the screams of the injured over the noise of the guns. Should they close and board? But *Celerity*'s full complement was at least a score more men than she had. Even with the casualties they'd inflicted, there was a good chance *Dawn Star* would come out the worse in that exchange.

She glared across the water at the crown ship. Was it listing to port? She lifted her glass again. Yes, it was definitely listing.

"She's taking on water!" she screamed. "Hold your fire!"

The guns roared as she gave the order, so she had to repeat herself. As Zek called the order back to her, she could see him squinting at *Celerity*. Arama's feet thumped across the deck as she went to stand beside him.

"We've sunk her, haven't we, Captain?" he whispered, still staring at the other ship.

"Aye, Zek, I think we have." She spread her feet and propped her fists against her hips, watching as *Celerity* tilted further, exposing more and more of her hull to Arama's gaze.

Siren's teeth, she'd sunk *Celerity*. Arama's stomach twisted suddenly. What had she done? She watched the mast crash down into the waves, her lips parted in horror—or was it awe? Her kicking pulse struggled against her churning stomach until she couldn't tell what she felt anymore.

Dawn Star's crew raised a cheer that seemed louder than

any she'd ever heard them give, Zek leading them in the triumphant, "Huzzah! Huzzah! Huzzah!"

Arama swallowed against a strange thickness in her throat and strode back to the quarterdeck. "Mister Carig! Set course for the open sea!"

"Aye, mum!" His expression must match hers; his eyes sad, his gaze terrible, his lips twisted into a strange half-grin.

Arama spun on her heel, striving for an expression of fierce triumph as she faced her crew. "Fine fighting, lads!" she bellowed. "We've given them cause to fear the Storm Petrel and her crew!"

She turned away from the cheer that followed.

23

Lozarr stood in the door of Anderly's last remaining pub, arms folded across his chest as he watched his soldiers and Anderly's citizens working alongside one another. They had rebuilt two of the inns first and then moved on to demolishing the houses that had received the worst damage. Another group of soldiers labored to mend sails, their fingers clumsy compared to how an Anderly widow's fingers flew across the canvas as she demonstrated.

The surgeons had succeeded in driving out most of the sickness. The chief surgeon had said it had something to do with contaminated water, and once Lozarr had learned how to correct the situation, he'd stopped listening to details. How long had they been here now? Lo pondered briefly. It had been nearly a month, he thought. No, three weeks. He'd been gone from the capital a month.

"General!"

Lo turned to see Anmeir approaching from the direction of the camp. Anmeir had recovered from his initial shock at the destruction and had been one of the first of the soldiers to reach across the divide to earn the villagers' trust. Of course, Lo thought wryly, it didn't hurt that he'd been so helpful to Mirzana Ebb.

"Sir," Anmeir said, "a message for you. Red seal."

Lozarr's brows drew together as he reached for the message tube. The emblem on the seal was Vistaren's. What could be so urgent that he used the red? Lo broke open the tube and unrolled the paper inside.

He scanned the words quickly, feeling his mouth go dry. He went back to the top of the paper and read the words again. They didn't change. His heart began pounding in his chest, and suddenly his legs felt shaky. "Gods witness," he whispered.

"Sir?"

Lo stumbled a few steps sideways and dropped onto the rough-hewn bench that stood next to the pub door. He stared into the distance to the north, wishing he could see across all the scores of miles to the capital.

"Sir!" Anmeir lunged as if trying to catch him, then stopped and stared at him, arm outstretched.

With effort, Lozarr focused his gaze on Anmeir's face. He opened his mouth, hesitated, and then closed it again. How—what—There was no way to break this news gently. "I…gods, Anmeir." His voice cracked. He cleared his throat and tried again. "This letter is from Vistaren."

"Is he well?" Anmeir dropped his arm to his side. "Is it the king?"

Lozarr shook his head, fumbling for words.

"Are we under attack?" Anmeir persisted. "The Shroudlings!"

Lo held up a hand for silence, shaking his head. "No. Gods, no." That put it in some perspective, at least. "No, Anmeir. I am not sure if this news is better or worse than the possibilities you suggest." He sighed heavily and rubbed at his eyes.

"Wait, sir." Anmeir darted into the pub and came back with a hand-carved wooden cup. Whiskey fumes wafted up from it.

Lo took a single gulp and exhaled. "We *are* at war, though. There's no easy way to say this." He looked up at Anmeir, still hovering over him, his brows furrowed in concern. "The prince has rebelled against King Rekel."

Anmeir stared at him. "And the *prince* wrote to tell you that?"

Lo took a much smaller sip of his whiskey. "He has asked me to command his army."

Anmeir blinked. "Why?"

That gave Lo pause. He looked at Anmeir for a moment and finally said, "Well, the prince and I have been friends for—"

"Beg pardon, sir, that's not what I meant." Anmeir glanced at the glass in Lo's hand—somewhat wistfully, Lo thought—and said, "Why did the prince rebel?"

Lo held out the cup, studying Anmeir's face. Anmeir was a good man for all his youth. Would he try to arrest Lo? Or was he more curious than patriotic? Lo sighed.

"His father has honored a stormwitch who weaponized her magic. She sent an anomaly-strength storm into the towns of Jorey and Harkenerth." He licked his lips. "There are hundreds dead."

"Jorey and—" Anmeir broke off and drained the cup. "I don't understand, sir. You mean the king *deliberately* created two more villages like Anderly?" His lips twisted and he clenched his jaw.

On a moment's reflection, Lozarr should have expected this reaction from Anmeir. "The storm was heading straight for Maron, apparently. She turned it. Sent it south, aiming it at the fishing camps." He fought to keep his lip from curling. "She calls herself a stormweapon."

"And the prince protested, of course." Anmeir nodded as if to himself.

Lozarr nodded, too. "Princess Azmei has sided with the prince...and so has Lord Kedar."

"Mirzana's brother rebelled?" Anmeir straightened.

Lo rubbed his forehead and pinched the bridge of his nose, where he could feel the first blossom of a headache. "I did say I thought he might," he murmured.

"And Captain Dzornaea?"

Lo felt his cheeks heat. He had done his best to be circumspect, but Anmeir was sharp-eyed and clever. If he hadn't already figured out Lo's relationship with Arama before Anderly, he had certainly figured it out after last week. "She'll join Vistaren," he said quietly.

So would Lo. There was no question. He'd seen the

prince grow from an awkward, self-conscious lad uncomfortable with the fact he loved men. Now Vistaren was a knowledgeable, compassionate young man who was still struggling, perhaps, to accept himself as he was, but was at least wise enough to recognize the things he couldn't change. On top of that, Vistaren was right—they shouldn't weaponize magic, not when they had no need to. And they *absolutely* shouldn't use weaponized magic against their own people.

Anmeir gave a decisive nod. "We'd best tell the men, hadn't we, sir? And…and Mirzana."

Lo blinked. "Tell them?"

Anmeir shrugged. "So they can decide if they'll follow us or side with the king."

Lo's mouth dropped open. Then he shook his head. "Anmeir…" It would be the end of the man's career.

"Well, you can't do without me, can you, sir?" He grinned faintly. "If you've told me that once, you've said it a hundred times."

Lo just stared at him, unable to form a sentence.

"So I'd better just go with you," Anmeir said, his grin turning sheepish.

"You'd better…" Lo trailed off. "Anmeir, this is *treason*."

Anmeir nodded. "All the more reason you need me, sir. It's not as if treason comes naturally to you."

Lo choked a laugh. "Gods witness. I'd have to be a fool not to take you up on that offer. But still—are you sure?"

Anmeir's grin had disappeared entirely. "Sir, one Anderly was bad enough," he said, and the hand he lifted to wipe his forehead shook a little. "If the king's doing it to more villages…and *on purpose*!" He shook his head. "No, sir. I know what side I'm on."

24

Vistaren thought a prince who had just rebelled ought to be doing something more important than drinking coffee in front of a tent, but General Orshard had assured him that war was full of moments like this. "Hurry up and wait," he'd called it, and Hawk had laughed when he'd said it, so Vistaren supposed it was true.

All the same, he felt useless. What would his men think of a prince who cared more about his breakfast than about actually doing something?

They'd marched out west of the city. Just before they crossed the Gehb River, General Orshard had informed his men that their drill was actually a rebellion. He laid out Vistaren's reasons in bare terms. They had lost far fewer soldiers than Vistaren had feared. Apparently his cause rang true with the common soldier.

"You're fidgeting this morning." Azmei sounded much more awake than he felt. She had both hands curled around her coffee and was standing with her back to the fire.

"Sorry," he mumbled. He looked down into the murky brown liquid and wondered why he had thought this was a good idea.

Well. It wasn't a good idea. But it was the only idea that seemed valid. He took a deep breath and sat up a little straighter. He might not like the situation, but there was no need to punish the others.

"My lord prince." He looked up to see Orshard had returned.

Vistaren nodded to the pot of coffee that heated over the fire. "Help yourself, general. What is our situation?"

Orshard smiled. He looked like he was enjoying him-self. "Well, sir. We're well situated. I've got them drilling at the moment. Might as well make use of the time to keep them sharp. We carried with us supplies enough to feed them for several weeks, though we'll have to supplement that as much as possible by buying up local stores."

Vistaren nodded. "Won't my father punish them for selling to us?"

"We can hope not, highness. It would be bad policy."

"Good strategy, though," Hawk put in.

Orshard frowned at Hawk. "Yes, good strategy, certain-ly, if he wants to have no one to feed the crown soldiers as well."

"Peace, Orshard," Vistaren said. "General Hawk is an experienced veteran of the wars in the Kreyden District."

Orshard's brow cleared. "Oh, well. That sort of strategy makes sense over there. How long has that war been going on now, Hawk?"

"Too long," Azmei put in. "But the point stands. The king will likely not employ such strategy so early in our rebel-lion. It would create more unrest among the citizenry."

"Aye. For that matter, it would probably push more of them to join our cause than the king's." Orshard scratched his jaw. "Having more on our side wouldn't be a bad thing. I don't like our odds if General Balahar commits all his re-sources to defeating us while we stand here."

"Would it be better if we retreated?" Vistaren asked, his voice sharp. "It's obvious why we had to leave the city, but if we march off out of sight of the city, won't we look like we're running away?"

Hawk lifted a shoulder. "We have a good situation here, but we'd be better off behind fortifications. There's little enough to do here. We could throw up earthworks, but…"

"Agreed," Orshard said. "I'd feel better if we had a for-tress to protect, highness."

Vistaren frowned. They couldn't exactly build some-thing in a day, so he would have to think about what fortresses might best suit their need, and then wonder if he could persuade the soldiers manning the fort to join him—or if his army could take it. "I'll think on it," he said.

Orshard nodded. "In the meantime, highness, there are my men in Jorey and Harkenerth. I know my officers. A lot of them would join."

Vistaren shook his head. "They're needed where they are."

"My lord, I have four hundred soldiers committed in Jorey and Harkenerth."

"Who are doing what they can to mitigate suffering!" Vistaren snapped. "I had you avoid the fishing camps for that very reason—to allow relief work to continue uninterrupted."

"Yes, sir." Orshard sounded unhappy about that.

"Let me be clear with you, Orshard," Vistaren said. He stood, looking around and raising his voice to catch the attention of those working nearby. "Let me be clear with all of you. Captains, sergeants, soldiers. This is not my play for personal power. I am not impatient to be king. But my father has broken faith with the people of Amethir. I cannot allow that to stand. I have begun this war to protect our people. People like those in Jorey and Harkenerth. Whatever decisions we make militarily must take that into consideration."

Orshard nodded crisply as the soldiers nearby cheered.

Azmei had come to stand next to Vistaren. She spoke in a low voice. "People get hurt in war. Innocent people."

"Damn it, I know that," Vistaren growled. "But I will do what I can to mitigate that whenever possible."

Azmei smiled at him. He thought her golden eyes looked sad, but her expression was approving. Vistaren looked back down at his coffee, feeling just a little better.

He had just poured his second cup of coffee when the shouting began. First at the eastern edge of camp, and then drawing closer. General Orshard looked up from the map he had been studying just as a scout burst into their circle, breathing hard.

"General, sir—crown soldiers!" He bent over and propped his hands on his knees.

"How far?"

"They're still marching out of the city, sir. They're coming in our direction, though."

Vistaren thought about that. They'd chosen the high ground about five miles outside the city as their camp. It would take the crown's troops a while to get to them. How far had this scout run?

"Balahar's men?" Orshard asked.

"Yes, sir. There's a messenger riding ahead, looks like. He bears the truce flag, and he's just got a guard of two musketeers."

Vistaren nodded. "We'll make no terms, general."

"No, my lord." Orshard bowed and strode away.

"Bring my horse."

The rest of the camp burst into activity. Orshard was everywhere, issuing orders. A man brought horses for Vistaren, Hawk, and Azmei. They rode slowly through the camp, watching the soldiers prepare for battle.

"We need to assign you guards," Azmei said. "A regular rotation. I'm not enough."

Vistaren snorted, but nodded. His gaze was fixed on a man who was approaching, a white pennant fluttering from the pole he carried.

Hawk rode forward to intercept the messenger, who stopped where he was. He and Hawk exchanged a few words, the messenger shook his head, and Hawk backed his horse a few steps.

"The king sends this word to his son," the messenger called. "Surrender, and our merciful king will pardon everyone below the rank of general. He will not punish those who have been led astray."

Vistaren nudged his horse a few steps closer and raised his voice. "My father knows why we fight," he called. "There will be no surrender."

The cheer that broke out went on far longer than Vistaren had expected it to. He and the messenger locked eyes, and Vistaren recognized Itotia Avidius. Odd, that the chancellor had felt it necessary to come himself. Perhaps to assure his father that Vistaren was, in truth, rebelling. Whatever the reason, Vistaren nodded to Avidius. Avidius nodded in return and wheeled his horse around.

The men drew up into battle lines as Avidius cantered back to the crown army, which was cresting a small rise. Vistaren could see some of Orshard's men setting themselves at an oblique angle from the rest, infantry in front, screening the musketeers.

"They've given us plenty of time to set up the artillery," he remarked.

"They're testing us," Orshard said, riding up in time to hear that. "They won't fully commit today, I judge. Balahar wants to see if my resolve is as great as his."

Vistaren nodded. "What's our plan?"

"The infantry will screen the musketeers, giving them time to shoot. We have the cannon in position at the center of our line, there." Orshard pointed. "The cannon will hopefully shatter Balahar's formations, and once they're in disarray, we deploy the pikemen."

"Where do you want me?" Vistaren said.

"You can't be in the front," Azmei said quickly.

Vistaren glared at her. "I won't be seen as a coward."

"I don't see your father on that field," Hawk said, his voice mild. "For that matter, General Orshard will be directing the battle from back here. These soldiers are professionals, Prince Vistaren. They know their business. There is no need for a prince on the field."

Orshard was nodding. "Feel free to observe from here, my prince, but I must agree with Hawk. No closer than this, if you please." He saluted and rode away.

Vistaren, watching him go, sighed. "Would you be willing to stay by me as an advisor, Hawk? I will give you a command if you wish one, but clearly I am in need of your guidance."

When he looked back at his companions, Azmei was grinning. "One true mark of a good leader is his ability to recognize a man's talents and let him use them."

Vistaren huffed a laugh. "I take it you approve."

Hawk's smile was bright in his brown face. "I will be pleased to offer what advice I may, highness."

Vistaren nodded. "My thanks."

***

The battle took less than two glasses, all told. Even Vistaren could see that Balahar was only testing them. He sent his men forward against the left flank and the right. Hawk explained that the oblique angle of the men was to provide enfilade fire along the enemy's line, thereby discouraging Balahar's troops from getting too close. In the meantime, Orshard's artillery pounded into Balahar's formations.

"He won't charge up the center, will he?" Vistaren said.

"He'd be mad to charge in the face of those cannons," Hawk assured him. "Perhaps if this weren't the first battle of the war. But he's just taking stock. Remember, he's fighting troops that he knows. He has some idea of their ability, but not how they'll use it when they're fighting against him and not for him."

Vistaren nodded. "Where are the cavalry?" he asked after a while. "I haven't seen them on the field."

Hawk grinned briefly. "That's because Orshard has another job for them. They'll have been riding around to flank Balahar's troops. Don't worry, we'll hear from them soon enough."

And they did. Half a glass later a high-pitched keening erupted from somewhere to the enemy's right flank. Vistaren turned to stare in that direction. They didn't have long to wait. A well-organized mass of horsemen, some five hundred strong, was sweeping down a long slope towards Balahar's flank. Balahar's troops hastily began turning and forming up, but it was a ragged effort. The cavalry crashed in among them, sabers gleaming, and Balahar's flank crumpled.

Wild cheering broke out around Vistaren. He realized he was cheering, too, when he looked at Azmei and found her mouth wide open. She nodded at him and kept shouting.

We've won, he realized. He stared at Balahar's troops, who had dissolved into a rout. *The first battle of the war and we've won it.*

What would his father do when he learned of this? What did a victory mean? *We only won because they thought we wouldn't be prepared*, Vistaren thought. But he kept cheering anyway, watching the enemy's rout slowly organize itself into a more orderly retreat. Orshard's cavalry kept moving, chivvying them on. Would the king's troops retreat all the way to the capital?

"We'll have a celebration," he told Azmei as they rode back to their camp. "Not a big one, but the men must know I am grateful."

She nodded. "I'm sure Orshard will arrange it."

As the sun sank into the west, Vistaren stood in front of the assembled troops. He knew they wouldn't all hear him, but hopefully his words would be reported throughout the camp. He wanted to be certain to praise them well and keep up their morale. He might not be allowed to fight, but he could certainly speak to them.

"Companions!" he shouted, smiling at them. "Already you reward my faith in you, as I knew you would! Today was well-fought!"

Cheers erupted around him. He paused, waiting for it to die down.

"You have been told, I hope, why we rebel. But I wish to make it clear to every man and woman who fights with me. Let me speak plainly. I believe that Amethir's finest strength is her people. Her tradesmen, her fisherfolk, her farmers—and her soldiers."

More cheers. He let his smile slip into a grin for a moment, then reined in his expression.

"I believe the royal family has an obligation—nay, call it a *sacred duty*—to the fine people of Amethir. We must protect you, respect you. We must remember that you are the lifeblood of our kingdom." He paused, looking around, and let the smile slip from his face entirely. "And we must *never* hold that lifeblood cheap."

No cheers now. He'd caught their attention.

Vistaren drew in a deep breath. He was about to lie to them—or at least twist the truth a bit. But it was necessary. They didn't know his father as he did, and they didn't know the nuances of court as he did. He would simplify matters for them, and hope that didn't come back around to bite him.

"My father commanded a stormwitch to send the storm into Jorey and Harkenerth," he said. "He deliberately spilled some of our precious lifeblood to avoid harm to himself. He sacrificed hundreds of folk in cottages of wood and thatch out of fear for his stone palace."

There was murmuring as the meaning of his words hit them. Vistaren raised his hand for silence.

"I will not pretend that I did not benefit from my father's decision. I and all who stand here with me were at the palace. We were celebrating my betrothal to this lady, Princess Azmei of Tamnen." He paused as Azmei lifted her hand in acknowledgment.

"But I swear to you," he continued, "I would rather we had suffered the storm than allowed our people to die for our betrothal ball. Instead, my father sacrificed two fishing villages." Vistaren sucked in a breath, preparing for more lies.

"This was part of my father's plan to weaponize stormwitchery. My father wishes to use the blessings of our unique magic to wage war—and he is not doing it against our enemies, no! He is waging war on the people of Jorey and Harkenerth!"

The murmurings grew into a rumble. *Forgive me for mis-*

leading them, Vistaren thought. His father had not made the initial attack, had not drawn up plans for this. But he was happy to exploit these events, and if no plans had existed a week ago, they certainly did now or would soon.

"You may have noticed we do not have with us those soldiers who were assigned to Jorey and Harkenerth. It is not because they refuse to join us, but because I have not asked." Vistaren's throat felt dry. He fought the urge to cough. "We will not win our war at the expense of our people! We will not win our war at the expense of Jorey and Harkenerth!"

"And that's why we'll win!" someone shouted back.

Mad cheering erupted at that. Vistaren raised both of his hands, holding them out to his people. He smiled at them, hoping he looked benign and charismatic. Hoping he didn't look like a liar. Was it wrong to lie to them in service of good? Probably. Would he do it again? Probably.

"Now!" he shouted. "Companions! Celebrate our victory with me!"

The cheering turned into a roar, and Vistaren, smiling, stepped down from the table where he had been standing. He smiled at everyone around him, hoping Azmei wouldn't take him to task for the way he had twisted the events of their betrothal ball.

But she was beside him, cheering as well, and Hawk and Orshard with her. They gave him approving smiles and walked with him as he passed through the crowd, greeting his soldiers and allowing himself to be touched by them. The light pressure of fingertips against his shoulders and elbows seemed to buoy him up as he walked back to his tent.

Once he was allowed to escape the general celebrations, Vistaren let Isden settle him with a meal and some wine. Azmei and Hawk had joined him, and Orshard had come in long enough to share a glass of wine with the prince, but had left again, citing his need to work.

They had finished their meal and were sitting in the front chamber of Vistaren's tent. It was hot in the tent, but

Vistaren didn't want the entry flaps open. He couldn't shut out the sounds of celebration, but he didn't want to join in them.

Azmei sighed. "I wonder if this is how people felt at the beginning in Kreyden."

"You celebrate every victory won honorably," Hawk said softly.

Vistaren looked over at her. The lanterns were turned low, making shadows flicker across her face. "I'm sorry if I've made things difficult for you, Azmei."

She shook her head. "You know I'm with you. I don't love war. I worship a god of peace. But I can see when war is necessary."

Vistaren nodded. "My father has to learn that I am serious about this."

"I daresay he's realized it after today," Hawk said, his voice light.

They were silent for a time, listening to the cheerful voices and singing from outside. The men were heartened by their victory, and Vistaren didn't grudge them that. He only hoped it didn't make them overconfident in their next engagement.

He couldn't wait for Lozarr to join them. He trusted Orshard, and he knew him for a competent general, but Lozarr was his friend. Lozarr wouldn't lead him astray. By now, Lo should have received the letter Vistaren sent, outlining his cause and what actions he had taken. Hopefully Lo would already be on his way to join them.

Where would Kedar Ebb meet up with Lo's army, Vistaren wondered. They'd parted in the stable yesterday, Vistaren going with the army west of Maron, Kedar riding one of Vistaren's horses south to Anderly.

Vistaren sipped his wine. "Where do you suppose Kedar is by now?"

Hawk and Azmei stirred, turning to look at him.

"He left when we did?" Hawk said. "He could have gone seventy miles or so by now, if you gave him a good horse and good advice."

Seventy miles. And it was another forty or so further to Anderly, Vistaren thought. "I commandeered what my groom said was the best horse for such a ride," he said, and then grinned. "And I asked the groom for advice. I knew I wasn't up to giving it myself."

Hawk nodded. "Then I imagine Kedar will arrive back at his village safely. He'll bring you more troops, no doubt of that."

25

"General." Someone shook him. Lo squeezed his eyes tighter. Hadn't he just laid down a few minutes ago? "General. You've a visitor."

Lo sighed and sat up, squinting against the lantern light to see Anmeir. "What is it?"

"Count Kedar, sir."

That opened Lo's eyes. The count had been in the capital with Arama. Did he have news? Lo left his camp bed and began dressing.

"What time is it?"

"Near midnight, sir."

"Go tell him I'll be out. See to his needs."

Anmeir went to the outer chamber of the tent. Lo could hear low voices speaking as he shoved his feet into his boots. He stepped out a minute after Anmeir.

"Count Kedar!" he exclaimed, shocked by the man's appearance. He was swaying slightly on his feet, dark stubble covering his jaw. "Is all well? Captain Dzornaea—"

"Had a different task for the prince," Kedar interrupted-ed.

"Sit down, please," Lo urged, and waited until Kedar had lowered himself to a camp stool.

"I'm here to rally my folk and bring you to join Vistaren," Kedar said, accepting a steaming mug that Anmeir brought in.

Lo nodded. "Then you're going back with us, rather than staying here in Anderly?"

After a long sip, Kedar lowered his mug. "Mirzana can run County Coman as well as I, if not better. I'll be more use to Vistaren if I'm there, as I see it."

Anmeir pressed a bowl of porridge into the count's hands, and the count set to with enthusiasm. Lo watched him gobble the food, wondering how long Kedar had been riding. Had the man not even stopped to eat or rest? When had he left Maron?

The questions could wait until Kedar was sated, though. Anmeir came back with half a loaf of bread and more porridge, and refilled Kedar's cup. Finally, the count slowed and looked around.

"My horse is spent—" he began.

"I had a man care for it, my lord," Anmeir interrupted.

Kedar nodded his thanks and looked at Lo. "It doesn't look like you're striking camp, general."

Lo shrugged. "Your sister had requests for us to finish repairing the docks and boats. I could not leave your folk unable to feed themselves."

Kedar gave him a faint smile. "You see? I might've come here and ridden immediately to join him." He sipped his cup and set it aside.

"I cannot fault a man for esteeming the prince so highly," Lozarr said, meaning to be kind.

He wondered if he had failed when Kedar flushed. Or perhaps it was a trick of the light, Lo decided, as Kedar ducked his head. "I can fault myself," the count said, "for allowing my emotions to rule me, as I have done. The prince said I had offended his father mortally."

Lo had feared that very thing. Vistaren hadn't mentioned Kedar in his letter, but Lo knew they must have arrived in Maron by the time Vistaren rebelled. "I hope, my lord, that you were not the instigator of this rebellion," he ventured.

Kedar jerked his head up to glare at Lo. "General, I knew nothing of it until Vistaren came to me and asked me to join." He paused, obviously struggling to regain his temper, and finally shrugged. "Indeed," he went on in a lighter tone, "he had me locked in my rooms up til then."

Lozarr stared at him, and that made Kedar smile faintly.

"To protect me from wandering back into the king's notice. Or charging headlong, perhaps."

Lo snorted in amusement. "Vistaren must like you. Good job winning him over. I don't relish the reality of civil war, but I honor the prince for acting on his convictions. Your village's plight clearly spoke to him in a deep way."

Kedar nodded absently, looking around the tent. "How close are you to fulfilling my sister's requests?"

"We'll finish tomorrow."

"And ride out the next day?"

Lo shook his head. "I judge the work will be done before the noon meal. We'll make a start after. An entire brigade can't travel as fast, my lord, as you must have done."

Kedar frowned. "I was two days coming from Maron."

Vistaren must have given the count a fine horse, for him to have made the journey so quickly. Lozarr nodded. "And we'll be four. Perhaps five. I don't want to arrive with my soldiers too tired to fight."

Kedar blinked and then nodded in understanding. He stood, swaying. "Very well. I'll spend the night in the manor, if you will lend me a horse to get there. I must speak with my sister, and there are legal steps I must take to designate my sister as my heir. I'll be back here before midday to join you."

"Let me send Anmeir with you, my lord," Lo urged. He didn't want the count collapsing on the way up to the manor.

Kedar nodded. "Thank you."

***

Yar was draped over the railing of the *Dawn Star*, watching a huge sea bird swooping over the swells. He wasn't certain how far they'd come, but they'd been sailing four days since the battle by the lighthouse.

You're dwelling on that again, Xellax murmured in his head. *Let it go, dearheart. It is done.*

"I didn't like the noise," Yar mumbled. Though at least there had been no seadragons this time. Nothing had been forced into hurting when it didn't want to.

That is what we attempt to stop. We hope that our singing cousins will know what has caused this. We may be able to make plans.

"I hope so," he whispered.

"Is all well, sir?" said a man's voice. Yar looked up and saw Mister Zek, a friendly man a little older than Azmei. He knew Zek was one of the ship's officers, but he couldn't remember which. Yar liked him.

"As well as I could expect," Yar replied.

Zek nodded. "Mistress Kinnet sent me to find you, sir. She said you'd know why."

Yar straightened, his heart thumping hard in his chest. She'd felt the singer, hadn't she? "Yes," he said, flashing a smile at Zek.

"Very good, sir. She's at the bow."

Yar trotted along the deck, dodging sailors and hopping deftly over the ropes. If he weren't tied to creatures of the air, he thought he might have liked being a sailor. Boats were nice.

Kinnet was standing at the bow, looking out over the water. "There you are," she said when Yar let his elbow nudge hers.

He grinned at her, and she grinned back. "It's time," she said. "He's coming. Look!"

She pointed out ahead of them. Yar looked and then flinched. A swarm of huge, serpentine creatures was swimming fast at the ship. Blue, red, and gold scales flashed in the sun.

"Seadragons!" he blurted. But Kinnet's hand was squeezing his upper arm.

"Look further. Behind them."

He strained, and he could see more huge figures, but these were bulkier. They weren't swimming as fast as the seadragons, but Yar could feel some power pulsing off them.

"The stormsingers are driving the seadragons ahead of

them," Kinnet said. Yar found her unmelodious voice fascinating. He knew she couldn't hear herself when she spoke, but her words were clear and spoken without inflection. He enjoyed listening to her.

"How?" he asked, turning his head so she could see his lips.

"With their songs. I don't understand exactly. They're so powerful."

He knew the seadragons were powerful, but he thought she meant the stormsingers. They must be creatures of immense power, if they were able to drive seadragons ahead of them. The seadragons swerved wide of the *Dawn Star* and soon they were only specks in the distance. But in the meantime, the *Dawn Star* had been surrounded by the bulky creatures. They spouted water into the air and slapped the water with their tails.

"He is here," Kinnet said as Arama came up to them. "His mate and child are not. They're somewhere safe. He brought only the males and childless females of his pod."

"Why is that?" Yar asked, just as Arama said, "They won't hit the ship, will they?"

Kinnet grinned at her. "No. But they wish me to take the Voice to them in your little boat."

"The launch?" Arama said.

Kinnet nodded.

"We're on the high seas, Kinnet!"

"They will let no harm come to us," Kinnet said, her expression peaceful. "They wish to touch him."

"Yes," Yar said, nodding. "That's why I'm here. Yes. Now."

Arama looked doubtfully at them, but she nodded. "Mister Zek! You and I will take them in the launch."

"Aye, captain," Zek said, and went to prepare the launch.

"Why didn't they bring the families?" Yar asked Kinnet again.

She was silent for a moment, her face scrunched.

"There is danger," she said. "To the young singers. Danger of their song being corrupted."

Yar nodded and followed her to the launch.

Soon they were being lowered to the surface. Yar closed his eyes, enjoying the swinging of the launch on its hoists. He could feel Xellax's eagerness humming inside him, but she said nothing.

Kinnet was laughing, tears glistening in her eyes. She had told him the story of her first meeting with this singer, three years ago. He had been swimming all alone, singing into the void, unable to connect with any others of his kind. It had taken Kinnet to realize that the singer could not hear his own song, just like she could not hear her own voice. But she had been able to hear his song with her magic, and so she had been able to alter it enough that his own kind could finally hear him.

Yar stared in wonder at the huge creatures that surfaced around them. Their skin was a blue gray, but he could see, when one rolled onto its back in the water, that they were white underneath. Dark, intelligent eyes were set back along their bodies, which were huge. They made even Xellax look small.

It is the buoyancy of the water that allows them to grow so large, she sniffed. *Were they aloft, their very weight would crush them to death.*

He had no doubt that was true. He wondered why they had insisted he come out in the launch. They could have easily come alongside the *Dawn Star* to touch him.

Arama saw him looking at the ship and back to the animals. "They could have swamped us," she said. "It's safer this way."

Yar nodded.

"Here," Kinnet said as one of the stormsingers surfaced next to them. "This is my friend. He wishes you to touch him."

Yar realized, as he stretched out his hand, that it was trembling. In fact, *all* of him was trembling. The dragons had lived in his head for so long as Voices that he hadn't feared them when they met; they had been the answer to an eighteen year mystery. But these…

The stormsinger surged up under Yar's hesitant hand. Yar's fingers slipped along skin that was smooth and slick, and he gasped.

Kinnet laughed at the expression on his face. "This is Qiaru," she said. "He is pleased to meet you, Voice of Dragons."

Tell him how we are with you now, Xellax said. Yar obeyed, speaking so Kinnet could see his face. She must have translated for him, because Qiaru let out a huge groan that vibrated Yar's bones within him.

"Qiaru says he and his pod greet their cousins of the air. Well met."

It has been long and long, Xellax said, and Yar repeated it.

"Too long, perhaps," Kinnet said for Qiaru. "But old powers stir again. The Sea Lord bids us guard against the Oorourrau."

Yar blinked. "The—seadragons?"

Kinnet closed her eyes in what looked like a brief exchange between her and Qiaru. Yar wondered if the stormsinger spoke to her mind the same way Xellax spoke to his, or if it were different somehow. "Yes," Kinnet said, and he had to think back to remember his question.

Yarrax told us of these Oorourrau, Xellax said, *He felt they were used against their will. That they did not wish to attack human ships.*

"It is likely," Qiaru told them. "The Poisoner of Fish has ever been one to take what he wishes."

How long can you defend against them?

It took longer for Kinnet and Qiaru to answer this time. Finally Kinnet sighed. "Our numbers are less, cousin, than they once were. We have lost one already in this."

Yar frowned. "One?" he asked softly.

Kinnet didn't pause to translate that for Qiaru. "They live long, long lives. Qiaru is older than I am by many years, perhaps two or three decades. Some of their oldest remember the lives of those whose parents first taught our ancestors, centuries ago."

Yar nodded. Like the dragons, then. It would be a tragedy for even one dragon to die, they were so long-lived.

Xellax had been listening. Yar could feel her grief along their connection. He wasn't sure how to convey it properly to Qiaru. "Xellax is grieved at that," he said, knowing it didn't begin to cover the emotions Xellax had.

Kinnet nodded, folding her hands in her lap. "It is our duty," she said for Qiaru, "given us long ago by Antos, Giver of Fish. We will abide."

Arama leaned in. "Ask if they know how many gods are awake," she said.

Kinnet blinked. "Poisoner of Fish. Antos, Giver of Fish. Still Waters has never slept. Renn of the Air touches us not. Morda sleeps deeply in his dark troughs. Thann dreams and shakes the world with it."

Xellax whispered into Yar's mind, *Renn slumbers yet, as does her mate Serl.* Yar repeated that to Arama, wondering if the gods of Amethir were the same as the gods of Tamnen. He only remembered five, but Qiaru and Xellax had named eight.

"Still Waters," Arama said. "That must be the god of peace? I never heard him named among the sleeping gods."

Kinnet nodded.

"And the Great Mother?"

Yar sent the inquiry to Xellax and was met with a blank silence that conveyed great distance. It was as if he stared into a void. He sent back his confusion but got nothing in response.

"The Great Mother is beyond," Qiaru said.

Arama, Kinnet, and Yar looked at each other in confusion. *Do you know what that means?* he asked Xellax.

The Great Mother is beyond, she replied.

"But what does that mean?" Yar demanded. He got no reply.

"There is a witch who twists the gift we gave," Kinnet said. Then she paused. After a moment Yar saw her realize she needed to answer aloud. It could be difficult trying to translate for them.

"Yes," she said, glancing at Arama. "She calls herself a stormweapon."

The water around them thrashed, their launch bobbing and heaving until Yar had to grab at the gunwales to keep from falling.

IT IS NOT TO BE DONE! THIS IS NOT WHY IT WAS GIVEN!

Yar wasn't sure if he was hearing Xellax in his head or Qiaru. Perhaps they were both speaking it together. He pressed his palms to his ears in a futile attempt to shut it out. Then he saw Kinnet's lips move and he lowered his hands.

"We know," she said. "I...I know. Not everyone agrees."

"Destruction. Pain. Death." Qiaru had a different feel even in Kinnet's odd voice. "These are all things that come to us all. But they should not be inflicted."

"Not even to eat?" Arama asked. "Fish probably don't appreciate being eaten."

The water churned again, but more gently, and they all felt some echo of the stormsinger's laughter. "Eating is the way of all. But humans do not eat other humans. They kill for no purpose."

"There's always purpose," Arama muttered. "Just not always good ones."

Kinnet met her gaze, but Yar had a feeling Kinnet didn't convey that to Qiaru.

"The gift is not to kill. Not to take. To give." Qiaru's words felt stern. "Once, this was known."

Kinnet bowed her head. "So are we the ones who brought this upon the world?" she asked. "Are we the ones who woke the gods?"

Into the silence that followed, Yar pushed the questions to Xellax as well. There was a long hesitation; he could feel

Xellax there, but she was not answering. Yet she didn't seem to be conversing with the other dragons either. Finally, she hissed a sigh into his head.

We do not know. But you have certainly not done well to kill with this gift.

"So what do we do?" Arama demanded. "It's all well and good to tell us we messed up, but how do we fix it?"

"Stop the misuse of the gift, lest the gift be taken from you," Kinnet said for Qiaru. Then she stopped speaking, her eyes and mouth open wide. "*Can* they take the gift?" she whispered.

The gods may do as they please, Xellax said.

That wasn't a complete answer, and Yar knew it. He could feel the edging away of Xellax's thought. She didn't want to answer that. Maybe because the answer was not that the gods *couldn't* do it, but that they *wouldn't*, even if they wanted to.

"To stop this, we'll have to keep killing."

"Perhaps with this news from Qiaru," Kinnet said, "we'll be able to persuade the others."

Arama's lips twisted. "Pralith won't listen. And if he won't, nor will the king."

Sometimes it is needful to eat those who obstruct, Xellax said, her tone gleeful.

"Xellax!" Yar exclaimed, shocked. Arama and Kinnet looked at him in inquiry, but he shook his head.

Tell them.

Yar sighed. "Xellax says…that war may not be good, but it's sometimes necessary."

That is not what I said, Xellax said as the others nodded.

"Can we help you, Qiaru?" Kinnet said, and then paused to listen.

"Not now, he says. Perhaps soon. I will sing to you."

Kinnet smiled, her face suffused with joy. "I have missed your singing."

"Return to your mates if you can," Qiaru replied. "A storm is brewing. We will continue to fight."

And just like that, the stormsingers dove and were gone. Yar felt Xellax withdraw as well, perhaps to share what they had learned with the others. The four people in the launch stared at each other.

26

Vistaren looked again at the map of central Amethir that was spread on the table. Longdale Keep certainly made the most sense for a rally point, but he couldn't help wondering if a retreat was truly the best course.

Nevertheless he dipped his pen into the ink and sighed. His handwriting was not so bad, but he missed Beyas right now. His secretary had been good at taking dictation, among his many talents, but it had not seemed right to entangle him in Vistaren's rebellion. He was beginning to regret that decision.

We have need of fortifications, and my council has settled on Longdale Keep as the most advantageous. I would ask you to join me, for the reasons cited above. I do not wish to force the issue, Commander Devlin. That is not at the heart of this rebellion. And so I ask.

My messenger will carry your response back. I will not trust this to a bird, which can be waylaid or diverted.

I give you my best wishes.
Vistaren, Prince of Amethir

It wasn't a very good letter, but he thought he'd at least been clear in his explanation of why he was rebelling. He shook sand across to dry the ink and gestured to Azmei.

"You'll give me your honest opinion?" She gave him a look so withering he had to laugh. "No, I'm sorry, of course you'll give me your honest opinion."

He stood and stretched, arching his back. Life in an army camp, he was discovering, was considerably less comfortable than life in the palace.

"Blast this weather," he muttered, peering out the tent flaps. "It shouldn't be raining at all, and we certainly shouldn't have fog. It's damned inconvenient."

"It might be more than inconvenient," Hawk murmured.

Vistaren nodded but didn't reply. Orshard had said he'd run pickets well out past the camp's perimeter, but Vistaren couldn't help thinking the fog could muffle the sound of troop movements until it was too late.

"I think it's quite a serviceable letter," Azmei said. "Clear and concise, which isn't always a talent of royalty."

Vistaren snorted at her.

"No, truly, I can see nothing I would change that matters enough to have you recopy the letter yet again." She smirked a little at him, and Vistaren rolled his eyes. He'd written the letter four times now, though only ashes remained of the first three.

"Very well. Orshard has a messenger he recommended, a woman who served three years at Longdale. She'll know Devlin, and she'll know the surrounding territory." He watched Azmei to be sure that met with her approval, but she just nodded.

"The sooner we get under a real roof, the better," Hawk muttered. Vistaren had noticed the man rubbing at his right leg, and he was moving more stiffly than Vistaren had seen so far. It must be an old wound, the prince thought. He ought to build the fire up; the rain had created a chill.

He was moving to do just that when the world exploded into sound.

Shouting, pounding footsteps, and then the worst noise of all—gunfire. The crack and sputter of musketry made all three of them drop to the ground, staring at each other with wide eyes. Vistaren heard one of his sentries cry out, "Stay inside, sir!"

Then Hawk was on his feet, moving with a noticeable limp to stand at one side of the tent's entrance. One of his swords was in his hand. Vistaren had wondered which of the weapons Hawk carried was his preferred, and now it was clear; Hawk was no lover of firearms.

"To me!" someone shouted. "Rally to me! Form a line—yes, on the oblique!"

Vistaren and Azmei exchanged frightened looks. What was happening out there? He could see she wanted to jump up and investigate as much as he did, but he forced himself to stay down as the sentry had ordered. He had realized in the last couple of days that if he died, the whole rebellion might die with him, and then the Stormweapon would have her way. That could spell the end of the world, from what Yar had said, so Vistaren had decided he'd better do his best not to die.

"Balahar's troops must have made it to the camp." Hawk was looking out the tent flap. His voice was low and calm. "They haven't overrun us yet, though."

A spatter of musketry punctuated this statement. Then came the welcome thud of the bigger guns. Someone screamed. Nearer, several voices cheered.

"There, we've got the cannons brought to bear," Hawk said. "I'll see what Orshard plans."

Without another word he slipped out of the tent, leaving Azmei and Vistaren to stare at each other.

"Damn him," Azmei muttered. "He knows I can't leave you, and he knows he *shouldn't*, but *can*, so he'll leave me here to stay safe while he goes off to risk his neck."

"Stubborn man," Vistaren said, smiling faintly at her.

The noisy chaos around them was slowly resolving into the sounds of marching, snapped orders, and the click and clank of muskets being carried and reloaded. "You, eleventh squad, form up here!" someone shouted.

Another volley of musketry clattered through the afternoon. It sounded further away, but the cheer it raised was nearby.

"We must be pushing them back," Vistaren said.

"I hope so." Azmei rolled over to her back and then sat up. "I think it's far enough away now," she said, and Vistaren sat up too.

"I feel a fool, waiting for someone to come tell me what's happening," he admitted.

"I understand," she said, giving him a sympathetic smile. "But you aren't, you know. Foolish, I mean. It's never a foolish thing to recognize what you need to do and to do it."

Vistaren shrugged. He was still trying to think of something to say in reply when renewed shouting broke out closer to them.

"Fall back! Re-form in front of the tents! Protect the camp!"

He and Azmei were looking at each other in alarm when Hawk ducked back inside. "Get back down," he said, his voice even. "Orshard mounted a counterattack, and it initially pushed them back, but they've rallied. He's re-forming the lines just outside the camp."

"We got that much," Azmei said dryly, but she rolled down to lie on her stomach again and propped her chin on her hands.

"Is Balahar likely to overrun the camp?" Vistaren asked, trying to make his voice as even as Hawk's. He was fairly certain he'd failed.

"I hope not." Hawk sounded grim rather than certain. "Just be ready to move if I say so."

27

"General Algot, we need to hurry!" Kedar Ebb was scowling at him. Lo wasn't sure how the man could even manage to sit a horse after the ride he'd had.

Cannons boomed again and Kedar's head jerked in that direction.

"We are moving as quickly as I deem wise," Lozarr assured him. They'd been hearing the noise of the guns for almost half a glass, and Lo was certain Vistaren must be engaged with the crown soldiers. He didn't want to rush his troops and arrive spent at the battlefield, though, and he was having a terrible time trying to explain that to Kedar.

"We'll arrive too late to do any good!" Kedar snapped.

"If we arrive too exhausted to fight, we might as well never arrive at all," Lo replied. "We'll get there. The battle sounds worse than it is."

All the same, Lo's heart was pounding in his chest, and he kept having to rein himself in. He understood how Kedar felt. Everything in him pulled to put his horse into a gallop and ride to Vistaren's aid. He managed not to by reminding himself that he would need to fight when he got there.

He glanced back along the column of march, mentally calculating how far they had to go. They had been four days on the march, and they'd woken this morning to a downpour. They'd marched for two glasses through a fog and disheartening mizzle of rain. That in itself had the troops uneasy—it shouldn't start raining for another fortnight, and the fog was unseasonal as well.

"General—"

"Please, my lord, I ask you to trust me. I fought the

Shroudlings when I was younger than you are. I did not rise to this rank so young as a matter of politics." Lo gave Kedar a reassuring smile. "We will arrive in plenty of time to help the prince, and we will do so better if we still have some strength to spend in the fight."

Kedar looked at him, mouth still open to protest, for several heartbeats. Then he closed his mouth and nodded. "My apologies, General Algot."

Lo shook his head. "Not necessary. I, too, wish to do nothing more than gallop to their aid. But experience is better than impulse."

Kedar nodded again.

They rode without speaking for another quarter glass. The next time the guns opened up, Lo could tell they were much closer than they had been. And on top of that, Maron's walls were in view.

"Look there, my lord," he said, pointing at the city. "We're in sight of the capital."

Kedar stood in his stirrups. "Then whoever's fighting the prince will be cut off!"

Lo shook his head. "Not my intent. We'll split the brigade, send half around behind him, under the city walls. The other half we'll take with us, directly for the fight."

"Why not just cut the other fellow off?" Kedar asked. "Caught between us and the prince—"

"Caught between us and the prince," Lo interrupted, "he'll fight like a demon, and my men there are likely outnumbered. I'd lay money it's General Balahar there, and he's the best; I learned from him. Right now, as we are, I can't beat Bal. We want him to quit the field."

"But—" Kedar protested, and Lo interrupted again.

"Do you know how many troops Vistaren has? How many cannon? How much ammunition?" He shook his head, seeing the answer in Kedar's eyes. "Nor do I. I can't take the risk of putting too much on the prince."

Kedar frowned. "So why go between Balahar and Maron at all?"

Lo grinned. "Because he'll know we've done it." Seeing that Kedar still looked confused, he gestured. "It's about morale, and maintaining an unbroken line to your supply. If my troops hit from the north, having marched from Anderly, he'll know he's flanked and *could* have been cut off. His instinct will be to pull back, check his lines."

Kedar was nodding slowly.

"It's what I would do," Lo said, "and as I said, Bal trained me."

"I shouldn't have doubted you, general," Kedar said.

"No matter." Lo grinned at him. "Will you join me with the main group, lord count?" Without waiting for an answer, he called over his shoulder to the troops. "At double-time now, lads! Let's go show General Balahar what we're made of!"

The soldiers behind him cheered as they picked up the pace. Lo urged his horse into a trot and saw, from the corner of his eye, that Kedar had done the same. Prince Vistaren's army would be reunited in short order.

***

The rest of the battle went much as Lo had expected it would. Once Balahar realized he'd been flanked, he began drawing back, and Orshard obviously realized what had happened; he kept firing as Bal retreated, but didn't pursue.

The half of Lo's brigade that had flanked Bal's army would chase him all the way to the city and bring back word of what had happened. Lo left them to it. They wouldn't have enough for a pitched battle, but if Bal turned and tried to make a stand, he would hear it. He'd be able to send more fresh troops, and Bal was likely as aware of that as Lo.

When Lo and Kedar rode into Vistaren's camp, a great cheer went up. Vistaren was there, Azmei next to him, both of them on their feet and looking hale. Lo swung out of the saddle and saluted the prince, as was proper etiquette in wartime.

Vistaren, neglecting to return the salute, threw his arms around Lo, pounding his back. Lo grinned and hugged him back. When Vistaren pulled back, he was beaming at Lo.

"You saved the day, old friend."

"It was good timing," Lo said modestly, "and Bal's mistake of leaving himself open. He should've been waiting for me. He has to know I've sided with you, and clearly the kingdom was more ripe for it than we thought, since we've walked off with two of his majesty's brigades."

Vistaren hitched a shoulder. "We don't have quite a full brigade, actually."

Lo waved a hand. "Close enough."

Azmei stepped forward and hugged Lo, too. She was a far cry from the anxious, awkward princess he'd danced with three years ago, he thought as her lips brushed his cheek. Her golden eyes danced with mirth as she looked up at him. "I missed you at our betrothal ball, Lo."

"My congratulations, princess. This wasn't exactly the welcome we had planned for you."

Azmei obliged him by laughing, though he could tell they all wished their reunion had been under better circumstances.

Orshard strode up to them then, clasping Lo's hand in both of his. "My thanks for your timely arrival," he said. "I'd say you've bought us time for our move."

Lo glanced from Orshard to Vistaren. "Move?"

The prince shifted his weight and looked at a darkskinned man standing behind Azmei. Lo hadn't met him, but presumed this was General Hawk, who had traveled with Azmei. "To Longdale Keep," Vistaren said. "Generals Orshard and Hawk have convinced me we need fortifications, and since we have no time to build them ourselves…"

Lo rubbed his chin, thinking. "And you believe…who would that be? Devlin, I think." He nodded. "Yes, he might join you. He's from the coast."

"I've written to him, giving him a chance to join us without coercion," Vistaren said. He grinned. "And yes,

Generals Orshard and Hawk have pointed out that's poor strategy. But this isn't about winning at any cost. It's about winning with honor."

Lo nodded, letting his approval show in his face. Vistaren obviously had a clear idea of how he wanted to run this campaign. Well and good. Lo would offer his experience when it was needed, whether it was requested or not—but he was more than willing to be overruled if Vistaren felt something was not honorable.

"If I may," Orshard said, "I'll get your troops settled alongside mine, Algot. Order of march tomorrow?"

"We're still fresh, I daresay," Lo said. "We'll let you lead, and we'll follow to guard the rear."

Orshard nodded gratefully and left.

Vistaren clapped Lo on the shoulder. "Come have some supper." He looked past Lo finally, a smile breaking across his face. "Count Kedar," he said. "Well met. Join us."

Lo glanced from Vistaren to Azmei and saw the same suspicion in her gaze that he felt. Vistaren liked the count. Come to that, so did Lo, but Vistaren *liked* the count. He glanced over his shoulder and found a pleased smile on Kedar's face. Well, perhaps it would be all right, after all.

"Yes," Lo said. "Let's go get some supper."

✳✳✳

The army camp had finally fallen silent. Azmei paused just outside her tent and looked up at the moon, which shone nearly full overhead. The ground was still soggy, and there was a rather dense ground fog, but at least the rain had let up. She pulled her cloak around her; with the damp, the night was chilly, despite the fact it was still more summer than autumn.

She could hear someone coughing in a tent nearby, and further off, someone called the midnight hour. Lozarr had set skirmishers and pickets out further than had been Orshard's practice, but after the surprise this morning, Azmei appreciated the precaution.

Oh, god of peace, this isn't how I thought my arrival in Amethir would go, she prayed. *I hope my actions have honored you, even if they haven't been entirely peaceful. Please keep Yar safe, and Arama. And please let me feel discord if this course I have chosen is the wrong one.*

She couldn't assassinate King Rekel, though that would be the easiest path and the one most likely to serve peace. Vistaren had reacted with such horror at her oblique suggestion that she knew he might never forgive her if she went against his will. Not that she intended to. She could see how difficult the decision to rebel had been for him. She didn't want to be the person who tipped his delicate balance in the wrong direction.

But she couldn't just sit here in the camp, staying out of trouble and hoping victory would come to them. She had been trained as an assassin, and Amethir was her kingdom now, or soon would be. It was her chosen home, and her chosen kingdom of service. If she couldn't serve Amethir with her blade, she would serve the kingdom with her other skills.

She set out through the camp, moving purposefully but calmly. No one would stop her; her steps and posture were calculated for that. Hawk had agreed with her reasoning, even if he hadn't liked the ultimate outcome of it. But he had never once suggested that she be anything other than who she was.

Hawk was not a man who would love a woman who changed herself for him. He was not a man who would tame a woman or tie her to him to keep her safe. Oh, he wanted to, she was certain of that—because she felt the same way about him. She would love to keep him by her side and keep him safe. But Vistaren would need him, and the work Azmei proposed was best done while she was alone.

Too, she wanted to make Hawk indispensable to Vistaren. She knew the prince would never go back on his word, once given. He would not want to dishonor Azmei, and he wouldn't ask her to give up her love for Hawk. But if Hawk filled a role the king of Amethir could legitimately need, it would be easier hiding her true reasons for keeping him around.

She drew up at the edge of the cleared space in front of Vistaren's tent, the large, double-roomed tent that served as the camp's command center as well as the prince's quarters. The sentries stood at either side of the entrance, properly alert. They hadn't seen her yet, but she had no doubt they would see her if she moved any further.

At her insistence, there were sentries at the back of the tent as well, and one to each side. She knew too well how easily an assassin could slip around the back of a tent and cut her way in, leaving a general—or prince—dead with no one the wiser. Vistaren had grumbled about it, but Hawk and Orshard had both backed her up, and Lo had commented on the wise precaution just a few glasses ago.

She stepped into the cleared area and the sentries were instantly even more alert, pikes held at the ready.

"Halt. Declare yourself."

Azmei lowered her hood a little, letting the pair see her face, and offered a sheepish look. The guard on the left, a tall, blonde woman, grinned.

"Let her through, Parl," she said. "Go on, put your hood up, m'lady. No slight to your honor."

Either the fact of Vistaren's being a same-lover wasn't as well-known among the commoners as it was among officers and the court, or the woman was willing to go along with the charade. Parl, however, was more stubborn.

"She might not be who she looks like," he said.

The woman sighed. "All right. Come four steps closer, m'lady."

Azmei obeyed.

"Now turn your face to catch the light."

Again, Azmei did as she was told. It would probably be more convincing if she were high-handed about it, but on the other side of the argument, she had come here in secret. If she was planning to spend a passionate night with her betrothed, she wouldn't want to raise the attention of every-one around her.

"It's her, Parl."

The man scowled and then, to her surprise, spoke to her in Tamnese. "Are there enemies about?"

Azmei blinked. "No enemies for five miles, it is to be hoped," she replied in her native tongue.

The man studied her for several moments and finally nodded. "My apologies, m'lady. Dax was right. But it can be hard to tell, and with the prince, we can't be too careful."

"Quite right," Azmei said, lifting her hood to hide her face again. "May I enter?"

"Aye, m'lady." Parl stood aside.

Dax added, "I don't think he's sleeping yet. We can still hear him moving around in there."

Azmei nodded and stepped inside the tent. Vistaren looked at her, unsurprised, from across the front chamber of the tent. Isden hovered, sour-faced, near the prince.

"I heard conversation out here and knew someone wanted me," Vistaren said. "Isden, go to bed, will you? I'll sleep soon, but I want a word with the princess first."

Isden's expression smoothed and he bowed, slipping in-to the prince's sleeping area.

"Can't sleep?" Vistaren asked. He poured a cup of something that steamed and held it out to Azmei. When she sniffed it, it proved to be spiced wine.

"It isn't that," she said. "I like darkness." She sipped and waited until he'd poured his own cup and settled on a camp stool before she sat down near him. They sipped in companionable silence for a few moments, then Azmei sighed.

"Vistaren, I'm not going to Longdale with you."

He lowered his cup, staring. "What?" Hurt began creep-ing onto his face.

Azmei shook her head quickly. "It isn't that I disagree with anything, or that I want to withdraw my support. But..." She looked down at the brazier, which glowed faintly with banked coals. "That rain and fog today wasn't natural. You said so yourself. But…" She looked up at him. "But was it a sign of the trouble we're working to prevent, or was it channeled by that Stormweapon?"

Vistaren frowned, the hurt dissolving into thoughtfulness.

"We need information. That is something I am good at."

"You're too easily recognized."

Azmei sipped her wine. "Not really. And I know disguising arts. I'll go to Lijka first. There may be enough she can tell me. But I think—" She took another sip of wine. Vistaren wasn't going to like what she was about to say. "I think I'll have to infiltrate the stormwitch academy."

"What? No!"

"No one looks at servants." Azmei smiled. "And I'm good at sneaking in the shadows."

"Does Hawk know about this mad scheme?" Vistaren asked, his voice cross.

Azmei arched an eyebrow at him. "Not that I need his permission," she said tartly, "but yes." She was pleased to see Vistaren blush. "I discussed it with him first. He agrees with me. Much as he might wish he didn't."

Vistaren rubbed his face, and Azmei heard the scratch of evening shadow against his palm. Finally he sighed. "Stay out of the palace," he said. "Too many people there would recognize you."

Azmei nodded. *And you don't want me to kill Rekel,* she thought, but she chided herself at once; Vistaren knew, she hoped, that she wouldn't cross him in that.

"I don't like it," he said frankly. "How do you know Lijka will help?"

"She's frightened of Eldry."

"All the more reason for her to refuse."

"No." Azmei smoothed a hand along her breeches. "She's afraid of what Eldry means. Of what Eldry will change. She doesn't want that change. She'll help."

Vistaren sighed. "How will we know you're safe?"

Azmei smiled. "I'll take some of your messenger birds with me. I'll send one a day with news. If you don't hear from me, assume I'm not safe."

"That's reassuring," he grumbled, standing to cross the room. He began rummaging in a chest. "Very well. You'll need money. I suppose you've already requisitioned a horse and food."

"Actually, I'm planning to sail." Azmei's smile widened. "It's much easier than riding to the light, and in a small fishing craft, I'm much less likely to attract attention than if I were riding."

"Right again," he muttered. He straightened and held out a leather purse. It was very heavy when she took it. "That should keep you a while. Be very careful, Az."

She drained her cup and stood, still smiling at him. "Don't worry. I intend to live a long life as queen by your side."

Vistaren hugged her tightly and Azmei relaxed into it, relishing the protectiveness and gratitude she felt in his embrace.

"You be careful, too, Vistaren," she said. "Listen to Hawk and Lo. They're both wise men, and I know they both want what's best for you." Then she tilted her head, conceding a point. "But if Hawk and Lo disagree, listen to Lo. Hawk would put my safety above yours, I am certain."

Vistaren chuckled and kissed her cheek. "Return safe."

Azmei nodded. "Look for me in Longdale. Probably when you least expect me."

Then she slipped out of the tent into the night.

28

Pralith Menever threw open the heavy mahogany door to his study and locked it behind him. No matter what he told the king, the witchery *had* been a great deal more slippery of late. He wouldn't want to be interrupted.

Eldry had upstaged him badly, diverting that storm that no stormwitch living should have been able to divert. Pralith had worked himself ragged calling up the steady downpour he'd dumped on the prince's army yesterday. The fog had been an accidental blessing, but the king had been so pleased Pralith had pretended he'd intended it.

And now there was the matter of the Storm Petrel. Two sailors had come in to harbor this morning, claiming they'd been on the *Celerity* when it sank. At first everyone had thought them mad, but once it became clear Arama Dzornaea had taken the prince's rebellion as an opportunity to return to piracy, everything made sense.

It wasn't storm season in Amethir yet, not for at least another fortnight, but the open ocean was another matter. Dzornaea might be savvy enough to stay inside Amethirian waters, but there had never been careful tests made of the boundaries of their seasons. The borders were shaky enough that Pralith felt confident in his ability to hamper the Storm Petrel.

There must be a storm brewing somewhere out at sea. Kinnet and Lijka Ardelis probably knew, out at their lighthouse, but there were two of them, and they were much closer to the sea than he was. Besides, Pralith wasn't certain they could be trusted. Kinnet was a personal friend of the prince's, and Lijka had been leery of Eldry's talents, so

Pralith considered it even odds that they would throw in with the prince.

Pralith cast his gaze along the shelves of artifacts, tomes, and witchery aids lining his study. He would need a map and something that had seen the deeps. He ran a fingernail lightly down the scar on his chin as he studied the objects on his shelves. Stone wouldn't allow a delicate touch, but it would provide brute strength, and perhaps it was strength more than softness the storm wanted. The stone was deep gray, about the size of his doubled fists. The surface was smooth after decades in the ocean.

He rubbed one fingertip across it, allowing his eyes to fall half closed. Would it tell him what he wanted? But no. Strength would be needed if he needed to wrest the storm from its course, but that was only half of his objective.

He turned to the next set of shelves, where he had row after row of sand bottles. Sand from every stretch of beach along the Amethir coast. Sand from the Sandswamp. Sand from along the Gehb Estuary. Sand from other shores across the ocean. He tapped the glass of a bottle from Tamnen, listening to his fingernail chime. But if he chose incorrectly, if the storm were not from Tamnen but from Strid, or if it had formed out over the open ocean, the sand wouldn't help.

Seaglass, then. It usually was seaglass. With one hand he clasped the pendant he wore even when he was sleeping. He sifted the other hand through his seaglass, letting each textured piece of glass or pottery slip through his fingers.

Often in the past, there had been a spark when he touched the piece of seaglass he needed. Strong witchery could destroy the piece of glass, or remove the virtue from it so it became brittle and eventually crumbled into sand. Stormwitches were always looking for replacement pieces of seaglass for that reason.

Nothing felt quite right.

With a sigh, he turned to the tall cabinet positioned behind his huge desk. He kept his larger pieces of seaglass in the lower vault. He suspected one of those would be needed. He pulled one of the drawers open and surveyed his collection. Colors from blue and green to deep red winked up at him. The red was not really a large piece, but the color was so rare that he put it here for safekeeping. There, a flat brown piece that was almost certainly the bottom of a rum jug. His fingers tingled as he rubbed them around the smooth rim of the circular glass.

Smiling, Pralith lifted it out and nodded to himself. This would do it. He carried it to his desk and sat down, placing his palms flat against the glass. Closing his eyes, he slowed his breathing. Feel the waves lapping against the base of the cliffs below the palace. Feel the pull of the tide, let it draw his awareness out further, out to where the ocean currents tugged at him. There! A small disturbance, an attraction of the water upwards, drawing moisture from the sea up into the clouds. Air currents roiling, carrying raindrops around with them.

Pralith breathed more slowly still, allowing the minute details of the building storm envelope him. He could almost feel the raindrops against his skin. His awareness floated like he was actually on the surface of the sea. Eyes still closed, he smiled, imagining himself opening his eyes to see where the storm was located. There was land within sight, he thought. He would just crack his eyes a little—

—and the storm twisted out of his grasp. He couldn't see the horizon. He couldn't see the sea. All he saw was the mahogany shelves and richly embroidered carpets of his study.

"Damn it!" he snarled, and gripped the brown platter hard. For a few seconds he fought the impulse to fling it across the room, then he mastered himself. He drew a deep breath. He would try again. In a moment. Just as soon as he calmed a bit.

The witchery had been doing this more often. Pralith was a master of stormwitchery. Forty-one years old now, he had first channeled the lightning on his seventeenth birthday.

He had trained diligently and discovered new techniques and new uses for the witchery over his years of service. He was the best stormwitch in Amethir, as evidenced by his position as king's adviser. There was no reason for him to lose control of the witchery.

And yet he had. He pressed his fingers against his eyelids and rubbed.

Damn Eldry for showing off the way she had. He'd begun working out a plan to introduce her to the king, to begin with small demonstrations of her power and then build to more dramatic ones. Instead she had, in one fell swoop, destroyed Pralith's plans and upstaged him to boot.

He hoped she was struck by lightning and left to rot.

He took a deep breath. This was not contributing to his efforts at calming himself. Very well, he would breath more slowly and imagine the sound of raindrops against windowpanes. It was a warming sound, pleasant and cozy, and it never failed to make him feel better. Imagine a soft patter against his study windows. Think of how it felt to be ensconced in his soft, oversized reading chair while wrapped in his favorite brocade dressing gown while the rain pattered against his windows. Pralith smiled involuntarily. His heartbeats slowed, his breathing calmed.

Now. Think of the storm. He opened his right desk drawer and pulled out a chunk of turquoise seaglass, which he set on top of the brown platter. Sometimes the right sort of seaglass could act as a magnifier. The two pieces together should focus and amplify his senses. He cupped his hands on the turquoise chunk and closed his eyes again.

The storm hooked his awareness and tugged. Pralith followed, exhaling. There were no ships in the storm yet, but they were close. He could sense them, but not identify their nationality. They didn't help him pinpoint the storm's location so he let the awareness of the ships slip away. Concentrate on the sea currents. Compare the feel of these currents to the maps in his memory. There, that northward swing felt familiar. Where was it? Was it the Dzornaea Drift? It could be, but that had a sharp curl to the east that he didn't feel. The Blade Stream? No, not cold enough or shallow enough. Pralith strained, trying to grasp the feeling more tightly. What was—

Light exploded in his study, visible even through his closed eyelids. He jerked back from it just in time—his fingers tingled and the hair stood up on his arms. Then sharp splinters drove into his thighs and a wall of sound crashed into him.

He screamed, though he didn't realize it until later. He shoved himself backwards. His chair tipped. The landing drove his breath from his lungs. His eyes flew open without his permission. Red afterimages flashed in his vision as he blinked. What had just happened?

He rubbed the back of his head where it had struck the floor. Blinking tears from his watering eyes, he pushed himself into an upright position. His desk was smoking. The surface had splintered. He glanced down at his thighs and winced to see blood seeping through his trousers. He had been stabbed by his desk. A woozy feeling seized him, but he dragged himself to his feet.

He'd lost the witchery again. He wiped tears from his eyes and stared at the desktop. What the blazes?

Lightning. He'd just missed being struck by lightning. Inside his study. He looked over his shoulder. The windows were closed. The sun shone outside. Inside, a thin spiral of smoke from the wrecked desktop was all that remained to show what had happened. Pralith caught his breath.

"Deep take me," he murmured.

The brown platter and turquoise chunk of seaglass were melted almost beyond recognition. The lightning had struck them instead of him only because he'd jerked backwards. The blue chunk of glass was fused to the platter, which had warped up around it in jagged claws. The path of the lightning, he supposed.

He rubbed his eyes and looked at the twisted seaglass again. Now what was he supposed to do?

As if in answer to his silent query, someone knocked on his door.

"Come," Pralith called, and then remembered, as the doorknob rattled, that he had locked it. "Blast," he muttered, and staggered to the door. He could see that he was leaving little blood droplets in his wake.

"Pralith—" Eldry began, sweeping into the room. Then she saw the destruction, the haze of smoke…the blood. "What in the name of the seven…"

"I was trying to find a storm to send after Arama Dzornaea." His voice was dull. There was no sense in trying to protect his pride from her; she had already trampled all over it.

Eldry's lips quirked a little, but she shook her head. "Pralith, you can't duplicate my talents like this. Here, you're bleeding. Wrap something around your leg and I'll help you call a storm."

Pralith dragged off the silk scarf he wore around his neck and wrapped it tightly around the wound, trying to pack the splinter of desk in place so it wouldn't move.

"You ought to see a surgeon," Eldry said, her voice kind.

Pralith gritted his teeth. "Not until I'm finished."

Eldry looked at him for a moment, then shook her head. "Very well. You were using—ah, that brown platter. Not quite right, I think. Here, let's…"

She fished around in the vault and came up with the piece of red seaglass he'd been saving. Pralith bit his tongue to keep from protesting. She obviously knew more than he did—or perhaps she sensed it, would be a better way of saying it. He was certain no one could *know* more about stormwitchery than he did.

Eldry gestured for him to sit down. When he had lowered himself gingerly into his chair, she knelt in front of him, bringing her hands up to cup the seaglass between her hands and Pralith's.

"Now, let me follow your thoughts," she murmured.

"Guide us back to where you sensed the storm."

He closed his eyes, easing them back to the northward-curling current, whichever it was. He heard Eldry hum in approval. She could see the potential just as he did. Good, at least he'd gotten that much right.

They followed the current, warming it, urging it on into a tighter curve. This would create the rotation the storm needed. But just as Pralith felt it building into something that would be bigger than them, something dashed across it, like cold water in the face.

"Ah," Eldry breathed. "You didn't fail, Pralith. You were thwarted."

"What?"

He heard laughter mixing with frustration in her voice when she answered. "Stormsingers."

"What?" Perhaps he'd lost too much blood. Her answer made no sense.

"The stormsingers are fighting us, using their magic to quell ours." Eldry's fingers tightened around his. "Push harder."

He tried, throwing his power out into the current. He felt Eldry's power seize his and guide it, but perhaps that was best. After all, as she'd explained it, she could actually *see* the weather. Surely she must be better able to direct the power than he was.

The push back was more obvious this time, like running into a stone wall. But Eldry hissed between her teeth and Pralith felt her fingers tighten more, crushing his fingers against the seaglass. It felt hot in his hands, though he knew that was just a trick of the pressure.

Then he felt a sense of immense power and ancient presence. Something repelled him, almost as if it were plugging the stream of his power like a brewer would plug a wine cask.

"No," Eldry hissed.

"Gods, they're so big," Pralith whispered, his mind trying to wrap around the edges of the stormsingers and sliding off. "How are they so big?"

"They've become monsters," Eldry snarled, and Pralith felt a hard tug behind his chest. He opened his eyes wide, losing his grip on the magic entirely, and so he was watching when Eldry's face twisted into an angry mask.

"I CALL YOU NOW!" she shouted, her voice deeper and more resonant than it ought to be. And then Pralith felt something *truly* monstrous approaching. He wrenched his hands out of her grasp and pressed himself into his chair, gasping.

Eldry let out a short, sharp cry and then her face smoothed with unnatural quickness. She opened her eye and rocked back on her heels.

And she smiled.

Pralith's hands were throbbing in time with his heartbeat. So was his leg. And Eldry was smiling at him as if she'd just found the most beautiful piece of seaglass in the world.

"The seadragons will take care of them," she said. "Our storm will get through."

"S-seadragons?" Pralith managed. "It was you who attacked the princess?"

Eldry rose to her feet, her upper lip curling. "Not I. The god I serve."

Pralith could only stare at her. His head was spinning, and something behind his chest felt hollow. Had he used up all of his witchery? He'd never heard of that happening.

Eldry's gaze dropped to his leg. "You've lost a lot of blood," she said coolly. "I'll call a surgeon."

29

A cackle cut through Eldry's meditation, and the Scavenger said, "She'll soon see, won't she?" Then he closed his eyes and began rocking in place, humming to himself.

Eldry opened her eye and glanced at him in annoyance. With every hour that passed, she wished she had accepted the larger rooms Pralith had tried to offer her the day after she saved the city. At the time, she had wished to look humble, so she'd replied that she was happy to return to the rooms assigned to her.

If she'd known how much more incoherent the Scavenger was going to become, she'd have said yes with alacrity. He spent hours humming or singing tunelessly to himself, picking at his hair or rubbing his hands together. His 'conversations' with his god were growing less and less intelligible, even when he spoke loudly enough to understand.

Then again, she thought, even if she'd moved into a larger apartment, the Scavenger would probably want to spend all of his time close to her. She had no idea if it was genuine affection or if he merely wanted to keep an eye on her. She wasn't sure it mattered, since the end result was the same—he was driving Eldry mad.

The tentative tap on her door was a welcome interruption. She went to open it and stared at Rhys, who shifted on his crutches and looked away as soon as their eyes met.

"El." He licked his lips. "You look busy."

She followed his gaze to the seaglass collection she had been sorting through. It had been a desultory thing, meditating for a bit, then shifting the pieces around, selecting one that spoke to her, and meditating through the piece.

"Of course I'm busy," she said, and smiled. "But I'm never too busy for you. You know that."

Rhys' lips twitched up in a smile. "I'm glad." He cleared his throat. "I've missed you."

Warmed by that admission, Eldry smiled more widely. "And I you. Come in." She stepped aside and moved a chair so it would be a shorter distance for him to cross.

She had missed him most at night. Her dreams of mist and Shroudlings and dead ends had been replaced with dreams of dark places in deep chambers under the sea, swirling with cold, black water. She always woke from those, chilled and shivering but slicked with sweat.

"How is your leg?" she asked, closing the door. "You look well."

It was mostly true. His movements were stiff, and she could tell by the set of his jaw that his leg pained him, but his eyes had lost the dark circles that used to be under them.

Rhys sank into the chair and gave a sigh. "I've had good care. And the man in the chamber next to mine has good stories to tell. He says it's just bad luck the *Elana Bey* went down. He's sailed for decades—most of the time without a stormwitch, even—and he's never wrecked."

"Without a stormwitch?" Eldry sniffed and settled back on her chair. "He must be foreign."

Rhys grinned. "Yes, Tamnese, and a fine fellow. But," he said, leaning toward her, "as fine a fellow as he is, he's no substitute for my best friend."

Eldry looked down at her hands as they clenched together. "I meant to visit you. I—I would have, but you were so angry..." She faltered, thinking of the expression on his face just before he turned away from her.

"By the seven, I'm sorry, El." Rhys put a hand on her shoulder. "I shouldn't have walked away in anger."

"No, I let you go. I should have apologized."

"Well." Rhys squeezed her shoulder gently and sat back. "Water under the bridge, eh?" He smiled. "Have they made you a master yet?"

Eldry shrugged. "Pralith has talked about it." He'd called her diversion of the storm her masterwork, in fact, and all but insisted. Eldry had feigned reluctance, though she wasn't sure now why she'd thought it was necessary. She had saved Maron; the stormwitches and nobles were falling all over themselves to thank her. "But mastery isn't really that important."

"Isn't important?" Rhys laughed. "When we got here, you said you wanted to be the youngest master stormwitch ever!"

Eldry smiled serenely. "I've learned that other things are more important." She had her cause now, the vow she had sworn, the tasks she had undertaken. She would rather be called Stormweapon than Master Stormwitch now.

Rhys' expression brightened. "Having a brush with death does put everything in perspective, doesn't it? I've been thinking…as soon as I'm healed, I'm going to rent a little stall in the market. Sell my bread and sweet rolls." He paused, tapping his fingers against his chair. "Maybe ask Genna if she'll let me court her."

Eldry looked blankly at him. Court Genna? Rent a stall? In the back of her mind she heard the whisper of a chuckle that somehow managed to be wet and amused and scornful all at once.

"Oh," she said, blinking. He was talking about the little lives they'd led before. "Yes."

The Scavenger shrieked with laughter. "You'll lose yourself!" he howled. "Already losing! Hee hee hee hee…"

Rhys jumped at the Scavenger's first shriek of laughter, and then scowled. "I know he saved your life, but doesn't he have a room of his own?"

Though she'd been resenting the Scavenger's presence just a few minutes earlier, she glared at Rhys. "He doesn't know anyone here in Maron. It would be unkind of me to ignore him." He did have a room of his own, in point of fact, just across the hall from Eldry's, but he barged into hers whenever he felt like it. She'd locked him out yesterday, but he just sat on the floor outside her room, singing to himself and cackling at everyone who passed him.

It seemed less trouble to keep him in her room.

Rhys shook his head, obviously dismissing the Scavenger as not worth the argument. "So what do you think of my idea?"

Eldry stared at him, trying to remember what idea he'd had.

"To get a stall in the market!" he prompted.

"Oh, yes," she said. "That's nice. It's a nice idea." She wondered if her ideas had ever been so mundane. If they had been, they were no longer.

Rhys' brows drew together. "A...nice idea? Eldry, this is what I've dreamed of since we were children." He tilted his head, eyes narrowed. "Don't you even care?"

"Well, yes," she said lamely. "It's just that...well. It's a very...small idea, isn't it?" Nothing like her ideas. She would change the world with her ideas.

My ideas, child. Not yours.

She would bring the stormwitches to their knees right along with the royal family. She would show them all how weak they had become, and then she would break them. She would use her power to cleanse away the timid ones.

My power, child. Lent to you, no more.

"Small."

Eldry blinked at Rhys. She'd forgotten he was sitting there. He was shaking his head slowly, his mouth open.

"Yes," he said finally, "I suppose it is small. After all, it's only feeding a few folk. Never mind that I might grow it into a fine bakery someday. Never mind that I might marry a talented cook who will help me turn it into a fine public eating establishment. It's too small for a great lady like Eldry Karayan."

Eldry blinked again, her attention snapping back to the present. "That isn't what I—"

"Of course it's what you meant." Rhys snorted. "Might as well admit it. I know I've never been as ambitious as you.

I guess I just always thought you cared about my dreams anyway, even if they were that much smaller than yours."

"I do! I just—" Eldry sighed. "Oh, I just have a lot on my mind."

"Like what?" Rhys scoffed. "Like this god you supposedly serve now?"

The Scavenger cackled. "The god who rides her."

"I swore a vow!" Eldry said fiercely. "Would you have me break it?"

"To which god?" Rhys demanded. He leaned forward and one of his crutches clattered to the floor. "Why haven't you been to the priests if that's the case? They could help you!"

"Maybe I have!" Eldry hadn't thought of going to the priests. Why would she, when she had direct access to the god herself? He wasn't even speaking through the Scavenger anymore; he was speaking directly to her. Who needed a priest?

Rhys was shaking his head. "No. I asked. No one's seen you anywhere except the palace or the academy."

Eldry stood, fists clenched at her sides. "Are you *spying* on me?" Her voice lashed out like a whip.

Rhys stared at her with wide eyes. "I'm worried about you! You aren't the Eldry I grew up with."

"You're right. I'm not. I can't help it if you're jealous of how I've changed." Her fingers were tingling. She wiped her palms against her thighs to soothe the itch.

"Jealous? I'm frightened!" He shoved his hand through his hair. She knew if he could walk he'd have jumped to his feet to pace by now.

"Of what?" Eldry's voice was rising as the tingling bit at her fingertips. "Of a little power? Of seeing me succeed? What's so frightening?"

"You are!" he shouted. "You're mad, Eldry! Mad!"

Sparks snapped around her fingertips and she pushed them out in front of her. The room exploded into light and Rhys screamed. The agony in his voice pierced her. Eldry sucked in a breath, jerking away from him, trying to escape his pain. She heard her chair crash to the floor as she stumbled backwards.

Then there was silence.

She couldn't see. The light had whited out the vision in both her natural eye and her seaglass one. She blinked rapidly, trying to dispel the tears that streamed from her good eye. Her breathing was too loud and ragged.

Then she heard the Scavenger giggling. It was a horrible sound, rising and falling along the scale like he was trying to giggle a tune. Eldry lifted her hands to stop her ears, but she could still hear it. She scrubbed her face against her arm and opened her eye again.

Rhys was lying on the floor, arms sprawled one way, legs sprawled the other. One of his crutches had fallen across his chest. His chest wasn't moving.

"Oh no. No no no…" Eldry whispered, stumbling forward. "No, not again, not this, this isn't what I bargained for—"

You said I could have whatever I wanted.

"If you saved Rhys!" she screamed. "This isn't saving him!"

I saved him once. You didn't ask for him to stay safe.

Her knees crashed hard against the stone floor as she bent over him. "No," she whispered. "No. Don't be dead. Don't—I didn't mean it, I was just angry, I just lost my temper and I didn't mean it."

You meant it, said the horrible, inexorable voice in her head. *I can see your intentions, and in that moment, you most certainly meant it.*

A sob broke free of her throat. Eldry lowered her head until it touched Rhys' chest. "No," she moaned, clutching at him. Don't be dead, please don't be dead, she thought, aching too much to try to speak. Her grief gripped her too tightly to even breathe. She would be dead too. If she were dead, she wouldn't have to fulfill her oath to the god.

It doesn't work that way, he whispered in her mind, and

she knew, with a horrible clarity, that no matter what she did, he would not allow her to die until he was finished with her.

The Scavenger laughed, and there was something terribly sane about that laughter. He knew—*knew*—what she faced, and he *enjoyed* it.

Eldry lifted her head, ready to lunge at him. He was sitting cross-legged, watching her and laughing. "Dead, dead, dead," he sing-songed. "And nothing you can do, do, do."

"Damn you!" she snarled, throwing herself at him. Her fingers were already crackling with power as she reached for him.

But he was quick. He dodged out of the way and slapped her hard across the face. Eldry fell back, shocked out of her rage and grief both. The power fizzled in her hand.

The Scavenger stood and looked down at her, his expression lucid and stern. "You have to get rid of him. Someone will come looking for him. That Tamnese ship captain, if no one else. Do it now. Get rid of that." He gestured at Rhys' body, sprawled across her carpet. "Destroy it."

Eldry sucked in a loud sob. How could she do that? She crawled across the floor and reached for the limp, pale hand. How many times had that hand stroked her hair until her fear calmed? How many times had that arm held her tight so she could sleep again?

She leaned down, pressing her face against Rhys' palm, and let her tears wet his skin. Then, sniffling, she kissed his palm and sat up.

Still holding his hand, she channeled enough lightning to consume Rhys' body entirely.

30

Longdale Keep loomed ahead of them, a huge, gray stone fortress built on the bluff overlooking the Singing River. It was a good position, there was no question of that. Anyone looking to attack the keep would have to fight up-hill. The keep's defenders likely had a good view of the long, rolling valley that gave Longdale its name.

There was no flag flying over the keep. Vistaren looked back along the line of footsore soldiers. They were in good spirits, and they'd collected a small group of followers in the three days they'd been marching from their camp. There would be no shortage of boys to run errands or women to do the washing. What there might be a shortage of was food to share with them.

"I'd feel better about this if we'd had an answer from the commander," he murmured to Lozarr. He tried to keep his voice quiet enough that the tramp of marching feet would cover it.

Lo gave him a sympathetic smile. "Your letter was a good one. And if it didn't convince him, maybe our arrival in mass will do it."

"That wasn't the point," Vistaren mumbled, but he knew he shouldn't quibble.

He guided his horse over to the edge of the road and reined her in. Lo followed, stopping next to him. Vistaren could feel the general's eyes on him, but he kept studying the keep. Longdale Keep was designed to be manned by four thousand soldiers. Vistaren had twice that number with him, as well as the new camp followers. Add that to the soldiers already stationed there, and he wondered if the keep could even house them all. He might have to turn the camp followers away.

"This is a good position," he said, hoping Lo would agree with him.

"It is. Longdale's been undermanned for a while, but not because it isn't a good fort. They built those garrisons at Estermere and Firebend thirteen years back, and that was fine, for the Shroudling War." Lo scratched his jaw. "There's a large garrison at Cragmond, too, to keep the Shroudlings from coming right down the Gehb into Maron."

Vistaren nodded. "We'll be able to command the valley from here, if your Devlin lets us in."

"I think he will, highness. As I said, your letter was a good one, and he's from the coast. He'll know how devastating one of those storms can be. The thought that his majesty allowed one to hit and then did nothing to speed the recovery…that doesn't sit well with me, and I'm from inland. It's sure to bother Dev."

"I hope so."

The column was winding around a long bend in the road as it approached the river. Once the front of the column passed around the bend, it would be under the keep, and possibly within range of their guns.

Vistaren straightened in his saddle. "Have the column halt there. We should approach the gate first."

Lo whistled a series of sharp notes and one of his officers shouted something. Then a trumpet rang out, signaling the halt. The column stopped in its tracks, spacing tidy and arms shouldered neatly. Vistaren couldn't help grinning.

"A well-disciplined regiment is a glorious thing."

Lo grinned back at him. "As I've told you more than once, I'm sure."

They rode along the column toward the front. Lo signaled several men to fall in with them, so by the time Vistaren reached the front, he had an impressive-looking honor guard.

They halted their horses just out of musket-range and

Lo hailed the keep.

"Is that Prince Vistaren?" someone shouted from the wall.

"It is!" Lo shouted back. "And the Second and Third Brigades with him."

The silence lasted so long Vistaren had begun to wonder if the keep was about to fire on them. Then a different voice shouted back. "Your highness, I am Commander Faradi Devlin. I surrender Longdale Keep to your command."

The troops behind Vistaren cheered and kept on cheering as the portcullis rattled up. Vistaren and Lo exchanged a grin and urged their horses forward.

Twenty minutes later, Vistaren, Lozarr, and Orshard were on the inside walk around the battlements with Devlin, watching as the sergeants and captains sorted out the disposition of the soldiers. Devlin thought the soldiers would all fit, though it would be a tight squeeze and, as he said, some of the men might end up sleeping in a stable.

Devlin had inquired after the towns of Rebena and Ratlin, but no one knew how they fared. Vistaren suspected the storm that had ravaged Anderly might have taken a toll on them, since they were out along Coman Head. Devlin's sister, it seemed, had married a boatmaker in Rebena, and their children were apprenticed in nearby Ratlin. Devlin hadn't heard from his sister in a month.

"Will Balahar come after us?" Vistaren asked. *Will my father send him after us?*

"He'll have to," Orshard said, leaning his elbows on the stone. "Can't leave us free to wander, and he won't know about us taking Longdale Keep if Dev's been as successful at stopping messages as he says."

Devlin swiped at Orshard, who ducked, grinning. "I stopped the messages, all right," Devlin said. "As soon as your bird came in, I locked the cotes and crushed our lodestone."

"That's why we didn't hear back from you," Vistaren

said.

Devlin nodded. "I thought it a necessary precaution. I can vouch for which of my soldiers are loyal, and the ones I thought might not go along with it were dispatched to one of the garrisons nearby without a word as to what was happening."

"Well done, Devlin," Lo said.

Devlin ducked his head. "Just trying to think of what I'd do if I were in Balahar's position," he said. "And the first thing I'd do is try to find someone inside the fortress that wasn't happy about the change."

Vistaren nodded. "My father will want me brought to heel quickly, I suspect." He suppressed a flash of guilt. "We'll have to take every precaution, but I trust your assessment of your soldiers."

"With permission, highness," Orshard said, and when Vistaren nodded, he continued. "I'd like to have skirmishers out a day's ride in every direction. I wouldn't put it past Balahar to ride around and come at us from Raven Hill or even Estermere."

Lo was nodding.

"Very good," Vistaren said.

"I'm concerned about ammunition," Orshard went on. "We'll need to pay more attention than we're used to. Can't exactly get resupply now, can we?"

Vistaren tapped his chin. "I'm sure the Storm Petrel would be happy to requisition shipments from Tamnen. She took forty barrels of saltpeter from the ship that sank *Elana Bey.*"

"It isn't just the saltpeter," Lo said. "There's sulfur and charcoal, and the ability to mix it safely."

"We don't have a powder-maker that could supply all of us, highness," Devlin put in.

Vistaren sighed. "Then we make sure we're well supplied with bows, and a large stock of arrows. I hate these damned muskets, anyway. I can't be the only one."

The others laughed. Devlin grinned at him. "We do

have two companies of crack bowmen here. Some of our older veterans, who prefer the bow, keep them in fighting fit."

"And a well-trained bowman *can* loose arrows faster than a musketeer can fire," Lo said, nodding.

Orshard was nodding as well. "Right, so we'll have archery practice. And pikes, I suppose?"

"Most of the infantrymen are proficient with pikes, but it won't hurt to drill them."

"Good." Vistaren clapped Lo on the shoulder. "Gentlemen, it is a source of comfort that I have such experienced men fighting for me. I rely on your judgment." He smiled around at them. "Carry on."

He strolled along the battlement walk, watching the men and women below as they went about their tasks. He felt suddenly very tired. How could he lead a rebellion if he forgot about things like powder-makers and supply lines?

He settled at one of the crenellations and looked out. He'd been right; he had a sweeping view of the golden fields in the valley. He resolved to speak to Lo about detailing some of their soldiers to help with the harvest. They would have to requisition enough to feed the troops, so they ought to work alongside the farmers. He wondered suddenly if he'd carried off enough gold to pay for everything he was going to need to sustain this war.

It wasn't long before he heard footsteps approaching. He glanced over and saw Lo approaching. He looked as tired as the prince felt. Vistaren felt a sudden rush of love for his old friend. He'd asked a lot when he asked Lo to follow him into treason. And Lo, bless him, hadn't even flinched. What he'd done to deserve such a friend, Vistaren would never know.

Lo smiled and leaned against the wall. "Vistaren, if I may ask…"

Vistaren nodded.

"Have you considered what will happen if we lose?"

The question made Vistaren's knees feel weak. Was

their situation as bad as that? Did Lo think they were doomed from the beginning? He gave Lo a sharp look.

"Not what will happen to us," Lo said. "Not directly. But—to Amethir. Or the world, perhaps. If we lose, your father and his stormwitches will be able to move forward with these plans of his—or Pralith's. To be honest, these plans sound more like Pralith than your father."

Vistaren nodded. "And if they're able to move forward, then Amethir gobbles up her enemies, or destroys them. My guess is that the seasons will continue shifting. Common folk starve. Nobles too, eventually—once it's too late for them to do anything about it."

They stared out across the valley. Here and there smoke rose from a crofter's cottage. Vistaren could see herds grazing in a pasture to the east.

After a while, Lo stretched and sighed. "What is our aim? Specifically, I mean."

Vistaren was glad he had an answer for that, at least. "If I can force my father's abdication, I think I will also have the strength to force the academy into submission. We root out those who are in favor of weaponization, first of all. Then we bind the academy to new rules."

Lo let the words sit between them for a few breaths. "And if it's too late to save the academy?"

Vistaren licked his lips. He hadn't wanted to think about that. He knew he would have to plan for that possibility. But it seemed too final. "Then I suppose we force them to abstain from witchery."

"That might be impossible, unless we kill all the stormwitches," Lo said.

A horrified silence blanketed them then. Vistaren knew he couldn't do such a thing. Being king might require many terrible acts for the greater good, but slaughtering every single member of a group of people? No. There could be no good reason for that.

"That wasn't a suggestion," Lo said.

Vistaren huffed out a breath, trying to shake away the

thought. "I hope that the Voice of Dragons will have alternatives for us before it comes to that."

Lo turned to face him, leaning his shoulder against the stone. "What's he like? The Voice?"

Vistaren grinned before he could school his expression. "He's odd, but in all the best ways." He tilted his head back, watching as swallows swooped over the walls. "Thoughtful, honest, determined. Brave. I can see why Azmei took to him as she did." He paused and glanced sideways at Lo, thinking of all he'd learned about the past three years of Azmei's life.

"It was his sister who nearly killed us in Ranarr, you know," he said, watching in gratified amusement as Lo's jaw dropped.

"*Orya?*" he said, staring at Vistaren.

Vistaren nodded. "She'd told Az about her brother, that he was different. Special. When Az…cleaned up…the rest of the Perslyn family, she found him."

Lo shook his head. "And kept him."

Vistaren shrugged. "She could see he had a higher calling."

He only wished it were so clear about his own calling.

***

Arama told herself she wasn't hiding. She knew it was a lie, but as long as she didn't inspect it too closely, she didn't have to think about the look on Kinnet's face when Arama told her that, close as they were, they'd have to wait for better seas to get her home. It was just too choppy to get a launch in close to the lighthouse without it breaking on the rocks.

"Unless you can calm it a bit," Arama had said, but to her surprise, Kinnet shook her head.

"I am afraid of the things Eldry might be able to do," she said. "That storm night before last, that was witched. Qiaru and his folk tried to fight it, and they managed for a time. But if she was strong enough to send that at us from

Maron…"

Arama nodded. Kinnet had said at the time that the storm had been set on them, but Arama hadn't thought about the power it would have taken to do such a thing.

"Then, if you can't channel the magic, we'll have to wait for the seas to calm naturally," she had said. "I'm sorry, Kinnet."

And then she'd retreated to her cabin, resolving to write a letter to Lozarr and perhaps a second one to Vistaren, just in case her first message hadn't gotten through.

She'd covered one page in her cramped handwriting and started on a second when she heard the lookout's call.

"SEADRAGON!"

Arama swore and folded her letter without regard for the drying ink. She jammed it into her vest pocket and ran out on deck.

Kinnet had said something about the stormsingers being attacked by seadragons during that storm the night before last, too. But Arama had brushed it off, too concerned with the repairs that had to be made to the ship. Now she wished she'd listened more closely.

Dawn Star was lying some distance out from the lighthouse. Rising from the ocean beyond the ship was a silvery-blue seadragon—the largest Arama could remember seeing. It had glowing green eyes that were fixed on the ship. Its neck arched high into the air, while its tail thrashed the sea an impossibly long distance away from the neck.

"Gunners!" Zek shouted, which prompted a wail from Yar.

The Voice of Dragons was amidships, staring out at the seadragon. His fists were clenched at his sides, his feet planted wide. Every line in his body was tense. Arama wondered if his dragon, Xellax, could lend him strength or magic, or if Yar was on his own.

"Belay that!" Arama said. "Make the guns ready, but don't fire. *Don't fire!*"

Every instinct in her screamed to fire at the dragon before it got any closer. But she remembered what Yar had said about the seadragons not wanting to attack the people. Not to mention the two other times she'd seen seadragons, the great serpents had been largely uninterested in human crafts. They ate fish as well as large marine creatures, but apparently had no taste for human flesh.

Yar strode fiercely to the rail and shouted words Arama couldn't understand at the seadragon. To her shock, the seadragon dipped its head—not as if it were answering, but as if it were attempting to understand. That was a good sign, wasn't it?

As her hands went through the routine of checking her guns and cutlass, Arama kept her gaze on the strange interaction of seadragon and boy. She wondered if Kinnet could use her stormwitchery somehow to distract the seadragon or drive it off. But Kinnet had never been shy about suggesting ways to use her magic, so if she hadn't said anything yet, Arama didn't suppose she was going to.

"What do we do, captain?" Zek was a few steps behind her. His face was paler than she'd ever seen it.

"Wait and see if the Voice of Dragons can manage to be Voice of Seadragons, too, I suppose," Arama said. She didn't lift her hand from the hilt of her cutlass, though.

Yar shouted something else, and a moment later they had their answer. The seadragon's neck straightened, its head bolting up into the air—and then it dove, launching itself forward at the same time. It was coming directly for *Dawn Star*.

"Fire!" Arama shouted. She heard Yar screaming, but she wasn't going to let the monster sink her ship because she was trying not to hurt it. A cannonball or two probably wouldn't do much to a beast this size, anyway.

The guns roared and then the ship lurched. Arama swore. It wasn't the usual recoil of the cannons. That mad beast had rammed the ship!

"Fire as soon as it surfaces!" she shouted. "Large ordnance only—don't waste the small shot!"

Yar was screaming. He was standing stock still, hands clenched into fists at his sides. His eyes were squeezed shut. But his mouth was open in a gaping cavern as he screamed. Arama wrenched her gaze away from him and looked for the seadragon. It would surface eventually.

She hoped it wouldn't surface *through* her ship.

When it did come up, it was between *Dawn Star* and the lighthouse. "Damn it, hold your fire!" Arama shouted. She couldn't risk striking the lighthouse. She saw a figure—it must be Lijka—standing on the top of the tower, watching them.

Yar stopped screaming. "Don't hurt it." His voice was tight and somewhat absent, as if it were an effort for him to speak. "Let me…"

Since the seadragon wasn't moving, Arama was content to let him—whatever he was trying to do.

"…just tell it…" Yar had gone pale underneath his tan skin. Arama thought his entire body might be trembling.

"…who we…"

Yar broke off with a scream as his legs crumpled under him. Arama lunged to catch him, but she was too late, distracted by the sight of the seadragon breaking away from whatever spell Yar had managed to weave it in.

The seadragon, with a furious bellow, doubled back on itself and charged straight for the lighthouse.

"Lijka!"

As Kinnet ran, screaming, past her, Arama managed to catch an arm around the woman's waist. Kinnet swung them both around with the force of her movement. She hit at Arama, trying to wriggle out of her grip.

"Don't," Arama said shortly. She was trying to keep her face towards Kinnet whilst watching the seadragon's unswerving drive for the lighthouse.

"It'll kill her!" Kinnet screamed in her face.

"It won't—she's already down off the tower!"

"Let me go! Let me go!" Kinnet twisted in Arama's grip.

"I can't." Arama looked over her shoulder and found Carig watching from the tiller. "Take us away from here!" she snapped.

He jerked his gaze away and eased the tiller to port.

"Get those sails out!" she ordered. She hoped Kinnet couldn't read her lips. "Where's Zek?"

"Here, captain."

"Take her. Don't hurt her, but keep her from going over the railing."

Zek closed large hands around Kinnet's wrists, pulling her as gently as possible amidships.

Arama turned to look for the seadragon—and almost wished she hadn't.

The creature was bashing itself against the stone lighthouse. It was large enough that bits of the stone were crumbling with every hit. The damned thing was trying to take down the whole tower, she thought.

Closer to, she became aware of a drumming, thudding noise. She looked down to see the cause and realized Yar was in the throes of a violent fit, his heels and head driving against the deck.

"Surgeon!" Arama shouted, ripping off her coat and shoving it roughly between Yar's head and the deck.

She looked back up in time to see the tower shiver. Behind her Kinnet wailed. Zek swore.

Arama ground her teeth and glared around her at all the things she could do nothing about—the helpless Yar, the collapsing lighthouse, the half-deployed sails, the frantic Kinnet. Damn it! Give her something to blow up and she was fine. But in a situation like this, her hands were tied.

"I've got him, captain," said a breathless voice, and Arama looked up to see their surgeon was trying to force something into Yar's mouth.

Arama stood and strode over to Kinnet, who spat at her.

"Stop that," Arama said with a calm she didn't feel. "Calm down."

"You've murdered her! You just let that monster murder her!"

Arama snapped her fingers in front of Kinnet's face, trying to get the woman to focus on her enough to read her lips. "There was nothing we could do that wouldn't endanger her further."

"You've always hated her!" Kinnet shrieked. "You can't just let her die!"

Zek was watching their exchange, his eyes wide. No one spoke to Arama like this normally. She gave him a tight smile. Then she gripped Kinnet by the shoulders and shook her hard.

Kinnet stopped screaming and went still, though her chest heaved as she gasped for breath. After a few moments, she turned her head a little and looked at Arama's face.

"Good," Arama said crisply. "First of all. She'll be fine. She'll have realized the dry cellar is the safest place for her. The seadragon can't get to her there." She hoped.

Kinnet's gaze was slowly focusing on her.

"Secondly, I haven't murdered her. I wouldn't do. I may not see eye to eye with your wife, but any idiot can tell she makes you happy. Our past history aside, I would not wish harm to someone who brought you joy."

Kinnet took a deep, shuddering breath.

"Thirdly, we don't have the resources to rescue her. The academy does. They'll know the light's fallen. They *don't* know, hopefully, that she's with us. They'll send a rescue team, and she'll be better off for it. The best thing *we* can do for Lijka is to get far enough away that those rescuers don't realize we're involved."

Finally Kinnet nodded slowly. Zek hadn't let go of her, though his grip had obviously loosened. Arama gave Kinnet an encouraging nod and then turned to look at the lighthouse—

—just in time to see the upper half of the tower shiver, slide, and crash down into the sea.

31

Pralith was just entering the academy grounds after council at the palace when he heard a breathless voice call his name. He turned to see who was hailing him. One of the academy stormwitches, plump and bearded, puffed up to him. As well as serving on the academy council, Malinche Bernays was one of their more popular instructors, and fairly powerful in the witchery. Pralith greeted him with a smile and outstretched hand. He liked Bernays, but the man's furrowed brow worried him.

"What's wrong, Bernays? You look as if you'd reached for a fish and caught a siren instead."

Bernays pursed his generous lips. "That might be it exactly, Menever. My seventh-level students and I were conducting routine scrying exercises when one of them detected some sort of anomaly out at sea. She reported it to me, as is proper, and the six of us worked together to perform a stronger scrying. We all saw it, but…" He wiped sweat off his forehead.

"Well, get on with it," Pralith urged. "What sort of anomaly? What's it doing?"

"It appears to be a storm, but it's…well, it's creating itself. There are no weather patterns that are contributing to it, and we could detect no stormwitch responsible."

"That isn't possible." Pralith ran a fingernail across his lower lip. "Creating itself? Not possible."

"You and I know that, but the storm doesn't appear to," Bernays replied. "I dismissed my students, with orders to keep silent, and came straight to you."

Pralith sighed. "Well, you'd better come to my study. I

want a look at this impossible, self-creating storm."

Bernays heaved a sigh of relief when they reached Pralith's study. Pralith gestured for him to enter ahead of him.

"Did you bring a focus?"

Bernays fished a large amber seaglass pendant from the front of his robes. Pralith nodded after only a cursory inspection. He trusted Bernays to know his business. Amber. He fished around in one of the seaglass drawers until he had found a piece that matched Bernays' in color, if not size. Then for good measure, he selected a creamy-white piece the same size as Bernays' piece.

"Now," he said, "let us just see."

Bernays was right. Pralith had to fight not to recoil from the unnatural sight of the storm energies swirling slowly to the right. The energies were not formed by sea current or wind. Pralith could detect nothing that influenced their formation. He strained, gathering yet more power and channeling it at the anomaly.

Instead of being deflected off course, the anomaly *ate* his power. Ate it! Pralith did recoil, shaken, as Bernays laughed grimly.

"You see," the instructor said. "It makes no sense, Menever. And yet it exists."

"Indeed," Pralith whispered. "I must think on this." He licked his lips. "Let us…let us keep this between us for now, yes?"

"It won't stay between us for long," Bernays pointed out. "It'll be on Maron before we know it."

"I may be able to divert it."

Bernays shuddered. "With Eldry's help, you mean? May you have the joy of it. She frightens me."

Pralith shrugged. Eldry's power was frightening, viewed a certain way. But viewed another way, it was just another tool to be used. He was sure that, given time, he could shape her power to his ends.

***

When Eldry arrived in answer to his summons, she showed none of the humility or honor a journeywoman stormwitch should show to her master. Pralith shoved away the thought that he had offered her mastery just a few days ago. She had refused it, after all, so she should still behave as if she were a journeywoman.

After he explained what Bernays had told him, and what they had seen together, she huffed a sigh. "We'll have to look together," she said. "I don't want to waste time looking for it by myself."

Pralith raised an eyebrow at her. Just two months ago that had been all it took to make the girl blush and apologize, but she had changed too much for him since departing on the *Elana Bey*. Eldry just met his gaze with her weird, wintergreen gaze.

Pralith shivered and turned to pick up his focus.

As they channeled together, Eldry allowed him to guide her, right up until the moment the rapidly-growing anomaly became apparent. Then she took control of their witchery, so deftly Pralith only noticed when that strange emptiness tugged at his chest.

"We can push it over the Blades," Eldry said. "You'll have to help."

"I am helping," Pralith muttered, but he tried to feed her more power. He squeezed his eyes shut, trying to envision what she was doing despite being unable to actually see it.

"More!" she snapped.

A low groan escaped his throat as he thrust more power at her, feeling her whip it away and demand more even before she snapped, "More!"

"I have nothing more to give!" he snapped back.

He felt the witchery between them stretch thin, thinner, felt her winding it around herself, almost as if she were wrapping herself in his magic. Then, to his shock, he felt something stab into his side just below his ribs.

He screamed.

No, he *tried* to scream. No sound came out of his O-shaped lips.

Heat seared him, driving the breath from his lungs. Cold flooded him. Pralith's eyes flew open and he stared at her face, twisted in a livid mask of hunger.

She smiled at him and he turned his gaze slowly down to where her hand was pressed against his tunic. Her hand—clutched around the sharp piece of seaglass she had just driven into his torso.

"*More*," she whispered, and light flashed so brilliantly he thought he'd been blinded.

Almost before the light was gone, Pralith's skin burned so cold-hot that he screamed aloud, and this time the sound escaped, blood-flecked.

"That's better," Eldry said. Her voice was calm, satisfied. Pralith stared at her in shock.

She lifted a blood-coated palm and covered his eyes. Reflexively, he closed them, and in an instant he could see— actually *see*—the anomaly breaking up into wisps of cloud and moisture.

"You just had to give me more, Pralith." When he opened his eyes to stare at her again, Eldry was smiling at him.

"More—" he wheezed.

"More. You gave me this idea yourself, Pralith," she said sweetly. "What a fine Stormweapon you'll make, once you've learned."

She smiled at him and walked out of the room, leaving Pralith to watch her, open-mouthed.

After several heartbeats he looked down, expecting to see the front of his tunic soaked and gushing with blood. There *was* blood, but less than he'd expected. His tunic had a ragged, vaguely round hole in it, but the seaglass he expected to see protruding from the cloth…wasn't there.

He lifted his tunic and then his shirt, and when his fingers touched bare skin he jerked them away with a hiss.

There, protruding from below his last rib on the left, was a smooth piece of red-streaked white seaglass.

32

The paper in Vistaren's hand crinkled as he yawned. He hadn't slept well the night before. He and Lozarr had sat up late with Kedar Ebb, and though they hadn't talked about anything in particular, it had been well past midnight when Vistaren finally found his bed. When Isden woke him this morning, Vistaren had been sorely tempted to exercise the privilege of royalty and stay abed…but he'd found himself unable to do it, knowing that the men and women who had pledged to fight and perhaps die for him were up at drill.

All the same, he'd drunk more coffee this morning than he was wont to, and even though he knew he would pay for it later with trips to the privy and jumpy nerves, he had poured himself another cup just before Azmei's messenger bird flew in.

Devlin had locked up the birds raised at Longdale Keep and destroyed the message lodestone, but Vistaren had been traveling with a lodestone keyed only to him. Only Azmei and Arama had birds whose leg-bands would guide them to that lodestone. Vistaren kept hoping for a letter from Arama, but so far his only messages had been Azmei's, arriving faithfully every day as she had promised.

I got to the lighthouse just after it was reduced to rubble by a seadragon. At least, that's what Lijka told me, and I have no reason to doubt her. The man who sailed me in didn't want to leave me here, but when Lijka appeared on the beach, he made haste to be rid of me and my packs.

Lijka reports that Arama tried to return, but the seadragon drove Dawn Star *away. Lijka knows Kinnet was on board, but she doesn't know why the seadragon attacked. I told her about the attack on* Victorious *when we were sailing to Maron. We'll have to save further speculation until we hear from Kinnet or Yar.*

Just a few glasses after I arrived, the stormwitch academy ship showed up with workers and two journeymen stormwitches. They expected to find Lijka and Kinnet dead in the rubble, but Lijka's injuries were convincing enough that they didn't come into the basement. She claimed I was Kinnet, suffering from a fever that set in after the light came down, and they seem to have believed her.

I can't swear they suspect nothing, so I will exercise caution in all I do. Nevertheless, I have learned much from Lijka that I did not know, and I believe I know enough now to begin to aid our cause using my own particular talents.

For now, Lijka maintains the light despite the tower's state of ruination. Tomorrow I will go to Maron and seek work at the academy.

Thank you for having faith in me. I wish you all best.

The letter wasn't signed, but Vistaren knew Azmei's handwriting. Vistaren read the letter twice and then fed the close-written page carefully into his fire. It was probably an unnecessary precaution, but it seemed a good idea to protect her.

Someone tapped at the door to his rooms. "Highness?"

It was Lozarr's voice. Isden opened the door without waiting for Vistaren's acknowledgement, and the general walked in.

"Isden," he greeted, and then, "Vistaren."

Vistaren turned in his chair, smiling at Lo. "What news?"

Lo wasn't smiling. "Balahar's army at our gates, I'm afraid."

Vistaren knew he ought to stand, but his knees felt weak. He gripped the arms of his chair, staring up at Lo. "What?"

"A skirmisher rode in on a lathered horse first thing this morning. He said Bal was on the move, and we began preparing."

"Why wasn't I told?" Vistaren demanded. At Lozarr's look of surprise, he felt his cheeks heat. He sounded like a petulant boy.

"I should have told you," Lo said. "I apologize. I didn't want to trouble you until we were certain."

Vistaren shook his head, acutely aware of how much more experience Lo had. "No, I'm sorry." He stood, reaching out a hand to grip Lo's. "I've given you charge of my army, and I need to trust you with it. I *do* trust you with it. My apologies, Lo."

Lozarr blinked and then smiled faintly. "You need not apologize to me. You are the *prince*."

There was something different, Vistaren had noticed lately, in the way Lozarr said that word. He didn't know if it was because Vistaren had finally asserted himself, shedding his old role of friendly, food-loving royal—or if it was because Vistaren had set himself against his father, attempting to claim a new role of Amethir's king.

He wasn't certain if he wanted to know.

After a moment, Lo sighed. "Anyway, Balahar's troops *were* on the move. We can see them from the walls now, and they're coming at a decent pace."

Vistaren's stomach jumped. He sat down and looked into his coffee cup, regretting the last refill. "What do you think, Lo?"

The silence lasted so long he looked up to see his friend frowning and rubbing a thumb across his lower lip. Vistaren bit back the questions he wanted to ask. Finally, Lo sighed again.

"They have cannon. My scouts report at least six four-pounders. The guns won't do much against a solid-built stone fortress, but they'll have brought sappers with them."

Vistaren nodded. He was still learning about how gunpowder and firearms had changed the profession of war. He'd studied the Shroudling War, of course, but that had been fought with cold steel and crossbows. At the time, gunpowder had been in short supply, so as Vistaren grew up, he had learned the sword. It had only been in the last five years or so that muskets became more readily available in

Amethir. Tamnen and Strid were still fighting their war mostly with swords and crossbows, and cannons—hard to move without wagons and teams—were of more use either mounted in fortifications or on ships.

Sappers, though…sappers had been in use for decades, and if the Amethirians had ever actually located a Shroudling fortress, they might have driven the Shroudlings back into their mountain stronghold much faster.

"Your recommendation?" Vistaren asked.

"I'm not sure I have any," Lo admitted. "We'll be ready to fire on them, of course. But we have the fortress, and we have the high ground. As long as we're supplied—and Dev assures me we're well supplied—we can hold out for weeks."

Vistaren nodded. "Very good," he said, and then his anxiety got the better of him. "What do you want me to do, Lo? Do you need me to make a speech? Should I just go out and watch on the battlements? I have no idea what my role is in this."

Lozarr looked at him for a moment and then sat in the chair across from Vistaren's. "I won't hide from you that your role is largely symbolic. You are a fine shot, I reckon, and well-versed in the use of several types of blade. But I can train a musketeer or swordsman. What I cannot train is someone to whom it is given to lead our people—someone to whom compassion comes naturally. You care about Amethir and her people, and you care about right and wrong." He paused, then ran a hand through his hair.

"I have served your father all my life, and I have respected him. But he is proud. You…" He huffed a laugh. "You have a natural dignity, and yet you never act as if you think yourself above me, let alone my soldiers. You care about the fate of the plain folk who live in towns like Anderly and Jorey. You care about those who make their living from the sea, those who might have lost loved ones in the recent anomaly storms."

Vistaren could feel his face getting hot. He hadn't meant to fish for compliments, but Lozarr was looking at him with an earnest expression, his eyes shining.

"You care, and you wish to do your best for this kingdom." Lo's lips curled faintly. "I wish I could explain it better, but that's what it comes down to. You actually give a damn. That's a gift beyond price."

Vistaren wanted to laugh. That shouldn't be anything to be grateful for. And yet Lo clearly was grateful for it. He realized his knee was bobbing nervously and stilled it. "I do care, Lo. It's hard to see each soldier as a person with a spouse and family, with desires and dreams…but I try to see them that way. I try to realize that every man or woman who fights—and maybe dies—for me is a person like me, someone who has a life of their own."

He shrugged. "Knowing you and Arama has helped. For so long, you were just this handsome, strong soldier I wanted. No," he added as Lo opened his mouth to protest. "No, you know that, and I know you know it. But you didn't let that put you off. You became my friend, and I learned to see you as someone apart from my image of you. And then I learned of your friendship with Arama, and I realized that your own desires and longings were as important as mine."

Vistaren felt his face heating, but he forged on. "And then I met Arama and learned her desires and longings. I learned to see her as not just the Storm Petrel, hero privateer of Amethir, but as a woman who had lost people she loved, a woman who knew more about sailing than most other people combined." He sucked in a breath. "And as a woman who was afraid to give her love to someone else." He hoped he wasn't overstepping, but then again, if he was overstepping, he'd done it long before this. "Along the way, somehow, I learned that *everyone* has a story to tell, if I will only listen."

He ran out of words and decided to stop talking instead of floundering his way through more incoherent half explanations.

Lo blinked a couple of times at him and exhaled. "And that, Vistaren, is why so many people love you and wish to follow you." He gave Vistaren a half smile and shook his head. "That is also why I know I am on the right side of this war. Win or lose, I will never regret following you."

Vistaren smiled faintly. "Win or lose, I appreciate that," he said. "But let us do our best to win."

Lo grinned at him and stood. "With your permission, I'll go see if I can't do something about that."

Vistaren stood, too. "I'll come with you. If nothing else, I can let the soldiers see who they're fighting for."

Lo nodded and led the way to the door.

***

Ever since the seadragon attack, Lijka's home had been plagued with errant breezes. She hadn't realized until then just how fond she'd grown of her stone tower surrounded by the sea.

She looked at Princess Azmei, who was huddled close to the fire, hands curled around a cup of hot tea. She'd had her doubts about Vistaren's choice to marry a woman he could never love. She'd been indignant on his behalf, unhappy that he felt forced to take a wife simply to breed children of royal blood. In the time that she'd known Azmei, though, the princess had begun to change her mind.

Lijka had begun to see that Vistaren's choice wasn't just about getting heirs of the body. Azmei had a good head on her shoulders, and skills that should be the envy of any queen. Vistaren was being shrewd about choosing his ruling partner. And if he couldn't feel anything more than friendship for her...Well, Lijka was beginning to see the benefits of that, too.

Staring at her wife across the gulf of tossing waves, a maddened seadragon between them, had been the worst moment of Lijka's life—worse, even, than the night the *Bounder* went down. She had been afraid for herself, of course, but harder still had been her fear for Kinnet.

The flutter of wings made Lijka look up. A messenger

bird was landing on what used to be a windowsill. She gathered the bird to her, gently releasing the paper from the message tube. "Bide here awhile," she said, finding a cracker to crumble for the bird.

It brought her a letter from Kinnet.

I pray to the gods you are well. Arama stopped me from leaping overboard to swim to you, and now that we are removed from the situation, I am able—grudgingly—to admit that is probably best. She pointed out how clever you are. I hope she is right that you took shelter in the cellar as soon as the seadragon began attacking the tower.

If she's wrong, and you are buried in a pile of rubble, I will kill her.

Lijka grinned faintly. Kinnet liked Arama, but even people she liked were less important to her than her wife.

We have met with Qiaru and his pod, and we know a little more than we did. The stormsingers have been charged by Sea Lord Antos to fight the seadragons. Apparently the god they call Poisoner of Fish has been urging the seadragons to harm us. The Sea Lord is awake, and the Ranarri's god of peace has never slept.

Thann sleeps restlessly and dreams. He may yet become a problem. The other gods are still deep asleep, save the Great Mother. She— well, we could get no answer. I wonder if she has not removed herself entirely from our concern. I believe we have nothing to fear from her, at least.

I love you, Lijka. I'm sorry I insisted on going. It was necessary, but after seeing the lighthouse come down. Several words were scribbled out. *I will not leave you again once we are reunited.*

Lijka looked up from the letter to see Azmei watching her.

"It's a letter from Kinnet," she said, and relayed what Kinnet had learned. "She was right to go, though. This is serious, and it is our duty. This is what we pledged our lives for."

Azmei smiled faintly. "She isn't wrong to say she doesn't want to leave you again, though."

Lijka nodded.

"So. Knowing what we know, that god you don't name

must be urging on the Stormweapon—Eldry, you said she's called?"

"Yes. A girl full of talent and ambition, but she's come back with a double measure of both. She has Pralith's ear, and Pralith has the king's ear." Lijka shook her head and prodded at the fire. "I fear that whatever we attempt, she will find out and sabotage us."

"We'll have to change her mind, if possible."

"Change her mind, when *that* one urges her on?" Lijka tucked her wife's letter into her skirt pocket.

"All right. I suppose if she's sworn herself somehow to a god, she won't be easy to sway." Azmei chewed her lower lip. "What about Pralith? Do you think he could be persuaded to see reason?"

"No." Lijka spoke the word automatically and then frowned. "Well. I could feel him out. It's possible he's been deceived by her."

Azmei tilted her head, watching Lijka.

"He's hungry for praise," Lijka explained. "He's a talented stormwitch, but he only became King's Stormwitch three years ago. My successor had stepped down, and the council… Well." She paused. The politics of the position were too complicated to explain, and they only mattered a little. "Pralith and I are close to the same age, and close to the same strength. But I was made King's Stormwitch at a young age. I left the position fifteen years ago, shortly after *Bounder* went down, and I was succeeded by a man in his sixth decade. When he felt he was too old to serve ably, he stepped down and we held a conclave. Five of us selected the next King's Stormwitch."

Azmei nodded.

"I voted for Kinnet, as did one other. But Pralith received three votes, and he assumed the title. It's been a point of contention between them ever since. It doesn't help that I married Kinnet a few months later." She bowed her head. "Pralith and I were close, once. He may not listen to me."

"Because of your marriage?" Azmei nodded. "But on

the other hand, he may listen to you, if you approach him *despite* your marriage and your support of Kinnet. Perhaps he'll see that you are not playing politics with him, but truly care about him."

"Perhaps."

Lijka wanted to believe it was possible. She and Pralith had come to the academy at nearly the same time. They had been well-matched in their classes, and had been friendly rivals all through their apprenticeship and journeyman years. He hadn't begrudged her the position of King's Stormwitch when it was appointed her.

Things had only soured between them when she supported Kinnet for the role instead of him.

Azmei nodded. "Do you think you could go to the academy tomorrow?"

"Yes. The supply boat only brought enough for a short while. And I have duties that take me to the capital once a week, as it is."

"Good." Azmei set her jaw. "If you can't turn Pralith, I'll have to kill the Stormweapon. I'd rather resolve this without killing, if possible."

"It may come to that anyway," Lijka warned her.

"Perhaps. But I'll save as many as we can."

Lijka nodded.

33

Lijka approached the academy building with more trepidation than she'd felt since her return following the *Bounder*'s sinking. This building had been her home for more than half her life. It provided stability, safety, and family—everything she'd ever thought she wanted. But if Pralith was truly in Eldry's thrall, and Eldry was truly in thrall to the Twister of Worlds, the academy was no longer the safe place it had always been.

Which is exactly why you're here, she reminded herself.

Taking a deep breath, she walked up the steps into the main building of the academy. She was greeted almost at once by friends and people she knew, and she spent nearly half a glass assuring people she was well despite the lighthouse's collapse. She spent another half-glass speaking to the academy quartermaster to resupply her usual needs and obtain supplies to refit the lighthouse.

It was past midday when she finally made her way through the passages of the main residential hall to Pralith's quarters. Her footsteps slowed as she drew near to Pralith's door, the fancy nameplate indicating he was King's Stormwitch.

She closed her eyes, reminding herself that she wasn't just here for herself. She was here for Vistaren and Azmei, for the stormwitch academy, and for Amethir itself. She was here trying to stop whatever horrible consequences were in store, should the gods continue waking. After a moment she found the courage to lift her hand and knock.

There was a long silence—so long Lijka lifted her hand to knock again. Then the latch clicked. After a moment the door swung slowly open, and Pralith stood there. He gazed at her with open curiosity, and Lijka thought he looked thinner than he had the last time she saw him. But after several heartbeats he licked his lips and smiled.

"I'm glad to see you unharmed," he said. "The report we received was that your lighthouse was severely damaged."

Lijka nodded. "It wasn't fun to witness it firsthand," she said. "May I come in?"

He stood aside, holding the door open wider. "Of course." The knuckles of the hand that clutched the door were white. Lijka wondered what strong emotion made him grip the door so tightly.

She stepped in anyway and paused in the small vestibule, waiting for him to indicate she could continue in. He swung the door closed with a definite thump and then turned. His movements seemed slow. She wondered if she'd woken him from a nap.

"Sit down with me," Pralith invited, indicating the sitting room to the left of the vestibule.

Lijka scanned the area and chose the chair that looked less used. She didn't want to put him on edge by taking his favorite seat.

"I just brewed some tea," he said, taking the chair opposite her. "Would you like some?"

"Thank you."

They made polite conversation while he poured the tea and offered her sugar and cream, then he lifted his own cup for a sip. When he lowered it, Pralith said, "What are you really doing here?"

His tone was so calm, so like the tone of his polite remarks, that it took a moment to register. When it did, Lijka tilted her head back, studying his face through narrowed eyes. But from his expression, it was a genuine question rather than a hostile one.

She looked down at her teacup. "Before I married Kinnet, you and I were friends. I wish we still were."

Pralith sighed, but didn't speak for a long while. They

sipped their tea. Lijka found herself reluctant to break the silence, so she waited for his response. The silence stretched until it was uncomfortable, but her patience paid off.

Pralith's cup clinked against its saucer. "You voted for her to be King's Stormwitch."

There was no accusation in the words, just an explanation. It was the explanation Lijka had expected, but she felt mostly relief that he had spoken it openly. It was between them now.

"Because I believed she was best suited to it," she said. "You are an amazing stormwitch, Pralith. But your skill at research was what we needed most from you. I have grown to love Kinnet, and I believe she has a fine analytical mind, but she doesn't have your curiosity. I thought she would serve better as an advisor, and you as a researcher."

He blinked at her, his mouth open. "I…I thought you had no faith in me," he said at last.

"Not that."

Pralith bowed his head. Lijka didn't wish to protest so strongly that he grew suspicious, and her answer had the benefit of being true, so she left it at that. He would have to think about it and decide for himself if it was reason enough. She looked around, admiring the mahogany furniture in his sitting area and the pale green and blue upholstery of the furniture. He had fine taste, there was no question of that.

After awhile he said in a low voice, "You're happy with her."

Lijka's smile was involuntary. "I am. She's renewed my joy."

Pralith nodded. He was studying his teacup. "I'm glad of that. I never believed the *Bounder* wreck broke you." He seemed not to notice how she flinched. "But I thought perhaps *you* believed it had."

Lijka's smile widened at the care in his words. So many people had thought either her nerve or her skill broken, and just after the wreck, she'd been content to let them think that. It warmed her to think that Pralith had known better.

When she lowered her empty cup, Pralith leaned forward to refill it. She heard his breath catch and he put a hand to his side for a brief instant. Before she could say anything, though, he angled his body forward at the hips and poured her tea.

She watched carefully as he sat back, and she knew she wasn't imagining that he was in pain. Something made him clench his teeth and suck his breath between them.

"Pralith?" she said softly.

He frowned. "It's nothing."

It wasn't nothing. She knew it, and she suspected he knew it as well. She simply looked at him, and after a while he heaved a sigh and set down his teacup.

"I haven't shown anyone," he said, his hand going to his side. He gathered the cloth of his tunic in his fingers and lifted it. She felt his gaze on her face, but she couldn't look away from the edge of fabric as it rose. When his side was bared, it took her several heartbeats to realize what she was seeing.

She sucked in a breath. Embedded in the pale skin just under his ribcage was an icicle-shaped, red-and-white piece of seaglass. The flesh puckered around the glass was an angry red, but there was no blood. It almost looked as if it had been cauterized somehow.

"What—" she breathed.

"I was joint channeling with Eldry." His words were clipped. She realized as she saw the glass heave with his breathing how much it must hurt him to breath, let alone speak or move. "We were watching a storm forming out to sea, and she wanted to shift it. I didn't have enough power to share with her."

"So she *stabbed* you?" Lijka couldn't stop staring at the wound.

Except wound wasn't quite the right word, was it? It was almost an alteration like that of Eldry's seaglass eye replacement. There was no bleeding or oozing. She would be surprised if it were infected. It was simply…embedded in him.

"She weaponized me." Pralith's voice was tired.

"Without asking you? Without even discussing it?"

He sighed. "It worked. I can't see it as she can, but I can feel the weather like a pulse now. It speaks to me through my blood, somehow."

"But your pain!" Lijka gasped.

Pralith shifted one shoulder. It might be a shrug. "Channeling lightning was never pleasant."

It always had been for Lijka. She felt lightning as a pleasant tingle across the surface of her skin, and when it was stronger, as a deep vibration in her bones. She had always enjoyed lightning. "Perhaps," she said slowly. "But you're so pale."

He shifted his shoulder again.

"And to do it without your consent!" Lijka felt herself growing angry. Eldry forcing her weaponization onto Pralith was like a man forcing his body upon a woman's. Done without permission, without welcome, it wasn't right. "Whatever the benefit, it was wrong of her!"

He sighed. "It's how that Scavenger fellow fixed her."

"And her passing it along to you doesn't make it right!" she snapped.

"What's done is done." He spoke dully but implacably.

"But—" she began, and he cut her off.

"Did you come to renew our friendship, or to judge me?" he snapped. "What's done is done."

Lijka bowed her head. "I'm sorry," she whispered. She had been judging Eldry, not Pralith, but she could understand why he felt that way. She hadn't meant to shame him for what had been done to him.

Pralith shook his head and let his tunic fall back over the seaglass. "It is good to sit with you like this," he said after a while. "I missed your friendship."

Lijka nodded. She could see that, despite Eldry's sins against him, he would only continue to dig in his heels if she kept pressing him on it. "Striving against you always kept me on my toes," she said, smiling faintly. "I had so few people who were working on the same level I was."

He chuckled. "As did I. I believe we learned from each other."

"Certainly," Lijka said. She wondered if Eldry outclassed both of them. She was hoping to turn Pralith against Eldry, but perhaps even the two of them working together wouldn't be strong enough to take her on.

"What brought you to Maron today?" he asked after a time.

"Oh, I needed some supply replenishment. Kinnet has taken a fever since the tower collapsed, and I'm nearly out of feverbane, among other things. And I hope to take a chicken home for a heartening soup."

Pralith nodded and lapsed into silence.

They made a few more desultory forays into conversation, but after another half-glass, Lijka thought she had accomplished all she could for a first attempt. She rose, making her excuses, and pretended not to notice how relieved Pralith was that she was going.

34

Thunder rumbled overhead. Lozarr glared at the clouds and tugged his cloak up to cover his head. It had been raining for a week, since Balahar's army arrived to camp outside the walls of Longdale Keep. Amethir's storm season was still a fortnight off, so they knew Balahar must have stormwitches calling the storms and keeping them stalled over the fort.

As far as tactics went, Lo had to admit, it was a success in terms of morale as well as battle.

The courtyard was a slippery, muddy mess. No one had been completely dry for at least three days. The keep cannons were sheltered enough to continue firing, but the soldiers had switched to bows to keep their powder dry. People were beginning to snap at each other, and even the affable Vistaren had declined to leave his comfortable fire today.

To Lo's mind, the rain was actually a blessing in one way—it had encouraged the keep's defenders to switch to bows earlier than they might have done on their own. He was worried about their supply, not of ammunition, but of powder. Lo and Orshard had agreed their powder supply was better used by the cannons to defend the keep, but as a result, the musketeers would soon be unable to use their weapons.

Another crack of thunder split the morning, followed by a scream of pain. Lo squinted through the driving rain in time to see a figure in mail topple from the wall.

"Damn them," he muttered. A score of soldiers had been struck by lightning so far, and he was convinced Bal's stormwitches were doing it on purpose. They hadn't all died, but falling thirty feet, even if you were landing in mud six inches deep, was incapacitating for most soldiers.

A bedraggled messenger bird fluttered down to land on the walkway near Lo's feet. He sighed and leaned over to scoop it into his arms. The officers had been passing the message lodestone between them as each man came on watch, so it was his responsibility to carry the bird to Vistaren, or send it with someone. Lo had assigned Anmeir to count the foodstores, so he would have to carry it himself.

Vistaren's rooms were inside the central keep on the fourth floor. He'd wanted a view of the surrounding countryside, and Lo had been happy to keep him further from the actual fighting, in case the walls were breeched. But that meant carrying the soppy messenger bird up several flights of stairs, his cloak dripping the entire way.

He knocked on the prince's door and heard a voice bidding him enter. The wall of warmth that greeted him did much to soothe his annoyance at the bird.

"Lo. Hullo." Vistaren's voice was dull, expressionless. He was sitting in front of the window, staring through the rain-streaked glass over the keep grounds.

"A bird, highness. Just arrived." Lo held out the bedraggled pigeon, which chose that moment to fluff its feathers, sending a spatter of raindrops across them both.

Vistaren took the bird without comment. Lo watched him unroll the message from the tube. He hoped Vistaren wasn't sinking into a gloom. The prince was prone to it at times, and while Lo had to admit it would be justified under the circumstances, it would certainly make their situation more difficult.

After a short silence, Vistaren grunted. "Azmei is well. She has Lijka attempting to change Pralith's allegiance, on the strength of their old friendship. Azmei's working as an errand *boy* in the academy." He snorted. "She likes passing as a boy, apparently, and I can't say it isn't better as a disguise."

Lo nodded. He didn't know what to say. As he understood it, Princess Azmei was trained as a spy and assassin and was a master of disguises. In Lo's opinion, Azmei might be their best weapon; she seemed to have an intrinsic hardness Vistaren lacked. Not that that was a weakness in Vistaren, necessarily; Lo thought it made Vistaren and Azmei a good team.

Vistaren had plenty of assets on his side. He had Arama, after all, and she was the finest sailor Lo had ever met. On top of that, they had the aid of Lijka Ardelis *and* her wife Kinnet—both of them stormwitches of strong talent.

Lo thought of Arama's old dislike of Lijka and hoped she would move beyond that for the prince's sake. He missed Arama. He wondered where she was. He knew she had taken the Voice of Dragons and Kinnet Ardelis to look for the stormsingers, but if Vistaren had any news of their venture, he hadn't shared it. Lo thought of asking, but thought it might seem churlish, since Vistaren had no one who was to him what Arama was to Lo.

The silence had stretched too long. Lo wanted to say something, but he couldn't think of the right words, so he kept staring at the fire crackling in the hearth. He was startled when Vistaren sighed explosively.

"We're in trouble, aren't we?" the prince asked.

Lo weighed his words before speaking. "Our situation isn't ideal," he said finally. "Our cannon shot runs low. The muskets have plenty of shot, but there isn't much powder."

"How long can we withstand this siege?"

Lo didn't think he was imagining the tremor in Vistaren's voice. He reminded himself that the prince was only twenty-three and had never seen war the way Lo had. He'd studied it, certainly, and was a swordsman and musketeer of some talent, but studying war was nothing like actually living through it. All the same, Lo knew Vistaren for a brave man, and he owed it to the prince to be honest.

"We have the food to last some while yet," he said slowly. "But Vistaren, I think that between Balahar's sappers and our powder running low, we should make a plan in case the walls are breached."

Vistaren nodded. "What do you think we should do if

his sappers are successful?"

"We'll have to fight, obviously," Lo said, thinking aloud. "They'll bring a section of the wall down, and there'll be fighting in the breach. If they bring their cannons up, that'll mean trouble. If it were up to me, I'd designate one brigade to hold Balahar off while the other three evacuate the keep."

Vistaren lowered his head and rubbed his face. "I thought we'd have more time."

"I did too." Lo couldn't suppress a pang of sympathy as he looked at the prince. "The fact is, Bal brought a lot of men with him, and he can probably get more shot and powder, while we can't. On top of that, the lightning. I'm certain he's using stormwitchery against us."

Vistaren nodded. "What plan do you recommend?"

Thunder rumbled overhead, rattling the glass in the windows as Lozarr considered his answer. He'd given the matter a great deal of thought following a conversation with Anmeir. He took a slow breath.

"I would have Orshard's brigade hold Balahar off. Order my two brigades and Devlin's to ride out, and march along the road north to Estermere."

"Didn't Devlin say he'd sent some of his questionable soldiers up there?"

Lo nodded. "I don't think we should march all the way to Estermere. I've been studying the map and talking to my aide, Anmeir. He's from Darkwell, and he says there's a local road that goes around Estermere. We could march along that and continue on to Firebend. There's no garrison at Firebend. We could rest our soldiers there for a night, maybe two. Then we head for Darkwell."

Vistaren was frowning. "I don't know where that is."

Lo imagined the map of Amethir. "Just outside the Sandswamp," he said, and licked his lips. "No one but locals do well in the swamp. We could take shelter there, and Anmeir says his people would shelter us on his say-so. His mother's the elder there, apparently."

He'd learned a lot about his aide in the past week, since Anmeir had recommended Darkwell as a refuge in case of need. He'd been surprised by much of it, but he was, more than ever, convinced of Anmeir's value as an officer of the Amethirian army.

Or the rebel army, as it were.

Vistaren stood, shoving his chair back, and paced across the room. He paused at the desk, looking down at some papers spread out across it. He pushed a hand through his hair and then let the hand fall back to his side. His shoulders were slumped.

Lo felt a pang of sympathy. "I don't think it will come to that any time soon," he said, and hoped he wasn't overstating the case. "We can hold Bal off awhile yet."

Vistaren had lifted his head to smile at Lo when thunder rattled the windows again. He nodded. "Keep me informed, please," he said. "But I shouldn't interfere with whatever you ought to be doing."

Lo gave him a faint smile. He knew Vistaren liked the idea of being a warrior prince who could lead the kingdom to victory and glory, but he was grateful that the prince was a practical enough man to leave the actual warfare to the professionals.

"I don't expect we'll have any trouble, but I'll report back at the end of my watch, highness," he promised.

Vistaren nodded and Lo let himself out of the prince's rooms.

35

Azmei smoothed her hair back from her face. She'd tied it at the base of her skull, but it was still short enough that a few strands escaped. With her breasts bound and hidden under the gray tunic of an academy servant, she ought to look like an anonymous boy running errands for the instructors. At least, that was her hope, and Lijka had said she passed.

This was Azmei's third day at the Academy. Lijka had sailed her in from the lighthouse and dropped her off at the public dock. From there, Azmei had gone to the academy's kitchens, carrying a letter of reference that said she had once worked for one of Lijka's cousins. The kitchens hadn't needed her, but the academy kept a small staff of errand runners, and they were short just now.

It was the perfect cover for her to gather information, and so far no one—not even Pralith Menever—had recognized her as their future queen. She'd only seen the King's Stormwitch once, and that a chance meeting in a hallway, but his gaze had skipped over the servant's tunic, just as she'd known it would.

She had managed to learn the general layout of the academy, including where certain important stormwitches were quartered. The academy council all lived three floors up, just over the kitchens and mess hall. The lesser masters were further up, the journeymen further yet, and the apprentices in one of three separate dormitory buildings, based generally on the length of time the apprentice had been there. Lessons were taught in one of three buildings that corresponded roughly with the dormitories.

Eldry Karayan's rooms were up in the journeyman floors. She'd been offered a mastery based on her deeds the night of the betrothal ball, Azmei learned, but had refused. To some who had known her before, it raised suspicions of disingenuousness. To several of the masters, who had only a passing acquaintance with Eldry, it looked like a fitting humility.

Azmei wanted to believe it was humility, but she couldn't bring herself to trust Eldry Karayan. The woman had called herself Stormweapon and had acted without even consulting with the king. Vistaren had said the stormwitches were independent of crown control, but that they were pledged to serve Amethir. Seen in that light, there was nothing wrong with how Eldry had taken control.

All the same, it seemed it would have been courteous of her to at least ask the king what he wished her to do.

"You there, errand lad!" A plump, bearded man wearing the insignia of a stormwitch councilor waved at her.

Azmei stopped walking and bowed, doing her best to look complacent.

"I need a message carried to the journeyman level. Journeyman Veit Tumaina." He held out a folded paper.

Azmei took the paper and bowed again.

"Quick now, lad. I want it to reach him before dinner."

"Right away, master," she said. The man nodded and turned away.

Azmei smiled to herself as she headed for the spiraling stairs that led further up the tower. This was just the excuse she needed. She would make her delivery, and then she would slip inside Eldry's rooms and wait for the right time to act.

***

Journeyman Tumaina tipped her a copper upon receiving his message. Azmei tucked the coin inside her waistband and bowed, but the door was already closing in her face.

Good. He would remember receiving a message, but not what the messenger looked like.

Not that Azmei intended for her message-boy persona to be connected to Eldry's death, but she didn't like sloppy work. She wanted to blend into the everyday workings of the academy. When the Stormweapon was found dead, everyone should be surprised and hopefully believe she had been the victim of her own witchery. Azmei had a fast-acting poison that would make Eldry's nerves and muscles lock up. She would suffocate quickly and fairly painlessly.

Of course, if things went badly and Azmei had to draw her knife, none of that would matter—but she didn't mean for it to come to that.

One drawback of the academy tower was its height. Azmei was skilled at climbing and negotiating rooftops, but while she had a long length of rope wrapped around her waist under her tunic, she hoped not to have to escape down the outside of the building. She didn't fancy the idea of climbing down some seventy feet of the smooth façade of the tower.

When she reached Eldry's door, she listened carefully for several minutes. In that time, no one passed through the hall. Azmei hoped that meant they were avoiding Eldry, her odd companion, or both. If the other occupants of the academy were avoiding her, it would be much easier for Azmei to make her escape.

Finally she tried the door. Finding it locked, she slid her picks from her pocket and quickly worked the lock open. Before opening the door she paused, holding her breath for a count of thirty. Finally satisfied, she eased the door open. If anyone was inside, they were asleep.

A quick check assured her the rooms were empty. Azmei did a routine search for weapons, but stormwitches were apparently a trusting lot; she found only a short knife Eldry probably used for meals. She tucked it in her belt and set about selecting her hiding place.

If she chose to surprise Eldry as the woman entered her

rooms, there was a good chance Eldry's body would show bruises later. It seemed a wiser course to bide her time and wait, perhaps until Eldry was asleep, and administer the poison then. It only required contact with the mouth, nostrils, or eyes to take effect. It would be best, Azmei thought, to catch Eldry if she dozed off in a chair. That would make it more plausible that she had attempted some weather working before going to bed.

Azmei considered the wardrobe and dismissed it; Eldry might be one of those folk who preferred to change into her nightclothes as soon as she retired to her rooms. The alternative was a small, unused area behind the door between the antechamber and the bedchamber. Azmei tucked herself into it, carefully positioning the door at the angle it had been before.

She sank into the aware state of half-meditation that she used while waiting to make a kill. *Please guide my hand,* she prayed to the god of peace. *Help me choose my moment well and act accordingly. Remember your servant in this hour and bless my effort to bring peace to Amethir through this death.*

She was unaware of the time as it passed, but when she heard a shuffle outside the door, she brought her awareness fully outward. Judging from the lighting in the room, it was dusk. A key turned in the lock and two sets of footsteps came inside.

Azmei frowned. Two sets. The Scavenger must be with Eldry. That was inconvenient. She would have to subdue him quickly in order to avoid killing him messily in Eldry's rooms.

"…doesn't matter how long, he sees you," said a sing-song voice. "He's awake now and he knows what you see and what you do and what you hear and what you think and…"

"Shut up." That was Eldry's voice, sharp and impatient.

The first voice cackled. "Wouldn't you like that? If I shut up and let him speak into your mind, into your thoughts, into your heart, into your head."

"I'd like it if you would be silent."

"Soon I will be silent as the grave, but you'll never have silence again. No, not in your time. You'll have to hear *his* voice, and you'll hear *His* voice as well, and there will never be quiet in your mind." He broke off in a high-pitched giggling.

"The gods damn you!" Eldry snarled. "Sit there and don't speak! I must have quiet for the work I am about to do."

"The storm will come to your call," he told her. "It will come, yes, and it will do its work. But you'll soon see he's woken more than just himself. He's called more than just the two of us. You'll see. It'll be beyond your control soon."

There was a silence then, and Azmei took a slow breath, listening to the sounds of someone pouring a drink. An exhalation told her the person had drunk, and then a clink indicated the glass being set down. Then footsteps crossed the antechamber. There was rustling. Azmei remembered seeing large floor cushions stored under a desk. Eldry was probably dragging a cushion out to sit on. Then there was a long silence.

Eldry must be meditating, or perhaps actually working her witchery. The Scavenger's breathing was very loud, but he didn't speak again for nearly half a glass. Finally he coughed and huffed a loud sigh.

"You're supposed to be getting a storm," he complained.

There was a pause, and then—"I *am!* If you would just shut up." Eldry's voice was annoyed. Azmei had gotten the impression Eldry and the Scavenger were of one mind, but clearly the woman was irritated with her savior. Or guide. Or whatever he was to her.

Azmei frowned. If there was strife between the two of them, that left her with more options. If she killed them both, she could make it look as if the Scavenger had killed Eldry and then died as a result.

The Scavenger grunted. "Can't shut up. Can't. He wants

me to remind you. Wants me to make you hurry. Something's coming. Something's going to interfere. You need to set it in motion *now*."

A chill ran down Azmei's arms. Did the Twister of Worlds somehow know she was there? Was he trying to thwart her?

Help me, she pleaded to the god of peace. She hoped the god would listen, would help her. She had often felt what seemed like a surreal peace, but she had never known if that was truly the presence of the god, or the god's blessing, as some of her faith asserted it was.

"I'm working on it," Eldry muttered. "The seadragon can see the *Dawn Star*. It says there are no stormsingers about, though I'm not convinced of that. I'm almost ready. Sit quietly, Scavenger. The stormcalling is almost ready."

Azmei chewed her lower lip. Was Eldry sending a storm after Arama? And if she was, could Azmei do anything to stop her?

Well, obviously, she could leap out and kill Eldry now, before she had a chance to complete her stormcalling. But there would be no element of stealth to that. It would be difficult to hide that Eldry had been slaughtered. Even if she disguised the work to look like the Scavenger had attacked Eldry, it would cause talk.

She would vastly prefer to keep people guessing about the nature of Eldry's death. If possible, she would like it to look as if the witchery killed Eldry, but without knowing much about the witchery, she wasn't counting on that.

Still, if she pulled out her cudgel and bashed Eldry over the head, it would clearly be murder.

On top of that was the question of what Eldry was actually capable of with her witchery.

Azmei knew a little of the basics about stormwitchery. There was the calling of storms and the calming of storms, the finding of water in the ground, wind-raising—the most common shipboard witchery—and rainmaking. There was also channeling, when a stormwitch touched or used lightning; Lijka had told her this was the rite-of-passage magic for many stormwitches, including Eldry.

Azmei had brought her sword and knife, but she earnestly hoped that keeping them in their sheaths would protect her from the worst of Eldry's lightning. She had never made a kill of a stormwitch before. She wasn't certain if it would be safe to use even a cudgel.

"You have to hurry," the Scavenger said, and Azmei, to her embarrassment, twitched as if he'd been speaking to her.

"If you can't be silent, you'll have to go away," Eldry hissed.

He made a grumbling noise but there were no footsteps, so Azmei assumed he had opted to be silent.

She bit down hard on her lower lip, wishing she could do *anything* besides wait while Eldry sent a storm after a woman Azmei liked and Vistaren depended on. But an outright attack would be too bloody. There was always the outside possibility Eldry would use lightning to kill her.

Azmei didn't want to die. She would, if she believed it was the only way to accomplish her mission—she had learned that from Master Tanvel's example, after all. But she honestly believed she would serve Amethir better as its queen than by dying for it.

She heard Eldry suck in a breath. "Scavenger! You didn't tell me she was *here*!"

Azmei's arms prickled as the Scavenger snorted. "Stupid girl. I did! I said something was going to interfere."

Azmei tensed. Eldry knew. Had the Twister of Worlds told her? Azmei had assumed it was the Scavenger who spoke to him—but perhaps they both did. She slipped her cudgel from the loop on her belt and gripped it, shifting her weight to the balls of her feet.

God of peace, help me, she pleaded.

Then, as footsteps approached her hiding place, she shouldered the door aside and leapt out at Eldry.

The storm witch's long hair fell around her face like a silver veil as she paused, raising a hand against Azmei's charge. The Scavenger was sitting on his bony butt, rocking from side to side.

"Who—" Eldry managed, and then Azmei's cudgel clipped the side of her head. Eldry staggered, but she flicked her fingers and something burned Azmei's hand, making her drop the cudgel.

"Careful, girl!" the Scavenger chortled. "She'll do you like you did Rhys!"

"Shut up, old man," Eldry hissed.

"Rhys?" Azmei sensed this was a weakness she could exploit. She hadn't missed the way Eldry flinched at that name. Her fingers stung, but she flexed them, planning a bare-handed strike. "Who is Rhys?"

"No one!" Eldry had staggered into the wall. She was leaning against it, but her hands were raised halfway in front of her, fingers crooked.

"Not anymore," the Scavenger said. "Hee hee hee!"

"*Shut up!*"

"Rhys," Azmei mused, drawing the word out to press Eldry's pain point. "Whoever he is, he must be gone by now. Did you drive him away?" She smiled. "Did you love him? Was he your brother? Your *lover?*"

"Shut up!" Eldry screamed.

"He saw too much," the Scavenger told Azmei in a confidential tone. He stood and began waving his arms.

"And he walked out on you, didn't he?" Azmei surmised. "You disappointed him."

Eldry lunged at her. "I'll kill you!"

Azmei sidestepped easily. "Is that what you did to Rhys?"

The Scavenger cackled, rocking harder from side to side. His head was tipped back as if he were watching something no one else could see.

Eldry threw her hands out, palms aimed at Azmei; Azmei had been expecting the woman to throw lightning at her, though. She dodged, scooping up the char basin to throw at Eldry. Eldry gasped and staggered, catching herself on a chair.

"He can see your heart's desires, he can make them change," sang the Scavenger, capering oddly about the room. "Find her, fix her, find her, fix her!"

Azmei was beginning to understand why Eldry found the man so irritating.

She struck at Eldry with the blade of her hand, aiming for the stormwitch's nose. She didn't feel it make contact, but another shock snapped at her fingers. Azmei gasped.

"I am doing the god's work!" Eldry shrieked. "I am doing what I swore I would do!" She shoved the Scavenger, making him stagger towards Azmei.

She hadn't really planned to kill the old man, but it was chilling how he laughed just before she struck him in the throat with her knuckles. She wondered, suddenly, if he had somehow known he was mad and had longed for death. Or perhaps he just didn't believe death mattered.

She skittered back as he fell in a heap on the floor, gurgling. She'd have to be careful not to trip on his body.

"You killed him!" Eldry cried.

"I'm here to kill you, Stormweapon," Azmei replied. "You've perverted the stormwitchery, sabotaging it. Breaking it."

"I'm fixing it!" Along with her words, Eldry threw a lightning bolt that sizzled through the air where Azmei had just been.

"It wasn't broken until you and your twisted god started messing with it." Azmei dodged sideways, hurling a throwing knife at Eldry.

Lightning shot from Eldry's fingertips, striking the knife and shoving it off course. Metal rang against stone as it hit the floor.

Damn it, this was not going well. No matter what she did now, Azmei would have a lot of cleanup work to do. There would be signs of a struggle to cover up, and there was the Scavenger's body—killed by physical force and not lightning—to explain away.

She and Eldry circled one another, each watching the other. Eldry's gaze was on Azmei's hands, but Azmei watched Eldry's eyes. The eyes always gave something away, except in the most cold-hearted of killers. But Azmei was a good judge of character. Eldry was no cold-hearted killer; she had reacted too strongly to the Scavenger's mention of Rhys. Her eyes would give something away.

By watching Eldry's eyes, Azmei managed to dodge the next two lightning bolts the stormwitch threw at her. Eldry was breathing hard now, obviously unused to the physical effort. Azmei waited until just after she threw a third lightning bolt. Then she drew her knife and threw it underhand at Eldry. It was a good throw, but not perfect—but the knife spun at Eldry and chunked wetly into the flesh at her hip.

Eldry screamed and staggered back into the wall. Azmei bared her teeth and started forward. No matter what Eldry did, Azmei had drawn first blood. There was no way for the stormwitch to save herself.

But Azmei had forgotten about the Scavenger.

His crushed windpipe was strangling him, but not quickly enough. His fingers gripped Azmei's ankle. Azmei kicked, trying to dislodge him, but Eldry threw lightning and Azmei had to lunge to one side. The lightning sizzled the air at her back, barely missing her. The Scavenger's grip on her ankle loosened too late for Azmei to regain her balance.

Instead of the graceful roll she would normally accomplish, Azmei landed badly, striking her head against the stone wall. Blackness shot across her vision, followed by odd sparkles of light that flooded her gaze. Azmei kicked out, her foot contacting something she couldn't see.

The gasp she heard in response sounded more like Eldry than the Scavenger. Something thudded against the floor. Azmei, still half blinded, fumbled her way toward the door. She couldn't defeat Eldry, not like this. Someone was shouting, though in her confusion, Azmei wasn't certain if it were Eldry or herself.

She jerked the door open and stumbled along the hallway, her steps faltering, her limited vision blurred. She could only pray the god of peace would see her safely out of the academy.

***

It had been another day of artillery fire and thunder. Vistaren knew the cannons he heard were their own, and they were keeping Balahar's forces from approaching with ladders, but that didn't stop the noise from grating against his nerves.

Azmei's letters had been a daily source of relief, but today's letter had been short, just two hastily scrawled lines so he would know she was safe. It had been signed with, "Wish me luck." He hoped that didn't mean she was planning something drastic, but he thought he knew her well enough to justify his fear.

He turned from his window at the sound of a teapot clinking against a cup. "Isden, this siege is driving me mad. Ask Lo, Hawk, and the count if they will dine with me tonight. I need a distraction."

Isden nodded. "At the usual time?"

"Yes…what time is it now?"

"Half a glass past the sixth hour."

"Yes. I'd better shave. That gives me time." Vistaren watched as Isden swirled a cloak around his shoulders in preparation to go out into the rain.

He'd been fighting a creeping gloom for the past several days. He knew it was caused by their situation, but somehow that knowledge didn't help him shake it off. Companionship often helped, though. Hopefully at least one of the men would be able to join him. He probably should have invited Devlin and Orshard as well, though at least one of them would be the watch officer and unable to attend. He hoped Lo wasn't currently watch officer.

Vistaren shook himself and went to the washstand in his bedchamber. He hadn't bothered shaving today, but he didn't want to appear slovenly in front of company. He made quick work of the stubble and then decided to change his tunic. He hadn't brought many with him, but he'd spilled his coffee this morning and not bothered to have Isden clean it.

Isden returned shortly with the news that the three men would join him, and Devlin had been speaking with Lo when Isden found him.

"I took the liberty of inviting him as well," Isden said in his soft voice. "It seemed it would be rude not to. I hope I did well."

"Of course you did." Vistaren smiled at him.

Isden nodded and began preparing the dining area for company. A short time later a keep servant arrived, laden with a tray of steaming food. Behind him was another with a bottle of wine. Vistaren's spirits began rising.

The keep bell was just ringing the seventh hour when his guests arrived. Vistaren greeted them all, noting the shadows under Hawk's eyes with a pang of guilt. He should have made an effort to spend more time with Hawk. The man couldn't like having the woman he loved endangering herself far away from them. Especially since she was doing it on Vistaren's behalf.

Once they were settled at the table, the conversation quickly turned to the topic of the siege. Vistaren was heartened to hear that the men all thought it was going well. The ammunition was holding out better than they'd expected, and with the rain, they were in no danger of running out of drinking water.

"Not that I was worried about that, highness," Devlin said quickly. "We've a well deep in the cellars, protected from sabotage."

"No, but it's good to see you so cheerful about the rain," Vistaren joked, and the others laughed.

"The food stores are obviously holding out well, if my table is anything to judge by," Vistaren said. He glanced around at the others. "I certainly don't expect to eat any better than anyone else. Drink better, perhaps, since I'm unlikely to be involved in the fighting…"

Devlin grinned. "The men on duty don't have a whiskey ration, but they're all eating pretty well, highness."

"I don't think we'll need to begin rationing it for another fortnight," Hawk said, and Devlin began nodding.

"General Hawk's been quite a source of information for me," he told Vistaren. "He was in command of Rivarden during the siege. They didn't have cannons, just trebuchets and catapults, and they managed to last four months holding off the Strid."

Vistaren nodded, seeing the respect in Devlin's eyes. Good. Hawk could do with another friend in Amethir, since Azmei and Yar were far away.

"We'll have to keep an eye on the flour, since the harvest was interrupted." Hawk lifted his wine glass for a sip. "But between the rations we carried with us and the dried meat in storage here, we're well off."

"If only the blasted rain would stop," Lo said. He held up a hand. "I know, I know, it means we won't run out of water. But I'm damned tired of slogging through that mire of a yard out there any time I want to get somewhere."

"Now, now," Devlin said. "Complaining won't get us anywhere."

Lo glared at him, making Vistaren snort in amusement.

Kedar had been quiet this whole time, aside from their initial greetings. Vistaren wondered if he were regretting his decision to come to Vistaren's side. Vistaren took a breath and lifted his cup.

"Kedar," he said, hoping this was not an unwise question. "I have never been to Anderly. Will you tell me what it was like before?"

The men around the table went still. Kedar looked at Vistaren for several heartbeats before he said, "It was a thriving town until a month ago. We have craftsmen of many trades. Three inns." He looked down at his plate. "Cooks that would put this keep's kitchen to shame. Our boatmakers were well respected. We—my father—had a strong voice in Council."

His voice was quiet, but he didn't sound angry. Thoughtful and a bit wistful, perhaps even sad, but not angry.

Vistaren nodded. "And you lived near Anderly, I understand."

"It was the seat of my father's county. Other nearby villages came to Anderly for anything their weekly market couldn't supply."

"I was there once," Devlin said. "Just after I enlisted, there was a spate of piracy along Coman Head. We were sent to clean up, and tracked them to a network of caves on the south coast, facing Swordfish Island."

Kedar nodded. "I remember that. Ten years or so back? My father was furious because they didn't just steal from our folk, they burned the fields as well."

"I didn't know you did much farming there," Lozarr said.

Kedar shrugged. "Not a lot, but enough to feed us— unless brigands burn the fields."

"There was an inn there, the Lame Tomcat," Devlin said, and Kedar began chuckling.

"Yes, it's still there."

Devlin grinned at him. "That cook there made the most exquisite apple tarts."

"Mistress Adra. She's still making those tarts." Kedar's chuckle trailed off, but he was smiling. "If I'd known she had admirers this far afield, I'd have brought some with me."

"You grew up along the coast somewhere, didn't you, Dev?" Lo asked.

"Aye, but far west of here, a little village called Hibbens Mill. West of Glimmerguard, almost all the way to the west coast." He leaned back in his chair. "I can still see the sunset sparkling off the water."

They fell to reminiscing about hometowns, then. Vistaren thought of all the things he loved about Maron—the markets, the library, the docks. He wondered if his feelings about Maron were anything like what these men felt about their hometowns. Hawk's descriptions of the Kreyden village where he'd grown up fascinated them all. They didn't have much desert in Amethir, and what they did was high mountain desert, much different from the huge stretches of sand and rock Hawk described.

When the eighth bell sounded, Lo pushed his chair back. "If you'll excuse me, I'm watch officer. I need to go relieve Orshard."

Hawk and Devlin were the next to leave. Half a glass after Lo left, Hawk finished his second glass of wine and stood. "Your pardon, but I think I'm for bed."

Devlin stood, too. "I'll walk with you. I have watch early."

Kedar was staring into the fire, his legs stretched out. He didn't look like he was planning to leave anytime soon. Vistaren shifted his chair a little closer to Kedar and the fire.

"I keep thinking of the ale at Foggy Creek Inn, the clang of hammers at Senia the smith's." Kedar's voice was low. "The music. The Foggy Creek innkeeper's husband was a harper. He sang the best songs."

Vistaren sipped his wine, watching Kedar's face as the count smiled faintly.

"My sister loved his music. He sang songs of Aevver and her sisters. Mirzana wanted to be Aevver. She's always said she wouldn't mind marrying for politics, as long as her husband wouldn't bother her beyond the children."

"A wise woman, your sister." As soon as Vistaren said it, he hoped Mirzana hadn't died in the storm. But he thought that was the name of the younger sister Lo had spoken with.

Kedar snorted. "I never admitted it to her, but yes. I hoped I could marry someone like her."

"Because of her political aims?"

Kedar didn't answer at once. He swirled his wine glass slowly and looked down into it. Finally he drew in a breath.

"For her self-sufficiency. I don't want to be responsible for someone else's happiness."

Vistaren tilted his head. "Is responsible the right word? I…well, I certainly hope I can do everything in my power to contribute to Azmei's happiness, should we end up married. But I don't feel it's my *responsibility*. We're each given the circumstances of our birth, but we make of them what we will."

Kedar snorted again. "I'd like to see what you would make of being born a fisherman."

Vistaren grinned at him. "I'd specialize in trapping sea-diamonds, and pair that with killing as many puff-skins as possible."

That made Kedar laugh. "No, that's a different trade," he said. "The puff-skin hunters extract their poison to make a liquid to coat your weapons with. That poison is good against sharks and sirens."

Vistaren sighed. "Very well, just sea-diamonds, then."

"Do you know how few sea-diamonds the fisherfolk actually get to eat? There's too much demand from the nobility." Kedar glanced sideways at him. "I believe the royal kitchen has purchased most of the catch recently."

Vistaren grinned. "I *do* love sea-diamonds," he admitted. "And I think I would like living in a village where the innkeeper's husband sang the Aevver stories on a regular basis. Perhaps I'd finally make myself learn to play an instrument myself."

"There was plenty of hard work to go around." Kedar's voice was remote. "We didn't have music every night. The fishing boats go out early in the morning, and we sail through the rainy season. It's only in storm season—"

He broke off, staring at the fire, his mouth still open.

Vistaren felt a pang of sympathy. Storm season had become Kedar's enemy now. Vistaren wished he could say something that would lessen Kedar's grief, but he couldn't think of anything that didn't sound stupid. He simply stared at the fire along with Kedar, giving him silent understanding.

He hoped that would be enough.

After a time, Kedar cleared his throat. "I play the flute. Perhaps another night I'll play some of our fisherfolk songs for you." He drained his glass and stood. "Your pardon, highness. I should go."

Vistaren stood, too, moving with Kedar to the door. "I enjoyed talking with you, Kedar," he said. "Thank you for sharing your village with me."

Kedar swallowed a couple of times and met Vistaren's gaze. His eyes seemed shiny, as if he were holding back tears, but he gave Vistaren a tiny smile. "Good night, my prince," he murmured, and let himself out of the room.

Vistaren sighed and closed his eyes, treasuring that smile.

36

Azmei blinked at the knots under her hands. She wasn't quite sure how she'd gotten here. Her head throbbed.

She squinted her eyes, trying to figure out why there were two knots holding the boat. Then she realized she saw four hands.

I'm seeing double, she realized, feeling clever.

She closed her eyes—that felt better anyway, and her fingers knew how to untie a knot in the dark.

She needed to get back to the lighthouse. She was proud of the fact she'd made it down to the docks, only stopping twice to vomit into a gutter. This boat rocked gently under her hands. She would have to find out later who owned it. Stealing was wrong, but she couldn't risk someone recognizing her.

I should have Lijka come get me. She had a bird from the lighthouse, but it was somewhere up in the academy, where she'd been sleeping. *Stupid.*

She felt the knot give under her hand. She opened her eyes, winced, and closed one eye. Looking with just one eye, she could almost focus.

Getting into the boat proved more challenging than walking had been. The boat moved just a little with every movement she made. At least the street hadn't been pitching under her, no matter how much it had felt like it.

She didn't have much time. She must have injured Eldry badly enough that the Stormweapon had been unable to follow her, but someone would be after her soon.

Azmei slumped back, holding tightly onto the rope. She couldn't let the boat drift away, but she had to rest for a moment. She was beginning to feel queasy again. She closed her eyes and concentrated on keeping her breathing steady. Exhaling heavily each time, she thought she could keep from vomiting again. She hoped she could. She shouldn't throw up all over this boat she was stealing.

She listened to the waves lapping at the dock and the creak of the wood. The breeze tickled the back of her neck and she shivered.

Azmei rose to her knees, studying the gunwales of the boat blearily.

If I fall in, I'll drown.

It was her first clear thought in a while. She pulled the boat tight against the dock and took a couple of breaths. Then she half-climbed, half-toppled into the boat. The impact jolted her head, bringing tears to her eyes. She breathed hard, unable to hold in a sob, and then leaned to one side and vomited again.

Damn it.

Wiping her mouth with the back of her hand, she sat up. She managed to wrestle first one oar in place, then the other. She eyed the mast dizzily—she knew it *must* be just one mast, with this size vessel, though she could see *two* masts—and dismissed the thought of raising the sail. That was beyond her.

Must get to the lighthouse.

She shoved the boat away from the dock and began rowing. Each pull made her stomach reel and she had to pause and rest between pulls. At this rate she would probably never get there.

Lighthouse.

She pulled on the oars until her strength gave out, then she slumped over them. Was the tide going out? She hoped the tide was going out.

She must have dozed off for a time. When she opened her eyes again, the stars were wheeling above her in a clearing sky. The masts swayed across her vision. She rolled over and vomited again, dry heaving since there was nothing left to bring up.

"What am I doing?" she rasped aloud. She was in a boat. She tried to remember what she'd been doing before the boat, but she wasn't sure.

Lighthouse. The word flitted through her mind and she sat up.

She was trying to get to the lighthouse. Yes, that was right.

She eyed the sail and saw how it went up. This was a small boat. The sail wouldn't be too heavy. She pulled the line she thought would raise it. Her arms shook as she worked, and she finally stopped when she'd gotten the sail up most of the way. That would have to do. She tied it off as well as she could and slumped back into the bottom of the boat.

Her head was throbbing. Azmei put her hand back to probe the spot that hurt worst. Her fingers came back sticky with drying blood. The smell made her stomach roil, but she swallowed hard and managed to keep from gagging.

Water. There should be water on the boat. She looked in the aft, where a small wooden compartment offered up a fishing pole, rope, some hard flatbread, and a skin of water. She took a few sips, hoping the water would stay down.

At some point she must have passed out again. When she woke next, it was because the boat bumped hard against something that scraped against the hull. Azmei jerked upright and then groaned, clutching at her head. Her stomach churned, but she didn't throw up.

She squinted. It was daylight, maybe an hour or so after dawn. The shore she had washed up against was rocky. When she turned to her left, she saw the ruins of the east light.

Thank you, god of peace, she thought, and tried to get out of the boat. Her foot caught on the gunwale as she tried to step over, and she toppled, skinning her palms as she caught herself. Water splashed up around her, soaking her clothes.

"Don't—" a woman shouted, and then booted footsteps hurried toward her. "I was going to help you," Lijka said reproachfully.

Then she gasped. "Sleeping gods," she whispered. "Princess, what happened?"

Azmei blinked at her.

Lijka shook herself. "Never mind. We need to get you inside and warmed up. Can you walk?"

"If…you help," Azmei said. She hoped it was true.

Lijka got an arm around her waist and helped Azmei up. She was only a little taller than Azmei, but she was strong. She supported Azmei as they struggled up the path to the lighthouse. Azmei tried not to lean too heavily on her, knowing she was getting filth and water all over the storm-witch.

When at last they were inside, Lijka stripped her down impersonally and wrapped her in a blanket of soft wool. She sat Azmei in front of the fire and began inspecting her head.

"What happened?" she asked.

Azmei had been trying to remember the answer to that question since the first time Lijka asked it. "I—I know I carried a message." She closed her eyes, which were stinging from the pain as Lijka bathed her wound with salt water.

"You carried a message?" Lijka prompted.

"Message upstairs. I…I think there was…he tipped me…and then…then I think I went to Eldry's rooms. I must have tried to kill her."

"That's what you meant to do when you went to the academy three days ago," Lijka said. "But *did* you kill her?"

"I'm not sure. I—I lost my sword?"

Lijka sighed. "This is more of an injury than I know how to treat. You aren't making any sense. I need to write for a surgeon."

"No!" Azmei tried to stand, but Lijka held her down with just a hand to her shoulder. "I have to help Vistaren."

"At least you remember that much," Lijka said. "I'm sorry, princess. But Vistaren, friend though he is, will have my head if I let you die because of a head injury like this.

They're nothing to play with."

Azmei closed her eyes, feeling her throat tighten. She had wanted to be *useful*. She'd caused so much trouble to Vistaren with the message she and Yar brought. She'd hoped she could at least help him.

"I'm sorry," Lijka repeated. Her fingers stroked Azmei's hair gently, far away from the part that hurt. "I'm going to send a message to the surgeon's school. I have friends there, and perhaps one will come out to help you without reporting it. I can't promise, though."

"Do what you have to," Azmei said dully. "I can't think, so you must be right."

***

Eldry's hip was throbbing. She knew she ought to act, but that boy had *stabbed* her. No, he'd stabbed the Scavenger. He'd just thrown a knife at her.

She groaned and rolled from her back onto her uninjured side. She thought the Scavenger was dead. She hadn't heard anyone else breathing, and surely he would have been talking to his god if he were still alive.

She rolled onto her front and managed to rock up to her hands and knees. Swaying, she let her head hang down for a moment as a wave of dizziness hit her. When she opened her eye, she realized she had been lying in a small puddle of blood.

The sight made her heart kick in her chest. Was she going to bleed to death? She took several panicked breaths and then forced her eye closed again. *Breathe in slow. Breathe out. Breathe in.*

After a few more careful breaths, she managed to stagger to her feet, clutching at a chair for support. She leaned against it with her good hip and looked around.

The Scavenger was, indeed, dead. He'd fallen on his side, facing her. His eyes were open, a grin frozen on his face. The boy's sword had fallen from his chest.

She suddenly became aware of a frightened pressure in her mind. The seadragon had felt her distress.

I'm hurt, but I will live. It's all well, love, she promised. *I need you to do something for me.*

She felt its devotion, its willingness to do whatever she asked. It had torn down that lighthouse because she had wanted Lijka and her wife subdued. It would do anything she asked—even throw itself into the teeth of the gale.

She didn't want that, though. Her seadragon was too useful.

Follow the storm, my love. Bring your fellows, as many as you can. There's a ship that must sink. Help it sink. She smiled to herself. *Thrash about to get the sirens to come.*

The seadragon sent its agreement and she let her awareness of it slip to the back of her mind again as her hip twinged.

She had to deal with the Scavenger. How would she explain this? Could she claim he had gone mad and attacked her? But how could she explain the sword? She'd never owned a sword in her life. Perhaps it was the Scavenger's sword?

She swore. If only that stupid boy hadn't injured *her.* She could have hidden the evidence of the Scavenger's murder, but the knife was stuck in her hip, and Eldry wasn't about to pull it out herself. She would need a surgeon, and that meant she would have to leave the Scavenger's body. Perhaps her story about his derangement would work.

If not, she would make Pralith fix it.

She stumbled to the door and fell against it, her hand slipping against the door knob. Finally she scrubbed her palm against her bodice to get the blood off. Then she gripped the door knob again and twisted.

She almost fell out of her rooms, startling the young woman who was passing in the hall. The woman jumped back with a startled exclamation, then leaned in. It was Councilor Mezika.

"Eldry? What—sleeping gods, you're hurt!"

"Scavenger…attacked…" Eldry whimpered. "Need surgeon. Please…"

"Of course! Don't move—I'll be right back!"

Mezika darted off down the hall and Eldry allowed herself to relax against the door. After a moment she slumped back and slid down the wood to sit.

Perhaps she would just close her eye for a moment.

37

Arama tapped the end of her pen against her lower lip, trying to think of anything she had failed to report to Lo and Vistaren. Her account of what they'd learned from the stormsingers and Yar's dragon had been sent three days ago, and the fate of the east light two days. She hadn't sent a letter yesterday, but she had been thinking of Lo all afternoon, so she'd taken pen in hand…and drawn a blank on what to write to him.

Someone pounded on the door to her cabin. Arama frowned. "Come in!" she called.

Instead of coming in, the person pounded again.

Arama swore at herself for a fool. It must be Kinnet, who wouldn't hear an invitation. She was just getting up to open the door when it burst open.

It was, indeed, Kinnet, her eyes wide. "I'm sorry for barging in. There's a storm coming."

"How close?"

"We have time. Qiaru felt it and told me. But he says it is the strongest he has seen. We must prepare."

Arama nodded. She bent and scrawled, "Storm coming. I love you," on the paper. Without waiting for it to fully dry, she rolled the paper into a tube and gestured for Kinnet to precede her out of the cabin.

She stopped at the dovecote and dispatched her letter, feeling vaguely embarrassed that Vistaren might think it was for him and open it first. But it didn't matter. She'd been thinking of Lo, and she thought it was probably good for him to know that, in case this storm was as bad as it sounded.

"Tell me everything," she ordered Kinnet, watching the dove wing its way from the ship.

"Qiaru felt the Stormweapon call this. She is calling on power he has never seen before in a human. She must be fed by the—by *that* one."

Arama nodded.

"There is a swarm of seadragons chasing the storm. He and his pod will try to help calm the storm, but there is only so much they can do, even working together. The seadragons attacked them last time they struggled with the Stormweapon's workings."

"Damn her." Arama looked around. "Do you know where Qiaru is? More importantly, where the storm's coming from?"

To her relief, Kinnet pointed abaft. That was better than in front of them. Turning the ship took time, and Arama suspected there was little enough to spare.

"Stay here for a moment," she told Kinnet, and strode across the deck. "Mister Zek! Prepare for a storm! Secure the guns in run-out position. Secure anchors. Place the weather cloths."

Zek appeared at the run. "Storm, captain?"

"The stormsinger sent us word. We have more time than usual to prepare, thank the Sea Lord." Arama tapped her chin and turned. "Mister Carig!" she shouted. "Make a bigger sacrifice than usual!"

"Aye, mum!" Carig called from his position at the helm. She saw him pass the tiller to another sailor and go to prepare his sacrifice.

"Where's the storm?" Zek asked.

"Abaft. I don't know how far, but the stormsinger says it's the strongest he's seen—and he's seen a hundred years of storms, I'd guess."

Zek swore.

"We'll set the lifebuoy and secure the reel," she said. "Who knows if it will make any difference, but we'll do it."

"Should I prepare the sea-anchor?"

Arama nodded. "We'll scud ahead of it," she said. "Try to get well away from the Blades, at least. We don't want to be there when the storm hits."

"Aye, captain. Foresail, main topsail?"

"And the fore topmast staysail," she said. "I'm going to see if Kinnet can give us a push."

Zek saluted and dashed away.

Arama went back to where Kinnet was waiting. Interestingly, the stormwitch wasn't looking around at the explosion of activity on deck; she was watching Arama alone.

"Can you put wind in our sails? We're still too close to the Blades for my liking."

"We are going to try to outrun the storm?" Kinnet was toying with her bracelet; Arama saw that it held several sea-glass charms.

"Not outrun it, exactly," Arama said. "We won't be able to outrun the waves. But if we sail with the wind, we'll lessen the impact of each wave as it hits."

Kinnet nodded. "Where would you like the wind?"

"Same direction as it is now, just more of it, if you please." It had been a fairly calm afternoon, and since *Dawn Star* had no assignment, she had been happy to let the ship have its way until now.

She counted her heartbeats as she watched Kinnet close her eyes, gripping a piece of glass from her bracelet in her other hand. Five heartbeats, six…nothing…seven…ten… Then Kinnet exhaled heavily and opened her eyes at the same time that Arama felt the sails fill.

Dawn Star responded keenly as the sails caught. Before long they were traveling fast, and Arama began to understand why a ship might enjoy having a stormwitch on board. Having the wind come at her call like that would be convenient.

Arama watched as her crew busied itself readying for the storm. She was pleased to see that no one looked frightened, even though they were making preparations without a storm in sight. Perhaps they thought it was just a drill, but she didn't think that was the case.

"I can't keep us ahead of the storm," Kinnet said. Her voice was tight. "It's coming fast."

Arama looked over to see lines of strain in Kinnet's face. She opened her hand and scattered sand on the wind, then jerked at her wrist again. To Arama's surprise, she realized the bracelet only had half the seaglass charms it had a few minutes earlier. As she watched, Kinnet squeezed her hand tight around a piece of seaglass and then swayed.

Arama lunged forward to steady her. Kinnet smiled gratefully at her and opened her fingers, scattering more sand.

"Is that—the seaglass?" Arama's stomach flipped. She had known the stormwitches used seaglass for their focus, and that powerful working would leach the vitality from the glass. She hadn't known it would crumble like that.

Kinnet nodded. "I have a few large pieces in my belt pouch and my pendant. Then I will have to look in my pack belowdecks to see if I have any left."

"Your earbobs," Arama said, and Kinnet smiled.

"Those are a last resort. They won't give me much power."

Arama nodded. Looking abaft, she could see the dark clouds approaching them now. The clouds were moving faster than she'd ever seen. As she watched, lightning flashed through the sky. The thunder that reached her didn't take as long as she would like.

"Mister Zek!" she shouted, and the mate was at her side a moment later.

"Let's get everyone possible into shelter. Put Master Yar in my cabin. Kinnet?"

The stormwitch shook her head. "I'll work out here as long as possible. The lightning won't threaten me."

Arama nodded and turned back to Zek.

"Check the well pumps and get a quicksaver on the foresail. That thing's coming fast." She put a hand on Zek's shoulder when he would have gone to do her bidding.

"Zek," she said, lowering her voice. "There's a swarm of seadragons following the storm. I think yon Stormweapon Eldry means to murder us all."

Zek's eyes widened, then he bobbed his head and ran off.

Arama sighed. "I'm going to the quarterdeck," she told Kinnet. "You're welcome to come with me."

Kinnet trailed her as she went aft to stand by Carig. He'd come back out to take the helm. The backs of his fingers were spattered with blood, so she assumed the sacrifice had been made.

"It's bad, is it, mum?" He wasn't looking astern. He would have when he made the offering, but he had a rule not to look astern during bad weather. That wasn't one of his superstitions; seeing enormous waves coming at the ship might throw him off and cause him to make poor choices.

"Bad enough," she said briefly. "I think it best we keep the wind directly aft, if at all possible." *Dawn Star* tended to roll, but Arama suspected the seas would be violent enough that rolling was a lesser danger.

She looked over at Kinnet in time to see the stormwitch loose the last of her bracelet to the wind. Kinnet met Arama's eyes, her mouth grim.

"I can do no more at this time." Indeed, she looked played out. Her eyelids drooped and there were smudges of gray under her eyes. As she lifted a hand to brush hair out of her face, her fingers shook.

Arama put a gentle hand on her shoulder. "Go to my cabin with Yar. Rest there. We may need the last of your strength later."

When Kinnet was gone, Arama looked at Carig to find him watching her.

"It's been a pleasure and an honor to sail with you all these years, Arama," he said. "I thank you for being the best captain a man could hope for."

A shiver ran down Arama's spine. "Don't talk like that," she said.

Carig's smile was oddly peaceful. "No worries, mum. It's in the Sea Lord's hands."

Arama licked her lips and nodded.

The storm hit soon after. The wind slapped at her so hard she staggered. Carig grunted as the ship began fighting the wind and the waves. Arama turned to watch the crew. Zek had them well in hand for the moment.

Thunder crashed so loud she felt her bones vibrate. There would be no hearing orders shouted across the deck in all this noise. Arama beckoned one of the ship's boys to her in case she needed an order run.

The wind howled around her, slinging rain so hard against her skin it felt like blades. In what felt like no time, she was soaked through. Arama looked around, trying to ascertain their position.

To port she could see a shining beacon cutting through the darkness. Praise Antos! They were east of Crescent Island, a large body of land that sheltered Ranarr from the wide expanse of ocean to the east. They shouldn't be driven back south onto the Blades, at least.

"Captain!"

Arama realized Carig had been screaming at her for several minutes. She swung around and saw that he was struggling mightily with the tiller, trying to keep his feet and keep the ship on course. She ran to help him with it.

"Lash me to the tiller!" he shouted in her ear.

Arama did as he asked, looping the line around his waist and securing him in place. It would give him more security, but she didn't like the terrible risk it posed. If *Dawn Star* went down, Carig would have a hard time getting free.

The ship was yawing heavily. Arama braced herself as the deck lurched under her. Twenty-foot waves were slamming into them. She squinted to port, shielding her eyes. The steady lightning hurt her eyes, but gave her a chance to see just how much the ship's direction changed with each yaw.

Carig shouted something—Arama didn't hear what—and the ship yawed hard to port. Arama grabbed for a line, turning to look at him. She froze for an instant as she realized the wind was hitting her in the face as she looked abeam.

"Broached to!" she screamed at Carig, but she could see he was already struggling with the tiller, trying to correct it. His right arm was bent at a sickening angle. He must have lost the tiller and snapped the bone. She leapt across the quarterdeck, trying to reach him. A wave washed over the railing, smashing her to the deck.

Arama jumped to her feet, gasping. No time to be dazed. She ran to Carig and wrestled the tiller alongside him.

"Can't do it!" he shouted. Arama shook her head. She wouldn't give up so easily.

Another wave dashed across them and Carig screamed in agony as the force of the water threw him against his broken arm.

"I'm sorry, Arama!" he said, looking at her.

"No!" she shouted back, though she wasn't sure if he could hear her.

"I'm sorry. I lost her." Carig's face had that peaceful expression on it again, though there was sorrow in his eyes.

"No!" Arama screamed. "Don't you give up on me! Don't you give up, Carig!"

"I'm sorry we never made it to Sea Lord Antos' temple."

She wrestled the tiller with all her strength, but *Dawn Star* had given up when Carig did. Or perhaps he had given up because she had. The next wave knocked *Dawn Star* on her beam ends.

Time seemed to slow around her as Arama watched the ship go over on her starboard side. Screaming crewmembers slid down the deck into the hungry sea. Arama clutched at the tiller, fumbling for her siren's tooth knife so she could cut Carig free.

His undamaged hand closed around hers. "Save yourself and Yar," he shouted into her face. "Save that boy!"

Arama met his gaze, feeling tears spring into her eyes.

But she nodded and climbed past him to get to the ladder down to the deck. She slashed a length of rope away from whatever it had been securing. She might need that.

Dawn Star rode the next wave on her beams. Arama fought her way to a position up the deck from her cabin door. She would have one chance. If she slid past the door without catching herself in the frame, she would go into the sea and Yar and Kinnet would be on their own.

"Sea Lord Antos, help me," she whispered, and let go of the ladder.

The deck scraped along her arms, making her wince, but she managed to dig her fingernails into the wood of the doorframe. She clawed her way closer, bashing the door with one bare foot until it crashed open.

Yar and Kinnet were huddled against the wall of the cabin that had now become the floor. The wind was a little quieter inside. Yar must have heard her kicking the door; he had turned to see what was happening. He grabbed Kinnet and jerked her chin up so she could see Arama.

Arama tied the rope around the ladder and dropped the free end down to them. "Climb up!" she shouted. "We're foundering."

Her throat closed on the words. She'd never thought she would see the day *Dawn Star* actually died. She choked back the fear and grief and reached out a wet hand to catch Kinnet's hand as the stormwitch climbed up.

Once she'd gotten Kinnet out, Yar came up the rope. He was quicker than Kinnet, but his arrival made Arama's uncertain balance even more precarious. Arama shook Kinnet to get her attention.

"Jump clear of the ship," she ordered. "Call your stormsinger for help."

Kinnet nodded.

Arama watched the stormwitch leap from the ladder with perfect abandon. She flew through the air, crashing into the water well clear of the railing and disappeared under the waves.

"You next!" Arama shouted to Yar.

He'd been watching. He jumped even further than Kinnet. Arama watched in satisfaction as his head bobbed back to the surface. One of the sailors grabbed Yar and tugged him away from the ship. They wouldn't last long in these rough seas, not if the stormsingers didn't come to their aid.

But Arama had done all she could. Maybe Zek had had time to cut the lifebuoy free, but if not, they would have to hope *Dawn Star* broke up. The flotsam would float, giving them something to cling to. She closed her eyes.

I love you, Dawn Star, she thought. *I'm so sorry I failed you.*

She had just opened her eyes to jump when the world crashed down on her. Arama lost her grip and fell, crashing into the deck on the way down. Then her ankle caught in the railing. She was dragged under the waves with barely time to suck in a breath.

She struggled for what felt like forever, tugging at her leg and then slashing blindly with her siren's tooth knife. At some point it grew too difficult.

Remembering the strength of Lozarr's embrace and the warm sound of his laughter, Arama surrendered to the deep.

38

"I hope we can continue these dinners," Vistaren said, smiling at Kedar and Devlin as they took their leave. Last night's dinner had succeeded better than he'd hoped. When he woke this morning, he'd been thinking about Kedar, full of ideas for the rebuilding of Anderly. He'd gotten out of bed and begun writing some of his thoughts down before he even had breakfast.

For lunch, there had been a brief cessation in the rain. Vistaren had gone out to move among the troops, thanking them for their courage and fortitude. He'd had lunch in the mess hall, speaking with some of the captains and lower officers. Wanting to stay energized and involved, he had again invited Kedar, Hawk, and the officers not on watch, to join him for dinner. Everyone but Lo had been able to join him. Devlin and Kedar were the last two to leave.

This had been a good idea, Vistaren thought as he stood by the fireplace, idly swirling the last few sips of wine in his cup. The dinners were different from meetings or council sessions, but they still provided a way for him to learn from his companions and for them all to trade thoughts and ideas.

He had just tilted his glass against his lips when the door opened. He heard one of the hinges creak and turned to see why Isden was leaving.

It wasn't Isden.

Four cloaked figures crowded into the room and closed the door behind them.

"Take him down," said a woman's voice, and they rushed him.

Vistaren threw his wine glass at them and then spun to snatch his musket off the mantel. He could at least take one of them with him. He turned and fired. The figure in front cried out, stumbled, and fell. Vistaren jumped back, trying to get closer to where his sword hung without turning his back on them.

Isden had come out of the bedchamber, pillow in hand, at the sound of voices. He swung the pillow, hitting the second attacker in the face. Vistaren took advantage of the attacker's hesitation to turn and grab his sword.

When he turned back, Isden was staggering backwards, his nose bloodied. Vistaren hoped the injury wasn't more serious than that. He leapt forward to slash at the attacker.

The door from the hallway burst open, hitting the last of the attackers and making him stumble. Vistaren's heart leapt at the sight of Kedar, a wicked-looking knife in hand. Kedar took only an instant to see what was happening and then jumped into the fray.

Vistaren's opponent was skilled with a blade. The hood of the man's cloak had fallen, showing a man of middling years with sandy brown hair and beard. His eyebrows were drawn together in concentration as he parried each of Vistaren's blows and tried to land one of his own.

"Who are you?" Vistaren demanded.

The man didn't answer. He just lunged in with such force that Vistaren had to sidestep before he could knock the blow aside.

One of the two figures lined up against Kedar laughed. It was the woman. "We are servants of the true king, here to end this rebellion at its birth."

Vistaren blinked, his sword dropping a little. He almost didn't get it up in time to counter the next stroke. Had his father sent assassins against him? His breath came faster as he renewed the fight with added passion.

He didn't see what happened to Kedar. He only heard the count's agonized cry and the sound of something heavy hitting the floor.

Vistaren lunged, his blade running through his attacker's shoulder. He tore the blade out, making the man scream. Vistaren didn't wait to watch his opponent fall. He stepped over him and ran to defend Kedar, who was hunched over, clutching his hands together at his belly.

Oh, gods, a gut wound? Vistaren choked off a cry of dismay and instead slashed at the woman.

If she was the one who had injured Kedar, it had been a lucky stroke. She had little skill with the blade. Vistaren overpowered her quickly and struck her down.

Running footsteps pounded along the hall. Vistaren hoped it was allies approaching and not more assassins. He didn't dare risk a glance at the door; the fourth attacker must have been the one who hurt Kedar. He used a short, curved blade, and he was quick with it.

"Fiend! Surrender!" shouted a voice, and Vistaren felt his knees weaken in relief. It was Orshard.

Then there was a surprised cry. "Dinya? What—no!"

Vistaren's opponent startled at the cry, and Vistaren was able to lunge in, catching the man's blade with his own and flicking it away. The man backed hastily, bumping into a chair and knocking it over in his haste to get away.

"Dinya, stop!" Devlin shouted.

To Vistaren's surprise, the man did stop. He looked around, saw his three fallen companions, and his shoulders slumped. He fell to his knees.

Devlin darted in and backhanded the man viciously across the face. "How dare you raise your hand against the prince?" he snarled. He pulled his hand back to hit him again.

"Devlin, stop!" Orshard cried. "We need him to talk."

Vistaren looked at Orshard, who was kneeling on the ground beside Kedar. He had wrapped his cloak around one of Kedar's arms.

Devlin turned, his face twisted with fury, but after a few heaving breaths, he nodded and lowered his hand. Without speaking, he turned back and yanked Dinya's arm up behind him. He twisted a piece of cloth into makeshift restraints and tied the man up.

"Your highness, are you hurt?" he asked.

Vistaren was breathless, but he didn't think he was badly hurt. "A few cuts, that's all," he said. He looked around for Isden and found his servant pinching the bridge of his nose, tilting his head forward. "Isden?"

"Udharbed aside frob by dose," Isden replied.

"Thank you for your quick thinking," Vistaren said to him. "You likely saved my life." He turned to face Kedar. "As did you, my dear Kedar."

He went to kneel in front of Kedar. The count's face was pinched with pain and white under his fisherman's tan.

"Here, lad, you're losing blood," Orshard said. He pushed Kedar's arm up into the air. "Hold that up there. The surgeon says it helps."

"Do I need to go for a surgeon, or have you sent someone?" Vistaren asked.

"I sent Harrs for a surgeon as soon as I heard the musket shot inside the keep," Orshard said. "I knew that couldn't mean anything good."

Vistaren nodded. "Kedar, how badly are you hurt?"

Kedar's gray eyes wandered down towards the floor and then jerked back up to hold Vistaren's. "My hand, highness."

Vistaren instinctively looked down where Kedar had looked and flinched. Kedar's hand was on the floor. Bile rose in Vistaren's throat, choking him for a moment before he managed to force it back down. "By the gods, I am so sorry," he rasped.

Kedar swayed and Orshard got an arm around his shoulders. "He needs to lie down so he doesn't hit his head by passing out," the general said.

"Let's get him down, then," Vistaren said, shifting to avoid Kedar's hand as he moved to Kedar's other side. Together they lowered Kedar to the floor. Orshard lifted Kedar's arm back into the air just as the surgeon arrived.

"See to Kedar first," Vistaren said as the surgeon tried to look at the cut on his upper arm. "I am in no danger of bleeding to death."

"Well, get someone to clean that," the surgeon ordered, and then knelt by Kedar. "And don't crowd him. Go sit over there."

Oddly reassured that, even in the face of assassins, surgeons would always be high-handed, Vistaren stood shakily and went to sit in a chair. Now that the fight was done, his hands were trembling.

Devlin had been checking the other attackers. "Two dead, and that one has a gut wound that will probably kill him eventually," he reported.

He came to kneel in front of Vistaren. "My prince, I am desolate. These are my soldiers. Soldiers I thought I could trust. I—gods have mercy, I failed you."

Vistaren rested a hand on Devlin's shoulder. "Not when it mattered, Dev," he said quietly. "You interrupted the attack. You subdued one without killing him. We'll try to get some answers out of him tomorrow."

He looked around. "In the meantime, let's get them locked up securely. Post some of Lo's men to stand guard over them. Get the surgeon whatever he needs."

"We need to get this fellow in a bed and get the bleeding stopped," the surgeon said. "Come, two of you help me carry him."

"Put him in my bed," Vistaren said. "I won't be using it tonight anyway."

He watched, slumped in his chair, as they carried Kedar into the bedroom. His legs felt so heavy he thought he might stay in that chair all night.

39

Lijka looked out the lighthouse door, hoping to see a sail on the western horizon. She had sent for a surgeon from Maron as soon as she'd gotten the princess settled in front of the fire. It was late afternoon, the tide turning, and she was beginning to fear the message had gone astray.

No—there *was* a white sail approaching. With a sigh of relief, Lijka closed the door and hurried back to the pallet she'd made up for Azmei.

"Princess," she said, shaking her gently. "Princess, wake up. You've dozed off again."

She was worried. She'd seen people die of head injuries before, and those were injuries that hadn't even bled. She had managed to stop Azmei's bleeding, but she thought it might need stitches, and there was no telling what damage had been done inside.

"M'awake," Azmei slurred. She pushed herself to a half-raised position and then groaned, slumping back down. "My head…"

"I know. It's why I sent for the surgeon." Lijka sat back on her heels. "I'm sorry. I'm sure they'll recognize you, and I'm not sure what they'll do at that point. But I'll do what I can to protect you. I just—I couldn't let you die."

"You sent for a surgeon?" Azmei blinked at her. "But I—wasn't I going to the academy to…oh." She frowned. "Oh, I *did* go. I remember delivering messages. But—are we back at the light?"

Lijka nodded. "I've seen this happen," she said. "You had a blow to the head. Sometimes that makes people lose time. It's a serious injury. I couldn't let it go without sending for a surgeon."

"Oh!" Azmei jolted upright and then clutched at her head again. This time she stayed up, though. "I—I need you to write a letter for me."

"To Vistaren? I will."

"No. Ranarr. Do you have—"

"I think I have birds for Ranarr. Who do you need to write to there?"

"One of my teachers. Revalis." Azmei sighed. "It's hard to think. Can you write it for me?"

"Of course." Lijka hurried to get paper and pen, then went back to sit next to Azmei.

"Revalis." Azmei's dictation was halting. "Amethir is at war with itself. I know I'm not Amethirian royalty yet. But I request Diplomatic intervention."

She waited until Lijka had stopped writing, then said, "My betrothed broke with his father for reasons I felt were justified. Reasons that affect not just Amethir but the whole world. Speak to Yarrax, Voice of Dragons. Stormwitches Kinnet and Lijka Ardelis. Count Kedar Ebb." She winced. "Pralith Menever." She broke off.

"Could I have some water?"

Lijka set the letter aside and brought her a cup of cold water, and Azmei continued, "Yours in service of peace, Azmei Corrone."

Lijka sprinkled sand across the letter to dry it and went to look out the door again. The ship was close. They would be here soon. She hurried back to the table and scratched out another short missive.

Prince Vistaren, I believe Azmei attempted to kill the Storm-weapon last night. I am not certain of the outcome, only that she managed to get herself back to my light with a nasty head injury. She is having memory trouble and dizziness, nausea. I apologize, but I have taken the liberty of summoning a surgeon. I fear we will soon be in Crown custody. I didn't know what else to do. Lijka.

She sprinkled sand across the second letter and then rolled the first letter, taking it out to send it. Thankfully she did have a bird trained to the Amethirian embassy on Ranarr. The second bird she took inside and set on the table to affix the letter for Vistaren. She would release it out the back in hopes no one on the ship would notice.

By the time someone loomed in the open doorway, Lijka was sitting next to Azmei, helping her drink. They had agreed it would be best for Azmei to appear more injured than she was, at least at first. When the person in the doorway came in and was no longer silhouetted against the sky, Lijka was grateful she'd thought of it.

"The surgeon's school told me you had requested a surgeon," Pralith said. He was moving stiffly. "I was concerned." He froze, gazing down at Azmei. "That is not Kinnet."

Lijka shook her head. "I'm sorry, Pralith. The princess came to me when Vistaren rebelled. She was afraid in the palace, and she'd just met me and Kinnet. She asked if I would hide her."

Azmei blinked at him. "We—Have I met you?"

Pralith's expression changed from one of suspicion to one of surprise. "Yes, several times, princess. I am Pralith Menever, the King's Stormwitch."

"She was injured when the tower fell," Lijka said. "She has lost some of her recent memories." Suspicion began creeping back across Pralith's face, and Lijka added, "Not many. She knows who she is, and that she's in Amethir, and that she came to marry our prince. She says she remembers coming here for help, though I'm not sure if that's just because I've told her that."

Pralith nodded slowly.

"If you're through jabbering, may I see my patient?" demanded an irritated voice. Lijka smiled to see a surgeon coming through the door.

"Certainly, Master Wasin," Pralith said, stepping aside. "Lijka, will you come outside?"

Lijka sighed and stood, following Pralith out to the terrace. From here, the damage to the lighthouse wasn't as easily visible.

"She'll have to come back to the palace," Pralith said. "You know that, don't you?"

"She doesn't have to be a part of this," Lijka said. "How could she have known Vistaren was going to split the country in two?"

"Perhaps she encouraged him to do so," Pralith said.

"I can't believe that."

"The timing is suspicious, Lijka. I can't take the chance." He looked around, frowning. "Where is Kinnet?"

Lijka ducked her head. "She said she needed to go to sea. Something about her stormsinger friend."

"When was this?"

She cleared her throat. "Just a few days before the lighthouse fell."

"Before or after the prince's rebellion?"

Lijka jerked her head up to stare at him. "Are you accusing her?" She hoped she sounded indignant enough. "Are you accusing *me*?"

"No, no, not at all. I was just wondering if…Well, the prince's prophet friend made certain allegations that…" Pralith shrugged.

"Ahhh." Lijka nodded. "You're beginning to wonder if he was right."

"No!" Pralith glared at her.

Lijka smiled. "Very well. Would you like me to accompany the princess to the palace?"

"That won't be necessary."

Lijka frowned at him. "How do I know she will be safe?"

Pralith's expression of hurt looked genuine. "I would never hurt her highness. As far as I am concerned, she is a member of our royal family, and even if she weren't, she is a foreign royal as well. To hurt her would be unconscionable."

Lijka sighed and nodded. "I'm sorry, old friend. I didn't mean to insult you. I—I suppose the prince's rebellion has made me more suspicious."

Pralith put a hand on her shoulder. "I understand."

The surgeon appeared at the door. "I will need two men to bring the stretcher up here," he said. "You were right to summon me, Mistress Lijka. The princess needs more care than I can provide here. We'll have to take her back to the surgeon's school."

"Certainly."

Lijka knew Master Wasin well enough to trust that once he took a patient under his care, he would fight to protect that patient, regardless of politics or personal feelings. Most surgeons were like that, she had discovered.

She watched as they lifted Azmei onto the stretcher and carried her out to the porch. They paused to let Lijka grip Azmei's hand. "I'm sorry," she whispered to the princess. "Rest and get better."

She held Azmei's gaze, hoping her friend could read everything she wasn't saying in her eyes. *I have alerted Vistaren. I sent your letter to Ranarr. I will keep fighting.*

She hoped Azmei would remember this.

****

Vistaren returned to his rooms after a frustrating interrogation of the lone survivor of the attack in his rooms. He had hoped the man would be persuaded to speak, but instead the man sat in stony silence for half a glass while Devlin and Vistaren alternated asking him questions.

Devlin *had* been able to tell him that Dinya was from an old Crelin family, not nobility, but highly regarded in and around Estermere. The woman who had been with the attackers had probably been the ringleader of the group, since she was easily the cleverest of them.

Vistaren had finally left to keep from shouting his frustration at Devlin, who didn't deserve it. Gods knew the commander felt bad enough for not having caught them before they hurt anyone.

How did it come to this? Vistaren asked himself. *All I want-*

ed to do was serve my country as best I could. I thought that meant marrying well and continuing my family's dynasty. I certainly never thought of myself as a revolutionary. How did I end up starting a rebellion and fighting off loyalists?

The guard accompanying him took up a post at one side of the door while the other guard opened the door for him. Vistaren nodded to them and stepped inside to the sound of shouting.

"—just asked for something to drink that wasn't bloody broth!"

Vistaren's eyebrows went up and he looked around for Isden, but his manservant was nowhere to be seen. He shook out his cloak and draped it over a chair to dry. He looked with distaste at the bloodstain on the stone floor where Kedar had lain. He wanted that stain gone, but it seemed petty to ask someone to scrub the floor for him when they were in the middle of a siege.

"No, I don't want your damned calming draught!"

Vistaren cleared his throat as the surgeon stormed out of the bedroom, a sour expression on his face. When he saw the prince he stopped short, obviously trying to school his expression.

"I'm glad you're here, highness. Perhaps *you* can convince Count Contrary that he needs to stay in bed and calm while his body recovers from the shock it got."

"I have found people very rarely listen to me," Vistaren said. "He sounds…energetic."

The surgeon scoffed. "He's just angry. If he'd give himself half a chance, he'd fall back asleep, and that's what his body needs most right now. Sleep and rest, a chance to rebuild the blood and recover."

There was the sound of muffled curses from the bedroom. Vistaren supposed Isden must be in there with Kedar. He hoped the count didn't do anything to further damage Isden's nose.

"How is he?" he asked the surgeon.

"Surprisingly well, all things considered. I've given him

a draught for the pain, and another to help rebuild the blood he lost. The initial amputation won't kill him. The question is really whether or not infection will set in. I've done what I can to prevent it, but it will require close watching."

"How long will he be bedridden?"

"The longer the better. At least a week."

Vistaren raised his eyebrows. "So long? It wasn't his leg that was cut off."

"You try having *anything* cut off and being strong enough to get out of bed in two days," the surgeon snapped. Then he shook himself. "I beg your pardon, highness. Yon count is easily the most irritable, trying patient I've had in a long time, and I haven't drunk enough to deal with his temper."

Vistaren fought a smile. "Whiskey or coffee?" he asked.

The surgeon sighed. "Either would do."

That made Vistaren chuckle. "I can provide both, but I am certain Isden has hot coffee already waiting for my return. He knows how much I dislike facing the day without it."

The surgeon looked surprised that the prince would pour a cup for him, but he accepted it with a jerky bow. "I'm afraid they posted me away from the capital because they knew I wasn't used to nobility, highness. I meant no insult."

"Of course not. Anyway, we're all rebels together at the moment, aren't we?"

Vistaren glanced at the bedroom door, wondering if he should go in and check on Kedar.

"You might as well," the surgeon said, lowering his voice. "He's been demanding to see you since he woke up. He was damned annoying about it, honestly, until your man Isden assured him you weren't badly harmed." He cast a sharp gaze at Vistaren's arm. "And since you had the good sense to have that arm seen to, I didn't have to contradict the fellow."

Vistaren sighed. "Thank you, Master Cordily."

Kedar's voice rose from the bedroom again. "Should

his highness ever stop being a coward—"

There was the sound of someone being hastily shushed. Vistaren, glowering, stormed into the bedroom.

"Ah," Kedar said. "I thought that would work."

Isden sighed.

Kedar was propped up against two pillows, his arm propped on another one to keep it elevated. He wasn't as pale as he had been last night, though Vistaren didn't think his color good.

"You look better than the last time I saw you," Vistaren said in relief.

Kedar tipped his head to one side. "Well, I'm not bleeding to death at the moment, which helps." His voice had a bite to it that Vistaren hadn't heard since their conversation in the palace.

Vistaren lifted a hand to rub his face. "I am…so, so sorry, Kedar."

"Why?" When Vistaren looked at him in astonishment, Kedar added, "Did you cut off my hand?"

Vistaren rolled his eyes. "No, but—"

"Did you ask those men to attack?" Kedar interrupted.

"I—no—" Vistaren spluttered. "But—"

"Did you force me to ride back with Algot to join you?"

Vistaren knew better than to try to reply. He gave an exasperated sigh and glared at Kedar. He had intended to apologize and humble himself to Kedar, offering whatever he could to make up for this. It wasn't actually going the way he'd imagined it.

"Good. I don't want you to apologize to me. I just want you to promise you won't give up."

"What?"

Kedar reached clumsily for a rough, clay cup on the bedside table. Vistaren moved to help him and was skewered by a glare. He stopped in his tracks, watching as Kedar took a long drink and then made a face. "Those bastards took my hand. Stole my livelihood. I want them to pay. Not the one who actually did it—I know *he's* dead. But they claimed they were fighting for the king."

Vistaren swallowed.

"They were fighting for a man who let a stormwitch destroy two villages just like mine. They were fighting to stop you from trying to protect people like my village. They were fighting for a man who wants to take our special magic and turn it into just another weapon to use to threaten and bully those who don't do as he wishes. I need you to promise me you won't stop fighting him. That you won't let your father win."

"But…" Vistaren shook his head, confused. "You aren't angry?"

"Of *course* I'm angry!" Kedar bawled. "I'm angry as a hungry siren! I'm angry I won't be able to work with my people! I'm angry I won't have two hands to pick up my children! I'm—" He was waving both arms around, his face darkening. "But I'm not mad at *you.*"

He stopped speaking, panting, and stared at the bandaged stump in front of his face. His expression changed from furious to queasy. "Oh, gods, my hand," he whispered. After a moment he lowered it to rest carefully on the pillow again, wincing.

Vistaren stepped closer, feeling his face twist in sympathy, and Kedar held up his remaining hand to stop him again.

"*No,*" he said loudly. "*Fuck* that. I won't let you feel guilty and I won't let them win. Just—promise me. Promise you won't give up."

"I won't give up," Vistaren said, his voice soft. "My anger at the injustice done to you and your people and those other villages—that's why I'm fighting. I won't give up."

There was a tap on the doorframe and Lozarr looked in the open door. His brows were drawn together apologetically.

"I'm sorry to interrupt, highness, but…"

"No, come in." For all it wasn't yet midday, Vistaren

wished that he'd offered the surgeon whiskey, and had some himself. "What is it, Lo?"

Lo was holding two rolled papers in his hand. He shifted his feet. "The birds came in at some point last night. In all the confusion, I wasn't paying proper attention. I'm afraid I opened one meant for you. I'm—I'm sorry, Vistaren." His voice was heavy.

"No harm." Vistaren took the letter. "You had a letter as well?"

"Yes, I—" Lo unrolled the paper and paled. "It…" He licked his lips. "It just says, 'Storm coming. I love you.'"

A chill ran down Vistaren's back. "I'm sure you'll get another letter soon. She must have been interrupted by preparations."

"I hope so." Lo looked back down at the paper in his hands, and Vistaren took that opportunity to read his own letter.

He reached the end and tried to read it again, but his fingers had gone numb. The paper fluttered to land on the bed. Kedar snatched it up with his good hand, his gray eyes scanning quickly.

Vistaren just watched him, thoughts swirling. This changed things. This…this changed everything.

"Prince Vistaren," Kedar read aloud. "I believe Azmei attempted to kill the Stormweapon last night. I am not certain of the outcome, only that she managed to get herself back to my light with a nasty head injury. She is having memory trouble and dizziness, nausea. I apologize, but I have taken the liberty of summoning a surgeon. I fear we will soon be in Crown custody. I didn't know what else to do."

"If they have Azmei," Lo whispered.

"They'll use her as a bargaining chip," Vistaren said.

They stared at each other. Vistaren was breathing too quickly. If his father threatened Azmei and Vistaren gave in, he broke his promise to Kedar. But if he didn't give in and his father hurt Azmei, then Vistaren had broken faith with her.

Oh, gods, what do I do? he wondered. *Silent god, Azmei's god, god of peace, what would you have me do?*

He startled when Kedar broke the silence by clearing his throat. "Well," Kedar said. "We'll just have to get her back."

40

Azmei stared out the window of her room in Maron Palace. The surgeon had been particular about getting her settled on the window seat and ordering her not to move around until he came back to check on her later. A servant had been assigned to wait on her and bring her what she requested, within reason, but it was obvious Azmei was a prisoner.

She wished her window didn't look out on the harbor. She didn't know what had happened to her, but she currently held no warm feelings towards the harbor. She would much rather be looking inland.

When someone knocked at the door, the serving girl answered without asking Azmei if she should. Azmei didn't protest. It was another sign she was not here for her own protection.

She was surprised to see Pralith Menever waiting outside in the hall.

The servant gestured him in, but he waited until Azmei had nodded. Then he stepped inside. He seemed to be moving stiffly. Azmei wondered if his back pained him. Vistaren had told her that stormwitches often lived very different lives before their talent manifested itself. Perhaps Pralith had been a soldier or a laborer in his previous life. He might have old injuries that protested weather such as the chill, gray rain that had settled around the palace.

Azmei wanted to ask why the stormwitches were allowing it to rain, if they had such good control of the weather. It wasn't storm season yet, after all. All that she had seen of the countryside had been crops growing well, but still not ripe for harvest. The rains would slow that process. Wasn't that part of why Amethir did so well?

She wouldn't be the first to speak, though. Pralith had chosen to come and visit her. She would let him speak first. She had no intention of being a polite prisoner.

Pralith approached her window seat slowly. He couldn't be much over forty, but he really did walk like a much older man. Azmei pressed down her curiosity and watched as he bowed. She heard the tiny, suppressed grunt as he straightened from that bow. He exhaled heavily when he sat on the chair facing her.

And then the silence stretched between them. The servant hovered nearby, watching to see if they needed anything, but Azmei wouldn't offer Pralith any refreshment.

Finally the stormwitch opened his mouth. "You lied to me, princess."

As an opening salvo, it was an interesting choice. "I'm sorry," Azmei said, her tone conveying very clearly she was anything but.

Pralith arched an eyebrow. "No denial?"

"No, I certainly *have* lied to you." Azmei folded her hands in her lap. "I am sorry it was necessary."

Pralith glared at her. "I have learned that you were with Vistaren when he attacked General Balahar, suborned half the king's army, and left the capital. You rode out with him."

"Oh." Azmei decided on honesty. "I don't remember telling you I wasn't."

Pralith sighed. "Lijka was the one who told me." He shook his head. "I was honestly concerned for Lijka, you know. I was pleased to renew our friendship." His glare sharpened. "I suppose you were behind her visit to me the other day?"

Azmei concealed the sudden rush of excitement she felt. She *remembered* that. "Yes. She was worried about you. You're wrong to trust Eldry, you know. We're just trying to keep you from making a dreadful mistake."

Pralith snorted. "I'm sure."

"Vistaren is truly doing what he believes is best for Amethir. We've been given plenty of evidence—"

"Save it for someone more likely to listen, princess," Pralith cut in.

Azmei stared at him, mouth open in outrage. That was *rude*. She might be a prisoner, but she had not been rude to Pralith. He had no call to be rude.

"I have learned a few things since I brought you here yesterday afternoon." Pralith folded his arms across his chest. "Not only did I learn about your part in the rebellion, but I also learned that something caused Eldry's devoted peasant to go mad and attack her. At least, that's the story she has given out. I can't help wondering, though…"

He gave her an unpleasant smile. "Why would Lijka wait several days to summon a surgeon after her tower collapsed on you? Unless, that is, she didn't actually wait, because the tower didn't actually fall on you. Perhaps you were only injured two nights ago. I have learned about some of your…unusual…abilities, and I can't help but think you might have been behind that attack on the Stormweapon."

Azmei smiled blandly. She didn't have to deny his allegations. "You have quite an imagination," she said, "but if I am perfectly honest, I have no idea how I was injured." And she'd be damned if she would let him see how much that bothered her.

He narrowed his eyes. "When I find out what your true aim is…"

"My true aim is to serve Amethir by helping Vistaren," she replied.

Pralith smirked at her. "That will be quite a task, since you're to remain here at the palace until Balahar and the Stormweapon are able to bring this unpleasantness to an end."

"If the Stormweapon wins, Pralith, the unpleasantness is only just beginning."

Pralith shrugged and stood. "I suppose we'll see, won't we? I wonder what will become of a foreign princess who colluded with traitors to the crown."

He took her hand and bowed over it. She nearly jerked away from his grip when she felt his lips brush over the back of her hand—but then she felt something else pressed into her palm. It rustled like paper.

She jerked her hand away, clenching it into a fist, and glared defiantly at him. "We aren't traitors," she snapped. "We're trying to save Amethir! Even the bloody-minded fools like you!"

Pralith merely chuckled and left.

When Azmei was certain her serving girl wasn't watching, she unfolded the tiny slip of paper Pralith had slipped to her. It had only two words.

Hold on.

Underneath it was a drawing of a thorn.

41

Arama woke to a blue world. Blue and cold. She groaned.

"Hold still, captain," said a voice. "You're not well balanced."

"Zek," she rasped. Her lips were dry and salt-crusted.

"Yes, mum. You're lashed into the life-buoy."

She grunted and turned her head slowly. Zek was crouched on a barrel. Beyond him she could see Kinnet and Yar, both clinging to pieces of flotsam she couldn't identify.

Arama closed her eyes and opened them again. The world was still deep blue. The stars shone above them. The sea was almost calm. When she turned her head the other way, she could see six or seven members of her crew all spread along a floating spar.

"How long since we went down?" she asked.

"Perhaps two, three hours," Zek said. "You'd swallowed a lot of water. Took us some work to get it out of you."

"How'd you manage that," she asked.

"Beating you, mostly," Yar put in. He sounded far too cheerful for their situation. "Your back is going to be sore."

Arama coughed and winced. "It already is."

"Qiaru is coming," Kinnet said loudly. "They'll be here as soon as they can. But there are seadragons in the way."

"The storm?"

Zek shivered audibly. "As soon as *Dawn Star* went down, the storm went with it," he whispered.

"We were some distance east of Crescent Island," Arama remembered.

"Aye, mum, and I think we're closer to it than we were. I'm not sure, but—"

And then Arama's skin crawled and her hair stood on end as a sound cut through Zek's words. It was a shrill, screeching cry that rasped into a low hiss. Her breath came faster as a second cry joined in, first discordant and then changing in pitch until it harmonized with the first.

"Antos defend," Arama whispered.

"What—what is that?" Zek asked. Gods save him. He was so young. Arama turned to look at him through the darkness.

The first voice was creaking low, the second voice screeching in rage. A third voice joined in, a low, throbbing vibrato. Then from behind them came a fourth voice and a fifth, until the night was full of eerie, soothing, inviting, terrifying sound.

Arama was eighteen again, and the ship she had just lost was *Bounder*. It wasn't Carig who had died, but her mentor, Raszel. The song throbbed around them and Arama's palm ached with a remembered wound.

"Those," Arama whispered, "are sirens." *Those are our death.*

The Storms in Amethir series will conclude in 2018 with *Witchery's End*.

ABOUT THE AUTHOR

Stephanie A. Cain writes epic and urban fantasy for fun, and a history blog for work. She lives in Indiana. She graduated from Purdue University with a Bachelor of Arts in History and Creative Writing, with a Medieval Studies minor. She enjoys hiking, reading, birdwatching, and general geekery. A proud crazy cat lady, Stephanie is happily owned by Eowyn, Strider, and Eustace Clarence Scrubb.

In her free time, Stephanie enjoys hiking (except for the spiders), bird-watching, visiting wineries, and collecting anything with owls on it. She likes to unwind by playing World of Warcraft and Skyrim. She enjoys organizing things, is overly fond of 3-ring binders, and visits office supply stores for fun. She owns way more movie scores and fountain pens than she can actually afford. She can be found online at www.stephaniecainonline.com.

AUTHOR'S NOTE

Thanks for reading my novel! If you enjoyed this, would you please take a moment to leave a review of my book online? Writing just two or three honest sentences is one of the best things you can do to support any author.

Thank you!

Stephanie